AFTER
December

JOANA MARCÚS

sourcebooks
casablanca

For every Jen
who tries to do things right,
who sometimes gets it wrong,
who keeps learning,
who falls over and over,
but who never stays down.
This book is for you.

Published by Sourcebooks Casablanca, an imprint of Sourcebooks
1935 Brookdale RD, Naperville, IL 60563–2773
(630) 961-3900
sourcebooks.com

Originally published as *Después de Diciembre* in 2022 in Spain by Montena, an imprint of Penguin
Random House Grupo Editorial. This edition issued based on the paperback edition published
in 2022 in Spain by Montena, an imprint of Penguin Random House Grupo Editorial.

Cataloging-in-Publication Data is on file with the Library of Congress.

Printed and bound in the United States of America.
PAH 10 9 8 7 6 5 4 3 2 1

1

HEALING WOUNDS

They say time creeps by when things are going badly…and I couldn't agree more.

I'd suffered, and the worst part of all is I was the one to blame for it. I'd made a decision that had seemed like the right one, but it was difficult to live with. I'd abandoned the guy I loved.

Maybe *abandoned* is too strong a word. The guy in question still had his friends on his side: Will, Naya, even his brother Mike. They were with him. I was the one who'd stepped away, who'd gone back to stay with my parents, who'd left everything behind.

A year before that, I'd decided to go away to college and study a major that didn't interest me, just to get as far as possible from the life I'd lived before. That's where I met all the people I just mentioned, along with Jack Ross, who was something more complicated than just a *friend*.

He helped me understand that my relationship with Monty wasn't love, that I'd need to learn to think for myself, that I had devoted my entire life to pleasing others no matter whether they wanted to make me happy.

I don't think he realized that the first decision I'd make for myself would be leaving him. Jack needed to chase his dreams, and I wasn't ready to accompany him. I needed to find out what my own dreams were.

I'd like to take the credit for these insights, which sound like they came straight from a self-help book, but the truth is I'd learned them from the woman who had been my therapist for the last year. My big brother and big sister, Spencer and Shannon, had helped me pay for my sessions with her until I managed to scrape together money of my own.

In a single year, I'd worked as a cashier, a gas station attendant, a warehouse worker, and assistant phys ed teacher under Spencer. Some of these jobs had overlapped, and they'd taken up so much of my time that all I could ever think about was how tired I was. And funny enough, that helped me a lot.

The chance to do as I wanted, make my own money, decide things for myself…it was a huge change. One I hadn't known how to anticipate. Along with my therapy, it allowed me to see things from a different perspective.

And one of those things was my family.

What Jack had told me once, that they always managed to make me do whatever they wanted, had gotten stuck in my head. For a long time, I ignored the truth, the hundreds of signs that he'd been right. I kept pretending everything was OK…but then one night, it all exploded.

I was sitting at the kitchen table with Sonny and Steve, my parents, and Spencer. The only sound was the game on the little TV by the fridge. My brothers and my father had their eyes glued to the screen, and Mom and I were picking apathetically at our meal.

That was probably what started it—the fact that she and I didn't like sports and couldn't distract ourselves—because it gave us no choice but to interact.

"You're not hungry?" she asked me, watching me push around a brussels sprout with my fork.

I was too tired to deal with her. I'd worked five hours at the gas station and four out on the fields, and I could hardly keep myself upright.

"Not really. I'll probably wrap this up and save it for tomorrow."

Mom glared at my basically untouched plate with resentment in her brown eyes, which looked almost exactly like mine. "Fine," she said after a moment. "I'm not hungry either. Maybe it's my cooking. Maybe it's just not good enough."

"Mom, I didn't say that," I responded.

"You don't have to. You never like anything lately."

"I'm tired."

"You always have an excuse."

She'd been snippy with me ever since I'd returned home, but this was the first time she'd just come out and attacked me, and I struggled to see why. Something was clearly up, but she wouldn't tell me what. And that meant I would have to be the one to pull it out of her.

"You want to tell me what's going on with you?" I asked. My tone was calm, but direct. *Assertive*, as my therapist called it. I had never spoken to my parents that way before, and everyone at the table turned to me with surprise.

My mother, of course, brought her hand to her heart. "What do you mean?"

"Mom," I told her, "you've been acting weird, anyone can see it. What I can't understand is why you won't tell me what's going on."

She and Dad exchanged glances. They'd been doing that a lot lately. I knew that they had talked about the situation, and it enraged me that they were both sitting there playing dumb.

"Well?" I insisted.

Dad warned me, "Don't talk to your mother like that."

"I haven't talked to her any way," I said, "I just asked what was going on and why you keep nitpicking at me."

Sonny and Steve burst out laughing, and I gripped my fork so tight in my fist, I was worried I'd bend it. Sonny told me I was out of my mind, and Steve added, "Yeah, since you came back, you think the whole world's against you."

"I don't *think* anything," I replied, "it's just that all of you are talking about me behind my back, and I'm over it."

"No one's talking about you," my father reassured me. He was lying, I could tell. He even blushed a little before he glanced over at Mom.

"Oh yeah?" I fired back. "Then why do you two keep looking back and forth like that?"

"We're not!" Mom shouted.

"You are!"

Steve pretended to cough, saying the word *psycho* as he and Sonny cracked up. I was furious and could feel the blood draining from my face, and that made me yell at my brothers for the first time in ages: "Can you shut up for once?"

"Jennifer!" my mother responded. "That's enough! No one's plotting against you! Stop being paranoid!"

"I'm not paranoid! Y'all are up to something!"

"Like what? Your brothers are laughing! What's wrong with that?" Mom asked.

"It's not that they're laughing," I told her, my voice getting louder, "it's that they're making fun of me! They've been making fun of me constantly, and you never say anything, and Dad doesn't either!"

My brothers turned irate, but Mom talked over them: "Where is all this coming from? Why now? When we're trying to have dinner in peace?"

I told her she'd started it, that she'd been acting weird with me ever since I'd returned home and I didn't understand why. I asked whether she even wanted me back, or whether I was just extra now. She shouted back that I was pushing it, and I saw my father's back straighten as he got ready to intervene.

"You're taking it too far!" he screamed. That wasn't like him. But I stood my ground and asked if he was really going to deny that Sonny and Steve made fun of me all the time. Sonny jumped in to tell me to stop making everyone feel bad, and to top it off, he threw a napkin in my face.

At that point, I lost control: "Can you not just leave me alone? Do you two really have nothing better to do than mess with your little sister? Shouldn't you maybe try to drag your garage business out of debt for once? Focus on your own shit and stay out of my business!"

That was the first time in history I'd gotten them both to shut up. But Mom was fiery red, which meant I'd really gotten under her skin. She pointed at me and said, "You can't just go through life making everyone else feel miserable, Jennifer!"

"Everyone else? What about me?! Have you ever asked yourself how I feel, or does that just not matter to you?"

"When did you decide it was OK to talk to people that way?" she screamed, and started burbling something about how I'd changed since I'd gone away to college, and I must have picked up my bad behavior from my friends there and the guy I had gone out with.

For some reason, since my return, Mom had refused to call Jack by his name. He was always *that guy you were going out with*, and her tone, which had once been affectionate, was now totally disrespectful.

I agreed with her, though, and I let her know it, slamming my fork down on the table: "You're right! Jack opened my eyes to lots of things!"

"Exactly," Mom said, and I realized that was the answer she'd been looking for. "He got into your head and turned you against us! He even got your old boyfriend thrown in jail!"

I couldn't answer—her words had shocked me too much. Frozen, I noticed that Spencer, who hadn't yet said a word, stood and warned her in a steely tone, "Mom, no. Don't go there."

She wasn't used to people defending me, especially not against her, and she almost flinched as she said, "I'm just telling it like it is."

"He was an asshole, and he got what he deserved," Spencer said, and when Dad stood up and shouted at him, Spencer cut him off. "Stay out of it, Dad."

Mom yelled that getting Monty arrested had caused all sorts of problems for them: "Do you know how the rest of the neighborhood has looked at us since then? Do you know what they say about us? It's like we don't even exist anymore."

"He was hitting Jenny, Mom!" Spencer screamed.

"That's what she says!"

That made me react. I had been miffed before the subject of Monty came up, but now I saw what was really going on, and it shocked me. Mom wasn't mad that I was back home, she was mad because things had changed in her life. She wasn't worried about some maniac who might come stalking me, she was worried about the inconvenience it might cause her.

Before I realized it, I heard my chair sliding backward and found myself running toward the stairs. My movements were at once robotic and enraged. Enraged at my mother, at the twins… I couldn't believe a year had passed and people still didn't believe me.

Because most of them didn't. A few people in the neighborhood, maybe, but even then, they weren't brave enough to say anything. Monty just wasn't the kind of guy they looked at as an abuser. He was handsome, funny, and good at basketball. For many, he was the perfect man. And I was the weird girl who had insisted on going off to college, returned home without warning, and ruined a guy's life by turning him in to the cops.

Of course people didn't believe me. How many people there even knew me, really? And despite the evidence, it wasn't in their interest to accept the truth. I could live with that, though. What hurt was my mother calling me a liar. She should have known better.

When I got to my room, I pulled out my suitcase from under the bed. I didn't know what I'd do when I walked out the door, but I knew I couldn't stay there another second. I wouldn't allow people to question my actions when I hadn't done anything wrong.

Monty had gotten what he deserved. I remembered the mistreatment, the crazy messages, the humiliation and insults. I remembered him tearing my clothing and breaking my glasses. I couldn't live with the fear of something like that happening again. I couldn't get back on the escalator that led from screaming to grabbing, from grabbing to shoving, from shoving to slamming me against the wall. One day, I thought, Monty would come for me again. I'd thought I was safe from him at home, but now I knew otherwise. And I wasn't just going to sit around and wait for him to hurt me.

Downstairs, everyone was shouting, but I didn't know what they were saying. I thought I saw some movement out of the corner of my eye. Spencer came into my room and shut the door in my father's face just as Dad appeared behind him, yelling. I'd never seen my oldest brother looking so indignant, and knowing that he was fighting for me, that he believed me, made me want to throw myself in his arms.

"Don't worry, Jenny," he said in a soft tone, almost a whisper. "I'll get you out of here, OK?"

I'm not sure if I answered him. I just remember jumping off the bed, opening my closet, and stuffing a bunch of clothes into my suitcase. When I had what I needed, I zipped it shut, and Spencer took it from me and carried it downstairs. I couldn't see the car keys in his other hand, but I could hear them jingle, and that meant we were really going.

My parents shouted at us. The twins did too, I think. But neither of us cared. I got into Spencer's car and he sped off—I didn't yet know where he was headed. Only when we were alone did I let the tears flow. He reached over and rested a hand on my shoulder, but he didn't say anything, and I was grateful for it.

He parked in front of our grandmother's house. She was sitting on the porch waiting. He must have talked to her before we left. As soon as she saw us, she stood and walked over with a melancholy smile.

"Come in, honey. Do you want a hot chocolate?"

That same night, I moved in with her.

It wasn't ideal. I was scared of being a burden for her. She was getting old, and she had her own problems to deal with. I kept offering her part of my wages, but she wouldn't hear of it, so I finally gave up and just tried to make sure the fridge was stocked with prepared foods so at least she wouldn't have to cook.

My parents talked to her that first night, and Dad kept calling afterward, but Mom cut me off completely.

That night had divided the family. Shannon and Spencer grew distant from my parents. The twins, I guess, wrote me off. I understood, sort of. Anyway, it's not like I wanted to talk to them.

I had stayed in touch with Naya after leaving school. We usually phoned each other once a week. I convinced her I was living my very best life: working as an assistant phys ed teacher, living with my grandmother to help her out around the house, with a family that adored me... She'd have liked to hear that Monty had fallen off the twentieth story of a building, but I didn't dare make up that much. I already felt bad for lying about everything else.

But the thing is, knowing Naya, if I'd told her the truth, she would have shown up at my doorstep and dragged me back to the old apartment.

One night, I had gone out on the porch to give her a ring, and in the middle of a conversation, she asked, "Are you sure you're OK?"

"Yeah," I said, sitting on the porch and hugging my knees. "Of course, why?"

"I don't know, you seem a little...quiet."

I wanted to tell her not to worry, but I couldn't fake it anymore.

"I'm tired," I confessed.

Naya didn't know how tired I meant, or that it wasn't just my body that was exhausted, but my soul, too. I hadn't told her I couldn't take it anymore. But she must have sensed something, and she consoled me as best she could. That's just how she was.

"Jenna, whatever it is that's bothering you, I can promise you it's not worth it. You deserve to be happy."

"Thanks," I said. "But I've got to be honest. If I'd known this conversation was going to get all deep, I'd have opened a bottle of wine before I rang you."

"I can wait," she responded, "but don't thank me. I'm just trying to make you feel better. But while I'm at it, let me give you some advice. You need a change of scene. I can feel it. Where you're living is part of the problem. I don't know why, but I can tell."

"You've hit the nail on the head, Naya. I'm sure of it."

"You could come back, you know? Give it another try for a semester. Disconnect from home, distract your mind with your studies."

Weirdly, it didn't seem like such a bad idea. I really did feel like getting the hell out of there. I wanted to forget everything for a couple of months. My worry was…

"I don't want to run into Jack."

"I know, but I don't think it will be a problem. When you guys split up, he went to study in France. There are days when I hardly remember he was ever here."

I knew that. He left not long after I did. Will had texted me the day he left. I was happy for him. I'd wanted him to pursue his dreams, and now he was doing it.

"Yeah," I told her, "but who knows if he'll decide to come back, to see his family or whatever. He still owns the apartment, and the program in France is just a year, I think. I'm worried if he ran into me, it would be uncomfortable for him."

Naya sighed. "I don't think that's an issue. Ross hasn't come back even once."

That surprised me. "Does he still talk to you guys?"

"Will calls him once in a while, but that's about it… And I'll tell you one thing: you should put Jack aside and think about you. I don't want you just sitting around there spinning your wheels, OK? The spring semester hasn't started yet, you've still got a few weeks to register. I know I'd love to have you back here."

"I'll think it over. But I'm not promising anything."

"Cool!" She sounded so legitimately excited that I could have hugged her. "When you do decide to come back, I want to be the first to know!"

"You always are!"

"Thank you, bestie!" she said.

I could imagine her smiling, and I told her, "Call you tomorrow, Naya. I've got to have dinner."

"OK. Hug your grandmother for me!"

"And you hug everyone else for me. But be careful with Sue. I heard she bites."

"I'll put on a hockey mask and a bulletproof vest," Naya said.

After hanging up, I looked at my phone for a few seconds before coming back to reality. I loved talking to Naya. She was my oasis. With her, everything seemed easier, as if my problems weighed less and my joys lasted longer. Maybe that was why she was the first person I thought of when I felt bad, and I liked knowing that went both ways.

But my good mood vanished as quickly as it arrived. It was an intuition—I didn't hear anything, but a shiver ran up my spine. I looked up and to my horror found myself face-to-face with Monty.

He was standing at the gate with his hands in his coat pockets and a hard-to-read expression on his face. All I could think was that I needed to take off running, now.

I stood and pointed at him, and before he had a chance to open his mouth, warned him, "Don't come a step closer."

Monty sighed, stepped back, and said, "Jenny, I only want to talk."

"I've got a restraining order against you, so I hope you feel like talking to the police."

I was too scared to turn my back, so I edged slowly away, my hand reaching out to grab the door.

"Stop running away, please." His tone didn't change, but he took a step toward me, and I got really scared. "I told you, I just want to talk."

I ignored him. I'd finally reached the door. But the worst thing I could have imagined just then happened: it was locked. And I hadn't thought to bring my keys with me. Dammit! Usually, when this happened, my grandmother would come out in five minutes or so to see what was taking me so long. But I'd talked to Naya for close to an hour, and she hadn't peeked out once.

In a panic, I rang the doorbell. I hit it three times while Monty was walking over with his hands raised to show he was harmless.

"I told you, stay back!" I wished I could sound less scared. I rang the doorbell again desperately. By now, Monty had climbed the stairs. What should I do? Jump off the porch and run down the street? I was a phys ed teacher, so I could manage that, couldn't I? But could I outrun him? Could I even get past him? Or would he trap me with those long arms of his?

I wasn't sure, so my best option seemed to be standing my ground and begging him to go away. Monty was close now, hands still raised, looking almost sad that I was so afraid of him. And that fake sympathy only pissed me off worse.

"Go," I grunted.

"I heard you were having problems with your parents," he said, now lowering his arms.

"Just leave! I don't have anything to say to you!"

"I don't know if you heard, but I've been helping out your brothers in the garage sometimes to make some extra pocket change," he went on as if he hadn't heard me. "I guess your mom really appreciates that, and..."

"I don't care!" I pleaded. "I don't want to talk to you—is that really so hard to understand?"

Why wouldn't someone come help me? Why had I gone outside to talk to Naya when I could have just done it in the living room? Why did I have to lock myself out on exactly that day?

Monty clenched his teeth. "I'm not leaving until you've heard me out."

I observed him carefully. In the time we'd been together I'd learned to see the signs that I might be in danger. If I got the least sense he might snap, I'd need to take off running.

"I'm just here to tell you that even though I'm glad to be helping out there in the garage and I'm glad your mom's taken a liking to me, if it's a problem, I'll stop."

That threw me off. Was he trying to be a good guy now?

"Leave me alone," I murmured, shaking my head.

"I hate seeing you like this, rejected by your family over a guy you're not even going out with anymore."

How did he know all this? Were my parents sharing intimate details of my life with *him*?

"For the last time, go before I call the cops."

"I don't understand how you can let this Jack guy push you away from your family when you haven't even seen him in like a year. Jenny, this is your family we're talking about. And they're really suffering over this."

So he's not just a good guy now, he's a family therapist in training?

"They adore you," he continued, "and they want the best for you. It may not seem that way because they don't use the right words, but I promise you they're worried and they want you back home. And if what you need to do that is for me to stay out of their lives, then just say the word and..."

He fell silent. The door opened and I almost fell backward, but I grabbed the frame just in time. My grandmother whizzed past me and Monty hurried away. "Get off my property!" she shouted. "Don't you dare come close to her!"

I was surprised my grandmother had scared Monty that bad, but then I saw she was aiming her brother's old hunting rifle straight at him. "Get out!" she shrieked, and he didn't try to argue. "Next time, I'll have the safety off, understand?!"

When he was gone, she lowered the weapon and asked, "Did he hurt you?"

"No," I reassured her.

"Are you all right? Do you need anything?"

Honestly, I couldn't have felt better. Seeing her rush to my defense had brought a smile to my face. Maybe it was the nerves. "Do you actually know how to use that thing?" I asked.

"This shotgun? It hasn't worked in twenty years. Come on, Jenny, let's go inside."

We decided to call the cops. Two officers came by, but they didn't seem to think there was a problem. As they took our statement, they kept pressing me on certain points, and I started to wonder if they even believed me. We had called Shannon, too, and their indifference made her so angry that once they were gone, she took it out on poor Owen, yelling at him to turn down the volume on his cartoons. The poor kid had no idea he'd done anything wrong.

Monty didn't try to contact me again, at least, and my life went back to its normal routine. Gas station, track practice, dinners with my grandmother, weekend nights watching movies with my nephew, and exhaustion. This went on until I decided to visit the college's website one day. Seeing the tuition, the deadlines, imagining getting back into the swing of it…it made me so nervous, but it was also so exciting. It had been a miracle that I didn't flunk out that first semester, and yet there I was, clicking through registration links for the five classes I had planned to register for before I suddenly decided to come back home. They didn't look much harder than what I'd already done, and as I looked at loan applications, I realized, biting my lip: *I can do this.*

It sounded so strange to say. I lay back on the sofa and, without knowing why, called the only classmate I had stayed in touch with since leaving, a guy named Curtis. We'd done a few group projects together. He had a special spark, and he was funny, and he'd always made class time pass more quickly.

"Jenna!!" he shouted as he picked up. "I sure didn't expect you to call."

"Hey, Curtis, can I ask you a question?"

Alas, my poor friend had failed half his classes after spending most of his first year partying. The good news, though, was that since he'd be repeating a bunch of coursework, we'd probably share some of our classes. He was optimistic: "Trust me," he said, "you'll do great. There's just one problem, and that's the dorms. I doubt you'll get a spot this close to the start of classes."

When I heard that, I called Naya, and she was over the moon when I told her I might come back.

"You think there's any chance you could talk to Chris and see if he can help me get back into the dorms?" I asked. "Imagine if we could be roomies again…"

"Eh…" Naya responded. "The thing is, I'm not in the dorms anymore."

Silence. I blinked several times as I asked, "What?"

"I'm living with Will and Sue. I moved in a few weeks ago. I forgot to tell you, sorry."

"Don't say sorry, I'm sure it's fun. I mean, you already basically lived there anyway."

"Well, Will's happy about it. Sue's a different story… But listen, I'll call Chris and see if he can pull some strings."

"Thanks so much," I said.

She was back on the phone a few minutes later with the bad news: "They're all full. But I talked to Will and Sue and we came up with a solution."

She sounded bubbly, and I thought I could sense where this was going. "Naya..."

"Just come live with us!"

"But..."

"No buts! We're all friends, and now there's an empty room!!"

"Yeah. An empty room that belongs to my ex-boyfriend. I can't!" I protested.

"Jenna, come on... It's been almost a year since he was last here. He's probably settled in, ready to make France his home. Do you honestly think he's just going to show up now?"

"With my luck, yeah."

"You want me to text him and ask?"

"Naya, it's not just that I'm worried he'll come around, it's that I don't want to sleep in his room. It's intrusive. It's weird. If someone did something like that to me, I'd be furious."

"Whatever..." she replied. "How about if we bought a sofa bed? It would at least give you somewhere to crash while you're looking for a room... Chris told me if something opened up at the dorm, he'd call right away."

We talked on and on for probably an hour, and predictably, Naya wound up convincing me it was a good idea. So soon afterward, there I was: I'd quit my two jobs, my bags were packed, and I'd made the first payment on my tuition. My grandmother had sewn me two wool hats, Shannon had brought over clothes from my parents' house, and Spencer was downstairs playing with Owen while he waited for me. I could hear them laughing from upstairs.

As I looked at myself in the mirror, Shannon sat on the bed behind me, asking, "So, are you nervous?"

I wondered... I don't know if it was just me, but *nothing* looked good on me that day. I was a disaster. My clothes sucked, my body sucked, my hair sucked. I took off what I was wearing and threw it into the pile on the floor. I had gone through what felt like a million outfits in record time.

My sister seemed to find the whole thing hilarious, and said, "Never mind, I don't know why I even asked."

"Why does everything look so terrible on me?"

"It's just how you see yourself, hon, because you're worried. I'm sorry, scratch that, it's your clothes. It's time to update your wardrobe. Thank God I picked you up a few things at the mall."

"My clothing is fine," I grunted.

"Jenny, you know I love you like no other and you're the best sister in the world, but your fashion sense is, um..."

I rolled my eyes and kept looking, finally managing to find a red sweater I used to wear my first year of school. "How's this one?" I asked.

"Obviously I like it, because it's mine."

"It *was* yours. It's mine now."

"Sure," she replied. "If I can have your platform boots and your blue necklace."

"Why don't you just take everything else while you're at it?" I asked. I was too tired to argue. The red sweater didn't look terrible, at least. I'd end up keeping it, along with a few other garments I'd packed. My sister spent hours throwing clothes at me, and I'd either fold them or cast them aside. I doubted I'd make a splash back at school, but at least I wouldn't have to go naked.

Neither Shannon nor I could get the suitcase to close, and I had to sit down on it as we each pulled one zipper, meeting in the middle. In the meanwhile, Shannon asked me to explain something to her: "It's been a year since you've seen your old friends, right? Naya, Will, and Sue…with everything that happened with a certain young man I won't name…aren't you worried about running into him?"

"No," I lied.

"But you're sleeping in his room."

"They're getting a sofa bed for the living room. I thought about asking to share Sue's room, but I dropped that idea almost immediately. And I won't be freeloading this time, I'm paying rent."

"I understand, Jenny, and all that sounds great, but…are you going to be happy?"

I understood why she was asking. I'd had a hard time that past year. It wasn't just the arguments with Mom and Dad and the thing with Monty, it was everything. And as for Jack, my sister knew the whole story. She was the only person I'd talked to, the only person I'd allowed myself to be vulnerable with. She remembered how I'd barely survived that first month back. She knew how much I'd missed him and how badly I'd wanted to talk to him. She knew about how I'd called Jack on his birthday, how I'd spent the whole morning fretting and checking the time in France because I didn't want to wake him, how I'd sat there on the edge of the bed with my cell phone trying to psych myself up.

I'd wanted to tell him happy birthday, but I thought maybe he'd forgotten me, or that he wouldn't be happy to hear from me, that he wouldn't want to even hear my voice. Anything could happen, but I needed to talk to him. It may have been selfish, but I wanted him to know I remembered him on his birthday and that I wished him well.

Ten times I tried to write a message, but I couldn't come up with anything, so I called. Would he respond? Would he hang up on me? Did he even have his phone on him? I remembered how forgetful he was, and how reluctant he'd been to make a big deal of his birthday. When we were together, I'd insisted we celebrate and we'd gone out. But now that our connection was gone, maybe it was better to leave him in peace.

I missed him so bad, though…

And I was so wrapped up in my thoughts that I hardly noticed when someone picked up.

"Yes? Who's there?"

I expelled all the air I'd been holding in. It was a girl's voice.

I couldn't answer for a long time. That was the one thing I hadn't prepared for. But it made sense. He must have rebuilt his life. It had been nearly a year, after all. What did I expect? That he'd still be in mourning for our relationship? Could I blame him for wanting to move on?

The knot in my throat grew with every passing second.

Finally, almost choking, I said, "Hi. I'm, uh, a friend. Of Ja—I mean, of Ross's. My name's Jennifer. Is he around?"

The girl paused in turn. She had a strange but elegant accent, with long, drawn-out vowels.

"Jennifer?" she repeated.

She'd clearly never even heard of me. So that meant Jack didn't talk about me. I hadn't mattered to him as much as I'd thought. Probably I overestimated how much I'd mattered to him.

"He's in the shower," she said. "Should I get him?"

In the shower? Had they…?

No—I couldn't think about that. It wasn't my business. I closed my eyes and shook my head. "There's no need to bother him. Just, when he comes out, can you do me a favor?"

I don't know why I pressed it. He didn't want me in his life. Couldn't I just drop the whole thing? When the girl said of course, I asked her, "Could you tell him Jen wanted to tell him happy birthday, please?"

The girl said, "Mm-hmm, I'll take care of it, au revoir!"

I never knew if she conveyed my message, though. Either way, Jack had turned the page. The same page I kept rereading over and over.

"Jenny, are you listening to me?"

Back in the present, Shannon was trying to bring me down to earth.

"Huh?"

"All I want is to be sure you're OK, you know? You had a really tough time, and I'm wondering, is it the best idea for you to go back there? It might be like reopening the wound."

"Shannon, I've made up my mind."

She groaned. "I guess you have. Come on, then, I'll ride with you to the airport."

I struggled to get my huge suitcase down the stairs. Biscuit, my dog—Spencer had brought him over—hurried up to me, looking sad. I think he could tell I was going, the poor guy. At least we could share one last cuddle.

When Shannon tried to get me out the door, Owen asked if he could come along, ending with a *pleasepleaseplease!*

"Sure, little guy," I said, and he cheered, "Cool!"

My grandmother walked up with open arms, hugged me, and told me to behave. "And if you change your mind..."

"I know, I know," I said, "there will always be a cup of hot chocolate for me here." All my nerves eased as I held her and told her, "Love you, Grandma."

She smiled. "I love you, too. And you'll always have a home with me."

"Don't get all sentimental," Spencer interrupted us. "We can go visit her anytime."

It was hard, staring through the car window and watching her wave goodbye. I was leaving my comfort zone. I was scared. But I also knew I was finally taking hold of my life.

My brother, my sister, and my nephew accompanied me to security at the airport. When it was time for me to go in, Owen was the first to hug me. He could still barely reach my knees. "I liked having you here, auntie!"

"I'll be back before you know it, buddy." I mussed his hair. "When summer comes, we'll make up for lost time."

He didn't seem convinced. "Not if you find a boyfriend."

My brother and sister looked panicky, but not because of him—it was because of me, because I always freaked out whenever Jack was mentioned, and I wasn't good at covering up my feelings.

Shannon reprimanded him: "Don't bother your aunt." Then, turning to me, she said, "Sorry. I told him not to say anything."

Owen started whining, wiped his nose, and said, "I don't want Jenny to go…"

Spencer asked if he wanted to go to the arcade later, and Owen stopped crying instantly, nodding his head. He was easy to bribe. Shannon gave me a bear hug and, as she was resting her chin on my shoulders, reassured me: "I'm so proud of you. Even if you're unbearable and your fashion sense blows."

I laughed. "I'll miss you, too."

Spencer stepped in, squeezed me tight, and planted a noisy kiss on my forehead. "Call me for anything you need."

"I know, Spencer, you've been telling me that all week," I replied.

"Anything," he repeated. "And do me a favor. Don't come home pregnant. This family doesn't need another surprise."

Shannon nudged him with her elbow. Owen didn't catch the reference. He had taken out his little stuffed horse with its brown spots and was busy playing.

"I doubt that's a worry," I murmured.

"Still, it's good advice," Spencer said. "Now have fun. I know it's not been easy here, but this is a new stage in your life, and I want you to enjoy it."

"Yeah," Shannon said. "It's just a few months, and we'll come see you whenever you want."

It was time to go. I picked up my suitcase, looked back, and got in line. Just before I passed through the detector, Owen tugged at my hand and said, "Auntie, take Spot."

That was the name of his stuffed horse. Surprised, I kneeled down and asked, "Are you sure, buddy? You're not going to miss him?"

He shook his head and shoved the horse into my hands. It was so soft! When he told me to keep the toy so I wouldn't forget him, that almost pushed me over the edge. Spencer smiled at us, Shannon's brows wrinkled with sorrow, and I assured him, "Owen, I could never forget you. But I'll take Spot along anyway. He'll be my perfect companion at bedtime."

Owen loved that, and then he turned quickly to his mother and said, "Mommy, we need to go buy another Spot, so Jenny and I can both have one to take to bed!"

Spencer laughed when he saw the frustration on my sister's face—Owen was spoiled, there was no denying that—and then I had to leave before I missed boarding.

2

BACK HOME

It felt like a lifetime since I'd last seen them.

I crossed through the arrival doors, my stomach feeling tight as I stared out into the groups of people waiting for their friends and family, and there they were, Naya and Lana, stretching out their necks to find me.

Wait a minute. Lana. Lana had come to pick me up? Lana? The same Lana as last year?

I was dying to know what that was about, and how she'd act.

I walked forward, dodged a few rolling bags, and just when I thought I'd avoided an embarrassing scene, Naya put in a star performance. Our eyes met, I smiled at her, and she shrieked as if she'd seen a monster, jumping over the barrier, which I was pretty sure was a crime and which pissed off all of the other passengers, and ran toward me, almost knocking me over as she leaped into my arms. As I made it into the hall, Lana grabbed hold of the two of us.

Naya I understood, but Lana?! We'd never gotten along. So what was going on here? Had I entered a parallel universe when I got out off the plane?

"I can't believe it," Naya said, jumping up and down. "Look at you!"

"It's been an eternity," Lana added.

"Nice to see you guys, too," I said, embarrassed because everyone was staring at us.

They both told me I looked amazing—*radiant* was the word Naya used—and they wanted to know if I was doing something different with my skin or hair. But there wasn't much I could say: I'd gotten a tan and I was in better shape, but my ass was still fatter than I'd have liked, my boobs were still too small, I had the same brown eyes and the same brown hair, and I still always had a frown on my face.

"I could say the same about you guys," I said. And it was true. Naya had cut her blond hair to shoulder length and was wearing a pastel outfit that matched her blue eyes and sharp features. She looked like a little doll. She'd always had style. As for Lana, she'd let her hair grow out and was immaculately made-up, in the same expensive clothes as always. Her smile was more sincere than I was used to, and I had the feeling I had missed everything there, including her.

When I could finally get them off me, I said, "I love reunions as much as the next girl, but how about we catch a cab?"

"No need, Lana drove," Naya said, grabbing my suitcase and running off. "And wait till you see her car!"

Lana grabbed my arm and told me, "I hope it isn't weird that I drove here. I was just excited to see you."

"No worries. I'm glad we're still friendly."

She smiled. "Naya's so excited to have you back… I mean, all of us are. We really felt your absence."

I didn't know what to say. As soon as we left the airport, I saw the snow all over the ground. That reminded me of the past Christmas, which I'd spent with my grandmother, Shannon, Owen, and Spencer. I missed them already.

Lana's car really was luxurious: I felt like a Hollywood star. She didn't seem to think much of it, though. Naya told me to take the passenger seat, and she kept poking her head between us, begging me to tell her what had been going on. I reminded her that we talked on the phone all the time and that she hadn't missed out on anything interesting, and Naya blurted out that Lana had a *super-super-hot* new boyfriend.

Lana rolled her eyes, but I could tell she didn't mind. "He's not just handsome, he has other qualities, too."

"Yeah," Naya responded, "but let's be honest, his looks are what really count."

"Well, I'm happy for you," I assured her. She wanted to know if anything was going on in my love life. I told her with so much work, I hadn't had time for anything. When the two of them stared at each other and Lana reassured me that they'd find me someone soon, I asked if that should worry me.

"No!" Naya objected. "I'm just saying, you don't want to waste your youth."

They caught me up on things around campus, like how Naya's brother Chris had come out of the closet. He and his parents hadn't talked for weeks. But then they relented and agreed to meet his boyfriend, and just as they were starting to accept the whole thing, the two guys broke up. Sue was the same, except more stressed out because it was her senior year and she had a capstone project that consumed her every second. Will was enjoying his internship, which he went to after class, and he couldn't wait to finish school and get an actual job. Naya didn't say anything about her own schoolwork, but she did go into endless detail about how she'd changed the decorations in her bedroom.

"I baked you some cakes, too! But, uh…"

Lana interrupted her: "You won't like them unless you enjoy the taste of charcoal."

"It's not my fault!" Naya screamed. "That stupid oven won't obey me!"

I told them I'd cook dinner that night. I'd never had any problems with the oven. Naya tried to get me not to, saying I was their guest and must be tired from traveling. That reminded me to ask whether the new sofa bed was comfortable, and once again, they exchanged weird glances. Naya told me they hadn't ordered it yet, and Lana said she'd remind her to tomorrow.

The drive was over in no time. Lana parked on the street, and I looked around nostalgically. The same old shops, the factories in the distance, the broad street, the lights overhead…it wasn't beautiful, not even with the snow, but I felt at home there, and I had missed it. As soon as I stepped into the lobby, then into the elevator, I was flooded with memories. Lana and Naya were as excited as I was. It was hard to believe I'd been away for so long.

"At last!" Naya exclaimed when we stepped out, removing the keys from her pocket. "I'm so excited for you to move in!"

She opened the door, and as I was taking off my coat and dragging in my suitcase, Naya skipped off into the living room, where I heard Will ask her what had taken so long.

"We brought a little surprise," she responded, and waved me over. I don't know what I expected, but it certainly wasn't the perplexed expressions that greeted me. The living room was the same as always, with its two couches, its two easy chairs, its shelf, its TV and video game consoles, the same old paintings on the wall, and the counter separating it from the little kitchen. Even the scent was the same. All that was missing was Jack. Will and Sue sat there staring at me as if they'd seen a ghost.

"What the…?" Sue asked.

"Surprise!" Naya shouted, with Lana joining in.

Surprise? They hadn't known I was coming? I'd expected a little warmer reaction, but Will and Sue didn't look happy at all, and I could tell something had changed. It wasn't their looks: Sue was still thin and wrapped in endless layers of clothes that didn't match. Her hair was pulled back sloppily, and she was staring daggers into me. Will was handsome as ever: black eyes, black hair, tight sweater, the spitting image of the guy your mother prays you'll bring home to meet her.

Feeling awkward, I joked, "I'm glad you're so happy to see me."

Will stood and glared at Naya. Was he…angry? Since when did Will get angry? Especially at Naya?

I really have just entered a parallel universe, I thought.

"I can't believe you," he said. "You know this isn't right. And you do, too, Lana. I don't know what kind of scheme this is, but you shouldn't have done it."

Well, then. I tried not to look hurt as Naya murmured an explanation I didn't understand, but Will noticed, then his features relaxed and he came over and hugged me.

"It's not you," he reassured me in a softer tone. "I'm happy to see you, Jenna."

"Happy to see you, too, I just don't…"

Sue interrupted me: "This is sure going to be interesting, as you'll soon find out. But hey, I'm glad you're here." And to everyone's astonishment, she hugged me. What the hell was going on? I asked Sue how things were. She told me she had just stocked up on ice cream, which was the same as saying things were going well. I couldn't relax and talk longer with her, though, because I saw Will looking pissed again and stomping around the living room, sighing and saying, "I can't believe it." *You can't believe what?* I wondered.

Lana flopped down in one of the armchairs and said, "Believe it. It's best for everyone."

Will seemed skeptical, and I was getting impatient. "Can somebody tell me what the hell's going on?"

Naya was sitting on the couch at a prudent distance from her boy-friend, looking guilty as her boyfriend asked her, "You're kidding me. She doesn't know?!"

What didn't I know?

Naya crossed her arms and said, "If I'd told her, she wouldn't have agreed to come!" This went on for a moment, with Will complaining that Naya and Lana had lost their minds and them making excuses, and finally, I interrupted their bickering to plead, "Can you all stop ignoring me?"

Will cursed under his breath and said, "You better take a seat." Nervous, I did so, sitting down beside him and letting him take my hand in his. The way he was looking at me, I'd have thought he was about to confess a crime. He asked me not to get upset, and I told him what was upsetting me was everyone leaving me in the dark. He responded that I wasn't going to like what I was about to hear. Sue growled at him to spit it out, but he hemmed and hawed a few more moments before finally confessing, "Ross is living here!"

My whole body tensed from head to toe. Surely he hadn't said what I thought he'd said.

"What?" I forced myself to say.

"Surprise!" Naya responded weakly.

I waited for someone to tell me this was all a big joke, but no one did. *Come on, Will,* I thought, and when I didn't get the reply I wanted, I tried asking again: "What?"

"Imagine how he's going to react when he sees her," Sue murmured. "I don't know about you guys, but I'm going to record it."

I passed in a matter of seconds from surprise to panic to rage, and I turned to Naya, letting all of those feelings out at once: "You said he was still in France! And you, Lana, you knew all this, and you didn't say a damn thing!"

"Yeah, but if we told you, you wouldn't have come!" Lana protested.

"Of course I wouldn't have, and that's my right!" I said, letting go of Will's hand and standing up. "This is an ambush, and you have no right!"

I couldn't believe Naya was still smiling and trying to tell me what she'd done was fine. She argued that Jack would be happy to see me, that we'd be like a little family again. Even Will wasn't buying that. He asked, "You really think he's going to want to see her after what happened last year?"

Naya looked down and admitted he wouldn't. "I just wanted everything to be the way it used to be."

"Well, this wasn't the way to do it," Will said. "So what are we supposed to do now?"

Sue, completely relaxed, responded that there was nothing to do but wait for Jack and hope he'd behave, and I looked up and asked what that meant. When there was no reply, I pressed them: "Is there something you all haven't told me?"

Lana started to try to explain, but trailed off, and Naya did the same. Finally, Will took the lead: "Ross isn't exactly like he was before."

Sue grinned. "You saw his good side. Hopefully you're ready to see the bad one."

"He's changed a lot this year," Naya murmured. "Or, like, he's gone back to the way he used to be. When he actually changed was when you were here…"

I thought he was in France! When I asked what he was doing back, they told me he had gone there and had started his studies, but then a good opportunity had come up in the US. He had a film coming out in three weeks, and he had gotten all kinds of press. So he'd made it. And yet…if things were going so great, why did it feel like bad news? I didn't know, but I wasn't going to wait for explanations. I jumped up and grabbed my suitcase, which I'd left by the fridge. I needed to go, now.

Naya ran over to intercept me, but I warned her to stay where she was. She had lied to me. I'd sworn I would only come if I knew I wouldn't run into him, and she had told me that was no problem. She tried to apologize, but I cut her off: she had done this on purpose. I was going home. This had been a terrible idea, a horrible idea, right from the beginning.

I should have stayed in my comfort zone with my grandmother, even if half the people in my hometown hated me. Why should I care? At least I wouldn't have to run into Jack there, and I wouldn't have to see the person I used to love replaced by some almost-famous director getting ready to make his big splash.

Will called out, "Jenna, don't rush. Maybe you don't have to go. There must be a solution…" As he continued musing and Naya went on apologizing, the front door opened, and we all froze. I was holding my suitcase, but I didn't dare move an inch as I heard those heavy, slow steps approaching. A ring of keys landed on the bar, skidded to the edge, but didn't fall. Only one person tossed his keys like that. *No…*

"Ross!" Naya shouted, trying to sound enthusiastic.

He hadn't noticed me, and I watched him from behind as he pulled off his jacket, looking at everyone and surely wondering why they all were acting strange. My heart was beating so hard I could feel it banging into my ribs. There he was, just a few feet away…and I wanted to reach out and touch him. I wanted to hug him. I wanted to tell him why I'd done what I'd done the year before, ask him why he hadn't called me back, find out whether he'd really forgotten me, and just know he was OK. But I couldn't, because he beat me to the punch, asking his roommates sarcastically, "What?"

I'd never heard him use that tone before, but the rest of them didn't seem remotely surprised. He asked Lana what she was doing there. Good lord, he sounded harsh! That wasn't like Jack. What was going on?

"Naya invited me," Lana said wearily, as if they'd been through this dozens of times. "In case you forgot, she lives here too."

"Speaking of guests," Naya butted in, looking over at me, "there's, uh, something you should know."

I could tell things were about to go south. Jack could tell something bad was happening, Will was trying to calm him down, Sue announced she'd had no part in this and Jack shouldn't blame her. I got tired of the tension and heard myself say, "Hi." A horrible silence followed.

My voice was soft, but it shut everyone up, and I saw the muscles tense in Jack's back as he froze. Will looked back and forth between us as Jack turned in slow motion. His hair was short, his beard had grown in slightly, and his expression was…different. He had bags under his eyes, he looked weary. How long had it been since he'd gotten a good night's sleep?

That was the last thing I asked myself before my mind went blank. His stare was nothing like it had been a year before. If you didn't know, you'd have said he hated me. Every pore in his body oozed contempt. Disdain. And despite myself, I could understand why.

I wanted to retreat, but I kept my composure. He looked me over from head to foot, and I felt a long-forgotten electric charge run through me. I wrung my fingers and opened my mouth, but I couldn't make myself break the silence. He was perplexed, and I was too, and I needed him to say something. I walked toward him, and he almost flinched. That brought him back to reality, and he looked away as Naya murmured, "Surprise?"

I couldn't tell what he was thinking, and that frightened me, and I closed my eyes.

"Fuck," he grunted, grabbing his things and slamming the door on the way out.

3

OF NIGHTS AND BARS

Jack didn't come back, and nobody seemed surprised. I was the exception. When night fell, I lay on the sofa and stared at the ceiling, and I couldn't get the way he'd looked at me out of my head. Had he felt sorrow, fear, anger? I still wasn't sure. Maybe it was all three, maybe something else.

Anyway, it wasn't good, and my only consolation was to hug Spot tight and imagine Owen sleeping soundly and doing the same. When I opened my eyes the next morning, Will was in the kitchen making breakfast. He didn't seem preoccupied. I asked him what was up with Jack.

"I'm not his babysitter, Jenna. He's a grown-up, he knows what he's doing, and when he decides he wants to talk, he'll show up."

I took that to mean Jack flipping out and leaving was nothing new. I didn't like the sound of that, though I didn't know why. I mean, he was right, Jack was an adult. But still…

It was a Monday morning, and I had a week till classes started, so I decided to take the light rail to the campus that had been my whole world the year before. On the way, I answered text messages from my siblings. I didn't mention seeing Jack.

I liked the feeling of familiarity when I arrived: the old station, the lawn by the administration building, the library, the bars, the school of arts and letters, where I'd taken my classes… The dorm was just past it, and I walked over. The feminist banner that had been there before was gone, replaced by a new one in favor of animal rights. I climbed the stairs with a smirk on my face. Nothing inside had changed. Even the front desk was the same, with a blond guy in huge glasses trying to hide the cell phone he'd been playing Candy Crush on just before.

I was about to speak when I noticed something: Chris was talking with Jack.

I could tell even from behind. He hadn't even changed clothes. He was wearing a black jacket and dirty white sneakers, leaning against the counter, exhausted. When he was tired, he got in a bad mood.

And I was pretty sure I was about to make it worse.

I tried to escape but didn't make it before Chris looked up and smiled. "Hey, Jenna!"

Mission not accomplished.

There was no point in trying to avoid it now, and I stiffened as they both turned, forcing a smile that must have looked alarming. I tried to say I could come back in a minute, but Chris was already waving me over, saying, "Come here…where do you think you're going?"

I looked hesitantly at Jack, at his elbows resting on the surface of the counter, at his fingers playing distractedly with a pen. *He hasn't slept*, I thought, but then, I'd thought that the day before, too. So maybe he just always looked exhausted now. It was hard to say.

I didn't want to complicate things, but I didn't know how to extract myself from this situation without making everything worse. Staying in Jack's apartment seemed out of the question, but it was also awkward to beg Chris to try to pull strings for me with campus housing when Jack was standing right there in front of me.

I leaned in a foot away from Jack, drumming my fingers, and said to Chris, "Hey! Nice to see you." I didn't dare look at my ex-boyfriend to my right. But I could feel him staring. My stomach was in knots. What was better: to ignore him, or to try and talk to him? I didn't want to upset him even more.

"I'm so glad you're around here again," Chris said, smiling innocently, with no idea of the tension all around him. "My sister must be happy, too."

"Yeah, she came to get me at the airport. She actually jumped over the barrier in arrivals."

"That sounds like her."

I knew Jack was watching. I could nearly feel his eyes moving up and down my body like some kind of scanner. I wasn't sure if I could keep from saying something to him as Chris informed me, "I hope you're not here trying to get a room. Naya mentioned it to me, but there's still nothing available."

Thanks a lot, Chrissy.

His mouth was just as big as it had been the year before. But what did I care at this point? I don't think I could have offended Jack any worse. I noticed something shaking out of the corner of my eye. Was Jack laughing as he rested his chin on his fist? I turned and found him staring at me, irked, almost indifferent, with a contemptuous smirk. "So you want to go back to the dorm?"

His voice was gentle. That caught me off guard. Wasn't he supposed to be mad at me? Or was I wrong in assuming I mattered that much to him? Maybe I barely existed for him now.

"Yeah…" I didn't like how my voice sounded…too soft. "Naya told me you weren't here and that there was going to be a sofa bed for me to sleep on, but now it seems like it's easier if I just stay in the dorms."

He toyed with a pen and responded, looking totally apathetic, "I guess."

What was with him? "Hey Chris," I said, "you sure there's absolutely nothing available?"

"Yes," he said, "I already told Naya."

Jack butted in, "Just call one of the hotels and put her up in a suite. She'll have no trouble finding some guy to pay for it."

He said that so blithely, I needed a few seconds to react. Even Chris seemed nervous as he continued, "If something comes up, I'll let you know, though."

I was no longer listening, I was just scowling at Jack. I'd never heard him speak like that to anyone, not even to Mike or his dad, and he'd had no problem giving them a piece of his mind. He looked at me smugly, almost waiting for me to snap. He was hunting for an argument. I remembered then something my therapist had said: that I had to pick my battles. And this one, I thought, I'd be better off ignoring. So I turned to Chris. "Yeah, keep me in mind if you hear anything."

"Oh, are you running away?" Jack said. "I mean, I don't know why I should be surprised." As Chris nodded, I apologized for bothering him, telling him I wouldn't have done it if it weren't important, and he mentioned a girl in an individual room who was supposedly having problems and might end up dropping out. "If she does, trust me, you'll be the first to know," he concluded.

"What's up?" Jack asked. "Are you in a rush to stop sleeping in my bed?"

I fell into his trap: "I didn't sleep in your bed, I slept on the couch."

"How sweet of you," he responded, "I guess that means you were worried about how I'd feel. Oh, no, I forgot, that can't be true, because a year ago you left me hanging like I didn't even fucking exist."

I could tell Chris was eavesdropping, but he didn't want to get in the middle of this and was pretending to dig around in a drawer. I tried to tell Jack I was sorry about what had happened between us, that I knew I hadn't gone about it the right way, but…

"Just drop it," he interrupted me. "Why would you even bother pretending that you ever truly cared about me? Or are you trying to say you're sorry? Because you can save that. I know you'd be doing it for yourself, not for me—you just want to make yourself feel better because you acted like a complete…"

He decided not to say the next word, stepped away from the counter, and looked down before pinning me in his stare, full of scorn. "Why did you even come back? Was it because you missed your little friends?"

"I wanted to come back to school, Jack. I thought you weren't even here. If I'd known…"

"I know, you wouldn't have come," he said.

"It's not that I wouldn't have come, it's just that this is so uncomfortable. I get it. But look, if you take your room and I just sleep on the couch until I…"

He laughed in my face. "Oh, wow, are you seriously giving me permission to use my own room? You know what, fuck it! You take the damn room."

"Jack…"

"No. No, no, no. Nobody calls me Jack. That was a special thing I let you do because you were my girlfriend. Now you're just some person. You can call me Ross like everyone else."

I tried to tell him not to be childish, and he stepped toward me—I don't know why. I was scared and stepped back and bumped into a short bookcase. I thought the argument would continue, but he turned around in frustration and walked out into the courtyard. Chris had seen the whole thing and still didn't look like he believed it. "Wow," he said. "And I thought he couldn't be any more unbearable."

"It's not that, Chris," I said. "He's just hurt."

"You're seriously going to defend him after he talked to you that way?"

"Whatever," I responded. "Just call me if a room opens up."

I spent the rest of the day on campus. Curtis, who was already living in the dorms, invited me up to his room to introduce me to his friends.

They seemed nice, and I was proud of myself for actually being social. I remembered how shy I'd been the year before.

Before we realized it, it was nightfall. I was lying in bed by then, another girl was lying next to me, and there were a couple of guys sitting on the rug. We were all staring at a computer screen where Gal Gadot was lashing shadowy figures with her golden whip.

"Wonder Woman's so hot," Curtis said. "I'd love to bone her with that outfit on."

The girl next to me giggled and kicked him in the shoulder. "Have you forgotten our conversation about objectifying women?"

"Hey, I don't discriminate, I'd do the same with Henry Cavill."

You could never know, but Henry Cavill sure sounded like a guy's name. Was Curtis bisexual? Awkward as it felt, I forced myself to ask, and he responded, "Duh! You don't have to say it that way, though. You make it sound like I'm a serial killer or something!"

"No!" I reassured him, "I just, uh…"

"Forgive her, everyone," Curtis said, addressing his friends with a relaxed smile. "Where Jenna's from, nobody's come out of the closet yet. It's like one of those tourist villages where they still have blacksmiths and water mills and stuff."

"That's not true," I protested. "It's just people there…they don't talk about their…sexuality or whatever." I blushed as I said that, but I wasn't lying. I couldn't even imagine mentioning something like that in front of my neighbors. People back home were close-minded about everything. Even I had found it hard to ignore all their dumb prejudices.

I tried to say it didn't matter, and everyone jumped on me, like *who are you to tell him it doesn't matter, nobody asked you*, and I could tell they were trying to teach me, but it was also a little mean. Thankfully, Curtis jumped in to save me with a joke: "Guys, she just got upset because for a moment she got scared she couldn't have me. It's OK, though, Jennifer. Just say the word, and I'm yours."

Things relaxed again after that, and I think the awkwardness even brought us closer. Curtis gave me a bear hug when it was time to go home and waved at me from his dorm window when I was outside. The two guys who had been with us offered me a ride. When I told them they could drop me off a few blocks from Jack's, they even offered to drive me home. I replied that there was no need, then said, "See you in class!" They told me to send Curtis a message when I got in so everyone would know I was safe.

Hands in the pocket of my sweatshirt, I walked the rest of the way home. It was a safe neighborhood, and I needed the fresh air and a few moments to clear my head. Just two days had passed and I already felt overwhelmed. I missed being home, living with my grandmother, when my biggest worry was whether my schedule at the gas station might clash with the time when I was supposed to be coaching. Then I found myself ducking before I even knew what was happening. Something flew past me: a beer can tossed by a drunk walking out of the one bar on the street. As the door slowly closed, I could hear loud music blaring. The guy laughed and flipped me off, and I crossed to the other side of the street.

That was when I saw the black car covered in stickers. I stopped. I knew those stickers. I knew that car. And I sure as hell knew its owner. I turned back to the bar—the only one in the area open on Monday nights—and asked myself: could Jack be inside?

I wanted to go in. At the same time, I wanted to take off running. I didn't like the look of the place and didn't want to push through the crowd—it grossed me out to think of all those people's bodies pressed against mine. The place looked like a dump, and I imagined everyone in there was hammered. But at the same time, I couldn't just leave, could I?

The drunk from before sat down clumsily and lit a cigarette, and I dialed Will's number. He was my one responsible friend, and he picked up on the first ring.

"Jenna, what's up?" he said cheerfully.

"Hey, uh…can I ask you something?"

Was that too direct? I wondered, because he took a moment before answering, "Sure."

"Does Jack like to go to bars on Monday nights?"

Silence again. Tenser this time.

"Why," he finally said, "did you see him?"

"I think so. I'm standing in front of his car, and there's nothing on this block but a bar, and…"

"The one with the palm trees on the sign? Like just two minutes from our place?"

"Yeah," I responded.

"Jenna, come home. I'll take care of it."

Take care of what? Will seemed worried. I guessed I should do as he said—he must know better. But then I hesitated. I told myself I wasn't the old Jenna, the one who just did whatever others said. And I wanted to know what was going on. I walked over to the drunk guy squatting there and asked him, "You didn't happen to see a tall guy inside, with shaggy brown hair, kind of tired-looking?"

"You mean Ross?"

"Yeah," I said, shocked. "Is he in there?"

The guy stood, crushed his cigarette, and sighed before walking back inside. For some reason, I forgot my common sense and hurried in behind him.

The place was as trashy as I'd expected, and so packed it was almost impossible to move. I kept getting shoved, and everyone was so drunk they didn't seem to care that I was trying to get somewhere. It was like I didn't exist. No one would move out of the way. And it stank! Of sweat, tobacco, cheap beer, and mildew. Disgusting.

The drunk guy reached a couple of tables and sofa where things looked calmer. Jack was there talking to a couple of guys. The drunk touched his arm and he turned. Then several people crowded past me, and I lost sight of him for a few seconds. When I pushed through again, Jack was looking straight at me. We were both paralyzed, then a huge smile crossed his face.

Wait a minute…a smile?

Wasn't he supposed to be pissed at me?

He was wearing a gray T-shirt, a black jacket, and some old jeans I'd seen him in dozens of times. He rushed over and brusquely shoved away the people nearby. "Jen!" he shouted.

I was so surprised that I didn't know how to react. That seemed to bother him, but it didn't stop him from wrapping an arm around me and dragging me over to his friends. I felt like a rag doll as he squeezed me and said, "Guys, this is Jen!"

That was all they needed to hand me a beer and give me a place against a column where everyone would stop pushing me. Jack leaned in close and shouted into my ear, because the music was so loud, "Did you come here to see me?" He sounded like a little boy at Christmas. "Drink your beer, it's on the house."

I tried to talk to him, but he wasn't listening. Someone had tapped him on the shoulder, and he turned around and started babbling like crazy. I stared listlessly at my beer. I hadn't drunk alcohol in forever, and these didn't seem like the best circumstances to start again.

Someone moved past, knocking him into me, and I stared at his chest, just a few inches from my eyes. He stank of alcohol. I could see the spots where he'd spilled beer on his T-shirt. He asked again if I'd come to see him.

"Are you drunk?" I asked in reply.

I'd never seen him acting that way. He'd always been one of those guys who could drink and drink without ever getting drunk. Now, though, he was pretty far gone: swaying, with a dumb smile on his lips, on the verge of dropping his bottle.

"Are you not thirsty?" he asked, trying to take my beer. So this was what he was like when he was drunk: unable to shut up or stop moving. When he wrested the bottle from me, he laid it on a nearby table and asked, "What's up? Are you OK? Is something wrong? You're cold, right? Of course you are, why do you always go out without your jacket, Jen, you're a disaster, but I'll forgive you, because you're my favorite disaster…"

He laughed, and in an instant, he was in short sleeves and I had his jacket draped around me. I couldn't react before he'd grabbed my wrist and guided me to the couches, pulling me onto his lap, because there was nowhere else to sit. He was talking and laughing with the person next to him, and I was disoriented: the lights were flashing, the faces were unknown, the place was weird, and my head was starting to spin.

Jack pulled me in close, and I remembered how he used to do that before. But it had been tender then. Now it was rough and jerky. I didn't like Jack when he was drunk. I felt…sorry for him. As if he were a baby I had to protect from himself. I could feel his forehead against my neck as he murmured, "I'm so, so glad you're back."

I wanted to be happy, I wanted to let myself go, but I couldn't. "You didn't seem very glad this morning."

"Oh, Jen. Things have gotten complicated. But it doesn't matter. You're here now."

"And you're drunk on a Monday night." I wasn't going to let him off the hook that easy. "Ross, don't you have a job? A movie to work on or something?" I had remembered what he'd told me, and I'd respected it—I was supposed to call him Ross now.

"Fuck the movie."

"But it's your dream…"

"Can we not just have fun for one night? Shit, Jen, I'm just trying to have a good time with you. I missed you."

I wanted to tell him I'd missed him too. But I wasn't sure whether it was him or the alcohol speaking. And anyway, I couldn't talk more because somebody grabbed me by the wrists and stood me up—a girl who wanted me to dance with her and her friends. I kept looking back at Jack, but the people on the dance floor all blocked my view. I didn't want him to get up and disappear. But then he was back, dancing beside me. The bright, colored lights shot across his face. He laughed, took a drink, grabbed my hand and pulled me close. But I wasn't dancing. I was desperate. I wanted to get the hell out of there. Will had to be waiting for us. How long had I been there?

Everything got confusing, and all of a sudden Jack was gone. I looked around for him, but there was no point. People were jostling me, and I didn't know any of them, and I was starting to feel scared. I was overheating in his jacket but didn't want to take it off. Eventually I found the girl who had dragged me onto the dance floor and asked her where Jack had gone. She shrugged and pointed toward some tables and said he'd gone to talk to a guy in a blue sweatshirt. Supposedly I couldn't miss him. When I found the guy in question, Jack was sitting across from him.

I found something else, too: lines of white powder being cut with a credit card. Next to them was a rolled-up five-dollar bill. Jack grabbed it, cackled, and sucked one of the lines up his nose.

I don't know what I felt then. I knew Jack had taken drugs before we met. I knew he'd done all kinds of questionable things in his past. But seeing it…seeing it happen again…made my whole world stop. He looked up and his eyes crossed mine. He stopped laughing and went pale. I guess I had done the same.

Jack was drinking. Jack was doing drugs. That's why he had those bags under his eyes. That's why he was acting so weird. Now I understood. He was the same ill-tempered Jack from before, the one they had told me about. Did his roommates know all this? Did they know that he'd relapsed? Did they know how long it had been? When had it started? If so, then why hadn't anyone told me?

I needed to go, and I needed to get Jack out of there. He got up, people told him to stick around, they complained, but he wanted to follow me. When he reached me, he didn't dare to touch me. His eyes were dilated, his breathing was labored, and I could tell he was afraid I'd turn and run off. When I didn't, he tried to hold me, but then he thought better of it and let his arms drop to his sides. He was sniffling, anxious, frantic, desperate.

"Jen, it's not…"

That was the moment when I dared to believe I still mattered to him. Maybe not as much as the year before, but still. And I used myself as an excuse.

"I don't feel good," I said. "I think I need some fresh air."

I was relieved when his expression changed, and he hugged me to him and pushed through the crowd to the exit. I kept looking over and noticing how strange he was acting, and it made me want to cry, but I knew that wasn't the moment. When we got outside, I turned my back. Maybe I did need that breath of fresh air. I was dizzy, even though I hadn't drunk a drop. Reality was weighing down on me like a ton of bricks.

"Jen?"

I didn't turn, but I could feel him coming closer. If he didn't touch me, it was because he didn't know how I'd react, not because he didn't want to.

In my head, I saw him taking coke again, and I closed my eyes as I heard him say, "Please, say something to me. Anything."

He touched my arm timidly, as if hoping to hold me back, and continued, "I didn't want you to find out this way."

He was still pale, and he looked upset, and I snapped: "How the hell did you want me to find out? Drugs, Ross? Really?"

"It's not such a big deal!"

I didn't know whether to laugh, cry, or both. I tried to step away, but he grabbed the sleeve of his jacket. He looked desperate as he told me, "I can quit whenever I want. It's just something I do when I party, when other people bring it. It's not a habit, Jen, you've got to trust me!"

"If it's not such a big deal," I challenged him, "then how about you swear to me here and now that you'll never do it again?"

As he stalled, a gray car screeched to a stop beside us. Will jumped out and hurried over, and Jack asked, looking betrayed, "Did you call him?"

"Of course I did, I was worried," I said. "And something's wrong with you. You need help!"

Wil tried to grab him, and Jack pushed him away. I was surprised by how strong he seemed, even when he could barely stand. "Fuck you both!" he shouted, "I don't need a damn babysitter, OK? I can take care of myself."

"Dude, just get in the car and stop being an asshole," Will said wearily. I guessed this wasn't the first time something like this had happened. They argued, then Will convinced him to get in the back seat and motioned for me to do the same. I didn't love the idea, but I also didn't want to fight about it. As I sat down, I noticed Jack barely moved. When the car took off, Will asked me to buckle Jack's seatbelt, and Jack snapped, "I can do it myself!"

I ignored him, leaning across the seat as he let his head fall backward. He was white as a sheet, and I worried he was about to puke. After buckling him up, I scooted in close in case he might need me and asked if he was all right. When he didn't answer, I continued, "Can you hear me?"

He grunted and turned toward the window.

"Just leave him," Will said.

Jack's chest rose and fell, and he shifted like a person having a nightmare. I was terrified. I had no idea what he was going through. When we parked, Will lifted him out of the car and helped him walk to the elevator.

Jack looked up a few times, but his head kept sinking, and as soon as we were in the apartment, he collapsed in a heap on the couch and started snoring. Will turned him on his side, put a pillow under his head, threw a blanket over him, and took off his shoes. I just stood there like an idiot the whole time.

When I asked if I could help, Will said, "Trust me, it's best to just leave him. As long as he's on his side, we don't have to worry about him aspirating. Will you stay with him a minute? I need to let Naya know we're OK."

I nodded, but stopped him. "Did you know he's been doing drugs?"

With a somber expression, Will replied, "Yes, and I know what you're thinking. And yes, we've tried to help him, Jenna. More times than you can imagine. But you can't help someone who doesn't want to be helped. All you can do is try to make sure he's all right and be there for him when he comes around. Now hold on, I'll be right back."

Wondering what it meant to make sure someone was all right, I turned back to Jack and saw him rubbing his eyes with his hands. He was awake, if barely.

"Feeling better?" I asked for some reason.

"It sucks that Will's such a party pooper. We were having fun."

"You were having too much fun," I told him.

He grinned. I didn't. Before I could add anything, Will came back in and recommended I sleep in Jack's bedroom that night.

I lay there a long time awake, feeling turmoil at the memories I'd spent a year trying to forget. The dresser, the closet, the posters, the trophies, the balcony... I'd never have guessed how much I'd missed all that. Nothing had changed in there but the scent, musty, dull. I could tell Jack didn't go there much, that it had mostly sat empty, and that saddened me.

I didn't get much sleep. I tossed and turned, and when the sun rose, I gave it up. I didn't get out of bed, though. I didn't have the courage to face what was awaiting me in the living room. Not, at least, until I heard someone come in and start moving things around, opening doors. It reminded me of that night Mike had come in, and Jack had thought he was a burglar. Could it be him again? I stood and looked at myself in the mirror in my baggy shorts, my T-shirt, and my red socks. It wasn't the most flattering outfit, but what the hell.

When I walked into the living room, I saw Jack opening and closing drawers in the kitchen, looking behind furniture, digging through the books on the shelves. He was frantic, and, unsure what to say, I just stood there watching him, feeling like an idiot. When he realized I was there, he turned and stared, acting startled, before finally asking with a furrowed brow, "What are you doing here?"

"I heard you moving all this stuff around…"

"No, I mean what are you doing in my apartment?"

Had he really forgotten everything from the day before? I reminded him that I'd asked Chris about getting a room in the dorms, that there was nothing available, that I'd found him drunk at the bar last night, that I'd seen him doing drugs. I tried not to sound judgmental, but I could tell he was ashamed. And he covered up for it by being rude, telling me, "Whatever, I'm busy and I need some time to myself."

"What you need, Ross, is to stop whatever it is you're doing. Do you not find it the least bit disturbing that you can't even remember what happened yesterday? That you completely forgot that I was here?"

"Leave me alone! Who do you think you are, my mom? Go deal with your own problems. From what I remember, you had more than a few."

"I don't think I'm your mom, but you're hurting yourself," I said. "You need help."

"And you need to learn when you're not wanted."

"You're not going to provoke me, Ross. I've got three brothers. I've spent my whole life learning to deal with that. And I'm not going to change the subject either. You're trying to make me a villain so you don't have to face your issues. I've been in therapy, I know about these strategies. Maybe you should give it a try…"

I was careful not to raise my voice, and I tried to pat his shoulder to reassure him. Bad decision. He jerked away, almost frightened, and said, "Don't touch me!"

Then he told me to get out, asked me why I was bothering him, asked if there wasn't somebody else whose life I could ruin. That hurt, but I tried not to let it get to me. "I want to help you," I said. "But you have to accept me for me to do that."

"I don't want your help! I don't want anybody's help! I'm tired of being treated like a baby who can't take care of himself! I know what I'm doing and I'm perfectly in control. Now where the hell is my damn jacket?"

He stopped. His chest was rising and falling dramatically. He collapsed in the middle of the room, pulled his knees to his chest, and started tugging at his hair so hard his knuckles turned white. "Shit, shit, shit!" he said.

I was taken off guard and needed a few moments before I had the courage to approach him.

Of course he couldn't find his jacket. It was in the bedroom, because I'd worn it home from the bar. I wanted to tell him, but then I stopped, thinking maybe the jacket didn't matter as much as a little bag of white powder that might be in one of the pockets. I crouched next to him, rubbed his hands to keep him from tearing out his own hair, and said, "Jack, what's going on?"

"Shut up," he grunted. "Leave me alone. Just go."

"I'm not going to leave you on your own like this. I'm trying to help you. But I need you to tell me how. And I need you to be honest with me about what's in the jacket."

I was surprised that his anger subsided for a moment. His body slackened, and he shook his head as he stared at the floor. "I fucked it all up, Jen," he murmured.

I hugged him and tried to reassure him. "It's probably not as bad as it seems."

"It is, though. You don't understand."

"Then tell me. Help me. Please."

For nearly a minute, he didn't speak. Then, finally, he admitted, "I owe someone money."

I hadn't expected that. And from his tone, I had to assume he wasn't talking about a little loose change. Hoping to encourage him, I reminded him, "Yeah, but I heard you have a movie coming out, right? Once that happens, you'll have more money than you'll know what to do with…"

"I wish," he responded. "I spent everything. And the premiere isn't happening yet, and I won't make another cent until then. Plus, what if it bombs? What if no one wants to see it?"

"Didn't you have a streaming deal or something?"

"My YouTube stuff. That's over. I haven't made any real money off that in forever."

"Is it urgent?" I asked, and when he nodded, I went on: "What will happen if you don't pay?"

He didn't tell me, but from the look on his face, I could tell it wouldn't be good.

"I've got two hundred on me. Would that work for now? I owe you way more than that for all you've done for me. I never paid you rent or anything," I told him.

He was hesitant, and for a moment he argued with me, but I didn't give ground, instead running back to his room and grabbing the cash out of my pants. I brought his jacket back with it. When he asked if I was sure it was OK, I responded, "Look, I've had two jobs for the past year. I'm not rich, but this won't bankrupt me, I promise you."

He thought it over, then accepted. As he counted the bills, he said, "I'll pay you back."

I agreed, but it didn't matter to me. Even if it was just this once, I was glad I could be the one helping him out of a jam. Now neither of us seemed sure what to say. He was calm again, and I was nervous. I decided it was better to leave him on his own. I tossed his jacket on the couch and told him, "Get some rest, Jack, you look like hell."

I think he might have mumbled *sure* in response.

4

BATHROOM INVADER

I managed to get another two or three hours of sleep, then drifted in and out for a while before giving it up and walking to the kitchen. As I passed the living room, I noticed Jack wasn't there. Sue was standing at the bar eating ice cream and pointed her spoon at me as she said, "He was gone when I got up."

"Is that common?"

"Is it common for him to spend all night sniffing coke and then vanish out of the blue? Definitely."

She must have seen the scandalized look on my face, because she asked then if she'd taken it too far, and when I nodded, she said, "All right, sorry. Yes, it happens a lot, unfortunately. He relapsed in France. He's been a totally different person since he came back."

That was like a punch to the stomach. He had regretted the person he used to be—why would he go back to it now? Had the pressure of being a filmmaker been too much for him? Was it his school? Something else? I didn't know, but we had to do something about it.

"He can't go on like this," I said. "He should… I don't know, I've never been in this situation, what do people do? Go to rehab, right?"

"I guess, yeah. I'm not really an expert," Sue replied.

"Good mooooorning!" we heard. It was Naya interrupting us, strolling over in a pair of panties and one of Will's sweatshirts. "I'm dying of hunger." She was so chipper, I assumed Will hadn't told her anything. He stomped in soon afterward, looking miserable, mumbled, "Hello, girls," and turned on the coffee machine.

"Did you get any sleep?" he asked me a second later.

"About the same as you, I'd guess," I answered. That got a slight grin out of him.

I heard a ding and took a look at my phone. Sue peeked at it over my shoulder, and when she saw what it was, remarked, "Damn, you didn't waste any time!" It was Curtis telling me there were *big plans* that evening. He was hosting movie night. Bring popcorn, or I'm not letting you in, he had written.

"Jenna, are you up to something naughty?" Naya asked.

"Her boyfriend wrote her," Sue cut in.

"Curtis isn't my boyfriend!" I shouted. But it was too late. Naya started repeating the name Curtis over and over, asking herself why it sounded familiar, and then announced that she remembered him.

"The handsome one, right? Weren't you with him late last night? Now I understand why you look so beat…"

"He's not that handsome," Sue interjected. I noticed no one had asked about Jack, and I wondered why, but also didn't want to bring him up. I thought the next best thing was to mention his brother, and said, "Hey, what's up with Mike?"

Sue murmured, "Who cares? He probably just found someone new to sponge off of. He'll show up eventually."

Will shook his head and said, "He's still with his band. They put out a song that did OK and we managed to get him to take some singing classes. He's gotten better, but obviously there was a lot of room for improvement. He's no Frank Sinatra, but at least he doesn't just scream into the microphone now."

My phone sounded again, and this time everybody turned. I had three messages.

I got that book you asked for! I left it in my underwear pile.

BTW, I disinfected it!

You want me to bring it by?

Naya shrieked, "Is it him? We want to meet him!"

"Fine," I said, "but he's not my boyfriend."

"So he's a friend, so what, I still want to meet him," Naya responded. "If we get along, maybe we can all have dinner or something sometime. I get bored with it always being the same people here. Not saying there's anything wrong with you guys, but a little new blood might do us some good."

Will stared at her as she spoke. He didn't seem to find it such a good idea. But I told Curtis sure, he could come by that afternoon, and I was actually looking forward to it. I mean, I'd met his friends and he'd gotten them to accept me, so why shouldn't it go both ways? He was a great guy, and I was sure everyone would love him.

Later, when he rang the doorbell, Naya was about to jump out of her skin. I opened the door to find him leaning on one side of the doorframe. He lifted my book up and winked.

"Special delivery," he said.

"Thanks. You want to come in?"

"Of course. You know how nosy I am!"

I laughed and stood aside, and right away I heard Naya greeting him. It was obvious that they would get along great: they were both super-social, and as soon as they flopped down on the sofa together, they were chattering away. Sue ignored them, flipping through her fashion magazine, and Will set a couple of beers down on the coffee table.

"I'm glad you guys have some classes together this year," Naya said. "I worry about Jenna being on her own."

"You sound like my mom," I told her, but Curtis said Naya was right, that I struggled to fit in, especially with big groups. "And my friends all love you," he added, pulling me into him and squeezing. I found that a relief—much more than I wanted to admit. Even if I had fun with people, I always wondered afterward whether they really liked me or were just pretending.

"Big groups suck," Sue said, turning a page of her magazine.

"Says you," Curtis responded. "I love hanging out with a bunch of people. It just means more people to talk shit to and embarrass."

Sue must have liked that—it fit with her weird sense of humor. She grinned slightly, and I had to admire Curtis's skill at winning over everyone in the house. I had needed weeks to get Sue to stop scowling at me when I'd first started coming over there.

Just then, Jack walked in and threw his keys on the counter. He had changed into a gray sweatshirt and a pair of jeans, all of it new looking. I felt somehow sad not to see him in clothing I recognized. Had things changed that much in a year? He didn't notice me, instead addressing Will and saying, "Hey, bro, have you seen Jen? I need…"

He turned, stopped talking, froze. And I realized Curtis's arm was around me. He withdrew it, clapped me on the back, and straightened up awkwardly. Jack didn't react. But you could tell he thought something wasn't right. He had reached into the pocket of his sweatshirt, but then he stopped himself instead of taking something out.

Will broke the tense silence: "Hey, man. This is Curtis, he's one of Jenna's friends."

I didn't like the tone of that word *friends*. It made it sound like he was trying to cover up for something. Jack's expression turned suddenly spiteful, the same way I had already seen him look—I guess I was naive to think something would have changed after last night—and he murmured, as if he couldn't care less, "Great."

He grabbed a beer, opened it, and sat on the other end of the sofa, leaving me between him and Curtis. Now things were actually getting weird.

"Our dear friend Jack here, who's swilling his beer and ignoring everyone, is a movie director," Naya announced, to try and make us feel less uncomfortable. "He's about to make his big debut."

"For real?" Curtis asked. "When?"

"Two weeks," Jack said.

"Look how overjoyed he is," Sue remarked.

Jack stared into the TV set. I wanted to ask if he was OK, but I was sure he'd be pissed if I did it in front of everyone. Will tried to force a conversation out of him again, asking, "Is Vivian going to be at the premiere?"

Vivian? I couldn't help but frown. That girl who had picked up the phone when I called on Ross's birthday…was that Vivian? What was the deal with them? I'd tried not to think about it before, telling myself it wasn't my problem, but if it wasn't, it sure as hell felt like it was.

"Obvs," Ross grunted.

"I can't wait to meet her," Naya told him courteously.

Why did I feel like everyone was being quiet for my sake? I turned to Will wide-eyed, pleading for help, but he pretended not to see me. Curtis, clearly tired of pretending everything was normal, told me with a smirk, "I gotta go. We'll talk, OK?"

"Sure," I said. "I'll walk you to the door."

I tried to ignore the sensation of being watched as he put on his jacket and I opened the door for him. He gave me a quick but friendly hug, which I was thankful for, then whispered in my ear, "One of these days, you'll have to tell me why the weirdo on the couch was staring daggers at me. I feel like there's some hot goss behind that."

I couldn't help but smile as I told him, "You can't even imagine."

"Now I'm dying to know."

"I'm sorry the evening ended up this way. If it makes you feel better, I think the rest of them really liked you."

"Of course they did, Jenna. I'm great."

I closed the door and felt everyone's eyes on me again. Jack had stood by then and was leaning against the wall. As cordially as I could, I asked him, "Did you want to tell me something?"

He arched an eyebrow, pretending to be apathetic, but he was squeezing his beer so tight, I thought he might crush it in his hand, and there was tension in his shoulders as he tapped his foot on the floor. It felt like a bomb was about to go off.

Jack didn't respond, so I tried again. "You said you were looking for me. Was it anything in particular you needed?"

"You seriously think I want to talk to you? Like you could possibly matter to me," he snapped.

"You literally said you were looking for me," I told him.

With a humorless smile, he responded, "Trust me, Jennifer, you don't want to hear what I have to say."

He'd said my name that way on purpose. To mark the distance. To tell me there was nothing between us. And there was defiance in his expression. He was daring me to say something. To keep from breaking, I announced, "I'm going to take a shower. Whenever you want to talk, come find me."

That sounded bitchy, but it made me feel better about myself. He never had a problem trying to irritate me, and he deserved a taste of his own medicine, even if it was just a small dose. I could tell it had worked by the way his eyes followed me to the bathroom.

What I hadn't expected was that he would take the words *come find me* so seriously, and so soon. I was still pulling off my pants in the bathroom when he opened the door. It scared me so bad I almost fell over backward, and to right myself, I had to step out of them. So there I was in a T-shirt and panties, wondering what Jack wanted. Strangely, he didn't even seem to notice.

"I need to talk to you," he burst out.

"Now?!"

"Yes, now."

"Do I not have a right to privacy? Get out of here!!!"

"Let me get this straight. You move into my house, take over my couch, leave me hanging like I was no one, then I come in and the first thing I see is you hugging up on some guy in my living room!"

He had come closer and closer to me as he said this, and I tried to shout, "Ross, get out!" But he interrupted me: "What the hell is going on with you? Is this who you always were? Because the Jen I remember was a decent person."

"Wait! I'm not a decent person? What the hell makes me not a decent person? The fact that I have a friend?! I need your permission for that now?"

"If you're going to bring them to my house, you damn sure do!"

"Fine! From now on, I'll go to his place instead."

That was mean, maybe. Inappropriate, maybe. But I couldn't help myself. And it was nothing compared to what Jack said next. Clenching his teeth, with a vein throbbing in his neck, he hissed, "Fuck you."

"Fuck me? Have I said anything about you and your female friends? Did I ever burst in on you in the shower?"

"Oh, please! You didn't even turn on the water yet!"

"Ross, I'm almost naked. Get out!"

Confused and angry, he looked me over and said, "It's not like it's anything I've never seen before."

Now I was pissed. I could feel myself turning red as I grabbed my pants and threw them in his face. He ducked, and I screamed, "You have no right to invade my privacy, and you have no right to stare at my body without my permission."

"Ross," Will interrupted us. "There's got to be a better time…"

"This is a great time," Jack cut him off.

"It is not!" I reprimanded him. "Now get out! And for your information, if I want to hang out or date people or whatever, I'll damn well do it, and I don't owe you a single explanation!"

He hadn't liked that. "Date? What do you mean by date?"

"JUST GO!"

I got him out the door and shut it behind him. Since I didn't hear anything more, I assumed he'd left. But no. A few seconds later, he tried to open it up again, and in a reflex, I threw my whole body into it and felt it slam into something.

"Shit!" I called out, realizing I had probably hit him in the face, then opened it back up and told him, "I'm sorry! Are you OK?"

He was rubbing his forehead but he seemed fine. Not hurt, just angry.

"I don't know, but since you fucking hit me, can you answer my question?"

I instantly stopped feeling bad for him. "Don't talk to me that way. Now I need to shower. If you really have something to discuss, you can wait for me out here."

I didn't think he'd do it, so I took my time, soaped up twice, washed my hair, used conditioner. I emerged a good while later with a towel wrapped around me, and there was Jack, sitting in the hallway, arms crossed, legs outstretched, looking like a sulky child.

"You done yet?" he asked impatiently.

"No."

I went to get my pajamas and shut myself up in the bathroom again. I took my time on purpose, getting dressed, putting on my glasses, combing my hair. Then I came out. He was in the same position but looked even angrier than before.

"Are you finally finished?"

I didn't answer. Instead I walked past him toward the kitchen and saw that in the living room, everybody had stayed where they were sitting. They were staring at me attentively. I walked to the fridge and grabbed a beer, but Jack, who had followed me, took it from my hand and slammed it on the counter.

When I protested, he told me he had done his part and waited, and now I had to talk to him.

"Has it occurred to you that maybe I don't feel like it?" I asked.

"No," he replied. He was hung up on that word *date*. He wanted to know who I had one with and when. I tried to dance around the subject, not because there was someone else, but because it was my right to live my own life, especially given how he was treating me. At one point, Will burst in and the two of us snapped at him, and he said, "You're both basically screaming at each other. The neighbors can even hear you."

"Screw the neighbors," Jack said.

"Ross!" Naya butted in. "It's not a date. She's just going to hang out with a guy from her class."

"Oh, just a guy from class?" he said sarcastically.

"Yeah," I shot back. "Is there a problem with it?"

"Do you like him?" Jack asked. Of course that was what he wanted to know. I hesitated. I didn't like Curtis. He was a friend, that was all. I wondered whether I should tell Jack that, but before I had the chance to, he had to get a dig in at me. "Are you going to tell him you love him too and then disappear for a year?"

Here we go. I was surprised it had taken him that long to get around to it. I looked away, ashamed, as he leaned in close. My fingers were tingling, and I clenched my fists.

He added, "Or are you just going to fuck him so you'll have a new place to live?"

"Ross, take that back!" Naya called out.

Looking at him, seeing how anxiously he was waiting for a response, I could tell what he wanted was for me to lose my cool. Maybe that's what I wanted, too, because all the concern I'd felt the night before, all my hopes that we could get along, had gone out the window. Our noses were practically touching, and I could see his dilated pupils and his bloodshot eyes. Everything about him made me angry. Without thinking, I told him, "You're a pig."

The whole thing was so weird. I almost wanted to punch him in the face. At the same time, having him so close did something to me. I was leaning against the counter then, and he reached around me, one hand on either side of my hips. "A pig?" he said. "Well, at least I'm not a liar."

"When the hell did I lie to you?" I asked. We were talking softer now, soft enough that our friends in the living room couldn't hear us, not that I cared. I could feel my hands slightly grazing his. I had to arch my back to keep away from him as I played the last card up my sleeve: "If you hate me so much, I wonder why you're so jealous."

"Fuck your date," he said. "I couldn't care less. I just thought somebody should warn the poor guy."

Those words broke the spell, and realizing I was letting Jack push me around and intimidate me, I shoved him with both hands in the middle of his chest, surprising him. "Warn him of what?"

"Of who you really are!"

"Oh sure! Like you're some saint!"

It was at that moment that Mike opened the door and walked in with a smile, shouting, "Hey, everyone!"

Jack and I went on arguing. This was the same guy who had confessed over beers one night to sleeping with God knew how many women, and he was seriously freaking out because I was friends with another guy? He kept saying that was different, that was the past, and so on, and I called him a creep, asking, "What kind of guy barges into the bathroom when someone's taking a shower?"

I could see Sue across the counter motioning for Mike to join her on the couch. "This is the best view," she said. Not wanting to be a spectacle, I grabbed my beer, getting ready to go to the bedroom, but Jack snatched it away and held it up in the air over my head. I told him to quit acting like a child. "You're the child," he said. And I jumped up in the air as best I could before finally giving up and telling him, "Fuck you."

I had admitted defeat and wouldn't have my drink, but at least I'd gotten under his skin, and that gave me some consolation. I walked past him and sat in the living room next to Mike, crossing my arms and legs. Jack followed me soon after, and I felt the sofa sinking as he grunted, "Move."

"Really, bro?" Mike said. "I don't know what's up with you, but why don't you open a beer and we can…"

"Move, Mike!" Jack repeated.

Mike tried to stand, but I grabbed his arm and held him back. "He's staying right here, Jack. You can go sit somewhere else."

This went on, with Jack saying he wanted to sit next to me, me telling him I didn't want him to, him telling me he didn't care, and Mike trying to still the waters, until Jack and I were on the verge of screaming. I shouted at him to shut up, he called me a child and blamed me for hitting him in the head with a door, I told him I hadn't done it on purpose, and he went back to the subject of Curtis, which was clearly his real issue. Jack tried to take his anger out on Mike, telling him to go sit in the chair, that it was his couch, his apartment, and so on, and we wound up yelling juvenile insults:

"Bitch!"

"Loser!"

"Narcissist!"

"Asshole!"

"Enough!" Will shouted, standing up. "I'm tired of this bullshit. You're both acting like children. I feel like you're trying to outdo each other to see who can be less mature. Well, it's time to grow up! You, Jenna, go to your room and yell into a pillow or something until you can calm down. And you, Jack, go grab a smoke and see if you can get your shit together."

That did the trick. Will was a sweetie, but he was a big guy and could intimidate anyone. So we both walked off, slamming the doors. When I was alone in the bedroom, I grabbed my phone and tried to entertain myself. I slipped between the sheets and watched TikTok videos of people drawing. That helped me relax.

An hour later, though, I was hungry. So hungry that my stomach was growling. I walked to the door and pressed my ear to it. The only voice I could hear was Naya's, and I decided to risk it, opening up the door and tiptoeing down the hall. I felt relieved when I saw she and Sue were the only ones in the living room.

"The men are up on the roof," Naya said. "Here, I saved you some pizza."

"Thanks," I said, grabbing the beer I'd left on the counter and sitting on the couch. "I was starving."

I heard something coming from Sue's corner of the room…was I crazy? That was my own voice. Sue chuckled, then noticed I had caught her and quickly tried to tuck her phone away.

"Are you serious? You actually recorded us?"

"It's for one of my Instagram stories. I need content."

"And you thought recording me in secret was appropriate?" I asked.

"What if Ross gets famous like the Kardashians?" she replied. "I need to get ready. This could go totally viral. I might be sitting on a gold mine. But whatever. I'll delete it if you want. I've already got more embarrassing material."

"Thanks," I murmured. "Please keep me out of it, but if it's just Jack, go wild. You've got my permission, after the way he treated me."

"I don't know," Sue said, "we've actually made a lot of progress. You may not realize it, but it's been forever since Ross has opened up like that. He's barely spoken a word for the last two months. I guess it would be better if he hadn't gotten all jealous and made a scene, but still, it's something."

Naya said talking was good, but he'd need to control himself in the future. Sue nodded along, and when I agreed, she offered to help out: "If he acts like that again, Jenna, just tell me and I'll stuff his head in the trash can."

5

SENSSSSATIONAL

The first day of class came upon me faster than I had imagined, and I spent the morning before with a sick feeling in the pit of my stomach. It had been a year since I'd set foot in a classroom, and I worried I'd never catch up, especially because I'd registered for almost all the same classes Curtis was in, even though I didn't know the upper level material too well.

I remember walking in and seeing him there with his friends and listening to our literature professor describe our project and exam schedule. I got my first syllabus, looked at the list of books, prayed they weren't too expensive, made endless notes, and all the while, Curtis just yawned and doodled and entertained himself by poking me with his pen.

On our way out, as we were discussing the midterm paper, which we had to pick a topic for soon, Curtis joked about our teacher and how she said our readings for that semester were *senssssational* as she swished her hips in her tight skirt. He had already repeated the word several times while we were sitting there, and it had been nearly impossible for me not to laugh. I'd had to hide my head and pray she didn't notice.

"Poor woman," I said. "She'll never hear the end of that."

"I doubt it," Curtis said. "Someone else will say something stupid, and we'll all forget about her." He held the door open, and I followed him to the parking lot. As I walked off toward the light rail, he asked if I wanted to meet him after lunch.

"Sounds cool," I responded. "Your room?"

He frowned. "Maybe not. My roommates are being a little annoying. Maybe we could do your place. Or do you think your boyfriend will try and beat me up?"

"He's not going to beat you up, *and* he's not my boyfriend. But yeah, that's cool, come by whenever. Jack hasn't even been home lately, so I'm sure we'll be able to hang out in peace."

How wrong I was.

The first thing I heard when I got home was Naya's voice. She didn't sound happy. I found her in the living room angry and yelling, which wasn't really like her. Jack was there, absorbing her insults as she called him selfish and self-centered. Ignoring her, he opened a beer and stared off into space. After a moment, while Naya was pausing to catch her breath, he asked, "Are you done now?"

That only made her worse. "I'm sure as hell not!"

"What's going on?" I asked.

Naya sat on the couch, crossed her arms, and said, "Nothing! I just can't stand him!"

I could tell she didn't want to talk more, but I double-checked anyway. "Are you sure you're OK?"

In a sour voice, Jack said, "Don't worry about me, I don't even exist." I pretended not to hear him and sat beside Naya as she tried to look over her notes. I guess she was trying to study, but whatever had happened had made things tense. I began to wonder if I should call Curtis and tell him not to bother. I put that off while I made a bite to eat and talked to my grandmother on the phone. When I returned to the living room, they were still sitting there ignoring each other, Naya with her papers and Jack with his laptop. I was nervous, but I had to interrupt them.

"Hey, guys…" They looked up at me, and Jack was glaring, as if he took for granted he wouldn't like what I had to say. "I've got a classmate coming over, we're going to make a study plan for our literature class, it won't be long, but…"

"Is it Curtis?" Naya asked.

I nodded. She smirked. She probably thought it was funny how much it would piss Jack off. I added that we could go somewhere else—it was Jack's house after all. "I'd be fine working in the bedroom, or I could tell him to meet me at the library."

"Stay here," Jack said brusquely.

"Even though you guys are here?"

He didn't answer. He just looked back at his laptop screen. I was worried about how he'd act. Curtis liked to pretend nothing bothered him, but it had to, sometimes—he was a person, after all. And I needed to hold onto my friends. I couldn't have Jack pushing everyone away. These thoughts were swirling in my head as the doorbell rang. I turned to go answer, but Jack jumped up before I could. Naya shouted, "Ross, get back here!"

It was too late. Try as I might, by the time I got to the entryway, Jack and Curtis were face-to-face, and by Curtis's expression, I could tell he wasn't happy about it.

"What do you want?" Jack hissed.

For God's sake…

"Is Jenna home?" Curtis replied.

Jack said no, but Curtis could obviously see me, and I tried to smile as I told him, "He's just kidding. Come on in!"

Curtis shoved past Jack and into the living room, and as he greeted Naya, I took his coat and turned back to find Jack with death in his eyes. "Ross, don't start, please," I said.

"Start what?"

"You know perfectly well what I'm saying. You remember what you did the other day."

With a mischievous expression, he leaned close and whispered that he just wanted to get to know my friend. He kept calling him *Charlie*. He knew perfectly well what his name was, but he loved getting on my nerves. He had done the same thing with Monty before. And when I corrected him and said Curtis was my friend, and we would probably have a lot of group work together that year, I added, "You really need to chill out. You look insane, and I don't want him to be scared to come over here."

"Why not?"

I ignored his question. I wasn't playing his game. "Ross, I'm serious," I said. "We've got several classes together, and I want him to do my group assignments with me. He's smart, and I didn't do well my first semester, and I'm really trying to turn my grades around. That's all there is to it, so can you just be cool?"

For an eternity, he didn't move and didn't respond. But then his face relaxed and he said, "Fine," between clenched teeth. "But tell him not to try to be friendly with me. I don't like him. He's a douche."

I decided there was no point in talking any longer. I had caught his wrist to keep him from walking into the living room. Now I let him go. I found Curtis sitting on one of the couches, drinking a beer that I guessed Naya had offered him. Jack sat on the other one, and I decided to stay standing to keep from provoking him. After some small talk, Naya pretended to turn back to her notes, but I could tell she was listening to every word we were saying.

Curtis complimented my apartment. Jack let him know it was actually his.

"You're right, though," I said. "It is really nice. But let's talk about schoolwork, that's why you're here, right?" And we looked at the syllabus for lit class and started brainstorming possible projects. It was easygoing.

Curtis was smart, but he also liked to fool around, and his pleasant attitude made an hour pass in no time. I told him how nervous I was about my grades that year, but I added that with his help, I was sure I'd make it through.

Curtis smiled. "You'll do *senssssational.*"

I couldn't help but laugh, and as soon as I did, I knew I'd made a mistake. Jack didn't say anything, but I felt guilty and decided to run and take refuge in the bathroom. I really did have to go anyway. I'd been holding it in because I was scared of what Jack would do if I left him and Curtis alone. But it seemed safe by that point, and anyway, Naya was there to run interference.

"Be right back," I said loudly. I must have set a world record for getting in and out, and I even washed my hands. But it wasn't fast enough, because when I returned, I found both guys sitting beside each other. Jack scowled, I asked what was up, and Curtis replied blithely, "Oh, nothing. I was just telling your, uh, *boyfriend* about our literature professor's favorite word and how we all were laughing about it earlier."

Uh-oh.

That bastard. Curtis knew perfectly well what he was doing. And he was having a damn ball. Naya didn't say anything. Jack didn't, either. Apparently everyone was more than happy to have me on the spot.

"He's not my boyfriend, he's just my roommate," I said, sitting down next to Curtis.

Jack snorted and said, "I'd say I'm a bit more than that."

Curtis looked from him to me as I responded, "Not much more."

Ignoring me, Jack informed Curtis, "I'm her ex-boyfriend."

"We broke up forever ago, though," I cut in.

"Define forever, *babe,*" Jack replied.

Babe?! Now I wanted to vomit. And I could tell he was loving every minute of it. "Let's say a year, for convenience's sake, *babe.*"

I'd thought that would knock him off his high horse, but he grinned back like a sly little child. I guess he was already planning what he was going to hit me with next. "Was a year long enough to forget what you and I used to do on this sofa, babe?"

Naya spit up a sip of beer and started coughing, and I turned red as a tomato. Curtis looked down at the fabric he was sitting on, as if worried he might get contaminated by body fluids.

"We never did anything in here, you idiot!" I shouted.

"Oh, that's right. We stuck to the bedroom. And the shower. And the counter," he said.

Naya didn't have room to talk—you could hardly enter the apartment without seeing her and Will getting it on—but it didn't stop her from overreacting. "The counter! Gross! Please tell me you guys disinfected it afterwards!"

I tried to no avail to protest that it wasn't true. Curtis, like Jack, was having a ball. I begged Jack to go out for a cigarette. He mimicked my own voice, reminding me of all the times I'd told him smoking was bad for him.

"Get some fresh air, then," I said, but that didn't interest him either. Fed up, I asked, "How about you go throw yourself off the roof then?"

He turned down that suggestion, too.

"Then at least go sit on the other couch," I said.

"Why, am I bothering you, Conner?" he asked. So we were playing that game again. I couldn't believe a man old enough to run for public office thought it was that funny to pretend to forget other people's names. Curtis corrected him, but he did it again, then I corrected him, adding, "Whether or not your behavior's bothering Curtis, it's starting to bother me."

Naya tried to help, saying, "Ross, shouldn't you be working on some PR thing for your film or something?"

Curtis's eyes got wide, and he turned, excited, as if he'd just heard the revelation of the century. "Wait a minute…are you Jack Ross?"

Jack responded smugly, "Yeah, why? You got a problem with it?"

"A problem? Hell no! I love your work!" Curtis gushed.

Great. Just great.

I rolled my eyes as I observed the malevolent satisfaction that overtook Jack's face. Surely Curtis noticed, too, but he didn't mind my nerves. He continued, "My friends and I used to love your YouTube channel! But since you never showed your face in your videos, I didn't realize it was you. The last time I was here and they said something about you being a filmmaker, I didn't put two and two together, probably because everyone calls you by your last name. When's your movie coming out again?"

Curtis almost blushed when Naya informed him, "In two weeks!"

"I'm buying tickets now!" Curtis exclaimed. Then, almost guiltily, he looked over at me. "I don't know if you're planning to go, Jenna, but I could get one for you, too."

"Whatever," I responded. "I hate movies anyway."

The silence that followed was as uncomfortable as could be, and when Curtis picked up on all the negativity, he stood and walked to the restroom. Once the door shut behind him, I grabbed a couch cushion and threw it at Jack's head. He ducked and stared up at me, murmuring, "What the…?"

I told him to leave Curtis alone. He protested he hadn't done anything. I reminded him he'd been calling him by the wrong name on purpose. He just chuckled, and Naya told us to lower our voices. I told him he was scaring Curtis, intimidating him, making him feel uncomfortable, and to hurt my feelings, Jack responded, throwing the pillow back at me, "I don't know, he seems to like me better than you."

"Does not!" I protested, hurling the pillow back.

"He said he was my fan!" Jack responded.

"He's just being nice. Your YouTube videos, your movie, I'll bet they're all trash!"

He threw the pillow at me again as he shouted that his film was *the shit*, and I told him I was going to put it up on the internet where people could download it for free so nobody would bother going to see it at the theater. We continued bickering back and forth until Curtis emerged, holding his phone, and announced, "It's getting late, I hadn't realized. Sorry, Jenna, but I need to go. It's been a long day, and I'm dying for a shower."

"Sure," I said, "I'll send you an email with all of our notes."

I followed Curtis out, and when Jack tried to stand, I pressed a finger into his chest, hard enough to elicit an *ouch*. He tried to swat my hand, but I dodged him just as Curtis, who hadn't noticed a thing, said, "Hey, it was nice hanging out with you guys," and Naya responded, "Likewise!"

Jack rolled his eyes and got one last dig in: "See you round, Curly."

I smacked him with the pillow again. I didn't care if Curtis saw. Instead of tossing it back, Jack grabbed it and held it to his face, his shoulders moving up and down with laughter.

On his way out, Curtis murmured, "I'm dying to hear you guys' full story, just so you know."

"Buy me a burger and maybe I'll tell you," I replied.

"That's all? Sounds worth it." He gave me one of his comforting hugs. "We could make it tonight, if you want. I was going to ask you if you wanted to come bowling with the guys anyway. The two of us can hang out after."

"I'd love that."

He patted me on the cheek and said, "Cool. I'll text you."

I shut the door behind him and stomped back to the living room. Naya looked uncomfortable, Jack looked smug, and I tried to ignore them both, but when I made it down the hall to the bedroom, I couldn't help but turn around and growl at him, "I hate you."

"I'll take that as a compliment," he responded. Why was he so good at provoking me, and why was I so bad at giving it back to him?

"You're a child," I fired back. "Curtis will probably never want to come back here again."

"Oh, no," he said. "Poor Curtis. I'm sooo sad."

I told him I'd never say anything if he came here with one of his girlfriends. He told me he'd never disrespect me enough to do something like that. I told him that there would be no issue, that I was mature enough to understand the entire world didn't revolve around me, probably because I hadn't been raised with a silver spoon in my mouth.

"Loser," he replied.

"Dumbass!"

"Loser."

"Dickhead!"

"Loser," he repeated.

"Moron!"

Jack turned to Naya. "I think she loves me."

Naya smiled and said, "I promised I wouldn't get in the middle of this."

I called him an idiot one more time, and he told me I was breaking his heart. As I slammed the door to the bedroom behind me, I heard him shout: "I love you, too, idiot!"

A few hours later, Naya was sitting opposite me on the bed with her legs crossed and rollers in her hair, which made her hard to take seriously. She was supposed to be going to dinner with Will that night. But in that moment, she was more concerned with digging into my friendship with Curtis.

"So…you two are going on a date then?"

"It's not a date. We're going bowling with some friends and then we're grabbing a burger."

"Riiiight." I tried to ignore the implication as I looked through my suitcase for something to wear—I still hadn't completely unpacked. Her stare like a hawk's, she asked, "You don't like him, though? Not just a little bit? Because he's nice, he's charming, he's attractive. I mean, you know how I feel about Will, but if I was single, I'd sure as hell bite."

"Yeah," I admitted, "Curtis is cool, but… I don't know. He's just…"

"He's not Ross, right?"

I didn't respond, instead just plopping down beside her. I hadn't gone out in ages and I was stressing about what to wear. The whole process was getting on my nerves so badly that I wanted to just give it up. Naya sighed and continued, "It's normal, Jenna. You guys had a very intensive relationship. I can imagine it's hard to turn the page."

"It's not really about turning the page, it's more like we're in totally different worlds and we can't even beam a message to each other."

"Does that bother you?" she asked, confused.

I didn't know. Should it? I mean, he was supposed to be my ex-boyfriend. I wasn't supposed to have feelings for him, good, bad, or indifferent. So why would any of this matter? Naya could tell I was getting uncomfortable, so she turned to my pile of clothing, fished out a skirt, and tried to change the subject. "You should put this on! And your black sweater with it! And some tights, obviously, so you don't freeze."

I wasn't sure a skirt was the best thing for bowling, but she told me since I'd suck at it, I might as well look good. I laughed and snatched the skirt away, shoving her. She shoved me in turn, and we cracked up as we got into a pillow fight. Then the door opened, and all of a sudden, Sue was there shouting at us to stop acting like a couple of six-year-olds. I guess we'd been a little louder than we'd intended.

Naya mimicked her: "Stop acting like a couple of six-year-olds!"

"You wanna die?" Sue asked her.

"You wanna die?" Naya repeated.

Sue told us we sucked, and Naya responded, "Come on, you love us. Why don't you grab a beer and come in here and hang out?"

"I'd rather die. Or what's worse, I'd rather hang out with Mike, who's actually in the living room right now," she replied. "Thanks for the offer, though."

Will peeked in behind her and asked, "What's going on in here?"

As Sue stomped off, she grunted, "Nothing, they're just reminding me of why I don't want to have kids."

Confused, Will stared at us, and before he could react, Naya jumped up, pulling him down onto the bed and planting a hard kiss on his cheek that left behind a big streak of one of the many lipsticks we'd tried on. He wriggled away from her, but I helped hold him down while she tickled him, kissing him all over the face and neck, until he announced, "I'm starting to understand where Sue was coming from."

Mike walked in and exclaimed, "Have I died and gone to heaven? Don't stop, girls, just move over and make a little room for me!"

Naya told him to get out and threw a pillow at his head.

I glanced at the clock. I only had about ten minutes left. I lay back next to Will, who was trying to wipe the lipstick off his cheeks as Naya chuckled and told him it looked good on him. "Maybe you should add makeup to your daily routine. More and more men are doing it."

"Very funny," he responded. She pinched his cheek, and he smiled and blew a kiss at her. They were so cheesy, they made me want to vomit. The way they looked at each other... I was probably jealous, but I didn't want to admit that to myself. She told him I'd been trying to pick out clothes for that evening and showed him which outfit I'd settled on, and he recommended a red sweater instead of a black one. When I said, "Great, so I've got two stylists now," Will told me, "Yeah, and we charge by the hour."

"No problem," I told him, "I worked in a gas station all year. I'm basically a millionaire. Whatever your normal rate is, I'll double it. I mean, I loaned Ross two hundred bucks the other day, why would I leave you guys out?"

As soon as I'd said that, I knew it was a mistake. Will stared at me with a confused expression, and Naya acted outraged. "Are you crazy? You better make sure he gives it back to you. I don't want to have to beat it out of him."

"What on earth possessed you to lend him money?" Will said. He sounded almost like he was accusing me of something. I nodded slowly, and he stood. Naya tried to calm him down, but he ignored her, hissing, "Jenna, don't give him shit! If he needs money, he can go to the damn bank. Do you know how much money he's made off that movie already? If he asked you for money, it was literally because he was too lazy or too fucked-up to go to the ATM."

I remembered him looking for his jacket like a lunatic. Maybe he'd forgotten where his bank card was? Will stalked out, and Naya and I hurried after him. Mike jumped back when he saw us. He'd been stealing a pack of crackers from the cabinet, and he quickly hid it behind his back. Sue saw him but just sighed.

"What's the big deal, Will?" I asked. "It's my money, I thought I was helping."

"Well, you weren't!" he shouted. That scared everyone. Will never got mad. It was almost as weird as Sue smiling or saying *I love you*. He didn't seem to care, though. He leaned his elbows on the counter and hid his face in his hands. Naya stood there next to him, unsure of what to do. I kept saying I was sorry, that I'd talk to Jack, that I'd get him to pay me back, that I'd...

"Just drop it!" he growled. "I'll take care of it. You just mind your own business."

The front door opened and Jack walked in. He had heard the end of Will's exclamation, and was looking at us tensely. I was fidgeting, but when I saw he was watching me, I let my arms hang loose at my sides and tried to act relaxed. But it was too late. He knew we were arguing.

"What's going on?" he asked Will.

Will smiled pretty convincingly and lied, "Roommate problems. You know how it goes."

Jack looked perplexed. "What kind of roommate problems?"

"The usual," Will responded. "Jenna, weren't you on your way out?"

I knew what he was thinking: I had screwed things up, and it was time for me to butt out. So I excused myself, saying I needed to get dressed. I rushed, skipping my makeup, but a quick glance in the mirror was enough to reassure me. I liked what I saw. I'd filled out in the past year, and I didn't look like a little kid anymore. I was a woman now—someone people would notice.

I walked past the living room and into the kitchen, where I found Will looking at his phone. I asked if he was sure he didn't need me to stay. He wasn't angry anymore, he just looked tired as he shook his head. "Go have fun. We'll figure things out tomorrow."

Figure out what things? I wasn't sure, but I could tell he didn't want me to push him. I grabbed my coat and purse and said a vague goodbye to no one in particular. Jack tried to ignore me. Naya, Sue, and Mike didn't even need to try.

I did as Will said and forgot everything and had fun. The beer Curtis got me at the bowling alley helped. I couldn't keep my ball out of the alley no matter how much I concentrated, so it didn't really matter to my team if I got drunk, and pretty soon I'd decided to just sit it out and let others take my turn.

Curtis drove us to some random greasy spoon. The burgers there turned out to be awful. I reminisced about how good the place Jack had taken me to a year before was. I had brought him up so many times that everyone was starting to make fun of me for it, but in a nice way, so I didn't mind.

For some reason, I'd decided to wear platform boots, and by the time Curtis drove me home, I'd taken them off because my feet were killing me.

When we got out of the car, I stuffed them under my arm. Curtis rode up with me in the elevator and asked me if I was drunk.

"If I was drunk, you'd be carrying me," I told him. "I'm happy, that's all."

Curtis reached out an arm to keep me standing as I walked toward the apartment, but I shrugged him off once we reached the door. We both leaned against the wall, and he said, "I'm glad you forced me to take you for a burger. Even if it was disgusting."

"I've eaten worse," I replied, making him laugh loud enough to alert Jack, who threw open the door with a grimace.

Curtis, chipper as ever, said, "Hey, hello again. I've been seeing a lot of you lately."

I chuckled nervously as Jack stared me down, focusing on my clothes, my shoes in my hand, my coat on the floor. "Are you drunk?" he asked.

"Are you really the person to be asking me that?" I replied.

Jack tensed up, and Curtis raised his hands in a sign of surrender, interjecting, "Listen, this looks like a couples' argument, and I'm not going to get in the middle of it. You two lovebirds have a good night!"

I waved. "See you, Curtis! You're sensssssational!"

I wondered if that was overdoing it. Jack sighed, took my boots from my hands, and bent down to pick up my coat, which I'd dropped. He guided me in gently, set my things down, and looked me in the eyes with an expression so tense I asked, "What's up, Ross? Did you have a bad night?"

"Not at all. What about you? Did you have fun with your friends?"

"I did," I responded defiantly. "It's been forever since I've laughed so much."

He turned and walked off, muttering curses, and started struggling with the sandwich press. He had apparently been trying to make dinner before I arrived. It was weird that he was up and dressed that late, but I didn't ask myself why. I was too entertained at the sight of him attempting to cook something. It was clear that he hadn't gotten any better in the kitchen in the year I'd been away.

He banged on the machine's lid and murmured, "If you had so much fun, how come you came back so early?"

"Why wouldn't I? I was just hanging out with a couple of friends."

"Friends…" he repeated. "Old Curtis, he's just the best, isn't he…"

"He's a good guy, Ross."

"He certainly makes you laugh a lot."

"Not like you," I blurted out before I could stop myself.

He looked up at me, and I blushed all over. Was it a mistake, being so sincere with him? I didn't know, but I came around the counter, looked quizzically at the sandwich maker, and said, "Let me lend you a hand…"

"I'm fine."

"It's not plugged in," I told him. As he blinked and stared at the machine, I proposed, "Why don't you go sit on the couch and I'll take care of this for you."

"Aren't you a little tipsy to be playing Gordon Ramsey?"

"Tipsy or not, I can do a better job than you. Now get out of my kitchen!" I grabbed a wooden spoon and raised it, and he smiled and ducked. I scraped out his first attempt at a sandwich—he'd squashed it flat banging on the lid—and grabbed the white bread, turning around to see him staring at me. My eyes swelled, and he scurried off to the sofa. He was right, I was a little drunk, and it took me forever to get out the cheese and turkey. I got mustard all over my fingers and nearly sliced my palm open cutting off the crust, but after ten minutes, I had two decent-looking sandwiches on two plates.

Jack looked relaxed as I sat next to him and set one of the dishes down on his lap. "I thought you went to dinner," he said.

"I did. It was disgusting."

I leaned into his shoulder and looked at the screen, where he was watching a show about people trying to fix their god-awful tattoos.

"I'm not surprised," Jack responded. "Not everybody knows where to get a good burger in this town."

"Don't blow your own horn."

"I can if I'm right."

"Fine, you're right. Are you happy?"

"I am," he said, devouring his sandwich while I tore mine into little pieces, nibbling them but leaving half of the sandwich. As soon as he saw I wouldn't eat it, he reached over for it, and in a matter of seconds it was gone. I didn't complain. I was tipsy, drowsy, and cold, and I got up for a blanket to cover us. I felt pleasant and warm next to him, and he didn't try to get away from me when I leaned into him. He even wrapped his arm around me so I'd be more comfortable. That made me smile, and I know he noticed. I could feel his eyes on me for a few seconds. Neither of us said anything. I guess we didn't want to ruin the moment.

After a while, I yawned, cuddled up closer, and said, "This is so comfortable." When Jack didn't respond, I glanced up at him. He was gawking at the screen with dilated pupils. That reminded me of my conversation with Will. But if he was high, what was I going to do about it? I decided just to try and take care of him.

"Why don't you put on your pajamas?" I asked. If I got him to stay home, he wouldn't do any more drugs, would he? Didn't people usually buy them and take them on the spot, at a crack house or something? I wasn't sure. I didn't have any experience with that kind of thing, but I had an intuition that if I could keep him there until he slept, he'd be out of danger.

"How come?" he asked.

"It's bedtime, isn't it?"

He waited almost an entire minute before responding. "Does that mean you, uh...that you want me to stay here tonight?"

Maybe it was the cowardly way out, but I gave him a vague answer: "I don't want you to go."

I was happy to notice he didn't pull away. And after a moment, he said softly, "OK. I guess… I guess I'll stay then."

I grinned more broadly than I probably should have and said, "Cool!"

His hands were on top of the blanket, and he was tapping his fingers compulsively. I could tell he wanted to ask me something, but I didn't know what. The silence was painful, and I was trying to think of some way to break it when he asked me in a strained voice, "Hey, Jen? That money you loaned me, it's in my jacket. Go ahead and grab it."

Why was he so tense? I thought about asking, thought about asking him if everything was OK, thought about asking him to open up to me and so much more. But he'd turned cold, and when I didn't move, he said, "Go on, please." I stood and did as he said, and the money was there, but the bills were dirty and wrinkled. As I counted it out, I asked, "Jack, do you want to talk, maybe?"

Instead of saying anything, he just stood. His whole body was tense as he snatched his jacket away and picked up his cigarettes and lighter. He walked out, and a few seconds later, I heard his steps on the fire escape.

6

TRUTH OR DARE

The next morning, I decided to go out for a run. I was full of energy when I woke up, and I jumped out of bed, got dressed, and threw on my headphones. I admit, part of my excitement was thinking I'd find Jack out there. I must have thought I'd saved him or something. But my hopes were dashed when I entered the living room and found it empty.

I stood there staring at the couch until Will emerged from his room, rubbing his eyes. Hoping he wasn't still angry at me, I told him good morning. He must have noticed how disappointed I sounded. As he trudged over to the coffee maker, he asked, "Are you all right?"

"Yeah," I said. "I just, uh… I thought Jack had stayed here last night."

He looked at me with an emotion somewhere between incredulity and pity, as if thinking, *you poor dummy.* "He doesn't usually sleep here," he told me, the way an adult tells a little kid there's no Santa Claus. "It's not you, Jenna. It's…the other thing."

"He gave me my money back last night."

"He did?" Will looked surprised.

"Yeah. Then he went up to the roof to smoke. I thought about following him, but he seemed on edge, like he needed time to himself. You think that's a good or a bad thing?"

He took a couple of cups from the cabinet and placed them on the counter almost automatically, as if his mind were somewhere else. "I don't know," he admitted. "I hope so, but I don't know."

So much for my run, I thought, sitting on a stool, crossing my arms on the counter, and resting my chin on them as Will served us. He remembered exactly how I liked my coffee. That's just the kind of guy he was.

"I'm sorry I yelled at you yesterday," he said, and I saw his shoulders tense under his blue T-shirt.

"Don't worry, I deserved it."

"No you didn't, Jenna. And I could have explained it better or been a little more mature. I shouldn't have flipped out like that. So just let me apologize."

"Fine," I said. "Apology accepted. And I'm sorry I'm an idiot giving that kind of money to a guy who has problems. So are we good now?"

He grinned. "We're good. But don't do it again."

"I'll try, but I can't promise."

Noticing the distracted way Will was stirring his coffee and the look of worry on his face, I asked him, "How much do you know about what's going on with Ross? You don't have to answer, I just feel…sort of out of the loop, you know? Where I'm from, drugs have never really been a thing. So I'm wondering if I should, like, do some reading or something…"

"How much do I know… Well, let's say I know the signs. It feels a little early to get all deep with you, but to hell with it. My brother died of an overdose when I was a kid."

He tried to smile, to let me know not to feel sorry for him, but sadness overtook his entire face and, for a moment, I felt myself turn to stone. I had realized our conversation might take a dark turn, but I could never have imagined it would be like this. I reached over and touched his arm. It wasn't much of a consolation, but at least it might make him feel a little less alone.

"It was a long time ago," he continued. "Just before my thirteenth birthday. He and my parents were fighting all the time. They'd tried to get him to go to rehab, I think they even succeeded once, but it was no use. He just kept relapsing, over and over. Then one day Mom found him lying on the floor in the doorway. He'd come in early one morning, when everyone was still in bed and no one could hear him. By the time we woke, there wasn't much we could do."

His voice was monotone, so different from his usual warmth. I wanted to hug him, but I let him keep telling his story.

"It tore my parents to pieces, and it wasn't long until they got divorced. I met Naya soon after that. She was my rock at that moment in my life, the only person who really supported me through it all. Ross and I were already friends then, but he was dealing with his own shit. I wouldn't say he abandoned me, he just couldn't be there for me the way I needed. You know, I can remember my brother before and after the drugs. I remember him smiling, going out with friends, walking me to school, standing up for me when other kids tried to beat me up…then, in the blink of an eye, all that was gone. He wasn't even the same person anymore. Drugs were everything for him, and he needed a bigger and bigger hit every time.

"He started stealing from us, from my grandparents, from strangers. He'd do anything, hurt anyone, and nothing was ever enough. It was pathetic, the way he used to beg and try to blackmail us emotionally. But it kept working. I barely had pocket change, and I still gave him money. My parents told me not to, but what can you do when it's your own brother? I couldn't tell him no. I wonder sometimes if I could have stopped him if I'd just stayed strong. But to hell with it. It doesn't matter anymore.

"All I'm trying to tell you is I know what it feels like when Ross comes to you asking for help and you can't say no even though you know it isn't right. I don't blame you. But think about what you're doing. Ross would never admit this to you, but he was in rehab before, when he was eighteen.

I'd been trying to get him to kick the drugs, but he wouldn't listen to me. Then everything came crashing down. His mother found him half dead and got him to a special facility, but they could only hold him for forty-eight hours without his consent. He kept swearing he would leave, and his mom asked Naya and me to go see him. I told him I'd already lost a brother and I didn't want to lose my best friend, too. And that I wouldn't walk with him down that road and watch him destroy himself. So he stuck it out for another month and a half, then he went to the lake house with his mom for a few months, then he was suddenly determined that he would take film directing seriously, and he got into school and was focused and doing great. And he met you. He'd never let another person get close to him like that. I liked it. I liked the new Ross."

That was touching, but it also made me uncomfortable. Was he implying that my departure was part of Jack's downfall? I wasn't ready to go there yet, so I joked with him, "Didn't you say it was a little early for deep conversations?"

He laughed and took a sip of his coffee, and I did the same, just to break the tension. "Sorry, I'm just worried. Something feels different this time, Jenna. I'm terrified for him, but I also don't think I or anyone else can get him to change. It's got to come from inside Ross. All we can do is try and help."

"But what if that doesn't work?" I asked.

He couldn't respond before Jack returned, laying his cigarettes on the counter next to his keys. I hadn't noticed them earlier. Wait—did that mean he had stayed here last night? The thought relieved me, but then I was startled because I realized Will and I were holding hands. It was nothing, we could never be anything but friends, but with Jack so sensitive, who knew how he'd take it. Will noticed at the same time as I did, and we both stood up straight as boards.

"Morning, partner," Will said in a far more natural tone than I could have mustered. "You want a cup of coffee?"

Jack narrowed his eyes, suspicious. "Nah, I'm going to grab a shower."

He ran his hand through his hair and walked to the bathroom. It was impossible to say what was going on in his mind.

Classes carried on, I started to get the hang of school, and I was surprised by how much I participated. Part of this was thanks to Curtis, who joked around but was sharp as a tack, and caught me up on the material better than I could ever have done on my own. He also did everything he could to help me fit in, but he worked his magic subtly and I barely noticed that I'd started forming new friendships on my own.

Jack didn't get better in all that time. He spent that one night at home but then he vanished, and we hadn't seen him since. Four days passed without a sign of life from him. He wouldn't even answer my messages.

It upset me. Will told me not to worry. I tried to listen to him, but it was hard. Jack was a grown-up, I tried to tell myself. If he wanted to be out on his own, that was his right. Saying that was one thing, though, and believing it was something totally different.

I talked a lot with Spencer and Shannon, and they kept me up to date on the family. My grandmother had started taking a water aerobics class and was with her new friends most of the day, and that was why she hadn't had time to call me. My sister told me she kept Grandma up to date on my life, though. She also let me know Owen was finally getting better at math, and I was relieved, because that was something he'd always struggled with. She didn't mind sharing her daily struggles and frustrations, and Spencer was open about that stuff, too. I liked that, but I couldn't do the same. I inevitably kept everything bad to myself and only brought up the good stuff.

I did some searching on the internet. Since I was clueless, I just typed in stuff like *How do you help an addict?* and *What do you do for a friend who's sad?* Naturally, I didn't find much that was helpful, but I did note a few things:

a. *Let the person know you're with them despite everything.* I had tried that, but I didn't think it would work. Jack was mad at me, hurt, bitter.

b. *Keep an eye on the person's habits.* But I didn't want to keep an eye on him, I wanted to help him!

c. *Seek professional help.* I didn't think that would work in Jack's case. He wouldn't go to a psychologist. Not now, anyway.

d. *Talk to the person.* That was obvious, but it sure wasn't easy.

e. *Hold an intervention with loved ones and friends.* I mentioned this to Will, but he told me Jack would get defensive and it would make everything worse. And he was probably right.

f. *Never stop being a helper, and never lose hope.* I guess that was my only choice.

I was glancing at these notes in the back of Will's car one day when I heard Sue yawn. We were on our way to a party Lana had invited us to that morning. It was the birthday of some friend of hers we didn't know the first thing about. As I adjusted my skirt, I thought to myself that I wasn't looking forward to the evening. But at least Lana and I got along better than we had the year before.

We walked into the sorority house, which still reminded me of a museum, and I took off my jacket and stared down at the violet top Shannon had bought me a few months ago when she invited me out with her and her on-again, off-again boyfriend—he was off-again just then, and soon enough, she met someone else. I hadn't actually worn it before that night, so this was its debut. It was a little tight, but I thought it looked good with my black Converse—no way I was making the same mistake with the platform boots again. I hadn't put on much makeup, and I'd pulled my hair back in a ponytail. I wanted to look good but in a casual way, since I wasn't interested in meeting anyone.

"Hey, guys!" Lana called out, coming down the stairs. She was dressed in a skimpy red dress that fit her like a glove. "Welcome, welcome. You can leave your coats over here with everyone else's."

She hugged all of us except for Sue, who stiffened like a cat ready to pounce when she got close. Then she guided us upstairs. People were crisscrossing the hallways going from room to room. The ballroom was packed, maybe even fuller than the last time I'd seen it. There was a poster that read *Happy birthday!* on one wall, but no one seemed to care who the birthday girl actually was. They were all just there to get drunk.

I leaned in toward Lana as we walked and said, "Looks like people are having fun."

Glancing back over her shoulder, she responded, "Yeah, this is the first party we've had since New Year's. We got noise complaints for our last one, and the school threatened us with probation. But finally we decided to hell with it. There's no way they'll actually do anything."

Looking at a group of guys passing a pitcher of beer around and drinking straight from it, I wasn't sure she was right. I could easily imagine things getting out of control there.

"I guess you're here because of Ross," Lana said.

That took me by surprise. No one had mentioned Jack. We were in the kitchen when she said that, and my roommates were getting their drinks. Lana continued, "He's here. He's with his, um, new friends. I just assumed you had come to see him."

New friends? I could already imagine what that meant. And as far as I was concerned, they sure as hell weren't his friends. A friend was someone who'd try to stop you when they saw you were losing control, not someone who'd push you to act even stupider. I was angry. I wondered if these were the same people he'd been with all those nights when he hadn't come home, and I tried to imagine what kind of horrible things they'd gotten into.

"Where is he?"

Lana motioned toward a small room with sofas and bookshelves, cushions on the floor, and lots of people sitting around a coffee table. Baggies were spread out on it, and a blue bong was standing in the middle of it. The scent was repulsive, and as soon as I walked in, I felt dizzy. They'd closed all the windows, probably to keep their precious weed smoke from blowing away.

The guys looked high as hell and were joking and laughing as they cut up lines. A few feet away, a group of girls were giggling and passing around a joint. Jack was sitting in a corner, eyes bloodshot, smoking. Just a cigarette, I hoped, but who knew. His look, partly somber and partly amused, turned blank as he saw me enter. A big lug with brown hair asked him, "Hey, dude. Do you know her?"

With a sneer, Jack told him, "Yeah. That's my mom."

The rest of the group thought that was funny, but Jack just frowned, stared away, tried to pretend I wasn't there. He must have thought I'd shown up to ruin his night. But I didn't care how mad he was. I stepped past the circle of losers around the coffee table and stood in front of him, forcing him to acknowledge me, however much he hated it.

"What?" he asked.

"Don't what me," I said. "Is this why you haven't responded to a single message I've sent you? So you can sit around getting high with a bunch of douchebags?"

Everyone was laughing at me. Well, to hell with them. Jack took another hit of whatever he was smoking, and I remembered how pissed he had been that time I'd smoked weed with his brother. How the tables had turned.

"Why should I respond to your messages?"

"Is it really asking too much for you to let me know you're OK?" I fired back. "If you're too childish to tell me, the least you could do is let Will know. He's worried, too. Is that so hard?"

He blew a cloud of smoke in my face. Everyone around me thought that was the funniest thing they'd ever seen. The big guy asked if I was Jack's girlfriend, and he responded, "Yeah, she wishes." My cheeks got hot as I felt everyone's contempt. I wanted to remind him of how much he'd cried when I left. But that was a low blow, and it would have made me feel guilty. And I tried to tell myself this was the drugs talking, not him.

"I'm his ex," I replied calmly, but loud enough for everyone to hear.

"Seems like you should get over him," some guy said, and more joined in, telling me to leave him alone. To relax. To stop being an uptight bitch. And far from defending me, Jack said, "Yeah, that's good advice, Jen. Why don't you worry about yourself and just let me be?"

I felt my eyes narrowing. I understood him getting mad, treating me badly, threatening to kick me out. It hurt, and I knew I'd never do anything like that to him, but I could accept that he was bitter and angry. What I didn't understand was his carefree attitude, as if we'd never been anything, as if we'd had sex and that was it and now he couldn't care less about me. I had mattered to him, and now he was using me to get laughs out of a bunch of weirdos who were no one compared to me. At least, not to him. Maybe we hadn't stayed together that long when we were going out, but it had been intense, and I knew how deep inside it had touched both of us.

I turned around, walked to an ice bucket, grabbed a beer, and sat across from Jack. The group chanted *oooooh!!* and I responded, "What? I thought I was supposed to relax. Well, this is me relaxing."

"Jen, be cool," Jack said.

"Be cool! Oh, I'm cool, Jack, I'm fucking cool." Espying a bottle of whiskey on the table, I picked it up and took a long swig. I saw one bubble, two, three, four, five, rise up through the glass. My throat was on fire and I wanted to vomit, but I wasn't going to let all these jerks win, and I sure as hell wasn't going to throw up after Lana told me the sorority house had already gotten in trouble.

Everyone cheered, and for a moment, Jack was speechless. I talked and joked, and watched Jack get more and more pissed with every word I uttered, but he couldn't bring himself to tell me off. He just clenched his teeth, opened and closed his fists, sighed, took drags on his joint. Trying to get a reaction, I threw an arm around him, took a selfie of us, and sent it to my sister. Then, I called out suddenly, "How about a game of truth or dare?"

The guys were into it. Why wouldn't they be? They were drunk and horny, and I was a warm body, which I was pretty sure was all any of them cared about. Most of them went for the dare, probably hoping they could get some action with me out of it, but I wasn't that stupid. I made two of the guys slow dance with each other, another one had to send a sexy voice message to his ex, and another had to show everyone the most embarrassing photo on his phone.

It didn't go much further for a while, but then a guy named Eric dared his friend Finn to kiss me from the tattoo on my hip all the way to my neck. When I first came in, Finn had been trash-talking me worse than anyone else there, so I was surprised to find him suddenly hesitant, even shy. But then I saw why. Jack was fuming, and Finn kept glancing over, uncertain whether this was a good idea.

"Maybe we should try something else," I suggested, afraid of what Jack or Finn might do.

"Come on," Eric said. "It's a couple of kisses. Trust me, if Finn wusses out, we'll come up with something even worse."

The tension was killing me, but I'd told myself I needed to get a reaction out of Jack, no matter what. So I agreed, "Sure, to hell with it. We're all adults, what's the big deal?"

I grabbed the hem of my top and pulled it up. Amid oohs and ahs, Finn bent down, ready to go. The thought of some stranger leaving a streak of his saliva on me grossed me out, but I took a deep breath, closed my eyes, and waited. Then I heard *hold on*, and looked up to find Jack clutching Finn's arm.

"I've got this," he said, sounding annoyed.

He handed me the cigarette he'd just lit and pulled me to my feet, pushing me against a shelf and resting his hands on either side of my hips. He got on his knees. People started giggling and making obscene comments I tried not to listen to. Letting a stranger do this had been one thing, but knowing Jack was about to touch me in that way drove me into a panic. Of course, he'd done it lots of times before. But this time, I wasn't sure he'd be so gentle—I wasn't sure that gentle guy was even still there—and I was scared.

I leaned my head back as I felt him tug my skirt down to expose my tattoo and deposit his first kiss there. His mouth was hot as it trailed up my abdomen and then between my breasts. He kissed my clavicle, licked the hollow of my neck. It felt raw, almost aggressive, and when he was done, he took back his cigarette and sat back down without looking at me. You'd have thought he'd felt nothing at all. He was calm, almost apathetic, as I turned red, bent over, and rested my hands on my knees.

"I don't know about you guys, but I've sure got a boner now," Eric said, getting a laugh out of everyone except Jack and me.

I was worried about what would come next, and I hoped the group would turn its attention to someone else. But I wouldn't get that lucky. We went around in the circle, everyone asked stupid questions or proposed stupid dares, and when I was up again, I said *truth*. But Eric knew how to get what he wanted, and he asked me a question so embarrassing, so personal, that I had to say, "Never mind, dare."

With a smile, he told me to do the same as Jack had done to me, but instead of finishing at his neck, I'd have to kiss him on the mouth, too. Everyone cheered except Jack, who hung his head in exasperation.

"No," I said.

"We can go back to truth," Finn responded.

"Fine, I'll do it, but it has to be like before," I suggested, "I'll go up to the neck, but I won't kiss him on the lips."

"What's the deal?" Finn asked. "Don't tell me you don't want to! Poor Ross, I know he's an ugly bastard, but he's a good guy, he deserves a real kiss! Don't be a chicken."

"It's not that," I said.

"She's scared she'll like it." This phrase came from Jack, who was rolling his eyes. *So that's how it is…* I wasn't going to let anyone put me down like that. I stood and turned to him, knowing he was manipulating me, knowing that he loved provoking me, but unable to stop taking the bait. I don't think he thought it would work, but there I was in front him, and neither of us could turn back.

He was sitting on the floor, and I grabbed his knees, kneeled down, listened to all the filthy comments everybody was making, tried not to let them get to me. Jack ignored everyone, too. He looked at me in shock, maybe with desire, and when our eyes met, he pursed his lips, trying to pretend he wasn't nervous.

"What are you trying to prove?" he asked.

"Shut up and let me do my dare."

"So you *do* want me," he said.

Was he sincere? Was he putting me down? I didn't know and didn't care. Nervous, I planted my first kiss just above the button of his jeans. He tensed beneath my lips and opened his legs to accommodate me. I gripped his legs tight as I rose up his abdomen.

I was less aggressive than he'd been, but that didn't stop him from reacting. He was still, but I could sense how he was throbbing inside. He didn't say anything cruel, didn't try to put me down; he just stood still, quivering slightly. I could feel his heart racing as his chest rose and fell. Mine was, too, as I reached his neck. His Adam's apple rose as I kissed it. The stubble on his cheeks poked my lips. I looked him dead in the eyes, ready for that last kiss. My mouth was open, our tongues ready to touch, and at the very last moment, I planted a finger in the middle of his forehead and pushed him against the wall. He blinked, baffled, as I murmured, "You wish," and sat back down.

People whistled and cheered, and I tried to ignore it. I had wanted to show him I could stand up to him, but I didn't want to see him hurt or frustrated. The catcalling and laughter ceased. The feeling in the room was unpleasant. I hadn't drunk that much, but I was feeling confused and woozy, and Jack was high as a kite. I could tell by the way he moved, his clumsiness when he grabbed at his drinks or his cigarettes, his glassy eyes when he was supposed to be paying attention.

When it was my turn again, I opted for *truth*, because who knew what they'd ask me to do next. Eric asked me, "Do you have a crush on someone?" and I almost blurted out Jack's name. *Get a hold of yourself*, I thought. But then I saw him staring at me intensely and thought it was time to take the lid off the charade. "I do," I said. "I'm in love with a complete idiot."

Jack slammed his glass down on the table, getting everyone's attention just before he stood and walked out, slamming the door. What the…? Maybe I'd overstepped a line a little bit, but was it really that bad? Was it too direct? Too soon? I wasn't sure, but I knew I had to follow him, no matter what the other people thought, no matter how much they kept shouting for me to come back and keep playing.

I could almost see the fire in Jack's eyes as he pushed his way through the crowd. Many of the partygoers stopped and stared. They could tell that there was a problem. Worst of all, Lana was there watching us with morbid curiosity.

"I'm sorry," I called out to Jack. "I went too far. Hey!" I grabbed his arm. He turned, an expression of pure hatred in his eyes.

Hysterical, he yelled out, "What the hell do you want? And why are you stopping me? Can you not tell I don't want to be around you? Can't you give me five goddamn seconds of peace?"

OK, that was a bit much. I knew I had intentionally baited him, but part of it was because, pathetic as it was, I thought if I told the truth maybe we could actually make some progress with each other. He continued, "Were you honestly not aware of what you were doing to me in there? Did you wake up today and think, you know what, I'll go find Ross and kiss another guy in front of him and see if I can drive him even further out of his mind!"

"What do you care if I kiss someone? What do you care if I kiss every guy in there? I mean, you don't want me, that much is obvious, so why should I have to explain myself to you?"

"Just go!" he shouted. "Go back and play your stupid truth or dare, I'm sure they have some super-cool idea for what you can do next!"

"Should I remind you that you're the one who stood up and decided you were going to kiss me?" I asked.

"And? What? You wanted Finn to do it instead? How would you feel if there was some girl in there who was going to kiss me?"

"How would you feel," I responded, "if you had to stand there and watch me taking drugs and destroying my life and there wasn't a damn thing you could do about it?"

That cut close to the bone, but I didn't care, and I didn't regret it. And he knew I was right—that was why his face went blank and all that rage drained out of him. "I can do what I want," he murmured.

"Fine. You do that," I said, turning around. Will, Naya, and Sue were there. I guess Lana had gone to get them. "Let's go," I told Will, then looking at Jack, I said, "Enjoy the rest of your night."

"Are you serious?" he shouted as I passed him. "You're actually just going to leave?"

"What the hell am I supposed to do?"

"Stay here with me. I'll take you home later."

"You've got to be kidding," I replied. "I doubt you could even get the car in gear in your condition."

"Do you have to criticize literally every single thing I ever do?"

"No, but I'm also not going to let you kill us both! Jesus! If I'd known you were going to blow up like this, I never would have let you kiss me again."

I hadn't thought about the consequences those words would have on him or me, or how our friends, who were watching us, would take them. I don't know why I kept thinking that hurting him would bring him closer…or did I want to push him away so I could stop thinking about him? He shouted something about how I could go back and make out with those other guys if that was what I wanted, and I told him maybe I would, that at least they knew how to have a good time. Naya interrupted us, saying, "Come on, you two," but neither of us listened to her.

"Here's an idea," Jack said, "since apparently I bother you so much. How about you pack your goddamn bags and get the hell out of my apartment!"

"I will!" I shouted. "Half my stuff is still in my suitcase, because I knew something like this would happen. There was no way you were ever going to be mature enough to deal with this situation."

"How am I supposed to deal with it? You do realize you're the one who just abandoned me one day. And now I'm just supposed to forget that after a whole year of suffering and act like everything's perfect?"

"Whatever!" I said. "I'll be out of your life soon, and then you won't have me to blame for your problems anymore."

He stopped, panting from so much screaming, then started in on me again: "Sounds great! Go find yourself a place where you can bring home all the dudes you want."

"Sorry, Jack. That may be how you cope with things, but that's not who I am."

"You have no fucking idea how I do or don't cope with things."

"Screw this," Sue interrupted us. "I'm not going to sit here and watch two babies scream at each other all night. Will, either we can go now or I'm catching an Uber."

Will shrugged, told her to grab her coat, and hung back to talk for a moment with Jack. I walked off, thinking at least this was over for now, but no such luck. When Will met us outside, he had Jack in tow. We said nothing as we piled into the car, and I felt bad for Sue, who had to sit between us. Jack and I both looked out the window and ignored each other the whole ride home. In the elevator, I could feel his eyes on me, but I stared at the ground. I didn't want him to see what I was feeling, and I wasn't sure I wanted to know what was going through his mind.

Once we were back home, Will and Naya tried to start a normal conversation, but when that failed, they rushed off to their room, and Sue did the same. I was alone with Jack, who was sitting on the sofa with his back turned.

He surprised me with a question: "I want to ask you something. Were you ever unfaithful to me?"

His voice was quaking. I'd been holding my coat under my arm. But my body went weak, and I dropped it to the ground. Was he serious? I walked around until I could see his face, sad, desperate. That hurt: how in the hell could he even think that? I knew I had screwed things up, I understood why he was mad at me, I'd have even understood if he told me he never wanted to see me again. But he had to know me well enough to know I'd never, ever cheat on him.

"Jack, you know the answer," I said.

"Do I, though? Because every time I'm with you, I feel like you're more of a stranger to me."

"I could say the same to you."

"I was always honest with you, Jen."

"So was I, Ross."

"Really? Even that day you tried to run off without saying goodbye?"

He was right. I had hurt him, I couldn't deny it, and that frustrated me. But instead of understanding, I counterattacked. "What about you? Don't sit here and tell me you didn't have any secrets when we were together."

"I never lied to you, Jen. Never. Not once in all those three months."

"Maybe you didn't lie, but you sure as hell weren't honest. How much stuff did you keep hidden from me? You might as well tell me now, because it's not going to get any worse!"

"Whatever I hid," he said, "I'm glad now, seeing where we're at. And anyway, since when was it my obligation to tell you every single thing I've ever done?"

"I want to know you, Jack! I want to understand you! I always did, and you'd never let me!"

"What would you have done with whatever I told you? Used it to hurt me? Run out on me anyway?"

"I don't know, Jack, but at least you could have tried! You could have tried to give it your all, the way I did from the beginning! I tried to make you happy, I tried to let you in. You never had the decency to return the favor."

"My life's not your fucking business!" he shouted.

"Not anymore, I guess." I pushed him. "But it is your problem. And you're destroying yourself. After all I did, after how much it hurt me to leave, just so you could go to France and live your dreams… And what was the point?"

"What do you mean, how much it hurt you? You didn't have to go! I wanted you here, and you turned around and walked away."

"What do you care?" I asked. "You had the opportunity of a lifetime, and you wanted to blow it, and the only thing I did was try to make sure that wouldn't happen…"

"Don't start in about Paris. You don't know a damn thing about that, and it has nothing to do with you standing in my way all the time now, when I'm just trying to live my life…"

"This isn't you, though, Jack."

"What the hell do you know about who I am? Nothing! It's been a year since you left me. I've changed!"

"I do know you. Maybe I don't know every single thing about you, but you're not this, I'm sure of it. You're not an asshole, a drunk, a drug addict, someone who's just fighting with the world for no reason."

He grabbed my wrists and pulled me so close to him I almost fell into his lap. "Oh yeah? Who am I then?"

I didn't try to get away. I didn't mind that he was touching me. I was tired, I wanted to break down in tears, but I had to try to reach him somehow. "You're good," I said softly. "You're a good person, Jack."

I felt his fingers squeezing my wrists, and he didn't seem angry anymore, just expectant, as if he needed to hear what I had to say. I wanted to take it back. I was scared to say everything I was thinking. I had a knot in my throat and was worried I'd break down in tears. But it was too late to give up now, so I gathered my strength and let it all out: "Jack, you're funny, you're disgustingly charming, you say three words and you make the whole world adore you. You're a guy who loves movies and junk food and superheroes. You do everything for everyone, even if you pretend to hate it. You're my Jack, my errand boy. I can see you behind that mask. I know you don't want to take it off, because you're scared of getting hurt, but I also know one day you will."

I wriggled away from his grasp and held his hands, as he remained attentive to my words. "I know I hurt you, and I'm sorry. I wish I could go back. I know things were hard for you after I did what I did. And I know it's my fault. All of it. But you're not this person, and you don't need to be. You're still the same guy I met a year ago."

He looked up at me, and I wasn't sure what I saw in his eyes. Torment? Anguish? Confusion? I squeezed his hands, and he flinched. It was as though the spell was broken, and he reacted with fury.

"The guy you knew a year ago…he disappeared, thanks to you."

I shook my head. I thought for a moment I'd been doing things right. But now it seemed I'd made it all worse.

"I'm sorry…"

"Stop apologizing! I don't want your apologies! Why did you even come back? Did you think it was going to be nice and happy? That we'd have a beautiful second chapter and I'd drop everything and come back to you? Do you honestly think I would fall for the same fairy tale twice?"

"It wasn't a fairy tale," I tried to tell him, but he wouldn't let me finish.

"You left me! Don't turn around now and pretend that your feelings for me were real."

"But they were."

"Then why did you leave me?! Why did you go? Did I really screw up so bad that you had to leave me that way? I gave you everything! Everything! I'm not talking about money or the apartment or any of that bullshit, I don't care about that. I'm talking about me! I told you things I'd never told anyone. Whatever you think about it, I was opening up to you. I was trying, Jen! For you! You were the only person in the world who could have hurt me, and you did. And now you think you've got the right to teach me lessons about how to live. And I'm supposed to buy this shit about you being a friend who's concerned about me? You think I want to be your friend? That can't happen, Jen! Shit! You're driving me crazy. Every time I see you, all I can think about is how for three months, I lost my head over someone who didn't give a damn about me. Can you even imagine what that feels like? Of course you can't. Never in your fucking life have you fallen in love with someone that way. And yet, here you are, and you think you have a right to show back up in my life just when I was starting to turn the page."

He got up and walked away from me, leaning on the counter.

"I'm sor—," I began, then stopped myself, remembering what he'd said, and told him, "I didn't mean to barge in and mess things up for you. If I'd known…"

"What? If you'd known, then what?" He turned back to me. "You wouldn't have left? Well, it doesn't matter, because you did leave. And you knew perfectly well how much I loved you. And I still don't get it. It wasn't really because of your asshole ex-boyfriend, was it? Or was it…? You know what? I don't want to know. I should have treated you like any other girl, I should have hit it and quit it and forgotten about you."

I didn't respond, and he smiled maliciously. He knew he'd hit me where it hurt, and now it was time for him to pour salt in the wound. "Because you know that's what I was thinking when I met you, right? *I'll bang this chick and send her on her way*. And Will told me not to because you were his girlfriend's roommate and she liked you. Naya thought you'd never come back over if we hooked up. So I stopped myself. And you would have fallen for me, Jen, we both know you would have. You were desperate for a little affection."

He had said that to get to me, and now he was bent over, his face close to mine, trying to see how I'd react. He couldn't have really felt that way, could he? My eyes filled with tears of rage. He knew I was insecure, and trying to take advantage of that to make me feel bad was cruel. Well, if cruelty was what he wanted, two could play at that game.

"You know what your problem is?" I asked.

"I don't have a problem."

"You damn well do. And I'll tell you what it is. As much as you try to deny it, as much as it fucks you up, you're still in love with me, Jack Ross."

He laughed bitterly and came closer to me. I had to back away to keep him from touching me, but I didn't let him intimidate me. In a whisper, he responded, "And you're in love with me, too, Jen. I might be a fuckup, but you love me. And you'd be better off going ahead and admitting it."

"At least I'm not jealous," I told him. "You think I couldn't tell when we were playing truth or dare? It was so obvious how pissed off you were, all because I was trying not to kiss you. And when you thought another guy was going to get to kiss me, you nearly lost your mind."

"Fuck you. Like you'd do any different. You'd cry a river if you thought I was with another chick. You know you were dying to touch me back there. If you didn't take it any further, it's because you like hurting me more."

"That's a lie. And for your information, I couldn't be happier to be single."

He bent so close to me I could feel the heat of his breath. "OK, then. If you're not into me, then move away." His nose was touching mine, and I did want to get up and go. I swear I did. But I wanted to stay even more. He grabbed the back of my neck. Not delicately, not affectionately, but like a brute, balling my hair up in his fist. And it turned me on.

"Come on," he said, "tell me to stop."

His other hand was resting on my thigh, and his voice was huskier, but restrained. He was tense, angry, and something else, too… Something vague but undeniable shone in his eyes. Longing, perhaps?

I looked at his lips, and he drew in a breath before looking back at mine. Then our eyes met. Each of us was waiting for the other to take the first step: to turn away or to finally close what little distance still lay between us.

"I was right, wasn't I?" I said. "I could move if I wanted to. You can't."

"I could if I felt like it. But I'll admit one thing. I do have feelings I wish I didn't have. I still love you. And you don't deserve it. You never deserved for me to love you, Jennifer. And you never will. I'm an idiot, though, and I'll bet I could love you for the rest of my life."

I smiled, trying to hide what those words did to me, pushing further into him and saying, "Leave, then, Jack. If I'm so terrible, just leave."

He shook his head, sparks of rage in his eyes, and I spoke again: "You said you could do it. So go."

Then I saw it: a very slight movement backward. Before he could take it any further, I grabbed his T-shirt in both hands. I couldn't bring myself to pull him in, but I didn't want to let him go. I felt his hand on the back of my head, and all at once, his mouth was pressing into mine. It wasn't a tender kiss: the rage and resentment that filled every fiber of his body were palpable in it. But that didn't stop either of us. I came in for more, and he shoved me backward. I stumbled toward the counter, and I couldn't tell if we were attacking each other hungrily or trying desperately to get away from each other. My answer came when I opened my mouth to breathe and he dove in and his tongue wrapped around mine...

His hips, his chest were tight against me, his hand moved from my chin to between my thighs. He was brusque, and I wish I could say I didn't enjoy it, that I didn't yelp with pleasure when I felt him rubbing me. But I can't lie. I needed him, and he needed me as he pulled up my skirt. My knees went weak, and he held me up with his other arm as he rubbed me, finally reaching inside my underwear.

That touch—that shadow of a touch, because I didn't let him keep going—was like an alarm going off. Suddenly I realized what we were doing, and I pushed him away, rearranging my clothing as his words echoed in my head: *I'll bang this chick and send her on her way.* That was what he'd told me he'd said. That was what he thought he should have done. And the way he was treating me now—like a starving animal and not like a lover—made me wonder if that was what he was doing now. What I needed was the Jack I had loved, not the Ross his friends had known before I'd come around, the guy who hooked up with girls and left them hanging without a care.

Aching, on the verge of tears, I wrestled free of his grasp. He stood there watching me, his chest rising and falling. For a moment, our eyes locked, and neither of us said anything, but I could feel his stare following me as I ran off to the bedroom.

7

GOOD NIGHT, JACK

The next morning, I pulled the blanket tight around me and reached over for my phone. It was nine, and I had a message from Curtis from the night before. He'd been at Lana's party and heard I was there, but he hadn't seen me. He wanted to know if I was OK. Word had gotten around that I'd been fighting with someone. He added, with the obligatory eggplant and peach emojis, that he'd hooked up with some girl in the education program.

I'm great, I wrote him. I just woke up. I wasn't feeling well last night and I decided to go home early. Lying to my friend. What a way to start my day.

He asked if I was better.

Yes ☺, I wrote. Really? he asked. I told him to quit beating around the bush. I knew what he wanted was to tell me about his hookup. He sent me a GIF of a dancing monkey and told me all the gory details before inviting me to breakfast. He wasn't dumb, so he had to have known Jack was the person I'd been fighting with, and he probably wanted to offer me an escape hatch in case I didn't want to deal with it.

I told him not to worry, I was supposed to have breakfast with Naya. That was my second lie of the day.

I just wasn't hungry, and I didn't want to get out of bed. But I needed to wash my face. I had gotten into bed fully dressed without taking off my makeup, and when I turned on my phone camera to take a glance at my face, all I could think was: *You look like a hungover raccoon.*

I groaned and changed into a pair of pajamas. On my way to the bathroom, I noticed Will was talking in the kitchen and stopped. I knew that tone. The tone of a concerned father. I didn't want to eavesdrop, but I was curious about what he might be saying. I heard Jack's voice: "She still hasn't come out yet?"

"No," Will said.

I heard what sounded like a spoon stirring coffee. Jack expelled a breath in frustration. "I figured she'd be out for a run."

"Nah. She's given that up since she's been back. I don't think it's really her thing anymore."

"Something's up. She used to be a fanatic."

"Ross," Will said, "I know you're not going to like to hear this, but it's not your business anymore. She can run or not run, she can sleep in, she can hang out with other guys, it doesn't matter. It shouldn't concern you. You should just focus on your things."

"Yeah…"

They talked a bit longer, but I missed most of the rest of it, deciding I should really go to the bathroom instead of trying to get into their heads. I undressed, wiped off my makeup, and took a long, hot shower. When I was done, I wrapped up in a towel and put on my pajamas. I recoiled when I opened the door and saw Jack there, about to knock on the door. He stood stiff for a moment before letting his arm drop. For a moment, it seemed as if we were both about to ask each other something, but then I looked at the floor. He realized I wasn't in the mood to talk and walked past me into the bathroom without saying a word.

Will was gone, which was a relief, because he must have known everything that had happened the night before, and it was too early to get into something that serious. Mike and Sue were in the living room jabbering, and when he saw me, Mike said playfully, "Jenna! I heard you put on quite a performance last night!"

"What are you talking about?"

"Your argument with my brother."

"What do you know about it?"

"I've got a mole," he said, pointing at Sue, who grinned and rolled her eyes. Sue the snitch... I sat on the couch between them and they both looked at me like children greedy for a treat.

"Aren't you going to give us the deets?" Sue asked.

"Why do you two care?" I asked. "I thought you hated gossip."

"This is a question of self-interest," Mike replied. "The sooner Ross starts sleeping with you again, the sooner I can have my place on the couch back. It's not easy, you know, having to find a new place to crash every night."

"I don't know why you think he'd want to sleep with me," I said. "Things got pretty uncomfortable between us last night."

"Yeah, we know that much," Mike replied. "Your future husband didn't even want to let me in. There was quite a bit of tension in the air."

"There's nothing new for me to tell you, though," I continued. "I mean, I guess the argument touched on some deeper things. I told him he was still in love with me. He didn't take that well."

"I don't know why he'd be so upset," Sue said. "You're clearly still in love with him, too."

"I don't know," I responded. "Maybe."

Why was I talking about my inner life with those two? I liked them, but they certainly weren't the most understanding people I'd ever known. It was comfortable, though, natural, even if they kept grinning at me like a couple of morons.

"You know what I think, Agent Susie?" Mike asked.

"I don't, Agent Mike. But if you call me Susie again, I will gladly chop your balls off."

"That's affirmative, Agent Sue. Now as I was saying, this looks like a job for the Drug Squad!"

When I didn't react, Mike snapped his fingers in my face. "Hello, Earth to Jenna! The Drug Squad! Don't you remember?"

"Yeah, I remember when you guys convinced me to smoke weed and then Ross got all pissed at me. How could I forget?" I said.

"That was just one time," Mike objected. "The Drug Squad is about much more than smoking weed. The Drug Squad has magic powers. We can brighten your day, and even my cranky brother's, too. Maybe we can help bring you guys closer. It's obvious you both want it. You just need a little push."

"I don't know, I'm grateful for your help, but, uh…" Happily, I didn't have to keep making excuses, because my phone rang. Unknown number. I usually let those go to voicemail, but I needed an excuse to get away from those two. As I heard them chatting behind my back, I stood and picked up.

"Hello?"

"Hey, Jenny."

Monty. I don't know if it's because I was tired or emotionally drained, but Monty's voice didn't even scare me. It was more like an annoyance. I couldn't believe I was still dealing with him after all this time.

"Are you seriously calling me?" I asked.

"Easy, Jennifer. I don't want to fight."

"If you don't want to fight, leave me alone. Otherwise, I'll call the cops again."

"I just wanted to see what was going on," he said. "A year's passed. I'm a different person now. I'm starting a new phase of my life, and I don't want there to be bad blood between us."

I had the urge to curse at him, to tell him to drop dead, but the most important thing was for our conversation to end as quickly as possible. "Great, bye," I told him.

"Wait! I wanted to know when you're coming back."

"Who said I was coming back?"

"I just figured because of your grandmother…"

"What about my grandmother?" I asked, suddenly consumed with worry. "What happened?"

"I don't think it's anything too bad. But you should call your parents. I was hanging out with them yesterday, and you came up. They miss you, Jenny. You shouldn't be so hard on them. Anyway, I just thought I'd let you know something had happened, and if you need anyone to talk to, no matter what, my door's always open…"

I hung up. I'd wanted to tell him to shove off, but what was the point? He wasn't all there, and that would probably never change.

"Is everything OK?" Sue called out.

"I don't know, I need to talk to my sister." Thank God, Shannon is one of those people who always have their phone on them. She picked up on the second ring.

"Hey there, little sister!"

"Hey," I said, sounding more upset than I meant to. "What's up with Grandma? And how come nobody's told me?"

"Did Mom call you?" she asked.

"No, Monty." That opened up a can of worms. Shannon screamed about how dare he call me, and she'd sic Spencer on him and he'd beat his ass, and I had to struggle to get her back to what mattered—my grandmother. She told me not to freak out, that it wasn't as grave as it sounded, but Grandma had just had a heart attack. I started yelling. It probably burst her eardrum, but I didn't care. I needed every single detail.

"Jenny, it was a scare," she said. "She's fine, I promise. Spencer took her to the hospital and is staying by her side. We got her there on time, and they're taking great care of her. When he has to go to work, I usually go in to relieve him. Grandma's complaining about it, but we insisted. She isn't going to be alone, and when she gets to go home, we'll look after her, too. I was planning on telling you, but I didn't want you to drop everything, and…"

I yelled, "Was that shit about water aerobics and her new friends even true?! I thought it was weird that she would never pick up when I called…"

"I'm sorry, Jenny, but that was her idea. She didn't want you to be scared. Please don't be mad."

I pinched the bridge of my nose. I knew she wanted me to make her feel better, to tell her everything was fine and I understood. But I also remembered what my therapist had told me, that I shouldn't hold back my feelings just to please others. And it was true. I'd had all that I could take.

"Well, I am mad," I said. "And I don't care why you decided not to tell me. She's my grandmother, too, and if something happens to her, I deserve to know. I'm not a little girl, and if I want to go down there and spend a week with her, I will. I can make my own decisions, and you don't have the right to do it for me. So from now on, you are not to hide *anything* else from me. Understood?"

Shannon was silent for a few seconds, then responded, "OK, you're right. I'm sorry. I really am. I promise I won't do it again."

I phoned Grandma, and this time I got through to her. She told me basically the same thing as Shannon did: she hadn't said anything because she didn't want to worry me, I had my own life to worry about, and so on. Of course, I couldn't be angry with her, and what I cared about was being sure she really was all right and wasn't just lying to make me feel better. Once I was sure about that, we talked a little bit about school and this and that, and by the time I hung up, I felt better.

It was a lazy, boring day, and I spent much of it trying to get over the blow of what I'd heard. After my afternoon class, I had a small lunch, went over my notes, vegged out in front of the TV, watched my roommates come and go without really paying them any attention. They did the same, they were busy, and for me, that was for the best. I honestly wasn't in the mood to talk to anyone.

Jack walked in at some point, threw his jacket on the couch, and headed straight to the bathroom for a shower. I didn't even look up from my notes. When he emerged soon afterward, he was dressed in a pressed black shirt and a fresh pair of jeans.

"Did you go shopping?" I asked.

Grabbing his jacket, he answered, "Yeah."

"You look good."

"Thanks."

In the awkward silence my phone buzzed, and I nearly jumped out of my skin. Jack noticed. I thought it might be Monty again, but thankfully it was Chris. I picked up and he told me he had good news for me.

"Which is…?" I asked.

"A room's opened up for you."

"Seriously?" I responded, surprised.

Jack narrowed his eyes as Chris explained, "Yeah, this girl in one of the single rooms was bombing all of her classes. I don't know if she was drinking too much or had personal issues, but anyway, her parents came and got her. Her room's not listed with housing yet, so I can probably hook you up."

"Can I think about it till tomorrow?" I found myself saying. I don't know if it was the day I had, or seeing Jack in front of me, but something was making me reluctant.

"I guess so," he said. "You're being kind of weird, though. I took it for granted you'd be jumping for joy."

"I don't know. I've just got a lot on my mind."

"All right," he replied. "Well, don't think about it too long, because if someone else gets word of it, I don't know when another spot might open up. I'm going to let you go, OK, I have some calls to make."

"Sure, Chris, thanks."

I hung up and tried to pretend I was busy with schoolwork, ignoring Jack until he'd walked in front of me and was standing there staring at me, playing with his keys.

"You're leaving?" he asked.

"Chris found an open room for me."

"Are you going to take it?"

"It makes sense, right? We're clearly not comfortable living together. You didn't throw me out, and I appreciate that, I really do, but I can tell when I'm not wanted. And that's fine. Anyway, I'll be able to save money on my light rail pass, so there's that."

His presence, his cold stare, my inability to know what he was thinking—all that made me nervous, and I found myself babbling, as I always do when I feel uncomfortable. "I can probably take care of it tomorrow. Then you'll have your room again. I'm sure it sucks sleeping on the sofa. And another thing…"

"I don't want the room," he burst out. "I want…"

He couldn't bring himself to finish. But I knew what he wanted to say.

"Actually," he said, "just do what you want."

"It's not just what I want," I responded. "It's what you want, too."

"So what, then, Jen? Do you need me to tell you to leave? Is that what you're waiting for? Would that make you feel better?" He turned and grabbed his things.

I shouted, "Are you just going to run away every time we start to talk for real?"

"I'm not running away. I have a party to go to, and I'm late."

"Admit that every time things get difficult, you run away."

He looked over his shoulder before walking out. "I'd say that makes two of us."

For a moment, I stared at the door, then I tried to study, but couldn't concentrate. I thought about Jack, then about my grandmother. If everything was fine, as they said, why had they tried to hide it from me? For a moment, I'd convince myself that I was blowing things out of proportion, then I'd manage to look at my notes, but soon the negative thoughts would start creeping back in, and all evening it didn't get better.

I was alone until after night fell. Naya had a dinner out, Mike didn't drop in, and Sue stayed in her bedroom getting ready for an exam. Will came in around eight and asked if I wanted takeout. "Let me treat," I said, and ordered enough food for three. He thought that was weird, and I told him I wanted to get something for Jack. "If he doesn't come home, no worries, one of us can eat the leftovers tomorrow."

Will shrugged. "That's your call, but if I were you, I wouldn't wait up for him. You look like you could use some rest."

He was right, but relaxing was easier said than done. I kept watching a film scroll past in my head: Jack drunk, Jack high, Jack lost in some shady part of the city, Jack vulnerable, Jack hurt. It made me shiver, and I started to get desperate. And the more desperate I was, the more I worried—about Jack, about Monty, about my grandmother—and soon I knew there was no way I was going to get to sleep.

After an hour's tossing and turning, I went to the living room and lay on the sofa, getting under a blanket and turning on the TV. I needed a reality show about beach babes and meathead dudes—that would cure my blues. But when I couldn't find anything like that, I opted for a rerun of a radical makeover show, then toyed around with my phone when I got bored. I sent a few texts, watched some videos of artists on TikTok, then finally admitted to myself I was only wasting time because I was hoping Jack would write. I looked at his Instagram so many times, I started to fear he could feel me watching him. Then I told myself: *If he really matters that much to you, you could write him.*

OK. Fine. Hey, I typed. Sorry about what I said before. I just didn't want to get into an argument again.

I kept rereading my message until I got mad at myself. What the hell did I have to apologize for?

Actually, I'm not sorry, because I know I'm right, but I didn't want to argue.

Five minutes later: I mean, I'm OK with apologizing, I know I'm not perfect, but sometimes I'm just right and you really could try and listen to me.

Time kept passing, and then my screen lit up. I was so scared I twitched, knocking my phone into the air. I caught it just before it went careening to the floor. Jack was calling. I was terrified but I picked up anyway. "Yeah?"

"You sure are chatty tonight."

His words sounded a little slurred, and though I knew it might get on his nerves, I couldn't help but ask, "Are you drunk?"

"No."

"Where are you?" I asked, standing up and looking for my shoes.

"I'm around. Why do you care?"

"Jack, please… I just do, OK?"

"Fine. I'm right outside."

That bastard… I opened the door and found him sitting on the floor yawning. He had to blink a few times to see me clearly. Then he waved. "Hello again."

He was still holding his phone to his cheek. I wanted to tell him he could hang up now, but then I saw something else that upset me. His key was jammed into the door. His car key.

"Ross, seriously?" I said. I grabbed it with both hands and pulled hard to get it out. When I'd extracted it, I asked, "Do you need me to help you up?"

"I thought you might be in your new dorm room."

"I told you I couldn't deal with that till tomorrow," I said, reaching out a hand to help him. He refused it, trying to stand, almost toppling over. Once he'd crawled inside, he leaned against the wall and closed his eyes.

"Let me help you over to the sofa, Jack. I've got you, I can hold you up." I meant that in more ways than one.

"Be careful what you offer, I might say yes."

"Are you OK?" I asked, being serious.

He opened one eye and smiled bitterly. "What do you think?"

I grabbed his hands and tried to tug him to his feet. He swayed toward me, looked at my lips, seemed tempted, then fell back slightly. "I wish," he said, "that our second first kiss had been nicer than it was."

I didn't want to talk about that, so I responded, "Let's get you sat down."

He groused and grumbled, but eventually I managed to drag him to the couch, where he collapsed, sighed loudly, almost snoring, and struggled upright. I didn't know what to do for him. The only thing I could think of was to pour him a glass of water. His eyes lit up as he heard the faucet, but when I brought it over, he pretended he couldn't move. "I need your help. I'm paralyzed, and water's very dangerous for a man in my state. I might drown. Or I could spill it all over myself, catch a cold, and die."

He looked at me like a defenseless puppy, and I asked, "Do you honestly want me to pour this into your mouth like you're a baby?"

He nodded mischievously. Fine. I played along. He took a few sips, then stuck out his tongue. "Gross," he said. "I thought that was vodka."

"Sorry, no more alcohol for you tonight. You've clearly had all you need."

Jack leaned his head back and closed his eyes, accepting defeat. I waited for him to say something, and when he didn't, I thought he had passed out. After a few seconds, telling myself there wasn't any harm in it, I stroked his cheek with my palm, feeling the prickle of his beard. He tried and failed to say something. That scared me, and I asked, "Do you need me to get Will?"

"No," he replied firmly. "Please, just stay here with me. Please."

Please, I thought. *Now we're getting somewhere. I haven't heard Jack utter that word since I got here.*

"We'll make a deal," I told him. "You drink some water, and I'll stay."

"Fiiiiine." He pursed his lips, but he obeyed. When he had emptied the glass, he handed it back to me with an innocent smile. "So, first question," he asked. "Are you going to keep living here?"

I couldn't deal with that yet, so I responded, "I got you a burger in case you were hungry."

He smiled like a child on Christmas day. "You got me dinner! That means you've been thinking of me!"

"You wish. We just happened to have one leftover." I walked to the kitchen, heated up his dinner, put it on a plate, and handed it to him. He still looked overjoyed as he turned on the TV and gobbled up his meal. I sat there next to him, beginning to feel relieved. There was nothing on, just infomercials, and yet strangely, they captivated both of us, at least until Jack set his plate on the coffee table and rested his head on my shoulder.

"Well, well," he said, his eyebrows rising and falling. "Look at the two of us, all alone, with no one watching. What should we do?"

"Sleep."

"Funny, I had something else in mind."

I wanted to laugh, but all I could do was shake my head. He loved to embarrass me, and he had a talent for it. His expression turned serious, and he asked, "Why are you sad?"

Of course, I knew why, but I wasn't ready to tell him.

"Who said I was sad?"

"I know you. I know what your sad face looks like."

I hadn't seen that coming, and I wasn't prepared. I'd been sad all day, but Will hadn't noticed. Neither had Sue when she'd emerged from her room. Jack was different, though. Even when he was drunk or high, or maybe both, he could see straight into me with those big eyes peeking through his chestnut bangs. No matter how silly he acted, he never missed anything.

"It's my grandmother," I confessed. He was the first person I had told. "She was… I guess she got sick, recently, and nobody in my family told me."

"Why not?"

"They said they didn't want to worry me. Spencer and Shannon said that, I mean. They're the only people in my family I'm talking to right now. I basically cut my parents off. I decided one day I couldn't keep hiding who I really am and what I really think, and it turns out they don't like it."

Jack reflected for a moment and smirked. "To hell with them, then. I'm proud of what you've done, and if they can't take you as you are, then they don't deserve you. You're sweet, caring, understanding. You're just good. Too good for those people. And I'm sorry about your grandmother. That must hurt. I hope she gets better soon."

It was strange, him being so nice. Strange, but I'd take it. I felt relieved, as if I could finally breathe again after being trapped underwater, and even if I wanted to change the subject—because the pain of knowing Grandma was sick was still so raw—I was grateful that the real Jack had finally returned.

"How'd you know I was sad?" I asked.

Edging in close to me, he shook his head. "Jen, I can read you like a book. Well, not quite. It was obvious you were upset, but I didn't know why. I thought it was because of me. Vain, right? I don't know why I'd think I mattered that much to you."

"You know how much you mean to me, Jack."

"You don't have to pretend, Jen. You don't have to try and make me feel better. It's just… I've thought a lot about you this year. Not always good things. I'm OK admitting that. I can remember imagining you at home, in your room with those cheesy decorations and all those records you never listen to, opening your scrapbook with all those memories good and bad inside. I imagined you putting something about me on the last page. And… I don't know." His voice cracked. "I don't want to be one of your mistakes, Jen. I know I've been acting, uh… I know I haven't been easy to deal with. When I'm with other people, I can deal with my issues, but with you, it's too much for me. The idea that a person I love would want to leave me, that was hard the first time around, but to have it happen again… I just don't know how I'm supposed to act."

Even though all I could see was the top of his eyelashes as he nestled under my arm, I knew he was watching me, and I knew I had to respond.

"You could try being yourself," I suggested. My tone was joking, but I was dead serious.

"I don't know if you're ready for that…" he replied, smiling at first, then pursing his lips. "Let's imagine something. Let's imagine this is the real me. What if it's true, and what if the rest of the time, I was just trying to deceive myself and everyone else? It's funny, it makes me feel bad, because I think about my brother, how I've talked down to him and criticized him his whole life. Now look at me, I'm basically just like him."

"Jack, you're nothing like him," I said, shaking my head. "Don't say that. You may have your ups and downs, but you're incredible, and you always have been. I'm not letting you off the hook for being mean to me, but I can't act like I've always been perfect either."

Jack hesitated. "You are, though."

"Trust me, I'm not. And I don't want you to judge me, so I'm not about to tell you to judge yourself."

For a long time, we didn't say anything. Jack looked devastated. Sad— no, more than sad. I'd seen him sad before, but this was something else. Lost. Vulnerable. Fragile.

"Jen, the nasty stuff I've said to you since you've been back… None of it was true, OK? I feel bad about it all, I've been awful, I know, it's just that I guess I wanted you to feel some of what I've felt since you left."

"Is that still true?"

"No," he fired back immediately. "All I want is to see you, every single day. Don't go again, Jen."

That shook me a bit. I knew he was being sincere, but he stank of alcohol, his pupils were dilated, and I couldn't be sure those feelings would still be there when he came out of whatever state he was in.

"I'll tell you what," I said. "If you say those same words again when you're sober, I won't go. But I think this is enough deep conversation for one night. We should get you into some pajamas."

He looked down at his clothing and chuckled. "You want to strip me naked so fast? Come on, Mushu, have a little decency."

Oh no. Not Mushu again.

"Yeah, on second thought, maybe it's best if you do it on your own," I told him.

"Sorry, cancel everything I just said."

I went into his dresser and took out a pair of cotton pants and a T-shirt, and he stood up and tried to put them on. He started stumbling around—I don't know if he was serious or just acting stupid—and said he needed me to lend him a hand so he wouldn't fall over.

"Liar," I chided him, but I went along with it. I successfully forced myself to look away as he was changing his pants. But when he took off his shirt, I couldn't hold back any longer. And what I saw made my jaw drop.

"What the…?" My voice must have risen ten decibels when I saw the inky black silhouette of a buck with immense horns taking up the entirety of his chest. "Since when do you have that?"

Jack blinked, almost as if he didn't know what I was talking about. Then, when it dawned on him, he said, "Oh, this? I lost a bet."

"Jack!"

"What? I was drunk in Paris and I had a couple hundred euros in my pocket. What do you want from me?"

I had to stop myself from reaching out and touching it. It was beautiful, I admit, but it was somehow disappointing. And yet, why did I care? It wasn't my problem. It was his money, his decision, and I guess there were worse things he could spend it on.

"Don't you like it?" he asked.

"It's nice, but, uh, it's a little big, no?"

"You can do like last time and get a smaller version on your shoulder or something," he responded, and I jabbed my finger into his shoulder and knocked him back on the couch. He put up no resistance, just stretching out and waiting for me to cover him with a blanket. When he was all tucked in and comfortable, he smiled like an angel.

"Try and get some rest," I told him. "And if you need anything, you know where I am."

I turned, but he grabbed my wrist. "You know, I'll bet I'd sleep a lot better if someone kept me a little company," he whimpered. "I'm vewy vewy afwaid of de dark."

"Don't worry, I'll send Sue right in."

"Nah, you'll do."

"Thanks for lowering your standards, idiot."

Jack laughed and pulled me closer, not insistent, but as though pleading. And I knew he wasn't joking when he said, "Sleep with me. Please."

"Are you sure?" I asked, looking over at the hallway.

"I'm sure."

"Shouldn't we go to your room?"

"We'll be fine here," he said.

I wasn't so sure about that, and much as I was tempted, I didn't need the whole apartment talking about us. And I definitely didn't want him to wake up sober, regret what he'd done, and kick me out. He was being sweet now, but he wasn't exactly in his right mind.

"What if you regret it tomorrow?" I asked.

He sighed. "Do you think I haven't been wanting to do this since I first saw you again?"

He scooted up to make room for me and see how I reacted. I took off my glasses and laid them on the table. "OK," I said. I lay down next to him and pressed my back into his chest. Almost as if he feared I might reconsider, he wrapped an arm around my waist and pulled me in tight. We pulled the blanket around us, and I lifted my head so he could give me a bit of pillow.

"No escaping for you now," he joked. I could feel his warm breath on my ear, and something stirred inside me. I wasn't used to having him so close.

"Oh, so this was a trap?"

"Damn straight. You can forget ever seeing the light of day again."

"Damn it," I said. "After how hard I worked on my tan…"

"If you're a sweetie, I'll let you peek out the window sometimes."

"Thank you, sire."

Our bodies shook as we laughed, and for the first time, it felt as if no time had passed and nothing between us had changed. I wished I could freeze time and stay with him forever there on the couch, just as we were. Jack squeezed me tight and rested his cheek against mine.

"Is this OK?" he asked.

"Yeah," I said after a second. "It's great."

"Good." His lips still close to me, he continued, "Good night, Jen."

"Good night, Jack."

And finally, I fell asleep.

8

THE FLYING KNIFE

Naya wasn't the type to beat around the bush: as soon as I told her what had happened that night, she wanted to get me out of the house to a safe spot where she could hear all the deets. As usual, she took a century getting ready, blissfully ignoring the awkward silence between Jack, Will, Sue, and me in the living room. I nearly fainted, I was so relieved when she finally emerged, dressed to the nines and with her face impeccably made-up.

"All right, see you guys!" she shouted, then addressed Jack directly: "Ross, I'm going to take her off your hands for a while."

I blushed in record time, but I couldn't see Jack's reaction because my dear, dear friend had already dragged me out into the hallway.

"I love starting chaos," she said as she pushed the button for the elevator.

"Naya!"

"I'm sorry, I couldn't resist." She reached in her purse for her sunglasses and put them on. "It's just so sad things aren't like they used to be. You guys were so cute together! I liked you being all lovey-dovey more than this push-pull thing you've got going on now."

"Trust me, I did too. But no matter what I try to do, we always end up arguing."

"Of course you do. He's always drunk! And being drunk puts Ross in a terrible mood. You need to ambush him one day when he's calm. Like today. Today's perfect! And I've got a plan!"

"Which is…?"

She smiled and said, "A good magician never reveals her tricks."

I was glad we finally had some time to hang out together, just me and her. We had very different ideas of fun—she wanted us to get our nails done together, and I wanted to go to the arcade at the mall—but our conversations took me back to when I was living at home and we used to call each other late at night. I went shopping with her—not bothering to get anything for myself—then we took a stroll in the park and got ice cream. On the way back, we stopped at a grocery store because, unsurprisingly, there was nothing to eat at the apartment.

At some point she stopped bugging me about Jack, and I liked that, but I knew she could only hold out so long before bringing him back up. She held out until we were in the elevator heading up to the apartment, but then she burst out, "Maybe we're overthinking things with Ross. We're treating him like a child who doesn't realize what he's doing is wrong, when he's actually an adult who's perfectly conscious of his acts. I can tell because, believe it or not, he's straightened up since you've been around. I think he remembers how much better he was when you were here."

"Great," I said. "What does that mean for me, though? That I should start acting like nothing ever changed?"

It was a rhetorical question, but Naya grabbed my shoulders and started shaking me with excitement, shouting, "You're a genius! That's it, Jenna! We need him to realize everything he's missing out on by acting like such an asshole. Especially after last night. You've found the answer: just pretend you never left!"

"I don't think that's going to fly, Naya. And speaking of last night, I doubt he even remembers it."

Jack had woken up early that morning and could barely say a word. All he managed to get out was that he felt terrible. He ran off to the bathroom and puked, then collapsed on the sofa, covering his face with his hands. My only real interaction with him had been banging on the bathroom door and asking him if he needed anything. He had grunted for me not to come in, and that was that. Even once he'd had his coffee, he still didn't seem quite human.

"Maybe you're right," Naya responded. "And if so, we'll just let things run their course, then. Now shall we?"

We'd stepped out of the elevator, and she was twirling her key ring around her finger waiting for me to answer. "Sure," I said. What else was I going to say? We walked inside the apartment. Things were just as we left them: Sue in her chair reading a book, Will and Jack on the sofa watching TV, and Mike in the kitchen opening his first beer of the day (I hoped).

"Sister-in-law!" he exclaimed. "I've got to tell you, your butt looks extraordinary in those jeans."

Jack scowled at him. This wasn't a good beginning.

"I won't take that as a compliment," I told Mike, and Naya added, "Yeah, it's disgusting. But then, it's normal for your compliments to be disgusting since you're disgusting, too."

Mike shrugged and went about his business while she jumped into Will's lap. He knew her like the back of his hand and had probably already guessed she had some scheme up her sleeve.

"What are you up to?" he asked suspiciously.

"Saying hi to my boyfriend! Is that some kind of crime?"

"You're not sneaky, Naya," Sue said. "We can tell you're planning something, and you should just spit it out instead of trying to fool everyone."

As Naya objected, I went to the kitchen to unpack the bags we had left on the counter. When Naya told Will it was a nice day out and the two of them should go for a walk, I realized she was scheming to leave Jack and me alone. I guess she'd forgotten about Mike and Sue. I doubted either of them had the intention of leaving. There was no way I'd get the opportunity to talk to him alone…

"Want some help?"

I was bent over stuffing a box of cereal into a cabinet. When I looked up, I saw Jack standing there with his hands in his pockets. He had been looking worse for wear, but that day was particularly bad: the bags under his eyes were deep, his hair looked like a bird's nest, his T-shirt was wrinkled, his skin pale. It pained me to see him like that. I even wondered if he was sick. There was something different in his attitude, too. He seemed… uncomfortable. Nervous, even. As I analyzed him, I nearly forgot he'd asked me a question. When I came back to myself, I cleared my throat, saying, "Yeah, uh, sure."

I stood and handed him a bag. "Could you put this stuff up top? I can't reach."

Jack nodded. I got back to work and could feel his eyes on me. It was weird having him in there. He rarely offered to help around the house. He had been a little lazy even when he and I were together. But I wasn't about to look a gift horse in the mouth. I passed him the cans and boxes and watched him put them away in silence. I assumed the rest of the day would continue like this, but then he surprised me, saying, "Hey. I still want you to stay, you know."

My brain didn't know how to process that information, and as I gawked, he went on: "You said you'd only pay attention to me if I was sober when I told you that. Well, I'm sober, and I haven't changed my mind. I want you to stay. I really do."

He was embarrassed to admit that, and he covered it up by feigning indifference, hurriedly putting the rest of the things away before running back over to the couch. Naya noticed, and since she hadn't managed to convince Will to leave, she changed tack, almost yelling, "Jenna was saying while we were out that she wanted to make everybody lunch today. Isn't that right, Jenna?"

When I replied with a meek *yeah*, she added that I'd need someone's help. It was obvious she meant Jack, but he didn't volunteer, and when she repeated her request, Mike was the only one willing to join.

"You?" I said.

"Helping?" Will asked.

"Without asking for something in exchange?" Sue added.

Mike crossed his arms and responded, "I'm sorry, would someone like to explain what the big surprise is?"

Everyone was staring at him like an idiot, and he was twisting in the wind. After a few awkward seconds, I told him, "Fine, come on in and help me if you feel like it."

"Brilliant!" he responded. I hadn't expected such enthusiasm. He came into the kitchen just as I realized I had no idea what we were going to cook. The one thing that occurred to me was a roast chicken with vegetables. I told Mike to wash his hands as I got the ingredients out of the fridge. He seemed incredibly chipper, much more than the prospect of an afternoon spent in front of the stove would justify.

Naya tried to get Will to go for a walk with her again, and Sue asked if she could join them. "As much as I love hanging out here when Mike's around, I think I could use a little fresh air."

Will laughed and told her, "Fine, the more the merrier. Let's go."

As they left, Mike turned, rubbed his hands together, and said, "I'm ready! What's my job?"

"You can, um…cut the potatoes, I said." He nodded and I told him in the meantime, I'd be preheating the oven and mixing the seasonings. Then I heard the words, "I want to do something," and turned to find Jack standing there. His eyes were narrow, and before I knew it, he'd snatched Mike's knife away and pushed him to the side.

"What the hell!" Mike said. "That was my job!"

"Now it's mine," Jack replied.

"Jenna, tell my brother to piss off," Mike protested.

"There's work for everyone," I shouted, grabbing Mike's arm and pulling him over. As he went on whining about how he wanted to slice the potatoes, I ordered him to help me rub down the chicken and stop acting like a baby. That only made Jack angrier, and after the third or fourth time he scowled, Mike turned to him and stuck out his tongue. Sue had been right to leave. They were acting like a couple of six-year-olds.

I gave up on trying to impose peace and let them do as they wished. Every time I needed something, they vied with each other to help, and whoever was left out threw a fit. When I asked someone to cut the last batch of vegetables, they both started shoving each other and knocked over a jar of sauce, breaking it. Then they froze and stood there staring at it like idiots.

"See what you did?" Jack shouted, throwing a rag in his face. "Now clean it up."

"You're the one who shoved me, asshole, you should clean it," Mike responded, hurling it back at him.

"I shoved you because you're always in the fucking way!"

They went back and forth like this, the rag flying back and forth, as they chased each other around the kitchen. They were out of control, and it shouldn't have surprised me that just as I was slicing into a carrot, one of them bumped me hard. *Ouch.*

The pain radiated through my hand, and I looked at my palm, which had a nasty cut running across it. The sight of blood made me weak in the knees, and I dropped the knife on the counter. Jack jerked Mike out of his way and asked, "Shit, Jen, are you OK?"

Since an image is worth a thousand words, I showed him the cut. After a panicky second, Jack dug through a drawer, finding a clean cloth to press into it.

His eyes were wide, and he kept saying, "It's fine, it's nothing, You're OK." I think those words were more for him than me.

"It's just a cut," I told him, but he wasn't paying attention.

"You're such a dumbass," he told Mike. "If you'd just stayed there zoning out to the TV like you always do, this would never have happened."

"I was here first, Ross. And who are you to talk to me about zoning out? You look like an actual freaking zombie today, you're the one who should have stayed in the living room."

They continued arguing, with Jack telling Mike he never knew when he wasn't wanted and Mike countering that everyone in the house liked him best. "Guys," I kept shouting, "Guys!" But it was as if I wasn't there. Finally, I exploded and said, "Can you stop acting like children? I don't know if you noticed, but I'm practically bleeding to death over here!"

The cloth was soaked and dripping. "It's really bad," Jack remarked. "Why won't it stop?"

Mike started to panic and shouted, "You don't think she'll bleed to death, do you? I can't handle having a person's death on my conscience."

"Jack, I won't die, will I?" I asked, suddenly afraid.

"No! Of course not! It's just a little cut," Jack replied. "And you, shut up," he went on, turning to his brother.

"But what if, like, the knife's infected? With salmonella or something?" Mike asked.

"I said, shut up," his brother repeated.

Now I was getting scared. What if Jack was playing calm for my sake but knew the situation was critical? That question started to torture me when he recommended we go to the hospital.

"I thought you said it was nothing," I told him.

"Don't argue," he replied, and warned Mike, "you stay here, moron."

Mike didn't listen—he never listened to anything—and so, despite Jack's best efforts, he wound up in the car with us. In different circumstances, I might have felt some kind of thrill that Jack was driving me somewhere, but I was too worried about whether I'd survive the night. Not just because of the cut, but because of the way the car was screeching through the streets. Jack, as always, was driving like a maniac. I looked down as he blew through a yellow light and realized the sleeve of my sweatshirt was soaked in blood. Some of it had even gotten onto my pants.

"Shit," I said.

"What?" Jack asked.

"Nothing, I've just ruined my outfit."

"There's no way you're actually worried about your clothes right now."

"I love this sweatshirt, Jack."

"Let's just focus on saving your hand for now, and we'll worry about your wardrobe later," he said.

You'd better focus, too, I thought. Jack glanced at his rearview mirror, crossed into the opposite lane, and passed two cars that were already going well over the speed limit. Then he repeated the feat, blowing through a red light this time, and yelled back at his brother, who had lowered the window and was flipping someone a bird, "Get your damn hand back inside the car!"

"They started it," Mike said.

We parked in front of the emergency room, and Jack guided me inside with a hand on the small of my back. Mike followed close behind. At the counter, Jack explained calmly what had happened, and the woman told us someone would be with us shortly. Then we sat down, with Mike in the middle, uncomfortable.

"So, like, if you die, what happens?" Mike asked. "Not that I'm planning on it, but I'm just wondering who gets to keep your things? And my brother's old room? Because if you're considering leaving it to someone in your will, I wouldn't mind getting first dibs."

"Sorry to disappoint you," I responded, "but dying isn't on my agenda this evening."

"Mike, I've got an idea," Jack said. "There's some vending machines down that hall. Why don't you go buy something you can stuff in your mouth."

"I'm not hungry," Mike told him.

"I didn't say you were, I said you need to block the hole all those stupid ideas are coming out of," Jack replied.

Mike informed his brother that he didn't have any money, and Jack rolled his eyes before handing him a five. Mike snatched it and skipped off happily. A moment later, he was back with two chocolate bars and a Coke. I thought he'd share—you usually got a cookie when you gave blood, and I had to assume my blood sugar was out of whack after losing what felt like two gallons of blood—but no, he dumped everything down his gullet as if neither his brother nor I existed.

The woman at the desk called Jack over again. I overheard her say we'd left a box on the form blank. It surprised me how perfectly he remembered all my information. And that reminded me of something: I had a birthday around the corner. Less than a week away. Jack checked the box, handed the form back to the woman, and nodded as she smiled at him.

"Does it hurt?" he asked when he sat back down.

"Not much. Maybe we didn't need to come all the way here."

"Maybe we did," he replied with a raised eyebrow. "It's pretty deep. I'm surprised to see you acting so chill."

I shrugged and said, "Sorry, Dad." Jack complained that having a bit of common sense didn't mean he was acting like my father. Mike nudged me and said, "Hey, do you think that chick's making eyes at me?"

He was referring to a cute girl who was typing away on her phone. She looked up every now and again and took a glance at one of my companions. Alas, it wasn't Mike, but his brother. *Grrr.*

Jack didn't notice. All his attention was turned to my hand. He seemed to be genuinely worried about it. As for Mike, I guess he was seeing what he wanted to see. And who was I to stop him?

"Yeah," I responded. "I'm pretty sure she's digging you. You should go for it."

Now that's what I call strategy.

"Don't touch my Coke," he said, "there's still a little bit left. I'm going in for the kill."

"Good luck, soldier," I egged him on.

He stood and walked over to the girl with a smile, then sat down, ready to work his, ahem, magic. To my surprise, she quickly turned her attention away from my boyfriend and toward him. Sorry, not my boyfriend—just Jack, I keep forgetting.

"He's got one thing going for him," Jack murmured in my ear. "He's always had a talent for getting people to do what he wants."

"Must run in the family," I said after a moment's hesitation.

Before he could respond, the nurse called me over the speaker. She sent me to a doctor's office down the hall, and twenty minutes later, my hand was wrapped in bandages like a boxing glove and I had a tube of ointment and a bottle of pills stapled into a paper bag. All that over a stupid cut. I wanted to complain, but what was the point? At least it was my left hand, so it wouldn't interrupt my schoolwork.

The doctor had made a nasty comment about how I should be more careful in the kitchen, like I was a dumb girl and had cut myself on purpose. He went on about nerve damage, and what if I'd severed a tendon, and so on, and when I couldn't hold it in any longer, I told him, "Look, doctor, I don't need any advice. Accidents happen. And I'd like to go home."

This only angered him, and he started talking about infections and tetanus and staph and how dangerous it can be if it gets into your bloodstream. He sounded a little bit psycho and wouldn't shut up about my antibiotics. When I decided to storm out, Jack stopped me and said, "Don't worry, doctor, she'll do as you say."

"Excuse me," I tried to respond, but he stopped me: "Jen, you'll do it and that's that."

Carefully, Jack went back over every one of the instructions I'd received as I took my seat in his car and stared at my bandaged hand. It would take two weeks before I could use it again. It was sealed with Steri-Strips, which would come off in ten days, but for caution's sake, the doctor wanted me to keep my hand wrapped longer. Two whole weeks! That felt like forever.

On the way home, Mike was in a bad mood because the girl he had flirted with had told him to leave her alone. When we parked, he stomped off to the elevator, crossed his arms, and rode it up before Jack even took off his seatbelt.

Jack helped me out of the car, and I told him, "I guess at least I'll have a cool scar to show my grandkids." I thought that would make him grin. But his expression was hostile, and I didn't know why. Did he need me to thank him? Was he mad that I wasn't taking things seriously? I didn't know, and that made the ride in the elevator uncomfortable. All I could think of to say was, "Thank you for taking me to the hospital. And for worrying about me. I'm really grateful, I swear."

Jack didn't look at me, and I decided not to press it. Whatever it was, he'd talk when he was ready. When we reached the apartment, he stopped and turned, leaning against the door. I tried to reach past him, and he grabbed my hand to stop me.

"I need to tell you something," he said, his voice quaking with anger. "What you said to me the other day, how I supposedly cope with things by bringing girls home… I don't know where you got that from, but that isn't me, OK? I'm not my brother. I'm not Mike. I would never try to hook up with some random chick just because I thought she might be looking at me."

"OK," I responded. "I mean, I said it in the heat of the moment, like…"

"I hope that isn't what you think I did all year, just fuck every person who came past. Please tell me you don't."

I didn't think that, but if I was being honest with myself, I didn't *not* think it, either. I remembered what Lana and Naya had told me about the person he used to be. That wasn't the real Jack, I believed in my heart. But what if I was wrong?

"I don't know," I answered. "To tell the truth, I've tried really hard not to think about what you were doing. It just hurt too bad."

Jack looked perplexed, and his eyes roved my face as if trying to find an answer to something. I think he was shocked that I could even imagine he'd ever hook up with someone.

"You honestly think after that our breakup I'd feel like hooking up with anyone?"

"I don't know, Jack…when we're mad, we do things we wouldn't normally do."

He shook his head. "All that time, I wanted exactly one thing: For you to walk through my door again. To just magically reappear."

That sincerity—without drugs or alcohol to give him courage—caught me totally off guard. His body didn't move, but in his heart, I felt he'd taken a big step toward me. And then he clarified, because I didn't say anything in response, "Let me give it to you straight: I didn't sleep with anyone since you left. And I didn't want to. Ever."

I could see in his eyes he wanted a response. And thankfully, I wasn't afraid to give it to him. "Me neither. No kisses, no sex, nothing. I just couldn't."

"Not even with Monty?"

I was shocked he'd even ask that, but then I remembered I had used Monty as an excuse when I'd decided to leave. It was the only thing I could come up with that I thought would keep Jack away. Looking back, I saw how stupid I'd been, and I wished I'd made up something better. Jack's nerves were showing, and I knew I needed to reassure him before he exploded.

"Never. Of course not," I said.

Jack paused, took a deep breath, and walked inside. I followed behind him. Naya, Sue, and Mike were standing at the bar while Will was portioning out our chicken with vegetables, which they'd somehow managed to cook. It didn't even look bad, especially given the disaster that had preceded it.

Sue smiled. "I guess it wasn't fatal?"

Mike must have told the story to everyone. I held up my bandaged hand and tried to flip a bird as Will explained that he'd taken the liberty of popping our meal into the oven. I told him I adored him, and he said, "For one day, at least, we won't have fast food. That's already an accomplishment, Jenna."

"It's good that you took the wheel," I replied. "If my two helpers had stuck around here any longer, it would have turned into a massacre."

Spencer and Shannon freaked out when I told them about my cut the next day. Spencer reminded me what a klutz I'd always been and warned me to stay away from sharp objects, and Shannon worried about whether the hospital near school was good enough. But when I told them how jealous Jack was and how he was acting like a little child, I got them to laugh it off—and it really was ridiculous. They both informed me of all the goings-on back at home, none of which were particularly interesting. I was weirded out when I looked at the cut and didn't want to put the ointment on it myself. I asked Naya to, but she nearly fainted when she saw the wound, so in the end, Sue came to the rescue.

"This is nothing," she said, smearing the ointment all over it. "It probably doesn't even hurt."

It did hurt, but I didn't want to let on, so I nodded and tried not to wince. A bit later, Naya said we should go to the movies. I was sure she was just trying to come up with something Jack would be into, and he was almost always up for the movies. But this time, he surprised us by saying no, that he wasn't in the mood.

Even Will found that strange. Jack turned away, seeming to look for an excuse but not finding one. "Whatever," he mumbled eventually, and came along unenthusiastically. Will drove, and Jack sat with me in the back, looking like he was falling asleep the whole time.

When we were halfway there, I told him, "If you're not feeling well, maybe you should go back home."

He shook his head without looking over.

It was a cold day, colder than usual, and I was wearing my coat and my favorite scarf. Will and Naya were bundled up, too, but Jack just wore a light jacket. He'd been doing that a lot lately. It was like he just didn't care about himself. His nose was red, and he rubbed it and closed his eyes. He was stressing me out so much, I decided to just look at the landscape through the window. Jack's phone rang. Not wanting to be nosy, I ignored it as he stared at the screen.

"Who is it?" Will asked.

Rubbing his nose again, Will said, "My manager."

"Shouldn't you respond?"

Instead of saying anything, Jack just closed his eyes. There was a quick exchange of glances in the car. No one knew what to do.

Will parked far from the entrance. As I was rewrapping my scarf, I saw Jack leaning on the hood to catch his balance. He knew I'd seen him, and he overdid his reaction, standing up very straight. Will had noticed the whole thing, too, and grimaced.

"Let's go see what's on," Naya said, to break through the tension.

Jack somehow made it all the way to the theater, but he was weirdly fidgety, sticking his hands in his pockets, taking them back out, and scratching his scalp. He refused to look at me, which bothered me, and it bothered me to see him like this. There was no denying it: something bad was going on. Jack looked like a shadow of his former self.

For the first time since I'd returned, I asked myself whether he'd always be like this: if every time we took a step in the right direction, he would immediately step back and stumble. Because if that was the case, I didn't know if I could take it, if I could just stand by and watch it happening. Maybe the Jack I thought I knew was a fantasy, and if he was, it would be better to leave. Because then, at least I'd have my memories.

As we looked at the titles of the films playing that day, a group of girls stared at us and whispered. Did I know them? I doubted it, but anyway, it wasn't just them. Other people were gawking and murmuring, too. I looked down—was there something wrong with my clothes? Was there something in my hair? My friends didn't seem to have realized anything was out of the ordinary. They just squinted at the posters and tried to decide what to watch.

"How about a romance flick?" Naya said with an innocent smile as Will hugged her from behind.

"Jesus, no," Jack grumbled.

They turned to me for help, but I didn't want to be a part of this debate. I didn't care. I was just worried about the people there staring at us. Then it hit me: it wasn't us; what they were obsessed with was Jack. It was the same story as with the girl at the hospital the day before. Jack had been on the news, in magazines, all over Instagram and Facebook. I had nearly forgotten he had a movie coming out, but it was supposed to be one of the biggest hits of the season. Of course, people recognized him. Especially here, at a movie theater. We had walked him straight into the eye of the storm.

Two girls came close, one holding up her phone. They didn't even bother to ask permission to record him, they just did it and giggled. Jack pretended it wasn't happening.

"Let's do the mystery," I blurted out, trying to put an end to the torture. "Jack and I will buy tickets while you guys get drinks. See you inside?"

Jack looked relieved as we walked in. But that didn't last long. No sooner than we'd sat down did people start peeking up from their seats, making remarks under their breath. Jack sank down and pretended not to notice, but he was clearly about to jump out of his skin. I couldn't blame him. Did these people not know how to behave? It was so rude! Two guys were talking so loud, I was pretty sure they wanted Jack to hear them and join in.

This wouldn't end well. That much I already knew.

The two guys were seated directly in front of us and turned around every thirty seconds. It was getting on my nerves, and I was supposed to be the one worrying about Jack. Jack stared straight at the screen, but his jaw and fists were starting to clench. When one of the guys pulled out his phone shamelessly, I decided I'd had enough, but before I could say anything, Jack stopped me, saying, "Jen, just let it go."

I tried to. I really tried. But even Naya and Will started to get on edge. We couldn't watch the movie without the guys in front of us pointing their phones at us like we were animals at the zoo. I couldn't take it anymore, and I asked Jack in a whisper, "You want to go outside?"

"What about the movie?" he asked with a curious look on his face.

"I hate it," I lied. In fact, I hadn't even been able to look at it.

I stood, told him to follow me, and was surprised when he actually did. Everybody in the theater turned to watch us go. Naya and Will stood, too, but I motioned for them to stay put. I didn't really know what I was going to do, I just needed to get Jack out of there. As we walked down the hall, we saw an emergency exit, and without thinking, I asked, "Do you think it will go off if we push the door open?"

Jack grinned and said, "There's only one way to know." I shouted that I wasn't ready to go to jail, but he'd already run past me. Fortunately, nothing happened. He held the door, and I walked out into a stairwell. It was dark and cold, but Jack seemed fine in his leather jacket as he pulled out a cigarette and lit it and we sat on a step.

"Does that happen to you a lot?" I asked.

He hesitated, blew out a breath, and nodded. "Almost always. Especially at the movies."

"Why'd you agree to come then?"

"To be with you."

I smiled at his honesty. He was probably high, but in that moment I decided I'd take it. I leaned my head on his shoulder and grabbed his fingers with my good hand.

"Well, that'll be the last time we come here for a while," I told him. "Unless you get super-rich and we can rent the whole place out for ourselves."

"I'm not quite there yet, I'm afraid."

"That's too bad. At least we can always watch movies at home."

We didn't say anything for a bit, until I glanced over and saw him grinning.

"What?" I asked.

"Nothing."

"If it was nothing, you wouldn't be smiling."

"Nothing. I was just thinking about watching a horror movie later, and I was remembering the last time we did it and you freaked out and you wouldn't even walk to the bathroom by yourself."

"That's not funny!" I said. "I still have nightmares about that damn nun."

"It makes sense. Killer nuns are the leading cause of death among young women."

"I'm about to be your leading cause of death if you keep on like this."

Jack chuckled, stubbed out his half-finished cigarette, and said, "Let's get out of here."

We had to wait a while by the concession stand, but nobody bothered us there. We each had a milkshake, and when Will and Naya walked out of the theater without seeing us, we let them pass by and stayed talking for a little longer. Things were going better now, but I didn't realize how much better until he wrapped an arm around me on the way to the car. There was a problem, though: the guys who had bothered him before were back at it, trying to snap my picture. Jack pulled me close so they couldn't see my face and told one of them, "Watch your step."

"Is that your girlfriend?" his friend asked.

I had to push his phone out of my face, and Jack got so angry that the veins started swelling in his neck. A few steps away, some girls were recording the guys who were recording us. This had all gone too far. I pushed Jack toward the car as the other guy kept pestering. "Come on, bro, is she?" he asked. I didn't know how long I could keep the scene under control. Thankfully, Will told the guys to scram, and he was intimidating enough when he wanted to be that they didn't feel like waiting to see if he was serious. By the time he returned, Jack and I were in the car. Will drove us home in silence.

We had dinner and tried to relax, and at some point everyone went to bed. Jack and I watched some TV, and when the memory of what had happened seemed to fade, I turned to him—he was sitting next to me on the couch—and asked if he wanted me to go sleep in the other room.

I couldn't finish the phrase before he'd lain down and pulled me close. I noticed, though, that he wanted me with my back to him again, almost as if it bothered him to look me in the eye. I didn't want to overthink it, though. It felt too good to have his arms wrapped around me. But I couldn't resist stroking his hands with my fingers. He sighed, and I felt his face against my neck, his breath on me as he said, "I'm sorry I was so drunk the other night. I went to a party, and I got a little out of control."

I hadn't expected that from him. Especially not then.

"It's OK," I said. "You didn't do anything wrong. I just got scared you'd forget."

"Forget what?"

"How we had dinner together. And how we slept here together, too."

I wondered if he would answer, and he did, but not how I expected. "You're the one who's forgetting, Jen. You're forgetting how I asked you to stay here."

"You're right," I said. "It didn't seem like such a big deal."

"Very funny," he said, tickling my belly. "And I asked you again, and I was completely sober."

"I know."

"So are you going to leave, then?"

"Do you want me to?" I asked.

"No."

"Cool. I'll stay, then. Just to get on your nerves."

I could almost feel him smiling behind me.

"Good, Jen. I'm glad."

9

THREE MONTHS

Everything went well over the following week—except for my hand, which was still in bandages—but there was one thing I couldn't stop thinking about. Or not a thing. A person. A name.

Vivian.

Will had asked about her one day, and Jack had gotten defensive, and Naya was clearly watching to see how I'd react.

To say I was curious was an understatement. I'd already tried to find something about her on the internet, but with no surname to go on, there wasn't much I could do. I didn't even know what she looked like. She was a needle in a haystack.

But one afternoon, when Lana was over helping Naya with a project for her French lit class, Will went up to the roof to smoke and I saw my chance. It wasn't like I was interrupting anything: their so-called studying was really just the two of them gossiping. It was obvious why they got along so well: neither of them could ever shut up. I had to disconnect now and then not to go crazy when I was around them.

I cleared my throat to get their attention and said, "Can I ask you guys something? But promise you won't tell anyone. It's important."

That seemed to intrigue them, and Naya said, "Well, now, this is getting fun. Sure, I promise!"

"Me, too!" Lana added.

Anxious, I tapped my fingers on my laptop and tried to form the question in my mind. But there was no veiled way to ask, so I just came out with it. "Who's Vivian?"

I knew they'd think I was jealous. I was even ready for them to make fun of me. What I wasn't ready for was the stupefied look on their faces. When Lana seemed incapable of believing I didn't know who she was, Naya said her name: "Vivian Strauss. You know. *The* Vivian Strauss."

"I get that you two are trying to make me understand something," I said, "but I have literally no idea what you're talking about."

They pushed me off the sofa onto the floor and grabbed my laptop, and I sat there with my legs crossed while their heads nearly bumped together as they searched the web and stared at the screen.

"Show her this one," Naya said.

"That one's horrible!" Lana responded.

"She's gorgeous in it!" Naya told her.

"Honestly, I don't care," I assured the two of them.

Lana flipped the laptop around to show me a girl with delicate traits and dark eyes. Her hair, dyed so blond it was almost white, was pulled up on the top of her head in a perfect arrangement. It had to be the work of a professional stylist. Her body was tanned a perfect bronze, and she was wearing a red sequin dress. Was she pretty? Maybe. But it was more than that. She was special, attractive, magnetic. Her back was turned to the camera, and she was looking over one shoulder with an almost bored expression that nonetheless intrigued me.

"What is she, like, a model?" I asked.

"Bingo," Naya said.

"Wait till you see Ross's movie," Lana said. "She's the lead actress."

Aha. Now I got it. Staring at that image, I wasn't sure how I felt. She was gorgeous, and I assumed she was talented. But were those the only reasons he'd picked her for his film?

"They get along well," Naya told me. "I think he met her at film school in France. She was studying to be an actress."

"And apparently she made it," Lana said.

"Ever since the poster for Ross's movie came out, the press has decided they're an item," Naya admitted. "The whole thing pisses Ross off, but Vivian hasn't denied it publicly, and that means everyone just keeps talking."

"Because if they talk about them, it means they'll talk about the movie," I deduced.

"Exactly," Lana confirmed. "It's free publicity."

"Anyway," Naya said, "let me know whatever you want to know about her and I'll ask. I'm going to meet her tonight at the premiere."

Tonight?! It seemed like just yesterday that I learned Jack had a movie.

"I wanted to go, too," Lana complained. "I was hoping to hook up with some famous dude. But Ross is a jerk and didn't bother to invite me."

"I thought you had a boyfriend," I reminded her.

"You said it. *Had*," she replied.

Naya told me Jack hadn't invited anyone but her, Will, Sue, and his family. The rest of the people there would be friends and family of the cast and crew, some VIPs, and the press. I have to admit, it stung a bit, getting left out like that.

After all, things had felt normal between us since that night at the movies. I looked after Jack, asked him every morning how he'd slept, ordered his favorite food when he was hungry, made sure Naya didn't torture him with her horrible taste in TV. It was silly stuff, but I felt like it meant something to him. He helped me with my schoolwork, made the bed when I didn't have time to, accompanied me to the laundromat, bought me groceries... And we were talking finally. Not screaming—talking.

These may have been small steps, but they meant the world to me. We might not ever be a couple again, but at least we could be friends. I had missed Jack's company, and I didn't really care how I had him back in my life, as long as I did. I missed him.

And I knew a day would come when we'd be calm and trust each other again, and I could finally confess to him what had actually happened a year before.

But still, I needed time. And he did, too, I'm sure. I guessed that was why he hadn't invited me to the premiere—because in my heart I knew I mattered more to him than the people who were going.

This internal monologue went on and on, and I heard the front door open. Jack cleared his throat. Naya and Lana were suddenly horrified, and I soon knew why. Vivian's face was still there on my laptop screen, for all the world to see.

Lana slammed my computer shut and threw it aside, causing me to panic. All my work was on there! If it hit the floor and broke, I'd be dead! I jumped and caught it, and just before Jack walked into the living room, I sat on it, hoping he wouldn't notice.

Naya tried to strike a natural pose as she said, "There he is! He never shows up before dinner time, even when it's his day to pick where to order from!"

Jack was wearing an old sweatshirt and spinning his key ring around his finger. He looked tired, as always, as he smiled at me wanly. Then he froze. I think he could see through our awkward attempts at being normal. Disturbed, he stepped back and asked, "Do you want to tell me why you're all staring at me?"

"No reason!" Naya shouted. "Absolutely no reason!"

Jack turned to me. I was an easy target, and he knew it, the bastard. Plus, I was a terrible liar and hadn't even had time to plan. I didn't know what my face looked like just then. As soon as I opened my mouth, I'd give myself away. I was dying of embarrassment. What kind of idiot would look at sensitive information like that right there in the living room? Couldn't I have just held off for a moment?

"May I ask…" he said, "why you're sitting on your laptop? You're not exactly plus-sized, Jen, I can see it perfectly."

"I was just…" *Come on, think, brain!* "I was taking notes."

"And we were helping her," Naya added, probably making things worse.

He was clearly unconvinced and decided to stand there in silence, waiting for a better explanation. It only got worse when Will came in, holding his cigarettes. He was about to clap Jack on the back when he noticed something wasn't right. His smile straightened out, and he asked, "What's up with the silence?"

"These three were up to something and they don't want to tell me what," Jack said.

"We weren't doing anything wrong!" Naya fired back.

"Then you shouldn't have any problem admitting what you were doing," Jack responded.

"We were just showing Jenna who…" Lana blurted out, then covered her mouth. Will and Jack both narrowed their eyes.

"Keep going…" Jack said.

Lana stammered and coughed, and I realized I needed an excuse, fast. I looked around, trying to come up with something plausible, something he wouldn't expect; something that wouldn't make him feel mad, insecure, or jealous. I came out with the only thing that occurred to me: "We were looking for Mike's band!"

Will looked skeptical. I tried to tell him I was just curious. Jack shook his head and said, "You didn't get any better at lying in the year you were away."

I stuck my tongue out, he grinned, and the tension lessened slightly. Thank God, a new interruption soon came through the door. Speak of the devil, it was Mike, who smirked, flopping down in an armchair and remarking, "Feels kind of tense in here. Naya, did you do something wrong?"

"Why me?" she asked, offended.

"Well, all three of you girls look guilty," he said, "and you're the one who usually starts things."

"OK, I admit it," I said. "It wasn't Naya, it was me. I was looking for Jack's movie."

That was true-ish, true enough to throw Jack for a loop, anyway. He blinked, and his expression changed, and I couldn't tell if it was curiosity, surprise, or terror he was trying to express. "Why?"

"Because your premiere's tonight, Jack," I told him.

When I saw his face, I wondered if I'd made a mistake. He ran his hands through his hair and opened his eyes wide. "Shit! I've got to put on my tux."

"Haha, someone's forgetful," Mike said. Lana threw a cushion at him.

"Why are you so worried about the tux?" I asked him.

"I hate that shit," he responded, "I hate fancy clothes, I hate tying a bow tie…all of it." There was some confusion when Mike thought he'd have to wear a bow tie too, but Jack made it clear that only the cast and crew had to go in formal wear. Seeing him so stressed, I reassured him: "You're going to look great. You should try it on and give us a sneak peek."

He hesitated, then ran off to his room, and Naya announced she was getting changed, too. That's when the chaos began.

Lana left, and I stayed sitting in the living room, since I was the only one who didn't have to dress up. When I got bored, I took a walk and called Spencer and Shannon. When I came back, it looked like a bomb had gone off. There were dozens of high heels thrown out in the hallway in a pile—Naya's rejects. She ran out a second later, barefoot, in a pretty pink dress. I smiled at her, and she sobbed: "I look terrible!"

Before I could say anything, she ran back inside, slammed the door, reopened it, and threw out a few more pairs of shoes.

Sue emerged and started playing with her phone. She was wearing a button-down shirt and black slacks, and honestly, she looked amazing. She had on lipstick, and had pulled her hair back, which was, to my knowledge, a first. Did Jack's big day mean that much to her? If so, it showed she was a good person deep down. Though, to be honest, I'd never doubted that.

Will soon joined us in a black suit, looking like a gentleman. I gave him a thumbs-up, and he blushed. Since Jack hadn't revealed himself, I walked down the hall to his room. Behind me, I could hear Sue cracking jokes about him having stage fright.

It was weird seeing Jack in our former room. Since I'd come back, he'd avoided it like the plague. His black jacket was on the bed; brows knitted, he was staring at himself in the mirror and trying to tie his bow tie. He was concentrating so hard, he didn't notice I was there until I walked up behind him.

"Don't laugh," he murmured.

I hadn't known I was doing so. I needled him a bit. "Looks like someone never learned to tie a bow tie. You want some help?"

"Can you?" he asked, trying even harder to do it on his own, and failing more spectacularly.

"For your information, I can. Here, step aside."

Jack straightened up, and I tried to undo the mess he'd made. I could feel his eyes on me as I worked, but I ignored them. I didn't want to get nervous. He was handsome, and he smelled amazing, and feeling him so close was electrifying. Finally, I untangled the ridiculous knot he'd made in the middle of the delicate silk, smoothed it out, and retied it, centering it under his Adam's apple.

"You look great," I told him, and he thanked me.

"And your bow tie is gorgeous," I joked.

"Don't torture me."

"Trust me," I said, "I'm just getting started."

He lifted his chin so I could adjust his shirt collar and said, "If I had it my way, I'd go in a sweatshirt. One with Mushu on it, maybe."

"Keep talking and I'll turn this thing into a noose," I warned him.

"Sorry, sorry. I'll shut up."

I was surprised at how good he looked when I was done. I hadn't tied one of those in a long time, but I hadn't lost the knack. I fixed the wings of his collar, smoothed down his lapel, and gave him a soft pat on the chest.

"All set. My perfect little gentleman. I guess it's close to time for you guys to go, right…?" I said.

He interrupted me. "Why don't you come along?"

Me? With him? Now?

"I can bring a date," he added. "I'm probably supposed to, actually. It just… I didn't think of it before, and then I was too nervous to ask."

Maybe he startled me too much, or maybe he sounded too wishy-washy. Either way, to my surprise, I found myself telling him no. It was his big day. He needed to focus on what mattered. I argued, "Jack, I don't have a dress, and I can't let the prestigious director standing in front of me show up at his premiere with someone looking like this. I'll watch the coverage on TV or YouTube. Or maybe I'll go on Twitch and see if someone's live streaming it from their phone. You know me, I like to live on the edge."

I smiled at him, but he didn't smile back, so I murmured, "Come on, we should go check on the others."

He nodded. I knew he wanted to say something, but he didn't manage to. He followed me into the living room. Everyone was ready to go except, arguably, Mike, who was wearing a wrinkled shirt unbuttoned halfway down his chest. He looked drunk. I mean, he didn't just look it. He sounded and smelled like it, too. He had a half-full bottle of champagne in his hand and shouted, "We've got a whole limousine to ourselves!" Trying to moonwalk, almost spilling his bottle, he continued, "This is the life I deserve to live!"

Behind him, we heard the door opening and a familiar voice saying a timid hello. Mike turned, and there was Chris. I don't think anyone was expecting him. His hair was gelled back so close to his skull it looked plastered down. He was proud of it, though, and no one dared to make fun of him.

No one but Sue, that is.

"Did I miss the memo about dressing up as Dracula—?" she started to say, and I butted in: "My lord, Chris. You look…spectacular!"

Jack was skeptical. Everyone else tried to go along with me and encourage him. Naya gave her brother a once-over, patted down the shoulders of his jacket, and buttoned a shirt button he'd missed. "Don't be nervous, pal."

"Why should he be nervous?" Will asked.

"Oh, he shouldn't be," Naya informed us. "It's just that Ross had an extra ticket, I gave it to Chris here, and apparently he's bringing a date along."

"Not a date, just a friend," Chris emphasized.

A friend I happened to know quite well. A friend named Curtis. A friend who made me crack up laughing when he strolled into the apartment looking like a stockbroker with his tailored gray suit and winning smile, ready to conquer the world. Naya smiled. Chris was shaking like a leaf. He ran to the door so quickly, he tripped over his feet and struck the wall. Will tried to catch him, but he was too late. Blood dripped down from his nose onto his chest, and Chris howled and covered his face with his hands.

"MY SHIRT!" he moaned.

Sue found the whole thing hilarious, while Curtis observed the scene with irony, wanting to help, but not really sure what he should do. "Excuse me, were you supposed to be my date?" he asked.

Chris nodded. "Yeah, just give me a second, I need to wash my face."

"Did you break it?" Curtis asked. Chris swore he hadn't. Naya seemed to think otherwise. Chris ran off to the bathroom, embarrassed, and soon returned, slight bruises already appearing under his eyes, with a ball of tissue stuffed up each nostril. Naya buttoned his jacket to cover up the bloodstains, and Curtis reassured him that if he started feeling off, they could stop along the way. Naya tried to follow them out the door, but Curtis turned back and shooed her off.

"I'm starting to wonder if this apartment is haunted," Mike said. "First Jenna's hand, now this. It's getting creepy."

"The weird thing is this time it wasn't your fault," Sue responded.

"Now is that any way to talk to your handsome date?" Mike asked, winking.

"We haven't even left yet, and I already regret saying I'd go," she told him.

He tried to cheer her up, telling her there was an open bar and they should celebrate. Just then, the door opened again, and Mary and Agnes entered in elegant gowns, talking softly to each other. I was excited to see them, but not for long, because a second later, Jack's father appeared behind them.

Uh-oh.

Both women were surprised I was there, but in the good way, I was pretty sure. Mr. Ross, on the other hand, didn't make a secret of how unhappy he was. Mary rushed over to me. "Jenna! I had no idea...but I'm so happy to see you!"

That was a surprise. I'd have assumed she still held my sudden disappearance against me. I mean, I had left her son hanging, and apparently the aftermath hadn't been good. But maybe Jack hadn't told her all the details of our separation, or maybe she wasn't aware of how he'd spiraled downhill?

"I'm happy to see you, too," I managed to get out as Mary swallowed me in a bear hug. Over her shoulder, I saw Agnes narrowing her eyes. She never missed anything, and I could tell she was taking stock of the situation.

"I hope you've shown back up to straighten out this clown," she said. "Since you left, nobody can get him to behave."

Jack shouted, "Grandma!"

"Whatever, boy," Agnes justified herself. "I'm too old not to tell the truth. Your mother didn't give you enough discipline, that's why you can't stay out of trouble."

Mr. Ross grabbed his wife's shoulder and pulled her aside. It was the first time I remembered seeing them touch. He was smiling politely, but his eyes looked dead as he said, "Nice to see you again, Jennifer. Will you be accompanying us to the premiere?"

Translation: how long will you be here leeching off my son?

I had thought about Mr. Ross a lot over the past year, and I was increasingly convinced that my separation from Jack was his fault. He was the one who had suggested I should go, acting all sympathetic and pretending it was the best for his son. Everyone had told me he didn't care about Jack, so why had I convinced myself otherwise? Or was I just looking to cast blame elsewhere because I didn't want to admit I'd hurt the man I loved? Maybe I was making too much out of it. Maybe Mr. Ross had tried to be sincere with me and really was looking out for his son's future. I doubted it, though. Jack had warned me about him from the very beginning. I hadn't listened too closely then. This time I would.

"No," I responded, a little surprised at how blunt I'd managed to be. "I'm living here, but I'm not going tonight."

It was almost funny how quickly his expression changed. Mary seemed happy about the news, Agnes just grinned, and Mr. Ross nearly turned to stone. "Since when?" he asked.

"What do you care?" Jack asked.

The atmosphere turned uncomfortable, as it always did when father and son locked horns, and Mary took her husband's arm to distract him, saying, "We should go. We don't want to be late."

Agnes must not have heard me, because she protested that we couldn't leave until I was dressed, and when I repeated that I wasn't going and she asked why, looking almost hurt, Naya informed her, "Ross didn't invite her."

His grandmother scolded him, and poor Jack found himself retreating. I was almost worried she'd thwack him over the head with her purse. I needed to step in before something terrible happened. I cried out loudly, "I've got a big exam tomorrow. I couldn't go if I wanted to. I'll be up cramming all night."

That lowered the temperature a bit. With just an hour to go, the last thing we needed was another spat. Jack told them to leave without him, that he needed to organize a few things and he'd see them there. I could tell that was a lie, and I think everyone else could, too, but we collectively agreed to let it slide. Even Mr. Ross grunted in agreement on his way out the door. Mike reached out and mussed my hair, then dragged Sue out behind him.

Once we were alone, I asked Jack, "Why'd you stick around?"

"I just wanted a few seconds of peace and quiet. And I wanted to let you know I'll be home early." He came close, grabbed my chin, and gave me a peck on the corner of the lips before departing.

There was supposed to be something about the premiere on the news at nine, and I went ahead and turned the TV to the right channel. For the moment, it was just ads and some dumb sitcom I didn't care about. Nervous, I started pacing the room and biting my nails, then I decided to distract myself by calling Spencer. That did the trick, but soon his droning on about the exciting life of a track-and-field coach started to bore me, so I let him go and went to the kitchen to make something to eat. Flopping down in front of the TV again, I noticed Jack's phone was on the counter. Maybe he'd left it on purpose? I wasn't sure, but I couldn't imagine it really mattered.

I tried to call Naya and Will just in case, but neither of them picked up. They probably had to turn their ringers off once they hit the red carpet. So I put my phone aside, stared at the TV in anticipation, then almost jumped out of my skin when someone called me. I looked at my screen, perplexed: it read Unknown Number.

"Hello?"

"Hi, is this Jennifer?"

"Yes?" I responded, thrown off.

"Cool! This is Joey, Ross's agent. You're at home, right? Well, apparently Ross left his phone there. He's panicking about it and things are crazy over here, so there's really no one I can send to pick it up. Is there any way you could take down an address and bring it over for us?"

I said sure and looked around for a pen and paper. Joey told me just to ask for him once I arrived. In my sweatshirt and tights, I headed off for the light rail, totally underdressed for the social event of the season.

The festivities were taking place at a grand old movie palace that was now surrounded by security guards, with a thick black curtain over the door to protect the guests from prying eyes. There were still some stragglers walking up the red carpet, and the press snapped photos frantically while a detachment of muscly men in dark shades with earpieces kept away the shrieking and applauding fans.

If I hadn't seen this with my own eyes, I'd never have thought a movie Jack directed could cause such commotion. And I couldn't help smiling. I was proud of him. As I approached one of the security guards, he thrust a fat hand in my face. He was obviously trained to know who was and wasn't supposed to be there.

"Authorized persons only," he warned me.

"I'm Jennifer. I'm supposed to talk to Joey."

The man looked at his partner, disconcerted. The other guy spoke something into a small microphone on his collar. A few seconds later, they called over a colleague, a gruff guy with a neck tattoo peeking out of his shirt, and told him, "Take her around back."

I guess they didn't want me to be seen with the famous guests, but that was fine. My goal was to get in and get out. Holding my purse tight, I tried to dodge the few people running around frantically. There were people carrying what looked like posters, others with audio and video equipment...it was chaos. "Go through that door," the guy said, and when I entered, I was almost knocked over by the flood of voices. It was the same energy as outside, but ten times worse, with people screaming into their cell phones, chasing each other around, an actress shouting to a makeup woman that her eyeliner wasn't dark enough, a dark-haired diva scowling... Finally, a guy caught sight of me and hurried over. He had to be Joey.

"Jennifer?" he asked.

"Yeah, here's the..."

Before I could get the words out, he shouted, "Thank you, you're my savior, I'll give it to him right now, gotta run!" And he vanished, screaming at a man pushing a trolley of speakers on his way out. I'd thought we'd exchange a few words, but I didn't mind that we hadn't. My mission accomplished, I was ready to get back home and stepped into the alley, where I found a young woman standing with her arms crossed, smoking a cigarette.

I didn't need to ask who she was. With her perfectly sculpted platinum blond hair, her shiny gold dress, her fit body, those piercing eyes and delicate features—she was exactly like in the photos. This was Vivian in the flesh.

She grinned as she noticed me and said, "You know, you might want to throw on a gown if you're thinking about staying."

I hadn't imagined our first meeting would be like this. Well, actually, I hadn't imagined there ever would be a first meeting. "I know, right?" I said sarcastically, wondering where the slight accent I heard in her voice was from. Germany, maybe?

She continued: "I don't know why we have to get so fancied up. No one here likes it. I'm sure they'd all rather be in sweatsuits."

I giggled nervously as she tapped the end of her cigarette with one of her long fingernails, which were coated in white polish. As the ash fell, she looked up, her stare magnetic. I could see why the press adored her. And she was probably even more impressive on camera.

"You should start the trend," I joked. "If you wore a sweatsuit here, I bet everyone would start copying you."

"Too much responsibility, having the masses look up to me like that," she said. "I wouldn't mind, though. This dress is squeezing my boobs terribly. And it looks like shit on me."

"I'd hardly say that."

"You're too sweet. But whatever. I hate it."

I tried and failed to imagine a single outfit that wouldn't look stunning on her, but it was impossible. She could have thrown on a potato sack and been a runner-up for Miss America.

"Are you sticking around?" she asked me. "I have a whole trunk of dresses with me, I'm sure there's something in there that would fit you."

It was a kind offer, and it surprised me. She was the second girl I'd met from Jack's life who wasn't a roommate, and I certainly liked her more than Lana. Granted, Lana and I got along now, more or less, but I could tell she still hated me deep down, and I was pretty sure I felt the same about her. Vivian was different, genuine. Or so I thought in that moment. I'd learn right away that it was all a facade.

"Thanks," I said, "but I've really got to be getting home. If I don't hurry up, I won't catch the ceremony on TV."

"Yeah, you should do that," she said. "Hopefully you'll enjoy it."

"I'm sure it will be great. Just seeing Jack get some recognition for all his hard work means a lot."

Perplexed for a few seconds, Vivian then inquired, "You call him Jack? You do know he hates that, right?"

"Yeah, maybe. I mean, I've done it so many times, I'm pretty sure he's used to it."

"You must be a friend of his. Naya, I'm guessing?"

"No, Naya's already inside. I'm Jennifer, nice to meet you."

I offered her my hand, but she didn't take it. As soon as she heard my name, her attitude changed. All the niceness was gone. Now her face was pure contempt.

"Jennifer," she repeated coldly. "I see…"

So she did know who I was. And she evidently didn't like me. "Ross told me about you," she added.

The old Jenny would have felt insecure, but the new one just lifted her chin and looked Vivian in the eye. If she wanted to turn a nice conversation into a face-off, well, two could play that game. "I guess he didn't have very nice things to say."

"What could he say about a girl who left him to go back to her abusive ex-boyfriend? That's hardly a way to treat someone, is it?"

I smirked at her defensively. A part of me wanted to throw caution to the wind, shove her, and dare her to keep mouthing off to me, but she was right. From her perspective—from Jack's, too, I guess—that was exactly what I'd done. And even if my motive had been different from what I'd pretended, even if my intentions had been good, the result was the same. I had broken Jack's heart.

"Yeah, I could have treated him better," I said, sticking my hands in my pockets. "But I'm back, and I'm trying to fix it."

"I doubt you can fix this. You ruined his life."

That put me on the defensive: "Listen here. Jack's a grown man. He doesn't need me or anyone else. I know I hurt him, but he's getting over it, and he's doing great things. You should know that, since you're the star of his film. Now whether or not he wants to forgive me is another question, but that's between him and me, and it doesn't concern you. It's been a real pleasure meeting you, Vivian, but I've got to be on my way."

She dropped her cigarette, crunched it out with the toe of her shoe, and went inside as I walked away.

When I got home, there were still fifteen minutes left before the broadcast, so I took a shower and put on my pajamas. I wasn't in the mood to cook, so I filled a big bowl with cereal and milk and got under a blanket on the couch. On the screen I saw the same red carpet, black curtain, and security guards that I'd seen in person just an hour before.

The poster for the film flashed on the screen. You could hardly focus on anything except for Vivian's eyes. In front of her was a guy, and she was resting her head on his shoulder. His hair was dark, his face visible in profile, and from what little I could see, I could tell he was a looker. Behind them was a setting sun. Simple but effective.

Good going, Jack. He knew how to pick a designer.

I remembered him telling me one time never to overcomplicate things, and he was right: the poster focused on what mattered, the main characters and the title, which appeared below them in curved letters: *Three Months*.

The camera cut to Vivian, who responded nicely to the interviewer's questions, the same way she had spoken to me before I revealed my name. She made a good impression on the screen: direct but polite, a straight shooter. If she thought something, she said it. And I had to admire that, especially because it was something I sometimes struggled with.

Three more interviews followed, including one with the guy on the poster, but I didn't pay much attention to him. I was more focused on my cereal until Jack's parents appeared on-screen. Mr. Ross said he was very proud, that his career as a pianist had taken too much time away from his children, but he was glad he could see them more often now. Mary, standing next to him, didn't get the chance to open her mouth, and I didn't catch a glimpse of Mike, Sue, Naya, or Will.

Jack looked uncomfortable during the interview with his manager. There were fans behind him begging him to turn around, but he ignored them, and I'm not even sure he really registered the reporter's presence. He answered the questions absent-mindedly, as though his mind were elsewhere. More people from the press soon crowded in, talking over each other so that it was impossible to hear clearly. The reporter asked if he was nervous about the film premiering in the city where he was born. He said no.

"How do you feel? Proud? Worried?"

"Indifferent," Jack responded.

What was going on with him? His attitude was worrying me, and I couldn't imagine what his agent was thinking as he kept glancing over nervously. The questions went on:

REPORTER: "How does your family feel about your success?"

JACK: "Ask them."

REPORTER: "Did you come here alone?"

JACK: "Yes."

REPORTER: "What about Vivian Strauss?"

JACK: "What about her?"

REPORTER: "You are in a relationship with her, aren't you?"

JACK: "No."

REPORTER: "Is there another special someone?"

Joey interrupted them. "Movie questions only, please. He's not here to discuss his personal life." Jack continued responding apathetically to the reporter's prying: No, the rumors of the film being based on a true story weren't real. It was fiction, imagination, not inspired by anything in particular. Eventually, Jack got pissed and told them to just watch the movie. Then all their questions would be answered. Joey could tell things were about to go south, and he smiled and dragged Jack off. Then the press attacked the producers and everyone else. None of what any of them had to say interested me, so I changed the channel to my favorite radical makeovers program and watched it till I dozed off.

I opened my eyes to find something else on and heard the door struck the wall. I put on my glasses, assuming the whole gang was back, but it was only Jack. He tossed his keys blithely on the counter. Was I seeing things? He looked like he'd just returned from smoking a cigarette on the roof.

"What are you doing here?" I asked.

"Nice to see you, too!"

He took off his jacket and tossed it onto a chair, struggled to get off his bow tie, finally gave up, and sat down next to me. I lent him a hand and then made space for him to lie down next to me. He looked tired. Noticing my empty bowl, he went to the kitchen and got some cereal for himself, then sat down and zoned out to the TV.

Perplexed, I asked, "Aren't you supposed to be at your premiere?"

"Yep."

"The movie's still showing, isn't it?"

"Yep."

"You don't care?" I asked.

"Nope."

I paused a moment, trying to analyze the situation, and when I couldn't, asked, "Do you want to tell me what happened?"

He swallowed an enormous spoonful of cereal and shrugged. "Is something wrong? You don't want me here?"

"Of course I do! That's not what I meant. It's just... You cut out on your own premiere!"

"No one's going to miss me. They're there to see the movie, not me. What's the point of me being there?"

That sounded absurd, but I couldn't think of a counterargument, so I said nothing as he wolfed down his cereal, took our two bowls to the kitchen, and walked back, unbuttoning his shirt and pulling his bow tie up over his head. I wanted to scold him when he wadded everything up and threw it into a chair, but it wasn't my place. Anyway, I had other things to worry about, like not staring at his bare torso as he walked back and forth. That required an Olympic level of effort.

Thankfully (or not), he threw on a T-shirt and changed into some sweatpants before grabbing his cigarettes and going outside to smoke. He was keeping quiet, and I decided to do the same in case he had something pressing on his mind. And he must have, because he couldn't stop fidgeting once he was back inside. Finally, he turned to face me and asked, "Can we sleep together again?"

"No," I said, eliciting a shocked reaction. I hurried to correct myself: "I mean, yeah! But this couch is killing my back. If we do it in a regular bed, that's a different story."

"Ah."

He looked down the hall to the room we used to share and considered my offer for a few seconds. Was it too soon? I didn't mean to pressure him. But then, he *was* the one who had asked. The tension was killing me. I thought he'd never respond, but finally he nodded.

"I'll need help moving my things."

"I'm on it!" I yelped, maybe a little too enthusiastically.

"Easy, now," he said jokingly. "What if I change my mind?"

"Too late, you're on the hook!"

I crouched and started opening the drawers of the sideboard in the living room where he'd been storing his things. I was shocked to find them almost empty. There were just a couple of sweatshirts and T-shirts and one pair of pants, plus some socks and underwear. I started making fun of him: "Jack, this is pathetic, you're famous now and you've barely got anything to wear. Look at this hoodie! It's been washed so many times, you can't even see the logo on it!"

"Sure you can. It's the *Kill Bill* poster. Look, it's perfectly clear!"

"It's full of holes, Jack. I don't even think the Goodwill would take it."

"I can't believe I'm hearing this from the girl who used to love to steal my sweatshirts!"

"Yeah, to sleep in, not to go to awards shows and banquets and things like that," I replied.

Frustrated, I pulled out all the drawers out and dumped them onto the floor. Everything he owned was balled up and in tatters. It reminded me of a crime scene. "Jack, none of this stuff is even folded," I told him.

"Why should I bother? It'll just get wrinkled when I wear it anyway!"

I rolled my eyes, grabbed everything I could, and walked off toward the bedroom. When I heard his footsteps behind me, I called back, "I *hope* you're not walking in here empty-handed, Jack Ross!"

He stopped and hurried back, fetching his T-shirts and underclothes, and together we sorted everything in front of his dresser. Inside of it was some more of his old clothing—whether it was fit to be worn was another question—like his Pumba sweatshirt and the one with the girl from *Pulp Fiction* on it. I turned toward the bed and started folding clothes, and when I looked back, I saw him stuffing them in the drawers by the handful.

"What are you doing?" I asked.

"You said I needed to put my stuff away!"

"Not like that, though! For heaven's sake. Now I know how my sister used to feel when I'd make a mess in our room. Just let me take care of it."

"If I didn't know better, I'd think you were Sue," Jack said. I pretended to throw a pair of underwear at his face, and he smiled and jumped back, leaning against the bed, where he alternated between watching me work and playing with his cell phone.

I felt satisfied when I was done, and told him so: "In the end, it wasn't as bad as I'd feared…"

"You're a neat freak."

"And you're a slob. You need some order in your life, not to mention some halfway decent clothes. This is embarrassing."

"It works for me."

"What are you going to do when you leave the apartment one day in these rags and they split open out on the street?"

"Why should I care? But whatever, Michelle, I'll go shopping if that's what you really want. While we're at it, we can do all the other fun things eighty-year-olds do. You know, mall-walking, coupon-cutting, all that fun stuff."

He tried to conceal his grin as I asked, "I'm sorry, what did you just say?"

"Nothing."

"I thought I heard something."

"You must be hallucinating."

"Don't act like you didn't do it," I told him. "I heard you call me Michelle."

"Oooh!" he shouted. "Now you've done it! You've said the forbidden word! We've got to punish you! And I think I know just the way to do it!"

He leaped up, grabbed me around the ribs, pulled me down, and started tickling me. *Run, run!* my brain told me, but it was too late. Jack grinned as I fought him off and struggled away on my hands and knees, then he grabbed my ankle and pulled me close to him. Laughing hysterically, I tried to stand up, but all I accomplished was knocking the sheets and blankets halfway off the bed. Jack turned me over and sat on my stomach, pinning me. I cackled and pushed him away with my one good hand.

"Stop!" I screamed, but amid all that laughter, it wasn't very convincing. "STOP!!!"

"Ask nicely and I'll think about it."

"JACK!"

"You didn't say the magic word…" he responded in a singsongy voice. He reached slightly under my shirt, and his warm hands made me shiver all over. I wasn't sure I could take any more, so I gave up and started begging: "OK, OK! Please! Please stop!"

He did as I asked, resting his hands on either side of my head with a smug expression on his face. I covered my heart with my hand, trying to calm down. I was almost hyperventilating.

"I hate you," I told him.

"Did I hear that correctly? Because if so, we might have to start again…"

"NO! It was a joke, I swear it was a joke!"

"See?" he said. "That wasn't so hard, was it?"

"I swear to you," I replied, "one day I'll find out where you're ticklish, and trust me, I'll get my revenge."

"Go for it. You have my permission to touch me wherever you like."

Irritated, I grabbed a pillow and slapped him in the face with it. It was a poor excuse for revenge, but it was at least something.

"Oh, so that's how it is? Now you're really asking for it," he told me.

"No! No more tickling! Anything but that!"

"Fine. We can try something else."

I felt him reach around my waist, and before I knew it, he'd stood and slung me over his shoulder. "Are you serious?" I asked.

Instead of answering, he took his phone out of his pocket and glanced at it briefly. When I tried to peek, he hid it.

"So we're keeping secrets from each other now?" I asked.

"Michelle, you know I'm a man of mystery."

"DON'T CALL ME—"

"Besides, you shouldn't be looking at my phone. Phones are off-limits. I hope you didn't turn nosy in the year you were away."

"For your information, I've always been nosy!" I informed him.

I could feel his shoulder bucking underneath me as he laughed. "Let's watch a movie," he said. "My pick. I'm going to die if I have to watch another garbage reality show."

"They're not garbage!"

"Like hell they're not."

"You're garbage!" I said just as he tossed me down on the couch. He rubbed his hands together as though he'd just finished a hard job, and I flipped him a bird. "You could have hurt my hand, you know I'm still wounded," I reminded him.

"Stop your bellyaching, Michelle."

"I told you, don't call me Michelle! I've been formally invited back into this house, and I deserve to be treated with respect. And if that doesn't happen, there will be consequences."

"Oh, I think I can take whatever you can dish out," he said. "And I can give it back, too. But then, you'd probably love that."

I tried not to let him see me blush. He pulled out his phone again. My curiosity was killing me, and I got on my knees and peeked at the screen. Jack tried to push me away, but I hopped up on his lap, straddling him. Before he could react, I snatched his phone and hid it behind my back.

"I won't give it back till you apologize," I said.

He looked down at his lap, where our hips met, and back up at me. "If you're going to stay sitting there, I'm not in any rush."

He tried to reach behind me and grab it, but I held it up over my head.

"Why should I apologize, anyway?" he asked.

"For calling me Michelle."

"Whatever. Give me my phone back. It's important!"

"I'm sure it can wait."

He lifted me up, took his phone back, and stared at the screen, almost obsessive. I tried to protest that he could at least pretend to pay attention to me, since I was right in front of him, but he shouted, "Silence!" and pressed his index finger into my lips. When I tried to peek, he opened his hand and covered my entire face, and as I struggled, he shouted, "Jeez, can you just wait patiently for one second?"

"Wait for what?"

"Hold it… Hold it… It's almost midnight…here goes… Happy birthday, Jen!"

What? He stuck his phone in my face. It was midnight on February sixteenth. "Don't tell me you forgot," Jack said.

"Of course I didn't forget!"

"You sure look like you did." he reached up and pinched my cheek way harder than he needed to, and I screeched. "I forgot, though, how old are you again? Was it twelve? No, it can't be twelve. Ten, right?"

"I'm twenty, jerk," I said, swatting him away.

"Wow. Twenty years old. It's just incredible how quickly they grow up. Did you behave this year? Should you get a present or just a lecture on now to behave now that you're all grown up?"

"You honestly can shut up now," I told him.

"Wow, no thank-you's for being the first one to wish you a happy birthday?"

"Wait…" I said. "Did you actually leave your premiere to wish me a happy birthday?"

He shrugged. "Maybe."

"Jack!" I said, tears coming to my eyes. "You shouldn't have. That's the sweetest thing anybody's ever done for me. But seriously, tonight is important. You're an artist. You should be there savoring your triumph."

He sighed and leaned back. "I have to be honest with you, Jen. I don't care. It's in the past now. And I'm trying to live for myself, not other people. What I wanted was to be the first to wish you a happy birthday, and I did it. Just let me enjoy that."

I rolled my eyes and wrapped my arms around his neck. When he kissed me, I wasn't able to duck him. It was awkward, and as his hands slid down to my waist, the only thing I could think of to say was, "Thanks."

"Whatever," he said. "I'll tell you one thing, when my birthday comes, if I you even think about forgetting it, I'm going to hold it over your head for the rest of your life."

My head resting on his shoulder, I told him, "I tried to wish you a happy birthday last year and you blew me off, jerk."

He had been rubbing my back rhythmically, but now he stopped. *Uh-oh*. Feeling the tension in his arms, I pulled away a bit and saw an exasperated expression on his face. I had surprised him, and I was afraid it wasn't a pleasant surprise. "What do you mean?" he said finally.

"Just what I said, I tried to call you. I mean, I did, and some girl picked up, and I told her to tell you so you'd call me back. But you never did, so I just figured…"

"Wait. What do you mean, a girl answered? What girl?"

"I don't know. She had an accent…"

"Vivian…" he realized. "She never told me."

Of course. How had I not realized earlier? I didn't know what to say, and I was scared, because he was furious. Whatever had been happening between us up to that moment had died. Jack cursed and pushed me off his lap, then stood and started pacing and running his hand through his hair.

"Jack, it's OK," I reassured him. "Let's talk about it…"

"No, Jen, it's not OK. She knew…she knew… Dammit! I was a wreck that day and she knew it! And still, she didn't say anything!"

I thought of suggesting she might have forgotten, just to talk him off the ledge, but if even I didn't believe that, how could I expect him to? It had clearly been intentional, and I needed to know what she'd done it for, so I asked, even as it made me nervous: "Why would she do that?"

"Because she doesn't think you're good enough for me. And she was there for a long time. She saw how messed up I was. I missed you. She knew I missed you. That's probably why she hid it from me. She didn't want me to ever have to go through that again."

I didn't know what to say. I could understand her reasoning. But I also hated her for it.

"The thing is, though," Jack went on, "whatever her motivations were, it's my phone! It's my life! If I want to talk to someone, it's my right! She doesn't get to just grab my phone and…"

"Jack!" I interrupted him. "Let it go. It's in the past. It doesn't matter anymore."

"It matters to me."

"Fine, but what is getting mad at her now going to do? It's not like she's here so you can tell her off. Save it for the next time you see each other, but for now, try to just appreciate your time with me."

That made him reflect, and he sat back down next to me. I scooted over and leaned into him. He'd gone from high to low and now just seemed confused and exhausted.

"What happened that day, Jack? Was it really that bad?"

"I don't know, Jen. It was so much all at once. Chaos, and then I found myself alone with her, and that's when it got really bad. I didn't want to talk, but she just kept pressing me, and she got me to let all this stuff out, about my past and whatever, and I couldn't shake the sadness. I got depressed. And that's when I wound up relapsing."

I already knew all this, but hearing it from his own lips shocked me. And the thought that I might have had something to do with it made it that much worse. The thought that maybe I could have done something if, instead of deciding to leave him on his own, I had kept calling and calling until I reached him. He might have relapsed no matter what, but shouldn't I have tried? I don't know. This, too, was the past, and there was nothing I could do about it anymore.

Ashamed, Jack confessed, "I didn't want to tell you. I didn't want you to look at me as someone with problems, someone who couldn't hold his life together."

"Jack, we all have bad times."

"I know, but…what if this is more than a bad time? What if this is who I am? Do you really want to be with someone like that?"

Was that what he was scared of? That if I knew the truth, I'd push him away? That was almost laughable, but this wasn't the moment to tell him that, so I just gave him a squeeze and repeated, "We all have bad times, and that's part of life. I'm not going to judge who you are because of one mistake."

"I haven't made just one mistake, Jen. I've made lots of them."

"Either way. It's not like I thought you were perfect." I smirked. "And I'm not either. I've made tons of mistakes. I made a mistake when I left you. But I know how to forgive. If I can forgive you for not liking barbecue pizza, I can forgive you for anything."

Since he didn't know whether to laugh or cry, I continued: "And as far as us being together, we can talk about that later, OK? Right now, there are more important things. Like you getting better."

"Getting better?"

"I know you don't want to hear this, Jack, but whatever you're taking, you need to quit."

"It's not that easy, Jen. I need it."

"You've spent more years of your life without drugs than with them. And that means that you can live without them. You just need help. And you've got it, right here. Everyone who lives here loves you, Jack. Your mother loves you. Your grandmother adores you. Even Mike cares about you. I know you guys don't always get along, but he'll always be there for you."

"Fine. But what does that mean in practical terms, Jen? What am I actually supposed to do?"

"You need professional help."

Bitterly, he replied, "Are you serious? You want to lock me up in some kind of jail for drug addicts?"

"Rehab isn't jail, Jack, these are specialized clinics that help people like you. You're an addict, Jack. You need to face up to that. You've got to get help."

"Yeah, you've said that about a thousand times."

He closed his eyes and shook his head. "Where's the money supposed to come from? My mom stuck me in one of those places one time, and they cost a fortune. I'm talking fifteen thousand a month, easy."

What the hell? I had no idea. Even if I asked my parents, my siblings, my grandmother, everyone I knew, there was no way I could scrape all that together. And I assumed Mr. Ross and Mary were done cleaning up their sons' messes.

"There's got to be somewhere cheaper," I objected. "Somewhere that's good but that's not trying to fleece you…"

"Jen, drop it. It's your birthday, you shouldn't be thinking about this stuff."

He wasn't reprimanding me. He said it sweetly, and for a moment we just looked at each other. I wondered if he'd say something else, or where things would lead next. But soon, Mike walked in. He'd lost his jacket and tie at some point in the night, along with several buttons from his shirt.

"The party sucked," he murmured. "What are you guys doing? Did I interrupt your long-awaited make-up kiss?"

"Very funny," Jack grumbled.

"I guess that's a no."

"It's Jen's birthday," Jack told him, giving him a stare that unambiguously said *beat it* but that Mike, for some reason, interpreted to mean, *Why don't you sit down and stay a while?*

"Hey, happy birthday, sister-in-law!" he told me, lurching forward and hugging me tight. He stank like a whiskey barrel. "You're twenty-one now, right? We should be celebrating! If you like, I can take you out partying and we can leave this boring loser behind."

"I'm twenty. I'm afraid I'm pretty boring, too," I told him, "so it's probably better if I just stick around."

"Whatever," Mike said, shaking his head. "I want to go to bed, and you're taking up my couch. Go find somewhere else to be cheesy."

Jack looked like he was contemplating punching him in the face, but instead he stood and walked out. I followed him. Behind us, I heard Mike chuckle: "See, you act all tough, but you always do what I say. Thanks for giving me my couch back, brother!"

As soon as he entered the bedroom, Jack jumped under the covers and started playing with a stuffed animal I knew very well. I thought he would tease me, but he just put Spot back on my side of the bed and patted it, inviting me in. I hesitated before lying beside him. He turned out the lights. I doubted I would sleep. After our conversation, I had more than enough material to spend the entire night thinking. I took off my glasses and set them on the nightstand and rolled onto my side, not wanting to bother him.

After a few seconds, he asked, "You really think I should go to a clinic?"

He was propped on one elbow, looking at me. His expression was vulnerable, and I thought my response must really matter to him.

"Yeah, I do."

"What if it doesn't help?"

"Then we'll find another solution. But at least you'll know you tried, and we'll be working on solving the problem instead of just waiting for it to go away."

I wrapped my arms around him and rested my chin on his shoulder, and he did the same. We didn't say another word for the rest of the night.

10

SURPRISE!

I woke in a good mood. Not just because it was my birthday, but also because I was well-rested. I could hear the water running in the bathroom—that had to be Jack in the shower—so I sat up and went to the kitchen to make everyone coffee. I decided to skip my run, even if it made me feel a little guilty. I hadn't exercised in forever. Spencer would kill me when he saw me next.

I was just taking my first sip when I heard the doorbell ring. I wondered if Mike had gone out to smoke again without his keys, since the couch was empty and everyone else must have been asleep. Despite everything, Mike made me laugh and was basically a good soul, so I was almost happy to see him when I opened the door. But any positive emotions I might have felt vanished when I found his father standing there.

Mr. Ross looked me up and down for what felt like an eternity. He was dressed impeccably, as usual. I was in a sweatshirt and boxers. It wasn't ideal, and still worse, I couldn't think of anything to say to him. Not that I had time to. He stormed past me, bumping my shoulder and nearly spilling my coffee.

"Good morning to you, too," I murmured.

He stopped in the living room and looked around. There couldn't have been a bigger contrast between the relaxed, informal look of the apartment and this stiff, bitter man grown old before his time. "Where's my son?" he asked.

"Which one?"

"You know which one, Jennifer."

"He's in the shower. If you want, I can go get him…"

"Leave him be. You're the one I want to talk to."

That was a bad sign, and I didn't like being bum-rushed like this, with no time to prepare. I pointed down the hallway and said, "Fine, let me go get dressed and—"

He cut me off. "No. Sit down."

Something about him—his forceful tone, the way he loomed over me, or the fact that he thought he could tell me what to do—gave me déjà vu, and I thought of Monty. He used to try to push me around like that, and the old Jenny had let him. The new one, though, wasn't about to, so I just stood there sipping my coffee as if he didn't exist.

He wanted to snap at me, I think, but he controlled himself, muttering, "I must admit, I was surprised when I learned you were back."

The sound of his voice was disagreeable, and I was torn between wanting to know what he was up to and wishing he would just leave.

"I didn't know I had to give you advanced notice," I replied.

"We had a deal, Jennifer."

"What deal?"

"You told me you loved my son. You remember that, right? You said you'd do anything for him, for his future. And yet here you are."

"I agreed to leave so Jack wouldn't sacrifice his opportunity in France, Mr. Ross. But he's back now."

"And I wish he weren't. He's not been right since he came home, and now you're living with him, and you have a terrible effect on him. You must know that. Unless you're blind or stupid."

He was losing patience, but I was, too. "I'm not blind or stupid, Mr. Ross, and I'm perfectly aware that Jack isn't well. But I've got to live somewhere while I finish my studies, they offered to let me stay here, and to be honest with you, I think your son needs me right now. God knows you haven't been here for him."

"Why can't you live in the dorms?"

"I can go wherever I want. I'm choosing to be here." I didn't know where this rebellious streak of mine was coming from, but it was working. I wasn't shaking, I wasn't standing down, I wasn't even ashamed or angry. I was just firm. I was finally standing up for myself, and it was satisfying.

"Of course," Mr. Ross said. "I mean after all, here you've got everything paid for. Who would turn that down?"

I was starting to understand what he was doing. Jack acted the same way when he was drunk or angry, picking fights that would lead to arguments he thought he could win. I was willing to let Jack slide because of his condition, and because I loved him, but his father was no one to me, so I went on sipping my coffee, watching him turn redder and redder.

"Are you trying to make things worse for him, Jennifer?"

"I honestly don't know what you're talking about."

"You know perfectly!" he exploded. "And what do you think? That you're going to come back into his life and solve his problems? That you understand him better than his own family? How long were you even together? A month? Two? I've had work trips that lasted longer than that, for God's sake. You're two children, you don't even know a damn thing about yourselves, let alone each other."

"I'm doing exactly one thing, Mr. Ross, and that's trying to take care of Jack. And that's what you should be doing, too, instead of trying to get rid of me. I mean, it's obvious to every single person who knows Jack that he needs serious help, and as far as I know, you haven't come around trying to offer it to him."

That seemed to hit him where it hurt, and for a moment, I thought he'd turn around and leave. But instead, he pursed his lips, reached into his jacket, and took out a checkbook and pen.

"How much?" he asked.

"How much what?"

"Come on, Jennifer, don't play dumb. How much to keep you away from him? Two thousand? Three thousand?"

I couldn't believe this was happening. Was he really insinuating that I could ever value money over a person I loved? Did he really think I could put a price tag on Jack, that I could just lay him on one side of a scale and a measly check on the other?

"Get out!" I growled.

"Fine…" he sighed. "Ten thousand."

"Are you out of your mind?" I asked.

"No. I'm worried about my son. I want the best for him, and you aren't the best. Now, twenty thousand is my final offer. If you're smart, you'll take it. Because trust me, if the carrot doesn't work, I can bring out the stick."

"I repeat: get out."

"Sorry to inform you of this, honey, but this is my son's apartment, not yours."

"Perfect. Then if you like, I'll go tell your son what you're up to in here."

That worked. Mr. Ross tore a check out of his checkbook and threw it at me in disgust. I bent over to pick it up, ready to ball it up and throw it in his face, but then I accidentally spilled a bit of coffee and stayed crouched, trying awkwardly to wipe it up with my wounded hand.

"If I find you here again, this will get ugly," Mr. Ross said on his way out.

I have to admit, that scared me. But it was also hard to take him too seriously. He wasn't Monty—I couldn't see him trying to hurt me—and bribery wasn't going to work.

When I'd finished cleaning up, I put my cup on the bar and looked at the check. Twenty thousand dollars. Wasn't that what Jack said a clinic would cost? Realizing this could be his salvation, I folded it up and put it in my pocket.

"HAPPY BIRTHDAY!!!"

I had just gotten back from class, and I found myself in the middle of a surprise party. Not that I was really surprised. Even before I left that morning, I'd seen Naya getting things ready.

She and Will were holding a giant card everyone had signed, Mike was double-fisting some beers, Lana and Curtis were blowing noisemakers, Chris was clapping, and Sue was in her armchair trying to pretend none of this was happening.

They'd gone all out: the coffee table was covered in my favorite foods, there were buckets of beer all around, chill music was playing, and balloons were floating up near the ceiling. I hugged Naya and Will, since it was obvious they were the ones who had done most of the work.

"Well, you've done the impossible," I said. "You've actually gotten me to agree to celebrate my birthday."

"That's the attitude!" Naya shouted.

But Jack was gone, and it took me an hour to start getting into the swing of things without him. I kept telling myself he'd be there soon. Supposedly he was at a party at Vivian's place. I got it: he must have wanted to talk to her about the phone call. I just hoped he'd still have some time left to come to my party afterward. Otherwise, it wouldn't feel very special.

I had fun, despite everything. I stuffed my face, then drank a beer with Curtis, who at some point forced me to dance with him. Chris stumbled over and tried to join us. He wasn't what you'd call suave, and when we cracked up at him, he crossed his arms and sat frustrated on the sofa. When Curtis winked and went over to console him, Mike tried to jump in his place.

"Aw, did he leave you all alone, sister-in-law?"

He was moving his hips suggestively. It was gross, but also hilarious, and I couldn't help but laugh. "You want to tell me what exactly you're supposed to be doing?" I asked.

"I'm seducing the birthday girl!"

"Failing to seduce the birthday girl, you mean," Sue said, taking a sip of her beer. "It looks like the mating ritual of a turkey."

"Whatever," Mike said, grabbing her hand. "It's time for the Drug Squad to bust a move!" Sue tried to get away, but Mike had her trapped, and once she was on her feet, we surrounded her. She pretended to be angry but gave it up after a moment and grinned, not exactly dancing, but bouncing slightly on her feet between us.

Naya got bored and tried to get us to play a game. First it was spin the bottle, but once she got Curtis and Chris to kiss, she didn't care about it anymore and changed to truth or dare. And since everyone kept picking truth (the best part was when Mike got offended after finding out Sue had been with more girls than he had), she finally just changed the game to dare and let her imagination run wild. She forced me to rewatch a clip from the movie about the psycho nun, Will had to do a sexy dance with Curtis, Chris had to do the same with Sue... The poor guy was lucky to make it through the experience alive.

It was fun, but something was still missing, and that something was Jack. I was thinking about my family, too. I knew some of them were mad at me, and I didn't expect them to call, but what about Shannon? What about my grandmother? Didn't anyone remember me? I mean, I forgot their birthdays all the time, but I was the youngest, I had a right...

Chris, who'd gotten a few drinks in him, was trying to dance with Sue again, and it was amusing enough that I knew no one would notice when I walked away and took out my phone, scrolling back and forth looking for Jack's number. I was too nervous to call, so I opted for a voice message, feeling a little pathetic: "Hey there…" I said, "I'm not trying to be needy on my birthday, but…you think there's any chance you could show up here before midnight? Pretty please? They threw a pretty cool party for me here at the apartment. I'm sure you'd have fun if you'd show up. I guess you'll see clips of it, I'm sure Sue's recording everything and putting it on her TikTok…"

I saw a call coming in, but my brain needed a few moments to grasp the significance of the letters on my screen. *Mom*. Now I was nervous. Was she just going to wish me a happy birthday like nothing had happened? Would she chew me out about something? I didn't know, and I didn't know which was worse, but I decided to stop thinking about it and just pick up.

"Hey, Mom."

"Hey," she murmured, sounding cautious.

I swallowed, trying to get rid of the knot in my throat.

"Sorry about the noise," I said. "My friends threw me a birthday party and it's starting to get a little rowdy. If I'd known you were going to call, I'd have gone up to the roof where I could hear you better. But if I start breaking up, tell me and I'll…"

"Jennifer!" she interrupted me. "Listen to me, OK? I'm sorry. You can't imagine how hard it is for me to tell you this, especially on a day like today, but…it's Grandma, honey. She died."

Those words seemed to float before me in the air as I stared at the wall in front of me. I'd have thought the joy would have drained out of me and sadness would have taken its place. But no, I didn't feel anything. I heard my heartbeat slowing down until my pulse seemed to fade away entirely.

"It was quick," she added. Her voice sounded as if it were coming from another galaxy. "It happened just a couple of hours ago. She said she wasn't feeling well, and Shannon and Spencer took her to the hospital. But there was nothing they could do. She didn't suffer. And she wasn't alone. They both were with her until the end. We'll buy you a ticket so you can come and say goodbye. Your dad can pick you up from the airport. We'll all be together, as a family. Does that sound good?"

Finally, after being frozen for several minutes, I managed to nod and say OK.

11

AN EMPTY HOME

Things at home were bad. Mom wouldn't stop crying. Dad tried to console her, but it was no use. The twins were fighting, Owen kept calling for his great-grandma, and my sister kept telling him she was gone, that now she was a star up in the sky. Spencer was trying to be the head of the family and bring some order to the house. And I was helping out as best I could.

In most families, people have set roles. The oldest child takes care of some things, the middle children have their duties, then there are other things left for the little ones. But when a tragedy strikes, all that goes by the wayside. I found myself running back and forth, doing everything in my power to make everyone feel better. And that meant that I never had time to cry or let someone else console me. Everyone was so upset, it hadn't even crossed my mind that I had that right.

That was how I started talking with my family again. Spencer, Dad, and I were the only ones who could hold them all together. The twins were too immature and self-centered, and it was all I could do to get them to make peace for a moment. Mom would gather her strength for a moment, come over and thank me for all I was doing, then break down again, and Dad would hurry over to dry her tears.

The funeral was more of the same: I cheered up this person, greeted that one, tried to keep everything running smoothly. We had a reception at home afterward, and Mom went up to her room because she couldn't deal with anything anymore. Shannon tried to get her kid to quit crying, the twins argued, Spencer sat in the corner ruminating. I hated to see him suffering, but there was nothing I could do.

People came over to clap me on the back and try to comfort me. Others talked about how wonderful Grandma was, how strong she'd been despite her age. I hated it. I hated it because I knew they didn't know her the way I did. Seeing her in the coffin, she hadn't looked strong at all. She was a tiny, ancient woman. I'd taken her hand in mine. It was fragile and cold. Mom had cried when she'd seen her. For me, the tears wouldn't flow. In some corner of my mind, I must have believed everything would turn back to normal all of a sudden, as if I'd awakened from a bad dream.

Unbelievably, Mom and Dad had invited Monty's parents. I refused to speak a word to them. But still. They came over and played sympathetic, just like all the other people who had called me a liar behind my back and complained that I'd gotten Monty in trouble and then run away when things turned ugly. Honestly, it didn't even get to me. Not that day. I just kept telling myself that no matter how I felt about them, these people had shown up for Grandma.

Dad came up to me at some point and said, "Jenny, why don't you get a little rest? Let me handle things for a while."

I nodded and thought about going upstairs but decided at the last minute that the back porch was a better place to be. It was February, and there was a thin carpet of snow glowing on the grass. I sat down on the bottom step. The cold afternoon air felt good. It cleared my head. I stayed out there a while just breathing and relaxing. But then I heard someone.

I thought it would be Mom, but it was my former best friend Nelle, the one who had stopped talking to me and then hooked up with Monty.

I had seen her once or twice because the gas station I used to work at was by her house, but we hadn't talked, and I preferred to keep it that way. Our friendship was over to me. There was nothing to go back to, and I just assumed she felt the same way.

Nelle was pretty. She always had been. Her hair was light brown, almost straw-colored, and she had big brown eyes and good taste in clothes. She stood out, and she liked to. That need for attention was one of her weaknesses. So I was surprised to see her in a black sweater and baggy black pants instead of some skimpy, low-cut dress.

I didn't say anything. I could guess who had told her she needed to dress discreetly. I could even hear Monty's voice in my head saying, *Nelle, you look like a damn whore.* I hated that word. He had used it with me, too. I wondered then what Nelle felt like when she heard it.

She must have read my mind, because she growled, "I'm dressed this way because I feel like it."

"I didn't say anything," I responded.

"You didn't need to."

I looked away. "Nelle, this isn't the day."

But she didn't care, and she didn't ask permission to come down and sit on the same step with me. I could feel her eyes on me, I could sense the tension in her, but she took a long time to talk. It was sad that after ten years of friendship, there was so much distance between us that even in a moment like that, we couldn't be kind to each other.

"I'm sorry about your grandmother," she finally said. "I mean... I know you loved her a lot. I won't pretend I understand what you're feeling, because I'd be lying. I've never lost someone who mattered to me like that. But, you know...if you need anything..."

They weren't the most touching words of consolation, and I had the feeling they weren't especially honest, either. I'm sure she felt bad or whatever, but the idea that I could turn to her in my moments of need was beyond laughable. Our friendship had never felt like it was entirely on solid ground. I'd always had the feeling one wrong step could shatter it.

But the tables had turned now, and she was the one who had screwed up. She was nobody to me anymore, not a friend, just another guest. Maybe she'd known my grandmother, but she wasn't mourning her, she had no idea how amazing Grandma had been. And somehow, I had the sense she was trying to make herself feel better, not me. Like she wanted to tell herself: *I did it, I said my condolences, I showed what a good person I am, now my job here is done.* That angered me, but I didn't bother telling her. I just pulled my knees under my chin and said, "Thanks," hoping she'd get the message.

Unfortunately, Nelle was too self-centered for that. "Are you mad at me?" she asked.

"Nelle, seriously…let's do this another time."

"When? Because you don't even live here anymore."

"You're right," I said, almost accusingly. "You could pick up the phone, though."

"I don't have your number."

"How is that possible?"

She didn't answer and turned away, almost blushing. Then I understood. "Let me guess. Monty made you erase all your old contacts."

"He didn't *make* me do anything, Jenna. I do what I want."

"Sure. Tell me something, then: last year, when I left, were you guys already together? Is that why you stopped answering my calls?"

"It's complicated."

I'd always suspected, of course. I'd been too blind to see what was obvious, or else I hadn't wanted to see it. Later, when she wasn't around to defend herself, I'd preferred to tell myself everything was Nelle's fault, because I wasn't ready to admit the reality that Monty was a bad person. Plus, he was scary, and she wasn't, and instead of confronting him, I took the coward's path, the easy path, believing him when he swore that it was Nelle who had seduced him because she was sly and underhanded and had never really been my friend.

That was easy to believe because Nelle had always been above me, she was never insecure, she was number one. Not that any of that was really true. Everyone feels insecure sometimes. Everyone has their weak side. The only difference is she hid it better than I did.

As I thought of all those things, it was hard to stay angry at her. I looked over, and what I felt wasn't anger, but pity. She reminded me of myself.

She didn't like me analyzing her, though, and defensively, she hissed, "What is it? You want to tell me to leave him?"

"That's not my place, Nelle. You're an adult. You have to make your own decisions."

"You're exactly right. And my decision is, I'm staying with Monty."

"If you think that's the best thing you can aspire to, then go for it."

I'd touched a nerve. "You wish you could aspire to something as good as Monty," she said. Before she could go on, I stood and went inside. That was the best thing for both of us. It wasn't long before I bumped into her parents. They looked older and much wearier than the last time I had talked to them. I had nothing against them. They were actually some of the only people we knew who had believed my accusations against Monty.

The reception dragged on, but I was done making nice with people. I sat on the couch next to Sonny and across from Steve, who was drinking a beer in the armchair and staring off into space. Sonny touched my knee softly and tried to smile, and I spent a while just staring at his scarred knuckles.

"I wish these people would fuck off so we could play some video games," Steve murmured.

"Is this really the time to be killing ogres?" I asked.

"What else am I going to do? It's a good stress reliever. I need it."

"He's telling the truth," Sonny interjected. "The thing is, though, everyone here's nosy as shit, if we turn the TV on, they'll be gossiping for weeks about how little respect we have for the dead."

I noticed someone new walking in and nearly cursed. I couldn't take playing the hostess any longer. But this wasn't some stranger who had known my grandmother or someone who remembered me from when I was a kid, someone who had popped in to be seen so everyone would say they had done their duty. No, it was someone I knew well, someone who'd had to catch an airplane to get there. I jumped up, and Jack looked over at me. He had deep bags under his eyes and messy hair, and his skin was much paler than usual. At any other moment, I would have been worried about him, but just then, I could only worry about myself. I ran over and hugged him.

"I can't believe you came," I said. I hoped it didn't sound like a reprimand, because I couldn't have been more grateful. I didn't see his expression, but I think he understood that.

"Yeah," he said, "I don't know. I just had this image in my head of you running around making everyone else feel better, and I told myself someone needed to make sure you were OK, too."

"What if I told you the only thing that would make me feel better was punching out every single person in this room?"

"I'd go outside and start the car first, so I could be your getaway driver once you'd done it."

Looking worried, he continued, "I'm sorry I wasn't there yesterday. I needed to clear the air with Vivian, so I went to her party. I didn't do anything wrong, though, I swear. I'm trying to be better. I listened to your message, too. I got in before midnight! But you had already left. They told me you packed your bags and caught a car like ten minutes after you got off the phone…"

"The important thing is we're here," Naya interrupted him, popping up behind him like a ghost. Will was with her. I don't know how I hadn't seen them. Jack was one thing. I wouldn't say I expected him to be there, but it was the kind of thing he'd do. He loved a grand gesture, but the other two…they had really gone the extra mile, and it was all I could do not to break down in tears.

Will noticed, and he pulled me in for a hug, and Naya joined in, too. I opened my eyes halfway through it and saw how many people were looking at us. I couldn't have cared less. But then my mother ran off into the kitchen. Jack noticed too, but he kept his thoughts to himself.

Will asked how I was. Finally, someone was asking *me* how *I* was for once. I admitted I didn't know. Everything had happened so fast. Naya nodded, a bit uncomfortable. Sorrow and mourning weren't really her thing. And she added, to lighten the mood, "We had to leave the apartment in Sue and Mike's hands, if you believe that."

"It's fine," Jack joked. "We don't need to worry about it because they'll have probably burned it to the ground before we get back."

"Two presumed terrorists are responsible for the explosion of a building…" Naya spoke in a newscaster's voice, and Jack laughed and said, "Exactly."

"I doubt it," Will said. "More likely, Mike will piss her off and she'll throw him out on the street. She's not the type to put up with anyone's bullshit."

That I had to agree with.

Thanks to them being there, things were more comfortable than before. Shannon and Spencer came over and talked. Even the twins tried to be sociable. Mom was a different story. She'd retreated to her room, and Dad made it clear that she was not to be bothered. Not that I was planning on it. I could imagine a fight happening, and today wasn't the day.

Once everyone had left, Jack, Will, and Naya helped clean up. My good mood didn't last long, because soon Dad came over and awkwardly said,

"Jenny." He cleared his throat and tried not to look at anyone else. "I'm not sure how to say this, but…it would be better if you didn't spend the night here."

Was he serious? Had Mom put him up to this? Could they not even bury the hatchet for one day?

Will and Naya stared at each other. Jack looked directly at my father with an expression that was hard to grasp.

"Are you kicking her out?" Shannon asked, indignant.

"I'm not kicking anyone out. I just think your mother needs some peace and quiet today."

"Did she say that?" Spencer asked.

Looking exhausted, Dad went on, "It's not about what she says. And it's not about you. If you want to stay here, Jenny, that's fine. But all these people…"

"I'm not kicking out my friends," I made clear. My tone was cutting. Dad sighed.

"It's just so we can have a little peace," he said.

I could have exploded, but I felt Jack grab my arm. His expression was surprisingly calm. "We're going back tonight anyway," he told me. "And you can join us if you want."

I can't even begin to describe how much those words relieved me.

We finished cleaning up, said goodbye to Shannon and Owen, and got in Spencer's car. He refused to let us get an Uber—he said a drive to the airport would help him clear his head. Jack sat up front with him, and the rest of us piled in the back. I was happy to leave, I admit it. I couldn't wait to get back, shower, and rest. I felt as if I hadn't slept in years. On the way, though, something occurred to me.

"Spencer, could you stop for a second?"

He knew why I was asking, and he had his doubts about it, I think. He gave me a long stare before parking in front of my grandmother's place.

Will remarked that he didn't want to be rude, but we were cutting things short for our flight. I assured him I wouldn't be long.

Going back in there was a shock. I hadn't ever been in there without her, and it was weird to find all the lights turned off. It felt so big, so empty. I crossed the vestibule into the living room, and for the first time I realized that there were dozens of photos of her sister and her grandkids, but not a single one of her. How could that have escaped my attention? In the kitchen, I found a bowl of dough in the fridge. Grandma had been getting ready to make a cake. I cleaned it out and washed it and left it in the sink.

Then I went upstairs to the bathroom, where I had left a hairbrush she'd lent me. It's not that I needed it, but it felt important to me. I walked downstairs and sat on the couch. At some point, I started crying. I guess I wasn't there that long, but it felt like ages that I clutched that hairbrush in the darkness. Finally, I walked out to the car, and no one said anything as we headed to the airport.

12

THE NIGHT OF TRUTH

Getting back to the apartment was like waking from a bad dream. I was so happy to put some distance between me and my parents again. I didn't cry when I talked about my grandmother, but there were days when it was hard for me to focus on anything. In class, I'd rest my chin in my hand and stare off into space, and even when a professor or a classmate tried to bring me back to reality, I still didn't really feel centered.

Curtis noticed, but he never mentioned it, and no one else did, either. I was grateful for that. I didn't want to talk about it, and I needed people to respect that. What Curtis did do was try to distract me by talking about other things.

I remember one day I asked if he'd called Chris again. We were sitting at a picnic table on one of the quads, and I was stirring a coffee I'd just bought. Curtis shrugged and sighed.

"I'll do it tomorrow."

"I swear, if you mistreat him, Naya's going to kill you," I warned him.

"We're not married, Jenna."

"Didn't you have fun on your guys' date?"

"It was fine. He's so awkward it's kind of sweet. But that's all I can say."

"He's a good guy," I said. "He's square, but you can't hold that against him. He was the first guy to be nice to me here, and he hasn't changed since."

Curtis nodded and tore off a strip of his cinnamon roll. "I know this is going to sound horrible, but I'm not sure *nice* does it for me. Or square, or whatever. Like I could probably use a nice guy in my life, but…"

"But let me guess: you want a bad boy?"

He smiled, and we went on talking about other things.

As for the rest, the days passed as they always did: Naya tried and failed disastrously to cook for us, Mike came and went, Sue grumbled, Will was his same kind, gentle self. Jack slept at home most nights, and we fell back into our routine from our first year together, or the part of it when we were still just friends. We left the room when either of us needed to change our clothes, we took turns making the bed, we asked each other how our day had been, we watched a movie on the laptop sometimes, had silly conversations… It was as if nothing had changed, as long as you ignored the bags under his eyes and how terribly thin he'd grown.

My hand was almost healed—in a few days I'd be able to remove the bandages—but I was still supposed to rub ointment on it, just in case, and Jack had taken over that responsibility. He was a little softer than he needed to be. I reminded him I wasn't made of porcelain, but still, every time he'd lean over me, biting his lower lip, he'd rub the cut in soft tiny circles and tell me he didn't want to hurt me.

For the most part, I liked how things had gone back to the way they'd once been. What I wasn't so happy about was Jack's constant arguments with his brother. Like the afternoon when I was going over my notes and they both sat down, one on either side of me. Jack was eating from a bowl of popcorn. Mike reached across me to grab a handful. Jack pushed him and Mike hit his head, and from the way he was rubbing it, you'd have thought he had a concussion.

"Careful, dude, that actually hurt," he shouted.

"You can take it," Jack replied.

"We'll see if you can take it when I do the same to you," Mike said.

"We'll see if you can find another place to live when I throw you out on your ass. Why are you here anyway? I thought with your band's overwhelming success, you'd be living in a penthouse in Beverly Hills by now."

I closed my eyes and tried to pretend I wasn't hearing their bickering. Mike accused Jack of not appreciating all he'd done for him; Jack called Mike a parasite and said his life would be easier without him. Then they stooped to kindergarten insults: *moron, idiot, loser, jerk.*

"You're both a couple of annoying babies!" I shouted, slamming shut the lid of my laptop. "You're acting like idiots, so stop arguing about which one of you is worse! It's both of you!"

They both looked at me with shock. If I wasn't furious, I would have laughed, because they could have been twins in that moment. Now, as if they were suddenly on the same team, they both accused me of taking it too far, with Jack reminding me I should show a little more respect to the guy who gave me a place to stay. I held my head in my hands.

"I can't believe that the one time you two agree on anything, it's to argue with me."

Mike laughed and gave me an unwanted squeeze and messed up my hair, and I screeched and stood. "I'm going to take a shower," I announced, "so I can get at least two minutes of peace and quiet."

"Getting all sexy for the big night?" Mike asked. "Oops, I wasn't supposed to say that."

I stopped in the hallway. "Sorry, what are you talking about?"

"Dinner at Mom and Dad's house tonight. You're invited," Mike said.

"Just skip it," Jack said. "It's dumb, there's no reason for you to go."

"What is?" I asked.

"My mom wanted to celebrate your birthday. I told her about your grandmother and she canceled for a little while, but then she got the idea back in her head."

"If I know Mom," Mike added, "she's got an entire banquet set up."

To say I wasn't in the mood would be an understatement, but just the thought of getting on Mr. Ross's nerves was almost enough to make me want to go. Since the funeral, something had changed in me. I wasn't as timid as I used to be. I honestly felt ready for a fight.

"I'm in," I said.

Jack didn't seem excited about it, but I could tell he didn't want to contradict me. "If that's what you want…"

"What about what I want?" Mike asked.

"Let me see if I care…" I mused. "Yeah—I don't."

Mike brought a hand to his heart as if he'd been shot, played dead for a few seconds, then sat up. "We've got time, though. What should we do till then?"

"I vote we take your brother shopping. I'm sorry, Jack, but it's time. If I agree to go with you to your parents', I'm not going with you looking like an absolute bum." Jack whined and protested, but I forced him to agree, and as soon as I showered, we drove to the mall.

Jack's attitude couldn't have been worse. He spent the entire time trying to make clear to me how much he hated the experience. He moaned, groaned, asked if it would take much longer, checked the time on his phone, took everything I picked out for him and hung it back on the rack… Mike, on the other hand, was acting like a model, taking turns in the mirrors with the most ridiculous garments. He never found anything he liked, but at least his ridiculous expressions lightened the mood.

I tried to offer Jack a blue cashmere sweater, then, when he turned it down, a sweatshirt with the Minions on it. I knew that would irritate him, and I was right. He admitted that he wasn't going to like anything, but I put my foot down: I wasn't leaving until he picked something. "Fine," he said, and grabbed a *Back to the Future* sweatshirt that looked like something a child would wear. It was horrifying, but Jack grinned and said he loved it. Mike distracted me, running over with a dozen garments under his arm that he said Jack was going to buy him now that he was rich. Jack shouted, "I'm not fucking rich!" and Mike recoiled—maybe that was some kind of sore spot for him.

Eventually, we made our way home. Mike had five bags of clothes—who knows where he got the money—and Jack had one, which I decided was a victory. Since everyone was home and sitting in the living room, Mike decided to show off for them while Jack and I went to the bedroom. He took out his sweatshirt, threw it on, and said, "Try not to salivate." Then he tossed his bag into the corner.

Sitting on the bed, I told him, "Yes, your taste is excellent, as always."

"Why didn't you buy anything?"

"I don't want to spend the cash, and I've got plenty to wear. And when I run short, I can always raid my sister's closet."

Saying that reminded me it was time for me to get dressed, too. So I told Jack to get away from the mirror and started trying on skirts, pants, sweaters. Nothing seemed to work that day. Everything was either too stuffy or too informal. I couldn't find anything that hit that sweet spot in the middle. As I was taking off my fourth sweater, Jack asked, "How many times have you changed in five minutes?"

"I can't help it! I hate everything!"

"Maybe you hate sweaters? Because that's the only thing you've tried on, and I can barely tell the difference between them. Anyway, I think you look great. I get that you're nervous, but you can't let that eat at you. Just throw something on, it'll be fine. Or, I've got an idea, let me pick."

Breathing a sigh of frustration, I replied, "That could maybe work." Jack dug through my things as I stood beside him with my arms crossed. There was only so much he could do. In the end, he was just digging back out the same things I had already tried on. He held up a brown sweater and grunted, "No, this one's horrible," then a yellow one, which he dismissed: "Sorry, you'll look like a bumblebee in this one."

Finally, he found another garment I'd stolen from Shannon and said, "This is the one. You had it on when you went to Mike's concert a long time ago. I like it, red looks good on you."

"Fine," I said. "The funny thing is it's not even mine. I actually gave this sweater to Shannon for her birthday one year, but then—"

"Shit!" Jack shouted, interrupting me.

"What is it?" Had I missed something? He opened a drawer in his dresser while I stared at him, wondering what he was up to, threw a few T-shirts onto the floor, and finally found what he was looking for: a big purple box.

"Thank God I remembered," he said, holding it up and saying with a smile, "It's your birthday present!"

I don't know what expression I had on my face, but he certainly found it funny. He continued, "I guess I was waiting for some excitement, a thank-you, or something."

"No!" I rushed to correct him. "It's not that! I just… I had no idea you'd gotten me a present. When? I guess I'd just assumed after all that time had passed and all that you were too busy, or maybe didn't feel like it."

"It's not that, Jen. I just…listen, I know I haven't been my best self. But I didn't forget, and I want you to know I never would. You mean too much to me for that." He tossed it to me, and I barely managed to catch it. Let's be honest: I'm not the most coordinated person. But it wasn't my fault—it weighed a ton! I have to give Jack one thing, though—the fear that I'd drop it startled me so much I stopped worrying about my damn outfit!

"Be careful with my present!" I said.

I sat down and opened it carefully. I was so moved by it, I didn't even want to tear the wrapping paper or the bow. Jack hopped down beside me and watched me impatiently.

"Can you get on with it?" he asked.

"Be patient, Jackie."

I finished, and I felt my heart stop. It was a dark wood box with the name *Rembrandt* carved on the top. I didn't say anything, and Jack got worried and started asking if I disliked it. If I did, I could take it back, he told me, but it wasn't that—I was moved, maybe more than I ever had been by a gift. I removed the sticker over the hinge and opened it. It had a silver palette inside, oil paints, brushes, charcoal, varnish…every single thing you could imagine or ever need. My fingers trembled as they touched the tips of the brushes. I could almost sense the tension coming off his body.

"Don't you like it? I got it because I hoped you'd start painting again. Honestly, I don't know the first thing about art, but I asked my mom what to get, and this is what she recommended. I guess it's her favorite brand… So are you going to say anything? I'm dying over here…"

"Jack, I just don't know what to say," I replied. And that was true. My mind was a blank. It had been years since I'd taken any art classes; at most I'd just doodled in my notebooks, and I hadn't touched a paintbrush since I was with Jack's mom at their lake house. The fact that he'd remembered that and had gone to the trouble to find something so perfect gave me a ticklish feeling in my stomach.

"You could say thanks," he suggested. "That would probably work for me."

"Thanks," I said. "Thanks a lot. I think this is the first time I've gotten a present and thought, *this person really knows me.* Sorry for making you nervous, I was just stunned for a second. It's wonderful!"

I threw my arms around him and, caught up in the moment, I kissed him. Jack didn't pull away. Still more, he stopped that awkward patting on the back that I think was meant to remind me we were just friends and reached down to squeeze my hip. I thought he would get on top of me, but then he pulled away and shook his head.

"No," he said. "If we start like this, I'm not going to go to that stupid dinner."

"Fiiiiine," I said, and set the box down beside the bed. I dressed and looked at myself in the mirror to touch up my makeup. Jack sat there staring at me in silence with a confused look on his face. He picked up the box and started interrogating me: what was all that stuff in there, what was the point of the different brushes, why would you use a stick of charcoal instead of a regular pencil. I thought he'd have known all that, having an artist for a mother, but his family life wasn't easy, and maybe they'd never been able to have those kinds of conversations. I tried to explain things patiently, but then I decided he was just acting stupid to get on my nerves, so I took the box from him, set it on the dresser, and said, "Thanks again, but we'll have to finish our art lessons later. For now, we've got to go."

I heard a voice in my head interrogating me insistently.

Why aren't you nervous?

I am!

Not nervous enough. You're walking straight into the lion's den!

I know how to take care of myself.

Sure you do. Wait till Mr. Ross ambushes you again...

"What are you thinking about?" Jack asked. I was glad he couldn't actually read my mind. Otherwise, I'd have a lot of explaining to do.

"I'm just thinking about how handsome you look in that sweatshirt," I responded. "You should be grateful to me for forcing you to go shopping." He grunted and looked at the road ahead of him. I was freaking out about seeing his dad—my eagerness for an argument was gone, and I was worried about making a scene—but I couldn't admit that without getting into the whole episode with him and the check, which I still hadn't told Jack about. Mary and Agnes would be there, too, and I didn't want things to be uncomfortable for them. And what if Jack's father brought it up—would I just admit in front of the whole family that it had been his mistake, and that I was keeping the money to send his son to rehab? On a day when everything had supposedly been planned in my honor?

In the back seat, Mike didn't say anything. That was weird for him. Maybe he sensed something bad was going to happen. Not that he needed psychic abilities to do so: that was par for the course when he saw his parents.

My premonition that things might turn ugly only got worse as I saw that huge white house with the black shutters again. In the garage was a Mercedes that I knew wasn't Mary's. After parking, Jack walked around, opened my door, and offered me his hand. I was surprised that he wasn't more stressed.

The house was just as I remembered it, but that didn't make it feel any less weird. We walked down the impersonal but very clean white hallway to the living room, where Mary was waiting for us in black jeans, a pink shirt, and oven mitts with a colorful pattern of cakes embroidered on them.

"Hey, guys!" she said and hurried over. The boys acted embarrassed when she kissed them on the cheek. I didn't mind one bit.

"How are you, Jenna?" she asked. "I'm so glad you were able to make it."

"I'm great," I told her. "Thanks for inviting me."

"Mike," she said, "may I ask what in the name of God you've done to your face?"

Mike had gotten creative with his morning shave and had decided to leave his mustache. He looked like a teenager who was trying to buy cigarettes. Sue had cracked up when she saw him. Now he crossed his arms, defiant. "Mustaches are coming back, Mom. You heard it here, first."

"Oh, honey," she replied. "You really should see a psychologist."

While the brothers sat on the sofa, I followed Mary into the kitchen, where she proudly showed off all she had prepared, noting humbly that she wasn't a very talented chef. There was a salad, a roasted sea bass, mashed potatoes, chocolate cake…it was too much for such a small group, but that wasn't my concern. It looked amazing, and she handed me a spoon to try the sauce for the fish, which I had to admit was incredible.

"I got the recipe from a cookbook someone gave me a few years ago. Trust me, none of this was easy, but I'm happy with how it all turned out. When I'm tired of the art world, I've got my next job all lined up."

"You could do both," I suggested, before changing the subject. "By the way, thanks for helping Jack out with my gift. You shouldn't have."

"Oh, did you like it? I'm so glad, the poor thing was an absolute bundle of nerves, he kept asking me over and over, *Are you sure, Mom? Isn't this other one better?* To tell the truth, it's nice to see him worrying about another person, that hasn't always been his strong point. I meant to tell you, too," she continued, her expression suddenly changing, "the boys told me about what happened on your birthday. You don't know how sorry I am. I know what it means to lose someone who matters to you on what's supposed to be a special occasion. My own mother died on Mother's Day, and it was a terrible blow. I was even younger than you were. And I lost my father not long afterward. I think he just couldn't bear the thought of living without her."

She was distracted as she said this, almost as if she were revisiting that moment in her mind as she stared into the oven and toyed with one of her bracelets.

"It wasn't long after that when I met Jack's father," she added softly. "I wonder sometimes how different things would be if I hadn't felt so alone in that moment."

Before I could stop myself, I asked, "Why? Do you think you might not have married him?"

That had to be one of the top ten least appropriate things I'd ever said, but Mary took it in stride, responding in a melancholy tone, "I don't know. He gave me the attention I needed at a very vulnerable moment, and I let that sensation carry me away. Would I have married him in other circumstances? Maybe, maybe not. But I have to remind myself that without him, I wouldn't have had my two kids, and they're what I love most in the world. When I consider that, I have to say, it wasn't such a bad decision after all."

The conversation turned back to my grandmother, and I nearly cried as I told her the story. I was thankful that she hadn't suffered, but I still missed her every day. As I spoke, I noticed Mary seemed impatient, and I wondered if I was boring her. Finally, I told her I was going to stick my head into the living room to see Agnes and the boys. Strangely, she seemed relieved to hear that.

Mike and Agnes were playing a shooter game, and for who knows what reason, his character was riding around in a pink tank wearing golden armor. The screen was split, and poor Agnes was just wandering around a bombed-out city with a slingshot in her hand.

"I want a gun, too!" she shouted, pressing all the buttons hysterically at once. "I can't do a damned thing like this!"

She hurled a stone at an old man passing by, and he responded by smacking her in the head with his cane. Her screen went black, and Mike cracked up laughing.

"Here, Grandma," Jack said, pushing a button on her controller. "You can change your weapons like this." Jack chose a machine gun for her just when Mike's tank rolled across her screen.

"TAKE THAT!!!" she shouted as Mike called out *Noooo* and she fired on him with Jack's help. The tables had turned, and for the next few games, Agnes kept changing to more and more destructive weapons as Mike tried to flee certain death. Mike was glowing with anger, but he was incapable of defending himself. I couldn't care less about video games, but even I found it too funny to look away. She only let him off the hook when a boss appeared on the screen and she decided to sabotage Mike, making excuses for why she couldn't use this or that weapon or how she didn't want to hurt their poor enemies. The whole scenario was so absurd that none of us could stop laughing, and I wished it would keep going for the rest of the evening. But then we heard steps. Jack was the first one to notice, though he didn't bother looking up.

Mr. Ross was wearing elegant slacks and a Ralph Lauren golf shirt, the one with the big pony on the breast so everyone knows how expensive it was. Looking through his square lenses, he took stock of the situation, then said with a frown, "Stop wasting time and go help your mother set the table."

"Stop being so stiff, son, we're all having fun," Agnes replied.

"I wasn't talking to you, Mother. Now boys, did you not hear me?"

Mike looked over at Jack, as though waiting for his reaction, and Jack responded, "how about you go do it and leave us alone?"

Mary rushed out just then, her arms full of plates and silverware and a nervous smile on her lips. "It's fine," she assured us, "I've got it, it'll just be another second!" From the dining room, we could hear the clatter as she set everything down.

All of us froze, pinned in Mr. Ross's stare, until I stood and said, "I'll help." Mike got up and joined me. We set the table in silence, and when we sat down, Jack and Agnes served us. After his outburst, I was surprised to notice that Mr. Ross didn't lift a finger to help. He just took his place at the head of the table and pushed his food around his plate. Mary seemed to be trying to get his attention, but he couldn't have cared less. I felt bad for her, knowing how hard she'd tried to make everything perfect.

"This is incredible," I told her, and I kicked Mike under the table just as he was stuffing an entire serving of mashed potatoes into his mouth. He tried to talk through it to congratulate his mother on the meal, but all that came out were impossible-to-understand murmurs. That did get a laugh out of her, though, so it was better than nothing.

"I have to give some of the credit to Agnes," Mary said. "The dinner was her idea, actually."

"Well, we had to celebrate our favorite girl's birthday, didn't we?" Agnes responded. "How old are you now, dear?"

"Twenty," I replied.

"Oh, to be twenty years old again…" she mused.

"You're almost there. Just multiply it a few times," Jack said with a wicked smile.

Agnes laughed and threw a napkin at her nephew. That elicited a grunt from Mr. Ross. "Can you all not share a simple dinner without acting like fools?" he shouted.

Agnes ignored him, asking Jack if he'd gotten me anything.

I answered for him: "He did. A set of paints. It's wonderful, and I didn't see it coming. I can't wait to break them out and start using them."

Jack grinned. Was he being bashful? That was so sweet… Mike, provocative as ever, asked what the point of painting was when you could just take a photo, and his brother responded by asking what the point was of screaming into a microphone and trying to burst your audience's eardrums. Mike defended himself, but without much luck. Unfortunately for him, everyone at the table had heard his music.

Mr. Ross frowned and huffed, but we all acted as if he weren't there. Even I nearly forgot him. It was as if we had tacitly agreed to ignore him, which he clearly didn't like, as I discovered when I left for the restroom and came out to find him standing there. A part of me had figured he might do something like that, especially when I heard footsteps outside as I was washing my hands. Because of that, I was ready for him, even if his bitter tone took me aback as he hissed, "You and I need to talk."

"We already talked the other day," I said, looking up at him from below.

"Why are you here, then? Did you come to hit me up for more money?"

Was he seriously trying that line with me again? I scowled as I shook my hands dry and said, "I don't know how to tell you this so you'll get it through your head, but I'm not with your son for his money."

"That certainly didn't stop you from accepting my check."

"You're the one who offered it," I replied. I'd bet he was dying to know what I'd do with that money. I'd bet he was asking himself whether he should threaten me to try to force me to give it back, but he had to have known that if he pushed his luck, I'd reveal what he'd done, and he wasn't willing to let everyone see how deceitful he really was. He reminded me of Monty, the way he liked pushing people around, and even something in the way he was standing resembled my old boyfriend's attitude.

"You really think you're smart, don't you?" he murmured. "Well, I've met a lot of smart girls before, Jennifer. Smarter than you. And you're all the same. You want money, something about it just draws you toward it like a magnet, and you're always on the hunt for someone stupid enough to let you have some."

"I'm sorry you see people that way, but nothing could be further from the truth. And you're the stupid one if you think Jack would ever fall for something like that."

I stopped, waiting nervously to see how he'd respond. It was clear he wasn't used to being talked to that way, and as he sputtered and cursed, I tried to slip past him, making it partway down the hall before he reached me. I could feel his hand reaching for my shoulder, and I turned and shouted, "Don't you dare touch me!"

I told him how arrogant he was; told him I'd never once thought about how much money Jack might or might not have; told him I loved his son, and he'd better get used to it.

"I'm just looking out for his future," Mr. Ross said.

"Bullshit!" I replied, unwilling to play nice any longer. "If you'd cared about your son, you would have known how he felt about me and how fragile he was last year. If you'd cared, you wouldn't have come up with that bullshit at Christmas about how what he really needed was to go live his life in France without me."

"I never told you to leave him hanging!" he said. "That may be how you remember it, but that's not how it happened."

"You didn't have to say it!" I responded. "You manipulated me, and you made it perfectly clear what you wanted."

"Look, Jennifer. I understand you don't want to take the blame. But if my son has suffered this past year, it's because of one person and one person only, and that's you."

"You never cared about his happiness," I fired back at him. "Not his or anyone else's, I'd bet."

"I care about him more than you know."

"Yeah, right. I guess that's why your whole family hates you."

With those words, I'd touched a sore spot, and I couldn't have been more pleased. And if there was anything wrong with it, I couldn't see what.

Mr. Ross warned me, "One day, when Jackie leaves you and learns what the real world is like, he'll thank me for trying to keep you away from him."

"Oh, like the way he thanked you for what you did to him when he was in high school?"

That had been a big risk: Jack never had told me what had happened back then, and I had no idea how bad it really was. All I knew was that Jack's father had done *something*, and whatever it was had pushed him into drugs, and that was when everything in his life had changed.

Mr. Ross put a finger in my face. "I don't know what my degenerate of a son told you," he began, "but I guarantee you it's not the whole story. You can't even imagine all the money I had to give to that school of his to keep them from kicking him out every time he got into trouble. Let alone the times I had to pay his bail because he'd gotten into a fight. If I told you all the money I spent on him in those years…"

"Right, because that's what matters, isn't it? Money and what other people think!" I shouted.

"Without everything I did, he'd never be where he is now! He should get on his knees and thank me for all I invested in him! Without me, he'd just be one more loser!"

"Without you, he'd be a normal, well-adjusted guy. I know you think he needs your money to make his dreams come true, but you're dreaming!"

"What the hell do you know about it?" he yelled.

"Maybe not much, but I do know that what little kids need isn't money— they need a father who loves them! It's great that you paid his tuition and his bail, but you what you should have done is sit down with him and try to figure out what was going on in his life that made him end up where he did. You should have tried to understand him! To let him know he wasn't alone! That's what a father who loves his son does, not just give him money and then throw it constantly in his face like he owes you something!"

He was momentarily too furious to speak. Then, very slowly, he asked me, in a tone that sounded like a warning, "Are you accusing me of not loving my son, Jennifer?"

"I'm not accusing you," I said. "I'm telling you. You don't love him. You only love yourself. Mike and Jack both needed love when they were growing up, and if they didn't get it, it was your fault."

"This, coming from the girl who caused him to start taking drugs again?"

That felt like a gut punch, and I couldn't say anything more. I turned around, ready to go back home, and that was when I found Jack standing there. His expression said something, but it was hard to tell what. He looked desolate, but also enraged, and his stare was frighteningly blank. Had he heard our entire conversation? Had he heard the horrible things his father had said about him? Did he know the truth now about what had happened a year ago?

He didn't say. All he asked was, "Did you take his check?"

Mary was behind him, staring back and forth between father and son. It hurt me to admit it, but there was no way to get around the truth. "Yes," I admitted softly.

"Twenty thousand dollars," Mr. Ross muttered. "That's how much she thinks you're worth, son."

I was in torment, wondering how Jack would interpret that. The subject of money had always irritated him, and the subject of his father even more, and I couldn't imagine he'd like the idea of what I'd done. But then, to everyone's surprise, he started to laugh.

Yes, to laugh.

Mary was as confused as I was. Or maybe it was terror in her eyes? She could sense something very bad was about to happen. Jack's smile was bitter. But still, he put a hand on my shoulder.

"You shook my father down for twenty thousand dollars?" he asked, shaking his head. "Jesus, Jen…just when I thought I couldn't fall any deeper in love with you…"

He pushed me aside softly and grimaced as he stepped closer to his father. Before he could say anything, Mary jumped between them.

"Jack, honey…" she began, voice trembling. "Why don't you go back home. I don't want you to do or say something you'll regret."

"Mom," Jack said, "take a look at yourself. This is the first time ever you've jumped in…and you've seriously done it to defend him?"

Those words were like a jug of cold water dumped on Mary's head. Jack continued: "You can't imagine all the times when I was little and the one thing I wanted was for you to come in and defend me. I always wondered what I could have done so wrong that my own mother could watch how Dad treated me and just let me absorb it. You never did anything for me, Mom, my whole life you stood aside. Well, don't bother doing anything different now. This is between Dad and me."

Mary started to say something: *Jack, honey*…but she ran out of words. Mr. Ross glared at his son, trying to maintain an indifferent facade, but he was uneasy, and had even begun to crouch, as if preparing to defend himself. Jack looked his father up and down before shaking his head. Then he lurched, and when Mr. Ross cowered, he shook his head and laughed. "Someday," he said, "life is going to put you in your place. But I won't be the one to do it. I'm not getting my hands dirty over you. I'll just let you know one thing: if I ever have kids, I can promise I won't treat them the way you treated us."

His voice was quaking, and though I was behind him, I could tell he was on the verge of tears as he continued: "You know what's pathetic is that I was actually scared of you when I was a kid. For most of my life, really. But look at you. You're just a sorry little man. And that's all you'll ever be."

Mr. Ross didn't speak, but it was clear that he was hurt. Jack turned to me, shoulders slightly sunken, looking weary, and said, "Let's go home."

I took his hand and pulled him back into the living room. His parents stayed behind us. Mike and Agnes were sitting on the sofa: she was fidgeting, he was looking down between his knees. "You two go on," she said. "Mike and I have things to take care of here."

They must have overheard the whole thing, and I could only hope that Jack finally confronting his father meant that Mike would do the same. There were things that family should have cleared up years ago, but it was better late than never. I nodded and walked to the garage with Jack, and when I saw how his keys shook in his hand, I recommended we take a taxi. "Nah, I'm fine," he replied, and he surprised me by driving more slowly and calmly than usual.

I felt I should say something, but at the same time, I thought I should respect the silence, so I just looked out the window on the way and let him have his space. When Jack parked in the lot, he didn't move for a moment.

His hands gripped the wheel, and he struggled to control his breathing. I sat there with him, waiting, telling myself I would stay as long as it took.

At last he spoke: "So now you know…"

"You don't have to say anything, Jack."

"What did you think I was going to say?"

It was such a painful subject, and there was no way of dancing around it. It had come up a year ago, and no one had wanted to tell me the truth. Now I was certain: "He beat you, didn't he?"

Surprise, pain, weariness crossed his face. "How do you know?" he asked.

"I know what an abuser looks like," I whispered. "And I know what it feels like to be a victim."

Jack leaned back. He looked so small, so vulnerable, like a little child. "It was just me at first," he said. "For most of Mike's life, it was like he didn't even exist for Dad. I don't know which is worse, honestly. My father always seemed to have this idea that he could shape me in his own image, whereas with Mike, it didn't matter what he did, Dad just looked right past him. Mike wanted his affection, but nothing he did was good enough. I know it sounds weird to say it, but the abuse…it wasn't that bad for me. After a while, it just became another routine. I know that's twisted, but it's how I felt. It happened all the time, and I took for granted that the same thing was going on in everyone's house. When I was in high school, I hit this kid and I got suspended for three days, and I think that was the first time I realized it was wrong. I mean, who was I supposed to learn that lesson from? Not Mom, she never said anything. I spent those three days sitting by myself at home, and I started thinking… I don't think anything Dad did to me could have shaken me, but the day I found him hitting Mike, everything changed. Mike had problems with drugs, you know. He always has, basically. And he had stolen money from Dad to get them. Dad lost it. It was really, really nasty."

"I thought Mike just drank and smoked a little weed," I interrupted him.

"He does now," Jack said. "He cleaned up a lot when he saw me going down the same road. I've seen him get close to relapsing once or twice, but he's kept himself under control, even if it doesn't always look like it. I'll never forget what he did for me…"

This was the first time I'd ever heard Jack talk about Mike like an older brother he cared about and not a mere inconvenience. It made me smile as he continued: "The way Dad was abusing Mike was different. Me he'd slap or shove, but he actually threw Mike on the ground and was punching and kicking him. Mike tried to cover his face, Mom was crying… And I freaked. I don't remember the whole thing very well, but I know I jumped on him. He was stronger, but I was younger, and I had more energy."

"How old were you?"

"Fifteen. I remember how he told me to stand back. *Your brother's a piece of trash and he deserves this*, he said. That's when I punched him in the face. I'd never done anything like that before. His nose started bleeding, and I got scared. He grabbed me by the neck, pushed me down on the glass table that used to be in the living room… That's when I hurt my back. I used to play basketball back then. You saw the trophies. I loved it, you can't even imagine. I was going to be captain of the team, probably the youngest team captain in the history of our school, but I had to forget all that. The trophies you saw were the last ones I ever won. The glass cut into my spinal cord. I don't remember exactly what the doctors called it, neuralgia something, but my whole body hurt, and I had trouble moving my legs and one of my arms. They operated on me, and I was in physical therapy for nearly two years. I guess I should be thankful that I wasn't handicapped for life, but I've never been able to play sports since, I don't have the coordination anymore. You've probably noticed I can be kind of clumsy sometimes, and my shoulder gets these sudden aches… So that was one dream down the toilet…"

"Is that when you started…?"

"Yeah. It was just smoking weed at first, but one thing leads to another, you know. I realize it wasn't the healthiest thing. If I could go back and change it I would, I promise, Jen. Mike really got himself together, and he tried to help me, too, but I cut myself off from the world. I didn't talk to my parents, I actually blamed Mom, if you believe that. I remember shouting at her one time that if she'd done something sooner, none of that would have happened. But she was scared, and I know it was really my father's fault. I couldn't bring myself to ever tell him, though. I mean, I was horrified to even be in the same room with him."

"So what did you do?"

"That's when I got into movies. They were my escape. My only one, honestly. Mom wanted me to forgive her, and when I was in the hospital, she brought me all these books I wouldn't read, but she also signed me up for a bunch of streaming networks, and something clicked. I'd watch four or five movies a day, then I'd stay up late reading about the film industry online…"

"And you figured out you wanted to be a director," I said.

"No. That still took a while."

I realized then that he'd gotten his first tattoo to cover the scar, and that was why he'd been so shy about showing it to me. I asked him when he'd done it, and he told me the story.

"I was pretty much healed by that point." He grinned, "I got drunk and I paid some bonehead ninety bucks to do it. It was horrible. Then a couple of years later, when I was off the coke, Will told me he'd pay for me to get it fixed. It was a celebration kind of thing, like he and I had talked about how my life was going back on course, I was getting better…and I wanted things to stay that way. That's one reason I didn't stop you when you wanted to get that same tattoo, Jen. Because I saw you as part of my recovery. And I don't want you to know about the scar underneath it. I want you to see the symbol of the new me that's on top of it. And I know you were trying to change your life, too, and I hoped maybe having that same tattoo could help you create a new you as well."

I looked down at my hip, where I had a little eagle with outstretched wings identical to the one on his back. I had always liked it, but it meant even more to me now. When I tried to catch his eye, I noticed his head was hanging. Did he really think...

"Jack, you don't think I'm mad, do you?"

"You went and got that tattoo with an idea of me in your head that wasn't who I really was. And that's my fault. If you were mad, you'd certainly be in the right."

"Jack..."

"I mean, honestly, I just assumed you'd regretted it as soon as you left," he remarked sadly. "I didn't tell you this, but the night of Lana's party, I saw it poking up out of your skirt, and even if it's cheesy, it made me so happy. This dumb part of me was worried you might have gotten it covered up."

"I would never do that."

I was still in shock, trying to absorb the whole story he'd told me. But there was one thing that was still eating at me. "I get that your mother didn't do anything. I don't approve of it, but I understand. It *was* her husband, maybe she was just too submissive or too traditional. But Agnes? She has such a strong character!"

"She never knew," Jack said. "She'd already had such a hard time with my grandfather, and I didn't want her to learn that her son was exactly like him. When we went to the hospital, we told her I'd had an accident on the court. If she ever found out what Dad had done, she'd have killed him."

I suddenly felt furious—at Mr. Ross but also at Mary. I'd never had a child, but in my heart I knew I could never do what she'd done, knowing how vulnerable young people are. I let all this out to Jack, and he responded with feigned indifference, "Yeah, well, believe it, because it's true."

He sounded crushed, and I wanted to help, but I didn't know what to do. Did he want a hug, a kind word, or just to be left on his own? Uncertain, I waited for him to react. After a few seconds he did. Clenching his jaw, looking so lost, he told me, "No one ever came to my defense. Not until tonight. Not until you did."

It took me a few seconds to speak: "Jack, I'll always defend you, no matter what. Even if you are an idiot."

I'd hoped to make him laugh with that last word, and it worked. He said, "I know you will. But it's weird for me. I've never been able to believe in anyone before. I've never just known that someone was there for me. And I don't know what that means for me, how I'm supposed to act, you know."

"Well, that makes two of us," I said, "because nobody in my life has ever supported me the way you have."

"Some fucking couple we are, right? I keep my whole life a secret from you, you dump me so I can go to another country to study…how the hell are we going to make this work?"

I forgot that he'd heard the part about why I'd left school so quickly. I felt guilty, and my eyes opened wide as I wondered what he was going to say next.

"If I didn't love you so much," he responded, "I'd give you hell for actually listening to my father. I warned you when we first met to stay away from him."

"Honestly, I deserve it," I said. "If you chewed me out, I could feel at peace with myself. Because I realize now how stupid I was."

"Fine. I told you so. But don't say you were stupid. You've been manipulated too many times. That doesn't have to shape you, though. And as someone who's known you for a little while now, I may as well tell you… you've changed."

"For the worse, I'm assuming."

"No, Jen, for the better. You're not the same person you were. You're not scared to say what you think, you're not scared to stand up to someone, even to my father, and make it clear that nobody's going to push you around. Last year's Jen would never have been capable of that."

I blushed, but his words made me feel good. And I knew Jack was picking up on something that had happened deep inside me. I had changed, I knew that, but he was the first one to notice, and I was so grateful I could almost have cried.

Maybe to take the edge off the moment, he added, "Listen, though. Don't let all these compliments go to your head."

"We'll see," I told him.

He reached out and took my hand. Then he turned serious again. "I heard basically everything you and Dad said to each other. The money you took from him… Is it true? Did you really keep it to help me?"

I nodded and squeezed his hand. "I did, Jack. And it's there whenever you're ready."

"I'm ready," he said. "Fuck it. I'm more than ready." He closed his eyes a moment. "I've been thinking, and… I'm supposed to go on tour for the film, and I don't want to be high when I'm doing it. When I'm old, I don't want to look back at my first big accomplishment and have that be all I remember. You've been right this whole time, Jen. I need help."

"We'll get it for you," I told him. "And all of us will be there for you."

He grinned as he murmured, "I heard you say something to my father about how you loved me…?"

Oh. That.

I'd be lying if I said I didn't start to panic a little just then. Of course, I loved him. But was I ready to say it? Was I ready to admit it to myself?

I could tell he was waiting. I could tell he needed me to confess. But I vacillated: "Come on, you have to know the answer…"

"Maybe. But if you don't say it, I'm worried I'll have a heart attack."

I laughed, felt my body relax, and finally nodded. Why go on hiding it?

"Yeah. I love you."

He leaned in and cupped my face. "Promise me something then, Jen. No more secrets, OK? Never again. Talk to me. Don't take off running because all of a sudden you've decided you know what's best for me."

"I'm sorry," I said.

"Don't tell me you're sorry. Tell me you won't do it again."

I reached up and held his hand to my face. "No more secrets. I promise."

He came in for a kiss, and it took my breath away. It was just a touch, a soft one at that, but it was unlike anything I'd ever felt, and when it was over, I was still trying to process it. Then he said the words I'd needed to hear, much, much more than I'd realized:

"I love you too, Jen."

We kissed again. It wasn't soft, wasn't slow—it was a kiss that showed the hunger he felt for me, a hunger he could finally express again after so long. I felt exactly the same, and I'm sure he could tell. Unable to contain myself, I leaned back into the seat and pulled him into me. But when my mouth opened to let him slip in his tongue, he stiffened and pulled back.

"No," he said, very determined. "I know where this is leading. I know what comes next when we kiss like that. And I don't want to. Not yet. Not until I'm clean."

I blinked and adjusted my clothes, feeling chastened, and said, "Oh, sure. Whatever you say."

We looked straight ahead for a few seconds, me tapping my fingers on my knees, him doing the same on the steering wheel. When I couldn't take it anymore, I asked him, "Jack?"

"Yeah?"

"That thing you said about waiting... I think it's really sweet. It says a lot about you. But I don't think I can. I don't think I have the patience for it. I'm sorry."

To my surprise, he breathed the longest sigh of relief in all of history. "Thank God. Because I sure as hell don't, either."

Now he didn't stop himself. He grabbed my neck and kissed my lips with so much intensity, he knocked me back. Then he jumped out, ran around, and opened my door. He gave me his hand, more nervous than he wanted to appear, and I let him guide me toward the elevator.

As soon as the doors closed on us, he couldn't decide what to do next. Well, if he wouldn't, I would: I grabbed the lapels of his jacket and pulled him toward me. He gripped my hips and pushed me back into the wall, pressing into me until the doors opened and started closing again. I laughed as I stuck a leg out to stop them.

By the time we made it to the apartment, we were both flushed and panting. Jack took out his keys but struggled to get them into the lock. After the third time, with me laughing at him mercilessly, he asked, "Is something funny, Michelle?"

"Yeah. Funny enough that I'll even ignore you calling me that."

I walked past him and he caught me, turned me around, and kissed me again. Now there was no more laughter—it was just passion, with his hand in the small of my back holding me tight to him and touching my chin with one finger so I would kiss him again.

I don't know how long we were there, but I do know I couldn't take it anymore. I could barely breathe. I felt like I was stranded in the desert dying of thirst. Jack grabbed my hand and walked me to the bedroom. He was still shy, still ashamed, I think, of his problems those past months. But that didn't matter anymore, and to get him past it, I shoved him onto the bed, straddling him as he rose up on his elbows.

He made a stupid comment: *If this is the new Jen, then I must say, I like it*. I told him to shut up or I'd tape his mouth closed. He replied, "I've never gone for the whole bondage thing. But hey, if you're in the mood to experiment, please count me in."

I helped him out of his jacket, and he tossed it into the corner, along with my sweater and T-shirt, which he pulled off in one go. His lips were cool on my abdomen, rising between my breasts and up to my neck. I remembered how we'd flirted at the party playing truth or dare. But this was no longer a game. As he kissed me, he sank a hand into my hair, and I wrapped my arms around him.

The rest of our clothes soon vanished, as did whatever misgivings we'd felt. I loved him, and I loved being with him. I loved the way he looked at me, the way he caressed me, the things he whispered in my ear, whether they were tender, ridiculous, or dirty. I loved how he made me feel. And even more, I loved the way I made him feel.

When we were done, I looked down at him, his cheek on my chest, his arms still around me. He was deep asleep. I caressed the tattoo on his back, felt the rough skin of his scar, felt him hold me just a little bit tighter.

No, Jack wouldn't be alone again. Neither of us would ever be alone again.

13

STARTING FROM ZERO

I was in the car with Will, who hadn't uttered a word the whole drive. Naya, sitting next to him, was looking at us with worry in the rearview mirror. I was in the back seat with Jack.

"How are you feeling?" I asked.

All morning he'd been silent, pensive, pacing back and forth in his bedroom. When I told Will, he said I had to give Jack his space. He was right, of course. At midday, Jack walked out with his hands in his pockets and asked to see the flyer for the facility again. There were several, but we had more or less settled on one, and gave it a last once-over. It was expensive—even more than the twenty thousand Mr. Ross had given me—but Joey, Jack's manager, had told us he'd pitch in. He'd been a part of the process ever since Jack had agreed to go to rehab, and had helped me do research and talked with Jack about where would be best for him. Jack had insisted on the center that was closest to home, about an hour and a half away by car. We wouldn't be able to visit every day, but at least we wouldn't have to catch a plane to get there.

I was happy. I'd spoken to the staff there on the phone, and they seemed kind. They talked about their patients like people, not just numbers on a list.

But on the way to the clinic, things didn't feel so good anymore. As soon as we were in the car, Jack started looking out the window frantically, and he hadn't stopped since. I asked him over and over if he was all right, but I was starting to feel like an idiot since he refused to respond.

To break the silence, Naya asked if we wanted to hear a little music.

"Sure," I said. Jack was silent. She took that for a yes.

The music helped distract everyone, but the sorrow returned when we got there. It had all happened too fast. I was so scared to leave Jack alone and vulnerable in a place like that, but at the same time, I knew I was doing the right thing.

The grounds were even prettier than I'd imagined. It was in the boonies, surrounded by farms and country houses, and in front of the building was a promenade lined with orange trees. The building was like a part of the landscape, with its ivy-covered brick walls and perfectly arranged pots with flowers and ornamental trees.

I think it must have impressed Jack, too. As soon as he got out, he covered his brow with his hands to see better and said simply, "Not bad."

Since he'd finally spoken, I thought it was time to take his hand. He didn't look at me, but he didn't pull away, either.

"It's pretty, right?" I asked.

"I mean, it doesn't look like the kind of place that ties you to the bed or whatever."

It was a weird time for jokes, but maybe his nerves were getting to him. He was smiling the way he did when he thought he'd done something wrong. Will and Naya had gone inside, and soon they returned with a short woman with curly hair. She looked sweet, and she showed us the facilities and then Jack's room, which he'd be sharing.

Naya laughed when she saw the bunk bed and announced, "I feel bad for whoever's your roommate."

Jack shrugged. "I shared a room with Jen, and look how that worked out. Maybe I'll get lucky again."

"You'd better not," I warned him.

By the time the visit was over, Jack's mood was less playful. He walked me to the door, and the woman who had shown us around stepped aside to give us some privacy. I didn't want to say goodbye. It felt too soon. I wanted to ask if there was something else to see there, if we could just stay a while until Jack had settled in, but then Naya interrupted me, giving him a big hug and telling him, "I'm so proud of you."

He stuttered a response. I don't think he'd ever seen her be so authentically affectionate.

"If you need anything," she continued, "let us know right away: food, clothes…cupcakes! I can make you some cupcakes and bring them if you want!"

"I've had your cooking, thanks. I think I'll just stick with the hug."

Will whispered to Jack, so quiet that I didn't hear. And when he stepped away, Jack smiled at me. I wasn't sure what I was supposed to do, but I didn't have to think too long before he pulled me close. We shared a brief kiss and he asked, "Any last words?"

"Just behave while you're here," I told him. "I'll try and make sure they don't destroy the apartment in your absence."

His laughter echoed in my ears, and that memory was my only company on the way home. Was it bad that I already missed him so much? I knew it was for his own good, but that didn't mean I could just act like he wasn't gone.

The first week was the hardest. They'd told me I shouldn't call him while he was settling in, and of course, every second I was thinking about him. He wasn't allowed to have a cell phone there, and phone time was limited, and I had to share it with his friends and family. Besides, he needed to focus on himself—I knew that—he couldn't make progress if he was constantly suffering because of all he'd left behind.

I eventually got used to everything—to sleeping alone, to hearing his voice once or twice a week, to dealing with Will, Sue, and Naya on my own… I have to say, school helped. I concentrated on studying, got close to my classmates, and my grades improved. Curtis started calling me a *nerd*. I guess there was a first time for everything.

April was sunny, and all over the quad you could find students lying around trying to catch some rays. Curtis and I were doing that ourselves one day after class, our heads touching, our feet facing in opposite directions. He was sipping a soda. My eyes were lost in the clouds.

"Curtis, Jenna!" I heard Chris shout. I looked up to see him walking over with a smile on his face and a bag of food. He must have been on his break. Curtis turned tense. He had been ghosting Chris for weeks. Weirdly, though, Chris didn't even seem mad. He just sat down and bit into his sandwich.

"I'm glad I found you guys," he said. "I hate eating alone. You want some?"

"Eh… I'm fine," Curtis said.

"I'll take some," I replied. "What is it?"

"Chicken salad," Chris said. "My recipe. It has feta, grapes, and almonds. Here, have half. You won't regret it. I'm sad to say that I inherited all the culinary talent in our family and left poor Naya unable to make a bowl of cereal without starting a fire."

Curtis chuckled as I took a bite. Chris was right, it was delicious. I told him so and could tell he was proud of himself. But then an uncomfortable silence followed. Or so I thought. Chris didn't notice it, apparently.

"How's Ross?" he asked. "Have you gone to see him?"

That was a complicated question. I frowned. "No. Supposedly visitors might be bad for his sobriety."

"Have his parents gone?"

Oh, Chrissy. If only you knew...

"I seriously doubt it," I said.

I felt more and more uncomfortable amid the sounds of our chewing and Curtis slurping his drink.

"How have you been?" I asked. "How are things in the dorm?"

"The job at the dorm is getting dull, if I can be honest with you. But I shouldn't complain. Anyway, there are lots of jobs out there and I'm sure I can find something as soon as I really start looking. As for everything else... It's hard, you know, working all day, trying to do your best, and then people treat you like you don't exist, you know? They don't answer your calls, they won't tell you why they don't want to see you again, and then you randomly bump into them hanging out with one of your friends... I don't know. I feel like I deserve better than that. Once you reach a certain age, you should be able to shoot straight with people, right?"

As Curtis blinked, Chris stood and balled up the bag he'd brought his food in. "You know what?" he said. "I just remembered I've got somewhere to be. See you guys around!"

We were both shocked as he walked off.

I told Naya the story that night. She clapped her hands and applauded, saying, "Now that's my brother! He's finally standing up for himself!"

Sue was sitting across from us and frowned. "I seem to remember you were the one who was obsessed with them going out."

"Listen," Naya responded, "I'm perfect at almost everything, you can't expect me to be the perfect matchmaker, too. Anyway, he's my older brother. It's time he learned to walk on his own."

It was hard to focus on our conversation because Mike was lying on the couch with his arms and legs in the air like a baby with a can of beer between his knees, trying to pour it into his open mouth. When he noticed everyone was staring at him, he asked, "What?"

"Nothing," Sue said, shaking her head.

Mike sat up, put his beer on the coffee table, and asked, "How is my brother doing in the nuthouse, anyway?"

"It's not a nuthouse!" I snapped.

"Mental wellness facility," Will corrected him, "but the answer is, we don't know. Not from him, anyway. We've talked to a nurse, she says everything's fine, but he's basically closed down. I don't know why. He told me the contact isn't good for him, that he can't work on himself with everyone bugging him and trying to make sure he's OK."

For a long time, Mike didn't say anything. We ordered some pizza, and when it came, he toyed with his portion and barely took a bite. Out of nowhere, he told us he'd be heading out early tomorrow, and he left before anyone could ask why.

The next day, Will spoke with the nurse at the facility, and she told him Mike had gone to visit Jack. Apparently, he'd stayed there the whole day. He must have said something to him, because Jack called me that night.

I didn't recognize the number, and I was shocked when I heard his voice saying, "Hey, Jen…"

I was down in the laundry room at the time, scrubbing out a stubborn spot in a pair of jeans. It had been forever since he and I had really talked. I called him whenever I could, but he always seemed so distant. This time, there was something different: a shyness, but also a presence.

"Mike was with me this morning."

Seriously? Those were his first words to me? I stopped what I was doing and grunted. "Great. And?"

"I don't know where to begin. Are you mad at me?"

That was a beginning, at least. But no, I wasn't mad. Frustrated was probably the better word. "You mean because every time I've called you it's been like talking to a brick wall?"

"Yeah," he responded. "Because of that."

"Look, I get it, OK? You need space. You're going through some shit. It isn't easy, but I can deal…"

"That's not it, Jen," he cut me off. I noticed then he sounded a little congested. "It's not that… It's not that I don't want to talk. I mean, dammit, you're all I ever think about, you and our friends, but especially you. I just don't want you to see me like this, though. I don't even want you to hear me like this."

He was silent so long, I wondered if he'd hung up. I knew what he was getting at. I had tried to remind myself of what he was going through. And I was sad for him. But he needed to know the rest of us had feelings, too.

"Jack," I began, trying to sound understanding, "we're here for you if you need us. Nobody's going to judge you. Nobody cares what situation you're in."

"It's easy to say that from a distance," he responded.

"Were you uncomfortable with Mike there?"

"No. But he's been through this, he knows the deal."

"Will does, too, doesn't he? Would you be willing to see him?"

"Will?" He thought for a moment. "Yeah. Yeah, I'd like to see him."

"Fine," I said, a little disappointed. "I'll tell him to go see you tomorrow when class is over. I charge for messenger service, though. You can pay me when you get out."

He laughed, and despite everything, I felt myself calm down. This was the most relaxed I'd heard him in ages. He asked how things were, how my classes were going. And finally, I got to tell him everything that had happened in his absence. It's not that it was much, but when you're crazy about someone, you need to share those things with them. He listened attentively, and when I was done, it hurt to realize the time had come to hang up. I hated thinking of him being there by himself. If only he were a little closer, I thought. I knew I wasn't supposed to visit, but if I could even walk past his window, it would have been a small consolation.

True to his word, Will went to see him the next day. Naya made good on her threat to bake him cupcakes, which were basically chocolate-flavored charcoal briquettes covered with a red icing Sue said looked like congealed blood. There was no way anyone ate them, but Will brought the Tupperware back empty and told her they'd shared them with the other patients and everyone had said they were delicious.

I admit it: I felt left out. Will and Mike could go see him, but I couldn't? I was trying to be understanding. I swear I was. But when insecurity struck, it was hard not to think Jack was slighting me.

More weeks passed, I lost myself in my routine, went back to jogging in the mornings, even talked to my parents now and then. They wanted to get close to me again, but they wouldn't say sorry. And I wasn't ready to let them off the hook. Our conversations were uncomfortable, but at least they were something. I remember one call in particular because I was walking into the apartment when it happened, and I found chaos: shoes on the floor, clothes thrown all over, and Sue beating on the bathroom door telling Naya to come out.

"Hey, Mom," I said, "I gotta go. I'll call you again soon." As I hung up, Sue kicked the door and shouted, "Open up, dammit! I need to piss."

"No," Naya responded. "Leave me alone!"

I was worried they might come to blows. Sue looked enraged, and Naya was screaming like a banshee. I asked what the hell was going on. Sue spun around, knees touching and one hand stuffed between her legs, and said, "If she doesn't come out now, I'm going into her room and pissing all over her carpet!"

It was clearly an emergency. I knocked softly, asking Naya if anything was wrong.

"No! Just leave me be!"

I heard her sniffle, and her little feet were pacing back and forth. In our good cop, bad cop act, I tried to play soft, telling Naya that whatever had happened, it would be OK, we'd understand. In the meanwhile, Sue's threats got more and more violent and demented.

Finally, Naya said, "I'm not sure if I should tell you."

"Naya, it's better to let it out than suffer alone in silence."

That convinced her, and she opened the door. We found her sitting on the toilet in a pink party dress with her mascara running down her face. She must have been crying all day. I instinctively hugged her, but Sue shattered the moment when she screamed, "MOVE, DAMMIT!"

I guess privacy didn't matter much to her. She shoved us aside, jerked down her pants, and sat down as Naya started weeping again.

"What is it, Naya?" I asked. I was torn between the worry that something awful had happened and the awkwardness of hearing Sue's piss streaming out right there next to us. As Sue blushed for what I assume was the first time in her life, resting her face in her palm and explaining, "I'm sorry, I just couldn't hold it any longer," I suddenly knew what was wrong with Naya. Could it be? I froze, and she saw in my eyes that I'd grasped the situation. If it was possible to cry any harder, then she did.

"Naya, are you…pregnant?" I asked.

In response, she handed me a white-and-pink plastic stick with a wadded-up sheet of instructions. "I think so," she said, "and I'm scared." Sue stood and pulled up her pants in silence. I think even she realized this was no time for sarcastic remarks. Naya was destroyed. Unsure what to do, I pulled her head close to mine as Sue grabbed the instructions from me and read them closely. The two lines on the test were plain as day. But maybe that meant *negative* on some brands?

I didn't know, but I tried to reassure her. "You know, these things aren't always right."

"They're 99 percent accurate," Naya sobbed. "I just looked it up on my phone."

"Still, we should do another," I said. "You can never be too sure, right? This is a big deal, no need to jump to conclusions."

But after two trips to the pharmacy and several more tests, all with the same result, it was time to jump to conclusions. Naya was shattered. I didn't know what to do, so I just sat there rubbing her back while Sue, on the floor, took charge of the Kleenex, passing her another one every time she needed to wipe her tears or blow her nose.

"My life's over!" Naya moaned.

"Come on, let's think," I said. "I know it seems like a big deal now, but…"

"It *is* a big deal, Jenna!" Naya screamed.

"How did it happen?" Sue asked. "Don't you guys use protection?"

"I'm on the pill," Naya said. "But you know how, like, there's the sugar pills in the packet that you don't have to take? I guess I got those mixed up with the other ones, and maybe my cycle was off, and something happened…"

"It's OK," I said, "let's calm down and be strategic here. Does Will know?"

Naya shook her head. "He's gone, he went to see Ross again. He won't be back till later. I was so excited, it's our anniversary, you know, and we've got a reservation at this fancy restaurant tonight…"

"Look on the bright side. Now you don't have to wonder what present to get him," Sue joked. It was irritating, and I tried to cover up for her by encouraging Naya. "Seriously, though. You need to tell him. You should go to the dinner and tell him there. He'll be in a good mood, and a restaurant is neutral ground where you guys can really talk."

"Are you crazy?" Naya cried. "Then what? I just tell him he's got no choice but to be a dad and I hope he's happy about it? He's going to hate me!"

"Will would never hate you," I told her, "especially not over this."

"She's right." At last, Sue had said something sensible.

"Either way," Naya replied, "there's a baby inside me now and it's going to ruin everything we've ever planned."

I frowned. "My sister had her kid when she was way younger than you, and she's always said it was the best thing that ever happened to her. My parents got married when they were twenty. I understand those were other times, but maybe people back then weren't wrong about everything."

"You don't have to keep it," Sue said. "I know that's not easy to talk about, but you do have options. I'd at least get some counseling and think it over before you decide. But then, you know me, I've got about the same maternal instincts as Cruella de Vil."

Finally pulling herself together, Naya admitted, "I don't think I could do that. I've always loved kids. I've always wanted them. And I never wanted to be one of those people who waited until they were in their thirties. At the same time, though, I didn't think it would be this fast. I haven't even graduated. I guess at least Will's almost done with school, but still…"

"Naya, you don't have to decide today," I told her. "Just talk to Will tonight, and then tomorrow, when you're calmer, the two of you can go to your gynecologist."

"Yeah," Sue added. "I'm sure a doctor will have better advice for you than we can give."

That seemed to cheer Naya up a bit. She had been hugging her knees. Now she stretched out, grabbed the positive pregnancy tests, stood up, and looked at herself in the living room mirror. "Jesus," she said, "I look like hell. Why didn't either of you tell me?"

"I thought it was on purpose, to make us feel sorrier for you," Sue said, and I elbowed her in the ribs as she laughed maliciously.

"This is a nightmare!" Naya screeched.

"It's not," I told her. "Sit down. I'm going to put on some music, and you relax. You're lucky you're in the hands of your own personal stylists this evening, and I can assure you, we're two of the best in the world…"

"Two?!" Sue protested. Then, when she saw my face, she said, "Whatever. Yeah, two…"

14

THE SIXTIES JOINT

I was fidgeting, and Will was next to me driving, looking highly amused.

"You all right?" he asked.

"Yeah, of course. Perfect. Just kind of wondering whether Jack will be happy to see me."

"Well, keeping in mind he was the one who wanted you to come…so I'd say yes."

Jack had been in rehab for two and a half months. This visit had to be a step forward for him, because a few weeks before, he'd kept insisting he needed space and time to think every time I brought the subject up. He finally told me one day he'd put me on the visitors' list, and I was over the moon, but I'd been so busy with exams that I'd had to put it off until now. It felt almost like I was meeting him again for the first time.

Will dropped me off at the entrance. I was nervous as I turned and waved goodbye to him. I hurried up the path, and almost as soon as I opened the door, an employee came to greet me. I was glad. If I'd had to wait too long in the vestibule, I'd probably have had a heart attack.

Still, the wait wasn't over. I was taken to a hallway with plastic seats, yellow walls, and a white linoleum floor. It was depressing the way hospitals always are, and looked nothing like any of the photos I'd seen in the brochure. I was wearing a sleeveless shirt and was self-conscious because I was sweating. It was hot for May. Or maybe it was my nerves. Or maybe both.

I heard steps approaching and looked up. The man who had brought me there was now returning, with Jack a few steps behind him. I stood, full of anticipation.

Jack had put on a little weight, but he was pale. His hair was cut neatly, and he was dressed like a jock in knee-length shorts and a grey zip-up sweatshirt. He had his hands tucked in his pockets. He smiled when he saw me, and in that moment, I learned all I needed to know: one, that he was fine, and two, that he hadn't forgotten me.

We walked toward each other and met in the middle of the hall, and I couldn't stop myself from jumping into his arms. I was lucky I didn't knock him over. I felt him laughing as he said, "OK, fine. I missed you, too."

"I'll leave you two alone," the attendant said, and walked back to where he and Jack had come from. Jack set me down, and as I held his hands, I looked at him more closely, trying to make sure he really was OK. He seemed to find that amusing.

"Did I pass the inspection?" he asked.

"The physical part. As for the behavioral part, that remains to be seen..." It was hard for me to joke just then, and I dropped it right afterward. "I know you wanted me to come earlier, Jack, but I had so much studying, and..."

"Relax," he said. "It's not like I came to see you, either!"

"That's different!"

"It still counts..." Guiding me toward a glass door, he asked, "You want to see outside?"

I hadn't imagined the grounds were so big. There was a soccer field, a pool, stables...it looked like some millionaire's estate. We didn't go far, though: Jack wanted to sit on one of the stone benches on the patio, under a wooden gazebo-like structure covered in ivy. All around, I could see other residents stretched out on the lawn.

It was hard to know what to say, and I found myself sticking to the obvious at first. "You've put on some muscle, it looks like. I guess they have a gym here?"

"Yeah," Jack replied.

"Maybe you'll start running with me when you get out."

"Sure."

"It's prettier here than it looks in the flyers. What's your schedule like? Do they give you enough time to enjoy all this?"

"More now than before," he said. "At first, I was under lock and key. Now, I have meetings and therapy in the morning and then I'm free the rest of the day. In the afternoon and evening, there's activities: meditation, yoga, swimming. I tried yoga, but I'm not what you'd call flexible. What I really like is the animal therapy, that contact with another creature is something beautiful. Art therapy on the other hand is lame. Speaking of art—"

"Yeah," I cut him off. "I've been using the paints you gave me."

"And...?"

"They're incredible. Like I said, school's killing me, so I've had to restrain myself. The art is my getaway, my happy place. Of course, Sue's bitching because the apartment smells like paint and turpentine, but I can't help it, I keep the balcony door open constantly and it doesn't help! I even tried covering up the scent with Mike's disgusting body spray. Thankfully, Will and Naya are cool about it."

"Those two..." Jack responded. "Will told me about *it*. It doesn't even seem real."

I smiled and said, "I'll bet it does to them."

He nodded. "Will's over the moon. I've always known he'd be an amazing dad."

I couldn't say I had as much faith in Naya. I wanted to believe she'd be a good mom, but I'd been trying to work on stuff with her, and the results were disastrous. All she had to learn was how to change a diaper, rock a child to sleep, give it a bath, feed it, but of the four dolls I'd bought her to practice on, she'd stomped on two of them in a fit of anger and thrown another one out the window, so... I wasn't especially confident.

I said that they were lucky they had friends to help them out, but it felt...not insincere, but beside the point, because we both knew I wasn't there to talk about Will and Naya. I was there to talk about him. But to do it, he'd have to make the first move. The ball was in his court, but he still didn't have the courage to open up to me. And I didn't want to pressure him, but I also didn't feel we could keep putting it off. To try to ease him into it, I reached out and touched his hand, and when he met eyes with me, I asked him, "How are things going here?"

He shrugged and said, "I don't know. I'm not sure if I'm ready to go back to the real world."

I hadn't expected that response. And though it hurt, I told him, "If you need time, Jack, take as much as you need."

"It's not that, Jen. I'm better. I can leave, I know I won't be in danger. It's not that, it's that I don't want to think about what's waiting for me on the outside: the movie, promotion, interviews. Just the thought of all that is, I don't know...almost irritating. Like, if I'm being honest with you, it makes me want to throw up."

He sighed and bent forward, resting his elbows on his knees. I tried to process what he was saying. "You want me to take the wheel?" I asked. "I can be your secretary. Trust me, I'll tell every last one of those people to go piss up a rope!"

He giggled. "That would be nice, actually. But no. I can't put my life off forever. At the same time, I want to ask, is it really too much to be able to come out of here and just take care of myself without having to worry about all those so-called obligations?"

No, it wasn't too much to ask. Not to me. I didn't know what his colleagues and manager would think, but I also didn't care. And if Jack was talking to me about this, it meant that he cared more about my opinion than anyone else's. The glitz and glamour, all that could come in due time. What mattered now was that Jack was OK.

"I've got two ideas," I told him.

Looking so small, so vulnerable, he rested his chin on his balled fist and asked me, "Which are…?"

"Number one: we could lock you in the apartment all summer and pretend you've been kidnapped. Number two: we could wait until my exams are done and get the hell out of here. Just you and me."

That made him think. Intrigued, he straightened up and asked, "And escape to where?"

"I don't know. Your lake house, maybe. Or if you're feeling adventurous, we could go overseas. I've never even been out of the country. I'm sure you find that hilarious, but whatever, there's a first time for everything."

"That could be nice," he admitted. "Traveling, I mean, not the lake house. I'd like to put a little more distance between this place and me, and obviously, I need to get away from my parents."

"We could go to my parents'!" I joked.

"Yeah, they're probably dying to have me show up there."

"I doubt that, but I am kind of dying to see the look on their faces if we did do it."

"Who are you, and what have you done with the sweet, innocent Jen I used to know?" he asked sarcastically.

"My sweet and innocent days are over."

He laughed and hugged me, smiling mischievously. "Tell you what.

Make a list of places you want to go. We've got a whole summer to start checking them off."

"And then the little shit goes and throws up all over me!" my sister complained. I rolled my eyes. I'd had one hell of a day: running back and forth, cramming between classes, and as soon as I made it home, with just five minutes before I had to leave again Shannon called. I was trying to hold my phone to my ear with my shoulder while I adjusted the strap on my bag, which was in danger of spilling all my stuff out onto the floor.

"What do you expect?" I asked her. "He's a child, he's not old enough to control himself."

"Whatever. It's not my kid, he's just some friend of Owen's, I agreed to play chauffeur, I didn't sign up for some little snotnose to puke on me five minutes into the drive."

"You did, though, Shannon. You did it as soon as you joined the Mommies and Daddies Facebook group I warned you about."

"Don't remind me."

Her talking about Owen made me think of Spot, the little stuffed horse he had given me, and I looked over to find him wedged between my pillows. I straightened him up and interrupted her: "Listen, all this sounds very dramatic, and I'm sorry to cut you off, but I need to go. We're going to pick Jack up from the clinic. He's finally coming home!"

"Oh, and I guess that's more important than someone vomiting in my car? I'm kidding. I hope everything goes great, Jenny. And if you need me, don't hesitate to call."

I hung up and tucked my phone into the pocket of my green shorts. I looked at myself in the mirror and wondered if they clashed with my mustard yellow T-shirt. I don't know why I was so worried, it's not like I had to impress Jack, and clothing had never mattered much to him anyway. Plus, I was sure he'd have other things on his mind.

"Jenna!" Will shouted. It was time to go. I almost skipped out of the bedroom, I was so excited. I found my roommates sitting there nervously, playing with their phones or watching TV. Will and I were going to pick Jack up, and that was for the best, I thought: I wasn't up for an hour and a half of him and Naya together. They'd barely spoken since their anniversary, and when they did, they argued. It was bad, and I didn't have the time or the energy to act as mediator. In my mind, I was already off on vacation, traveling the world with Jack, leaving all the drama behind us.

There was just one problem: Mary had shown up, too. That explained why Will didn't even have his shoes on, and why it got tense as soon as I walked into the room. Standing near the kitchen, she said a nervous hello, and I greeted her back. I was so shocked, all I could do was look around and hope someone had an explanation. But everyone there was as surprised as I was.

"I heard Jack was getting out today," she said bashfully. "And I thought it would be a good idea if you and I went and got him together."

That sounded like the exact opposite of a good idea to me, but I didn't feel comfortable telling her so. She continued: "I know things have been difficult. Bad, maybe I should say. But I need to talk to him, and I can't think of another way."

"You could call him," Will recommended.

"He won't answer me. This way, even if I make him mad, he won't be able to wriggle out of it," Mary said.

I hesitated, looking hopefully at Will, who was always the voice of reason. But he was as helpless as the rest of us. *I can't do this*, I thought, and I told Mary it might be better for her to go alone. "It'll give you guys the space to talk without anyone else being in the middle..."

"No," she responded. "Jack will feel more comfortable if someone he knows is there. I really think it should be you. If you're willing, I mean."

No, I wanted to tell her.

And I almost managed to say it.

But then I saw the pleading expression in her eyes. And Will noticed the resignation on my face and sighed, and thirty minutes later, I found myself in her passenger seat on the highway, asking myself just how bad an idea this was. Mary's luxurious car was racing through the suburbs, air blasting, upholstery soft as butter, and…she wouldn't speak a word to me. Was there anything to say? I wasn't sure, but if not, couldn't she at least put on some music? Something, anything, would be better than hearing her clear her throat, grunt, nibble the nail of her pinkie finger.

Things went on like that for about an hour, and then out of the blue, she asked how I was. *There's the million-dollar question*, I thought. "Fine," I replied.

I didn't say more. I wasn't sure what else I could say.

"I'm glad," she told me. "You looked so upset the last time I saw you."

She was right about that: the last time she saw me, I was yelling at her husband. But I wasn't ready to go into that, so I changed the subject: "I've been thinking about my grandmother a lot. I never realized how much I'd miss her."

"I can imagine, honey. If it hurts, don't feel like you have to say anything."

"No," I said, rubbing the corners of my eyes. "It's not that. I actually like talking about her. But it's weird, everyone avoids the subject with me."

Mary smiled with understanding. "I was very close to my grandparents, too. My granddad used to drive me to school every day. He loved to drive, he used to tell me I shouldn't bother to get a license, that he'd be happy to be my chauffeur forever. I had this suspicion then that he was being sexist, he was of that generation, you know, they had all these prejudices about women drivers…but now I realize it was the one time a day we were alone together, and he didn't want it ever to end."

"Is he…?"

"Oh, no," she replied. "He died ages ago. He was very old. It's funny, I realize now I haven't talked about him in years. The poor guy doesn't deserve that, he should be commemorated more often, but you know, people get weird when it comes to talking about death."

"People get weird when it comes to talking about anything serious," I said. I wondered if that sounded too forward, and I wasn't exactly sure why I'd said it. I mean, I knew she was avoiding *something*, but even I wasn't certain what I expected from her.

At any rate, she changed the subject. "How are your parents?"

It was a touchy subject. I stared out the window. "I guess they're fine. We don't talk much. It's OK, though. They do their thing, I do mine."

"I understand," she replied. I hated that. I hated how older people always told you they understood everything. And I didn't want her pity.

"You don't understand," I told her.

"But I do. More than you can even imagine. If you're upset with them, you must have your reasons, but I can promise you, they think about you and they're worried about you."

Something snapped in me, and I responded, enraged, "They weren't worried about me my first year of school, when they kept trying to undermine me so I'd come back home! They weren't worried about me when I had to go stay with my grandmother because they'd basically stopped talking to me! And they sure as hell weren't worried about me the day of her funeral, when they decided it was better to kick me out than let Jack stay with me so I could have one single day of peace."

"I understand."

"Stop saying you understand!"

I hadn't wanted that to come out so aggressively, but I couldn't help it. She took it well, though. "What I mean is, I understand them. I'm not saying what they did was right—it was wrong, and there's no justifying it. But being a parent…it's not what you think it will be. When you're a child, you take for granted that parents have access to some special wisdom, but they're just like you. Just as touchy as you. Just as petty as you. The only difference is, they're older."

"Are you talking about your own parents?" I asked.

"More about myself, actually. But it's complicated. Let me take a little step back here, and I'll make a confession. I was worried when you came into Jack's life. I'm embarrassed to say that, but we're being honest here, right? You brought out something in him I hadn't seen in a long time, and that was nice, but I was scared where it would take him."

"How do you mean?"

"OK…when the boys were little, Mike was…well, what can I tell you, Mike was Mike. He's always been wild and impulsive, he's always gotten into trouble. I love him with all my heart, but he just never grew up. He's never been serious, and he's never cared much about anyone else. He has a good heart, but he doesn't know how to use it. Jackie was the opposite, and that's why, despite Mike being older, Jackie's always been the more mature one. And believe it or not, he absolutely adored Mike when they were boys. You can't even imagine, he was his idol. If he got a good grade, he used to run to Mike's room to show him his report card. If he won a trophy, he'd go seeking his approval. And so, when Mike, um, turned down the wrong road… Jackie tried everything to help him. But at some point, I think he realized some people just can't be saved."

Wait…was she talking about me somehow? Because it certainly felt like it. I looked straight ahead as she continued: "Jack's always had this kind of savior complex, trying to help people who don't even realize they need help. He was that way from the time he was a kid. It only went away when he couldn't do anything for Mike. And then you showed up, and that part of him came back…"

Did she mean that in a positive way? I couldn't tell, but I was starting to feel attacked. Mary went on to say she thought it had something to do with the abuse Jack had suffered at the hands of Mr. Ross. That Jack felt bad for not being able to stand up to his father, and that made him want to stand up for other people. She finished: "What I admire about Jack is his understanding nature. But he's not that way with everybody. It's something he can turn on or off, you know? But you bring out that nurturing side of him, and that was why I wanted you to come."

I wasn't sure whether I was relieved or I resented her for using me. And did she think I was someone who needed saving? She implied that it was a good thing that I brought out the kindness in Jack, but was I comfortable with how ready she was to use that to her advantage? It seemed unfair to me, and downright manipulative to Jack.

She added, when she realized I wasn't going to respond, "But getting back to earlier, if I can give you some advice, Jenna…give your family another chance. I'm not saying everything will ever be perfect, but you'll have a relationship. And at least they'll know you're all right, and you'll know that they are, too. It may not seem like much, but one day, you'll be happy to have that, I promise."

She stopped talking then, and I was grateful for it, and by the time we reached the clinic, I was a little more relaxed. I wasn't sure what to think of everything she'd said, but I no longer felt like coming with her was a mistake. When she parked, I hurried out, excited and nervous: excited to see Jack, nervous about what he would say when he saw his mother. Mary was tense, too, and walked a few steps behind me with crossed arms. She knew as well as I did that this could all blow up in our face.

I walked inside, and after a few minutes waiting, the attendant I'd seen on my last visit brought Jack out, dressed in the exact same outfit as before.

He was smiling and looked ready to go. I smiled back at him convincingly enough that he didn't ask me if something was wrong. He clapped the employee on the back, adjusted the strap on the gym bag he'd brought with him, and trotted down the stairs arm in arm with me, looking ready to conquer the word. Then he looked up, saw his mother, and stopped. He clearly wasn't pleased that she'd come.

"What are you doing here?" he shouted.

"Hello, Jackie."

"Don't *hello, Jackie* me. I want to know why you're here. And Jen, did you know about this? Did you two come together?"

So much for our romantic reunion. I shrugged and said Mary had shown up to the apartment and offered to come get him, and everyone had agreed maybe it was a good idea…

"Well, it wasn't. It was anything but. So Mom, you can leave. Jen and I will take an Uber back."

Unsurprised, weary, Mary sighed and asked, "Don't you want to hear what I have to say?"

"Now?!" Jack growled. "You want to talk now? Twenty-two years have passed, and you still haven't figured this out? Hell no, I don't want to talk. Go home. I don't have anything to say to you."

"I'm not going home, Jack," Mary said. "I'm not moving until you talk to me. I'm not asking for much. I just want the three of us to go to lunch. You guys pick a place. I'm sure you're both hungry, it's almost lunchtime."

To our surprise, Jack shook his head and got into her back seat. We tried to ask a few questions, but he said he wasn't in the mood to talk. I devoted my time to scouring the internet for a half-decent place to eat and then reading the directions out to Mary.

We wound up at a cozy spot that looked like a place from the sixties, with puffy red vinyl on the chairs and booths, tables with plastic table-cloths, a black-and-white checked floor. I had read online that it was "quaint" but also that the food was delicious. I could smell meat roasting on the grill. Mary looked like she'd never set foot in someplace so vulgar. I think Jack found that amusing.

He sat next to me with his mother facing us, and we stared out the window at an indoor playground across the street where a bunch of kids were jumping in and out of a ball pit. A waitress came over and dropped off some menus, and I studied mine intently.

"Anything special you guys are in the mood for?" Mary asked, trying to sound normal.

Jack didn't answer. I responded, "Ooh, a barbecue burger. Jack's going to love that."

"I'm *off* drugs now, remember. A person would have to be high to eat one of those," he said.

He must have been the only person in the world who could come out of rehab and joke about being high just a few minutes later. He was grinning as he scrutinized the menu. He wound up ordering chicken fingers, loaded fries, and onion rings. I asked, "Do you honestly think you can eat all of that?"

"It's the men in this family," his mother answered for him. "They're all bottomless pits."

It was true. I remembered a time when Jack took me out, ate three burgers in a row, and then finished off with dessert. Since Mary and I just ordered burgers, we had to sit there watching him devour his appetizers when they came. I found it entertaining. Jack started to get self-conscious. Mary was too nervous to talk. She was biting her upper lip, and after a few minutes, she finally asked, "Is it good? Because if not, you know, you can always get something else. Or if it's not enough. Either way, it's your day is what I'm trying to say, and…"

Jack hissed, "Why don't you just say what you've got to say? That way we can finally get it out in the open."

She froze briefly, then cleared her throat and informed him, "Your father and I are getting a divorce."

Jack stopped chewing and looked up. He was so still, I had to peer close to make sure he was still breathing.

Time to go, I thought. I excused myself, said my phone was buzzing, and walked out. As I pretended to respond to a text, I tried to peek through the window and see if they were talking, and since they appeared to be, I sat on a bench by the front door, thinking it was best to give them some time.

Only when I worried things might be getting awkward did I go back. There was still an awkward silence, but it wasn't as tense as it had been. Mary was fixating on her burger, which she kept repeating was delicious. That was weird, but it was still better than before I'd left. Trying to make her feel better, I said, "Yeah, we hit a home run with this place."

Jack grinned. I could tell he thought it was funny, his mother writhing while I struggled to salvage the situation. "Who was texting you?" he asked.

"It was the clinic. They said you took some extra attitude with you, and they need it back."

Jack laughed hard enough to nearly spit out his food. Even Mary, usually so prim and proper, found it funny. Things weren't perfect—whatever the divorce meant for Jack and Mary, I couldn't even begin to grasp yet—but I was glad, at least, I'd be riding back home with two people and not two stiff statues.

15

BROTHERS VERSUS FRIENDS

"You know when you're watching a horror movie and the main character turns down the hallway, and you're like *don't do it* because you know it's suicide, but then he does do it, and you think, *What a dumbass?* Because that's kind of where I'm at now."

Jack's words, of course, coming from the back seat, as he stretched out and adjusted his dark sunglasses. He was grumpy. He had been ever since he'd returned home.

He was complaining because he didn't know where we were taking him. That was my plan, and I'd decided it was best to keep it a secret. The idea had come to me after a conversation with Will the afternoon before. He had been reading all these webpages with recommendations about how we should treat Jack once he was home. Jack had gotten cranky and said he wasn't a vacuum cleaner and didn't need an instruction manual, but Will didn't care, and he'd printed up a list. One of the things everyone agreed on was that people coming out of rehab should try to get exercise. And what better exercise was there than basketball, the sport Jack used to love?

Jack, Will, Mike, and I were in the car. I admit I was intimidated at being the odd girl out, but I was pretty sure I could hold my own with them, and if it made Jack happy, it was worth it.

"I'm assuming I'm the killer in this scenario?" I asked him.

"No, Will is, because he's the driver," Jack responded.

"You're one to talk," Will shot back, and we laughed. Even Jack was aware of how questionable his driving was. He rolled down the window and let in a gust of hot air. I couldn't wait to get there, and when we finally parked, I jumped out, while Jack dragged himself out like a lazy dog—he even groaned like a dog. He clearly wished he could just stay at home, but I wasn't going to let him bum me out.

Will had told me Jack used to spend his summers at his family's lake house, and that there was a half-size basketball court nearby where the two of them used to shoot hoops. It was run-down now, but it had something special about it. I could tell he had been right about that when I saw the gleam in Jack's eyes once he realized where he was.

I grabbed his wrist and pulled him around to the trunk to take out the basketball I had hidden there.

"I'm sorry," he said, "do you want to tell me what the hell we're up to out here?"

"You're a smart boy," I said. "You figure it out." I threw the ball into his chest. He caught it with surprising dexterity and glanced around.

"Don't tell me…"

Before he could finish the phrase, Will came from out of nowhere and jerked the ball from his hands. "Think fast," he said, dribbling as he ran away.

"Hold these," Jack said, handing me his glasses and chasing Will onto the court.

They laughed and shoved each other as Mike stretched his arms out lazily, standing next to me. "One thing," he said, "I hope me coming here doesn't imply I'm actually supposed to do exercise. Because, as you might have noticed, I'm more of a couch-beer-TV kind of guy."

"Yeah, but you're here now," I told him, "so hop to it!"

I clapped him on his back and headed to the court, and Mike grunted before finally joining us.

Will and Jack were taunting each other and running around in circles. At one point, Jack managed to get the ball, turn on his heels, and shoot, and even from the far end of the court, he swished it in. My jaw dropped, but Mike and Will didn't look especially surprised. Will caught it on the rebound and shot another two-pointer from close by.

As I stepped on the court, the ball bounced toward me and Will said, "You're up."

"I don't even know what rules we're playing!" I protested.

Sarcastically, Will responded, "Bounce the ball, throw it, try to get it in the hoop. It's not that hard."

"Hey!" I said, making a throw and aiming at his head.

As Mike stepped onto the court, he proposed, "Shall we play brothers versus friends?"

All of us agreed but Jack, understandably. Mike was an obvious handicap. But surprisingly, Jack didn't put up much of a fight before warning us, "Whatever. I can stomp you guys and carry this bum, too." He dribbled away, leaving me there with Will. I have to admit, Will was a gentleman and tried to school me as best he could. I also have to admit, despite what I thought when I got there, I was way, way out of my league.

We worked out a system: Will took care of offense and blocking Jack, who was as sticky as flypaper, and I did the dirty work: throwing elbows, shoving, stealing the ball… The one thing I'll say for myself is that my morning runs paid off: Jack could rarely catch me, and Mike didn't have a chance. They tried to make me stick to the rules, yelling, "You can't run without dribbling!"

"Tell it to the ref!" I fired back.

Ten or so points in, Mike was already taking rest breaks, along with sips from a can of beer he had produced as if by magic.

"Mike!" Jack shouted every time he caught him, "we're getting our asses beat! Stop drinking!"

"Bro, beer has electrolytes in it," Mike responded.

I had to admit it—Jack wasn't a clean player, but he was good. Almost impossible for Will and me to stop. We'd been at it for an hour before I blocked even one of his shots—or so I told myself, because I had the feeling he'd let me get in front of it.

At one point, he stopped, dribbling back and forth and mocking me. "You tired yet?"

"Nope."

"You sure are breathing hard."

"It's your handsomeness. It takes my breath away."

When he smirked, I tried to rob the ball from him, but he dribbled through his legs, caught it with the back hand, shot past me, and dunked. Humiliating. Will jumped up in a spiral and caught it on the way down. Before I even realized it, he'd passed the ball to me. That was the first time he'd done that, and I was nervous.

"Shoot!" he said.

Jack actually had the nerve to stop and fold his arms across his chest. "This should be fun," he said.

"Get ready to weep," I told him, instantly losing credibility when I dribbled so hard, the ball bounced off and I had to chase it down.

"You need to work on your hand-eye coordination, Michelle!" Jack called out.

"You need to work on your brain-mouth coordination!" I shouted back.

Rabid, I caught the ball and approached the basket close, dribbling just a few inches from the ground. Jack laughed and tried to steal the ball from me, and I clutched it tight in both hands, running off until he caught me and pulled me up off the ground.

"That's called traveling, and it's a foul," Jack said.

"Will, help!" I screeched.

But Will was having too much fun watching us as he leaned against the fence. Kicking in the air, I shouted, "Let me go! Red card! Red card!"

"Red cards are for soccer, Michelle. Get your games straight."

"WILL!!!!"

I threw the ball away desperately, and Jack dropped me and ran off to play some more. When we were done, Will and Mike went to the car for a cigarette and I sat down on the court. Jack was still dribbling. He crouched down in front of me, and I was tempted to push him over, but instead I just grabbed the ball and threw it as far away as I could.

"Come on," he told me, "don't be a sore loser. You want to give it a shot?"

"Give what a shot?"

"You want to try and make one in?" He stood and offered me his hand. "Come on, I'll show you how."

I accepted reluctantly.

"Let's start with the basics," Jack said, coming around behind me to set my shoulders. "Here, hold your arms like this…yeah, that's it…exactly. No, straighten your elbow a bit. There you go. It's not so hard, is it?"

I couldn't say if it was hard or not—I hadn't done anything yet—but I nodded and tried to play along.

"Now," he said, "just look at the backboard, and…wait, stiffen your fingers a little so your palm's not touching the ball. There you go! Now bend your knees slightly, straighten up, and throw."

"That's it…?"

"No, we need to work on your aim, too. Which, if it's anything like your coordination, means we're going to be here a while."

"I should remind you, Jack, that Will asked me to hold onto the keys while he played. They're in my purse. So unless you want to go walking home…"

"Did I tell you how good you look today?"

I grinned. I would never have admitted it, but I really wanted to make the shot. I squinted, bit my lower lip, got ready, and…

Not even close.

That time I'd gotten an F in gym class had been a prophecy.

Jack chuckled as he ran after the ball. I tried several more times, but it was clear I was no Caitlin Clark. I had no sense of aim, and no explanation of technique was going to change that. In the end, Jack got behind me again and wrapped his hands around mine. "Come on now," he said. "You and me together, no one can defeat us, right, Jen? One, two…"

All right, so Jack did all the work, but whatever: it went straight in that time. Ridiculously, I felt a tingle from head to toe and started skipping off toward the ball, which was still bouncing near the post.

"My God, that was one for the record books, Jordan himself would be impressed!"

"I'm so happy," I said, "that I'm going to choose to believe you're actually being serious!" I gave him a five, then pretended to be holding up a trophy. "First of all, I'd like to thank my coach, I could never have made it this far without him. I'd like to thank Will, who took a chance on a rookie player. I'd like to thank Mike for leaving the court to drink beer and making things easier on me. And of course, I can't forget my old gym teacher who flunked me…"

"How did you flunk gym?" Jack asked. "I didn't think that was even possible."

"It wasn't my fault! He told us we could pick our activities one day, and my friends and I decided we'd just toss a ball around, and he came over and was like *Less talk and more work, ladies, I want to see those butts moving*, and when he turned around, one of my friends flipped him a bird behind his back."

"That doesn't explain very much, Jen. I feel like you're leaving out some essential details."

"Fine, so we were all laughing afterward, and I acted like I was going to throw the ball at him, but it slipped out of my hand and hit him in the head. I didn't do it on purpose! My hands were sweaty!"

"Wait—you haven't made a single successful pass this entire game, but you nearly decapitated your teacher? Amazing!" Jack was laughing, and I might have joined him if the two other guys hadn't come over. But I wasn't in the mood to have all three guys making fun of me. Thankfully, despite his occasional fits of the giggles, Jack kept the story to himself.

That evening, Lana was having a party, and I'd agreed to go with Naya and Will. Sue had said she'd had enough of Lana to last a lifetime and was staying in. Jack, well… Jack's reasons for not going were obvious. He couldn't take the risk of running into people he used to get high with. I respected that. It had to be hard, and why let himself be tempted? Still, I felt bad, looking at him lying there on the bed with his laptop propped up on a pillow, and I asked, "Are you sure you don't want me to stay?"

It must have been the fifth time, and again, he gave me the same answer: "Go, Jen. Go have fun."

He was watching something, and he only ever looked up to see what I had on. I ended up choosing a pink spaghetti strap dress that hung to just above my knees. I thought it was cute. It had been a gift from Spencer, but I was pretty sure Shannon must have picked it out, since he had no taste and always got her to do his shopping for him.

"What do you think?" I asked him, my hands on my hips.

Jack's neck stretched out like a turtle's. In his tank top and cotton shorts—his summer pajamas—he grinned. I took that to mean he approved. But then he stopped me: "I'm not sure...maybe you should walk back and forth a little bit so I can get a better idea of how it fits..."

"Is it too short?" I asked.

"Is it ever too short?"

"Jack, I'm serious."

"It's perfect, Jen. You look amazing. I don't know who gave it to you, but if they were here, I'd kiss them."

"How do you know I didn't pick it out?"

"Jen, let's get real. I've seen the clothes you wear to school." There was no point in arguing. He was right: T-shirts and shorts, sweatshirts and jeans, that was pretty much all I ever donned of my own free will.

I looked at myself in the mirror and pulled my hair back into a ponytail. It was weird to me that Jack wasn't jealous—that he wasn't worried some guy would see me dressed that way and try something. Maybe that was my issue, though. Maybe I was so used to a guy trying to control me that I didn't realize the normal thing was to trust someone, accept that they cared about you, and let both people be free.

With my bag in my hand and a thin jacket draped over my arm, I bent over and kissed him on the lips. He kissed back, but he was reading an email on his phone as he did it.

"See you soon," I told him.

"Have fun, Mushu."

I flipped him a bird, putting my hand in front of his screen so I could make sure he'd seen it.

Naya and Will were in the living room waiting. Thankfully, she had already gone through her routine of hysterically pulling everything out of her closet while we were off playing basketball. For the first time in history, we wouldn't be late. Will asked if I was ready.

"Ready," I replied, then looked over at Sue, who was grunting as she tried to read some book. "See you later, loser," I told her.

I had the feeling she might have exaggerated her dislike of Lana. She probably did want to come to the party, but she felt someone should stay behind to keep Jack company. Sue was sweet in that way, even if she would never admit it.

"Sure. Try not to die," she replied to me, but then added, in a more pleasant voice, "Seriously, though. If anything cool happens, tell me."

Naya and Will barely looked at each other the whole drive. Things hadn't gotten better between them, and it was causing issues in the apartment. I didn't know if they were arguing, if they had finally made a decision, or if they were just going to pretend it wasn't happening.

For weeks now, Will had been telling her they needed to figure out what they were going to do. And Naya would always clam up, saying she had to think about it. Will would remind her that if they were having a kid, they'd need to get a bigger apartment, but whenever they looked at one, she always found something to object to. Will moved heaven and earth to make peace with her, but she was constantly snapping at him, crying, walking out of the room for no apparent reason.

It was uncomfortable, but I wasn't about to make it worse by getting in the middle of it. Naya had rarely been at a loss for words, so I was sure that sooner or later, everything would come out.

We arrived at the huge sorority house and walked up the stairway, which looked like something out of a Greek temple. It was early, but people were still roaming around, walking in and out, sitting on the steps with their drinks. We followed the music to the ballroom, which was lit up by sparkling lights that changed from green to pink to blue. Some corny song was playing, but everyone was excited about it, jumping up and down and shouting out the lyrics, which they knew by heart.

It seemed like the vibes were good, but that quickly changed when we went to the kitchen for drinks. Will reached into an ice bucket and pulled out two beers. Naya tried to grab one, but Will passed it to me instead.

Narrowing her eyes, Naya asked him, "I'm sorry, where's mine?"

"You can stick with water tonight," Will chastised her.

"Oh, so now you get to tell me whether or not I can drink?"

Pursing his lips, Will said, "I'm trying to look out for your health. For both of you."

"Are you serious?" she shrieked. "For me and the…what? The egg? The embryo? We don't even know what it is yet."

"It doesn't matter what it is," Will said firmly. "You shouldn't be drinking alcohol, and you know that as well as I do."

"Well, congratulations, mister father of the year," she said bitterly, in a whisper. She hadn't meant for him to hear her, but the music had stopped suddenly, and her tone had cut Will deep. He turned around and walked off into the crowd, fleeing the argument that was clearly about to happen.

Naya watched him go, and just when I was sure she'd start crying, she targeted me with her anger: "Aren't you going to say anything? Are you just going to take his side again?"

"I'm not on anybody's side, Naya, but any person in this room would tell you if there's a one percent chance you're having that kid, then you shouldn't drink—"

I didn't get to finish before she marched off. So there I stood, beer in hand. Surrounded by strangers. Another exciting night in the life of Jennifer Michelle Brown.

I didn't want to go home, but I also didn't really want to be there. I didn't want to drink, but there wasn't much else I could do, and I sure as hell wasn't in the mood to be out on the dance floor hopping around with a bunch of drunks. So I just took little sips of my beer, hoping that would liven me up a bit, and finally went out on the deck, which I assumed was where Naya had gone.

I found her sitting with Curtis in a wooden chair surrounded by a group of people, some of whom I knew from my classes. But instead of interacting with anyone, she had just crossed her arms and was staring out toward the city.

I thought she might feel uncomfortable if she saw me, so I started back toward the door. Curtis knew I was there, but he was distracted, with his arm around a handsome guy I'd never seen before. They were playing some game. Curtis held a card high in the air, then slapped it down on the table, and everybody cheered. After that, the two guys kissed. As I walked back into the kitchen, I found Chris looking out the window. He had seen everything. I could tell he was hurt, but that didn't stop him from putting on a cheerful face when he saw me.

I guess all of us were having a bad night. Except for Curtis, obviously.

Chris and I chatted a bit, and I went to look for Will, thinking it was best to go home. I found him in the corner drinking a beer, looking bored as he watched a game of beer pong. He didn't seem like he was in the mood to talk, though, so I walked off to a corner and took out my phone. I wanted to call Jack. Hell, I'd even have taken Sue over this. But I didn't want them to think we weren't having fun. Knowing Jack, he'd try to come rescue me, and keeping him away from the wrong influences was more important than me having a good time. So I found myself writing messages, erasing them, and scrolling through photos.

I looked up when I heard a scream. It sounded blood-curdling, but there was no danger, it was just some girl flipping out over the lead actor in Jack's movie. All heads were turned toward him, and people stepped aside to let him through. Just behind him, at the center of the entourage, was Vivian, looking much less formal than the last time I'd seen her. I guess she hadn't been lying at the premiere when she said she hated her gown: she was now wearing jeans and a plain black sweater. She looked hot, of course. She was carrying a fancy water bottle, I could see the glistening white enamel on her nails from where I stood, and she had a look of vague curiosity on her face.

I thought about saying hi to her, but I wasn't sure that was smart after what had happened the last time we were together. So I walked back to the kitchen and dumped out my beer in the sink, taking a drink of water instead. I heard her behind me:

"Hello again."

I nearly cursed. Things were just getting better by the second here. Vivian was beside me looking through the liquors on offer with disgust. Finally, she chose a cognac—*how European of her*, I thought—which she poured into her bottle before taking a sip. "I know it must look strange," she said, "but you never know how clean people are or aren't, and I really don't feel like swallowing somebody else's germs."

I had two choices: I could leave, and let her know on my way out what a snob I thought she was, or I could play nice and see if there was any chance we might get along.

"Sure," I murmured. "Nice bottle."

I remembered how at home, Sue would always scream at people for double-dipping, and how whenever she drank beer, she wouldn't touch her lips to the edge of the can. I guess Vivian had taken that to the next level. "I've got a friend I think you'd get along with," I said.

Vivian leaned against the counter and took another drink.

"Isn't that nice, you have a friend. Congratulations."

Was there something about my face that called out to people: *Hey, come over here and be an asshole to me!?* Was there something in my personality that brought out that side of people? I didn't get it. "Thanks," I grumbled.

"Is she your only one, or do you have others?"

"No, I've got quite a few. You might remember Jack."

"Ah, yes. I hope you treat the others better than you treated him."

Just as I was about to respond, I felt a hand on my shoulder. It was Lana, looking sweet and innocent, announcing, "I've been trying to find you! And you…you're Vivian, right?"

As Vivian nodded uncomfortably, Lana said, "Wow, Jenna, I see you're hanging out with high society these days."

Was that a joke? It was hard to tell, but there was a strange note in her voice, and one of her blond brows was rising in a high arch.

"Yes," I responded sarcastically. "It's only the finest people for me now. Preferably Europeans, I find they understand me better. I've even begun drinking cog-nac..." I deliberately mispronounced this last word.

"I'm sorry," Vivian interrupted us, "is this supposed to be funny?"

Lana turned to her with her hand to her heart. "Funny? What do you mean? I'm simply saying it's unusual for a woman of your status to bless us with her presence."

Vivian rolled her eyes and walked off. The crowd watched her. She pretended they didn't exist. Lana was proud of herself, and said to me, "See how easy it is? You can't let a person like that insult you to your face."

"Thanks for the lesson in evil, professor."

"No worries, you can pay me later." Lana winked. "What are you doing here by yourself? Where is everyone?"

"I kind of lost them on the way. Will and Naya are fighting, Curtis and Chris are, too, but they're in a spat of some kind. Sue and Jack did the smart thing and stayed home."

"Did you say Chris? Like, Naya's brother Chris? Because I think I just saw him, and I'm pretty sure he was crying. I would have said something, but I figured there was no way it could be him, I've never seen him at a party before."

"Where is he?" I asked, feeling worried.

"He was on his way into the bathroom."

The poor thing. We worked our way through the crowd, which was more complicated than I might have guessed and took the better part of five minutes. When we reached the door, Will was already there pounding on it, and Naya was standing next to him, looking nervous and biting her nails.

"Open up!" she ordered her brother.

"Leave me alone!" he said.

"Chris, I'm serious!" Naya shouted.

Lana asked them what was going on.

"Nobody knows," Will said. "He was walking around crying and when I tried to come after him, I found Naya here knocking. He says he wants to be alone."

"I think it's because of Curtis," I explained. "He just saw him with another guy."

"I thought that was old news," Naya replied.

I shrugged as Lana finished the drink in her hand, looking bored by all the drama.

Naya struck the door again, commanding Chris to answer her, and that made Will flip out. He asked how she expected anyone to talk to her when she was screaming like a banshee, and she accused him of being insensitive when her brother was clearly so upset. He told her to calm down, and she told him to calm down; he told her she was overreacting, and she told him there was no such thing as overreacting when a person you loved needed you. It was obvious that they were really arguing about themselves and their situation, and I worried it would get really ugly, but then Chris appeared, cheeks streaked with tears, a big ball of toilet paper in his hand. He was panting as he looked around at us.

Sounding strangely calm, he said, "Nobody tell Curtis about this."

I don't think anybody was planning to. He went on: "It's not him anyway. I don't even really like him that much. If we really gave it a chance, I'm sure we wouldn't last five minutes. It's just…" He sniffled. "Look at you, Will, you found the person you wanted to be with when you were basically a kid. And Jenna found Ross. Lana doesn't even need to worry about it, because she could get anyone she wanted, and Curtis is the same... I'm the only one who's always left behind. I'll never find anyone to be with..."

"Chris, don't say that," Naya told him, hugging him. "Of course you'll find someone."

"And plus, buddy," Will added, "it's not like you just meet a person and all of a sudden you're happy. Nobody's perfect, and relationships are a lot of work."

"It's not that, though," Chris said, "it's me. There's nothing special about me. I'm not funny, I don't have an interesting job, I'm not good at sports, I don't know how to talk to people, I don't have a good body, I'm not handsome. I'm nothing."

"That's not true," Will interrupted him. "You're...uh...you're really organized."

"What Will means is, you've got your life in order. You're solid, a guy people know they can count on. And that's one of the rarest traits there is," Naya corrected him.

Will nodded and said, "Yeah, and you're sharp as a tack. Even when we were little, Naya always said there was no puzzle you couldn't solve, no riddle you didn't get."

It was clear none of this was helping. Chris's head was hanging as he told his sister, "I sure never impressed Mom and Dad."

"Whatever!" Naya said. "Screw Mom and Dad! They've always just thought about themselves. Who needs them? You and I have got each other. We always have, and we always will. And since you apparently haven't noticed how great you are, let me tell you something else: I can't think of one other person who puts other people ahead of themselves the way you do. I know I don't, I never could. Do you have any idea how rare that is, how amazing? Just look right now: we're all standing here around you worried sick, because you mean that much to us. We wouldn't be doing that if you weren't the person you are."

Chris dried his eyes and asked Will to join him and his sister for a group hug. After a few seconds, he finally smiled and said, "Thank you guys. You're going to be amazing parents."

Lana choked on her drink and said, "P-parents...? What the...?"

"Shhh!" I said, covering her mouth. "Don't ruin the moment."

"I think Chris already did," Will said. "But it's fine."

Naya asked Chris if he wanted a ride home, and he nodded. I was glad, because that meant we were leaving. Thankfully, I didn't run into Vivian on the way out, and Chris didn't run into Curtis, either. Lana walked us to the door and waved goodbye as we were getting into the car. I treasured the silence once I shut the door, and almost instantly, Chris fell asleep next to me. I couldn't help but notice how Will and Naya smiled whenever they looked at each other on the drive home. I guess they'd finally made it through the crisis.

16

INTERVIEW TIME

I'd been trying and trying, but I couldn't hold it in any longer: "Naya, might I know what the hell you're doing?"

For ten minutes, she'd had her shirt lifted up and was moving some white thing all over her stomach. Whatever she was trying to do evidently wasn't working, because she wouldn't stop cursing between clenched teeth.

"I'm trying to hear the baby's heartbeat," she replied, very focused.

"How pregnant are you again?"

"I don't know. Six weeks, maybe."

"I think that's a little soon."

"Who asked what you think?" she snapped. "I want to hear it, and I'm going to hear it, and that's that."

Jack lowered the volume on the TV and asked me, "What's she doing?"

"Now you're jumping in," Naya jumped in. "Can't everyone just leave me alone? I'm trying to hear my baby's heartbeat, Ross."

"Did I miss the moment you decided to keep it?" Jack asked.

"I wasn't aware I had to inform you," she replied. "Anyway, yes, I'm keeping it, I'm going to be an excellent mother despite whatever you may think, and if you make any smart comments, I'll throw this thing at your head."

"Jeez. I was just asking," Jack said.

"Wiiiiiiill!" Naya cried. "I think something's wrong!" As always when she was upset, Will came running out of his room, looking pallid and scared, and asked her, "What is it? Does something hurt? Are you sick? Is it…?"

"I can't hear the baby's heartbeat!" she shouted.

Will closed his eyes, trying to gather as much patience as he could before telling her, "Naya, you're six weeks pregnant. Of course you can't hear the heartbeat. Now put that damned thing away! Doctors say they can be dangerous!"

"I've been reading tons of stuff on the internet, and I didn't see anything about it."

"Oh, the internet!" Sue piped up. "The same internet that tells you how Avril Lavigne is really a lizard person? Good job, you're a crack researcher."

I decided to try and help out: "It's too early, Naya. I think it's something like twelve weeks till you can consistently hear a heartbeat. And Will and Sue are right. Don't take this the wrong way, but you're not a doctor. Now just relax and take care of yourself and rest and look forward to when you can finally hold that baby in your arms."

"I like how you skipped on the gross part. The baby has to come out before she can hold it. You do know giving birth is the worst pain you'll ever experience, right?" Sue asked her.

Someone knocked at the door. Will went to answer while Naya, still looking suspicious, as if she didn't trust any of us, rolled up the cords on her machine and lowered her T-shirt with an expression of defeat.

"Does somebody want to tell me where the star of the show is?" said a voice that sounded vaguely familiar. No one else reacted except Jack, who instantly panicked, flopping on the floor and crawling behind Sue's armchair to hide, almost knocking it down in the process. Alas, his efforts were in vain. Joey walked in, crossing his arms and knitting his brow as he stood in the middle of the living room.

"There you are!" he called out.

Jack's butt was clearly visible from behind the chair. His eyes peeked around the other side. "I'm off today," he protested.

Joey was incensed. "You're off? You think you deserve a day off? Should I remind you that you took months off to go to rehab, and you've been MIA ever since? It's almost June! Now we need to talk. No more excuses."

"What's so urgent?" Jack asked. "I'm busy."

"He's busy watching television," Will butted in.

Jack's shoulders sank as he finally got serious with Joey. "Whatever it is, I don't want to do it."

"Ross," Joey began, "if it was up to me, I'd let you live your life, but you signed a contract, and you committed to promoting the film. Now, it's just two interviews. The production company can make you pay serious money for bailing on these things, and we're still at the very beginning here."

"I've been planning on going out of town," Jack said. "Jen and I were thinking of spending the summer somewhere."

Surprised, everybody turned to me. I smiled awkwardly and shrugged.

"Look, Ross," Joey tried to reason with him. "I know you've been through some tough times, and I'm the first person to give you credit for doing what you did, with the rehab and all that. But still, rules are rules. You can't just up and vanish right now. You're not the only person in the world with problems. I'm not asking a lot, but what I am asking, I need you to do."

Jack sighed, walked over to the couch, and slumped down next to me. Will asked when we were leaving, and I told him we didn't have a solid plan yet, but we were thinking sometime in the middle of June.

"Great," Joey said. "Let's do this, then: we'll go ahead and set up some media spots now, and I promise you whatever comes up afterward, I'll try to make it something you can do over email or Zoom. Then we can pick back up when you're home."

Jack frowned, but he really couldn't object. I thought it was a good idea, and I said so. And to relieve Jack's worries, I added, "You worry about your stuff, and I'll take care of the details for the trip, OK?"

"I'll help," Naya said. "I'm the queen of cheap flights and hotels."

Joey leaned over Jack and stuck out his hand. "So…do we have a deal?"

"I guess so," Jack replied.

"Good. Then get your ass up off the couch and throw on something decent, because I went ahead and set up an interview for half an hour from now."

Jack groaned and scuffled off to the bathroom.

"You're good at that," Sue told Joey. "None of us can get him to do anything. Maybe you want to move in?"

"Yeah…" he said, glancing at his phone. "I don't think so. What are there, like five of you here? I need my privacy, my days of living with roommates are over. Tell the little prince I'll be waiting downstairs in my car."

He turned, stuck his hand in the bag of cookies Naya was eating, bit into one, and walked out the door.

Jack did his part and dressed up, enough to elicit laughter from Will and Sue. Not Naya—she was already hypnotized by the internet, shouting out places we could stay, hotel prices, attractions. I didn't get why she cared, but since it kept her mind off her own issues, I let it slide and went to work on dinner. Jack gave me a kiss goodbye. When I was done and had set out everyone's dishes, Naya started grilling me:

"Somewhere hot or somewhere cool?"

"I don't know…it's summer. So hot, right?"

"OK, hot…" She was typing at an alarming pace. "Beach or mountains?"

"Beach. That way I can get a little tan."

I remembered how when I was little, my siblings always said I was shorter than them because Mom spent so much time swimming when she was pregnant, and the warm water had made me shrink, like wool when you wash it too hot. The pathetic thing is, I believed them. I thought the story would entertain my roommates, but when I told it, Naya responded, "Oh waah. That must have been so traumatizing. Now can we focus on planning your trip? I'm thinking Australia."

"It's a little far, isn't it?"

"Plus, there's all kinds of creepy animals there, it's like *Jumanji*," Sue piped up. "They've got sharks, alligators, kangaroos. A kangaroo can kick you and knock you out!"

"OK, fine," Naya said. "Then how about Italy?"

"I don't know," I said. "For some reason, Italy's never really attracted me."

"OK, well, you could go to Rangiroa in French Polynesia. That'll be something new for you."

I thought she was just saying that out of frustration, but I reminded her, "I think Jack already got his fill of all things French last year. What about… I don't know…what about Greece?"

I could tell Naya thought it was a good idea, even if she didn't like that I'd come up with it and she wouldn't be able to take credit for it.

"Done. Greece," she said. "Athens or the islands?"

"Islands."

"There he is!" Sue shouted. We all turned to see Jack on the television. He was with Vivian, sitting on a brown sofa on a stage set to look like a regular living room. Now and then, the camera turned to the public, which laughed at the presenter's jokes. He was a middle-aged man in small glasses with an energetic smile.

Images flashed on-screen of Vivian's and her fellow actors' promotional tour across the US, including events with fans. She was glowing, as always. Poor Jack looked nervous. He was playing with his water glass as she spoke, forcing a smile to pretend that the conversation mattered to him.

The presenter said, "I suppose you all must be tired of answering this, but I can't help myself. What does it feel like to be in your position? Did you expect to be this successful?"

I pursed my lips. Vivian seemed to relish the fame and fortune, and especially the chance to act like she was better than everyone else. Jack wasn't like that, though. He hadn't changed, and I was pretty sure he didn't want to. I worried the question would upset him, and Will must have, too, because I could see the tension in his shoulders.

"It's amazing," Vivian said, smiling her professional smile. "It's like a dream, really, like none of this was real, like I'll wake up tomorrow and be the same old me from before. Knowing people are so happy with the work we've done…is there anything more gratifying?"

The public applauded, and Sue rolled her eyes. "Aw, isn't that just so sweet? It makes me want to go jump over a fucking rainbow. I swear, I'm glad I'm not famous, I'd probably hate people more than I already do."

I think even Vivian knew how cheesy her response was. She looked too trained, too perfect. It was almost sad, like she didn't trust herself to just be a person and act sincere. Jack, though… Jack was a different story. He grinned uncomfortably, thought the question over, and started to speak, and I could just imagine Joey fainting as he watched him in the wings.

"Honestly," he said, "my life hasn't changed much. I've still got the same friends, I still live in the same place, I'm still writing scripts like before… really, everything's the same."

The presenter smiled, and I breathed a sigh of relief. "How interesting. So what do your friends think about this new aspect of your life? Have they seen your film?"

Everyone tensed up, and Naya and Will looked back and forth at each other. Was it because of me? Because I was the only one who hadn't seen it?

"Most of them have." Jack cleared his throat. "They liked it. But that's all, I don't have some sort of moving story to tell you about it. The joke people like to make is everyone took it for granted that my first movie would be horror. Nobody expected me to do romance."

"A tragic romance, you mean," the interviewer corrected him, looking interested. "That's something numerous people have remarked on. This sort of dark air that's always enveloping the characters. Do you have any-thing to say about that?"

Vivian looked like she was grinding her teeth. Jack turned serious. "Not every love story has a fairytale ending. I'm trying to be a realist here."

"Are you saying there are no happy love stories?" the presenter asked.

"In real life?" Jack responded. "Not many."

The interviewer narrowed his eyes. "I wonder if you're speaking from experience?"

Vivian burst in, and to tell the truth, I was glad she did: "What Ross means is that happy stories are nice, but they're not the only stories we can tell. Sad stories deserve to be told, too."

The audience seemed to agree. As for Jack... I couldn't tell what he was thinking. He was leaning forward, his chin resting on his fist while his other hand clutched his glass. Vivian looked over, trying to catch his eye. She was clearly trying to throw him a lifeline, but it was futile. The presenter knew this could blow up, and he was perfectly happy to let that happen. "Interesting," he said. "Do you agree, Ross? Do you think tragic stories deserve to be told? I'm asking because we all know you've been off the scene these past few months, and maybe there's a story there you'd like to tell us?"

I was frozen, as were my roommates. I don't know how Jack managed it, but he didn't give anything away. Only those who really knew him would have noticed the change in his expression. "There's nothing to tell there," he said. "I had a family member who was sick. Someone I had to take care of."

"Were you aware of this, Vivian?" the presenter asked.

"Of course. Ross and I are close. I was by his side the whole time."

As the crowd said *oooooh* and Jack and Vivian relaxed and the conversation turned to other subjects, I realized what those words had concealed: I hadn't been able to visit Jack in rehab, and Vivian had been going the entire time.

Will, Sue, and Naya all looked like they were deliberately avoiding eye contact with me. Did they know? Had they understood her words the way I had? I couldn't tell. They all kept eating in silence as Will flicked through the channels.

A few minutes later, Sue walked off to her room. Naya and Will started smooching, then disappeared as well. I tried to get a grip on how I felt. It wasn't as if he'd said he was in love with her. But he had admitted that when the going got tough, he had wanted her in his life and not me. And that had a weird sting to it. A kiss, a hookup…those were things that happened. But *trusting* someone…did that mean he didn't trust me? The thought scared me, because I already had a hidden fear that we would never get back the level of faith in each other we'd had when our relationship began. And now, he had almost confirmed it.

Was I angry with him? Did I have reason to be? I was asking myself this obsessively when Mike got home. He was twirling the keys on his finger and they took off flying, striking a glass on the bar. As he ran over to try and save it, he realized I was there and said, "Did you see that save? Just like a ninja. Admit you were impressed."

"Very," I responded. "That's why I didn't manage to say anything."

Mike flopped down next to me, completely oblivious to my mood, threw an arm around me, and pulled me close to him. His raggedy T-shirt was full of holes, and his Bermuda shorts looked like something from a thrift shop. "Good to see you, sister-in-law!"

"What is it?" I asked. "You only ever act this way when you want something."

"Ouch. That hurts. And it's not true, anyway, or not really. I was just wondering if you might give up the rest of the couch. I'm beat, I'm basically sleepwalking. I mean, you could share it with me if you like, far be it from me to repress a lady's desires."

"No thanks," I said.

But I didn't make it up before Jack walked in, dragging his feet just as when he'd left. He didn't look especially happy to see me. Mike, rambunctious as usual, told him how he'd seen him on the television and had said to himself, *Jeez, that's my brother.* "I forget sometimes you're actually famous now."

Jack ignored him. I don't know what expression he had on his face—I was resting my chin on my knees, turned away from him—but when he told me, "Jen, let's go to the bedroom and talk," I was sure I could hear the guilt in his voice.

Of course, I wanted to say yes—I wanted to know what was going on—but I also wasn't in the mood for a serious talk, especially one where I might get hurt. Not that night. So I said, "Why don't you go ahead? I'm not really tired."

I didn't mean that to sound angry, but I was sure it did. Jack groaned and said, "Come on. Please."

I didn't like to be ordered around, but I was also embarrassed to be doing this in front of Mike, who stood, to his credit, and said, "Look, guys, it seems like something's up with you all, so I'm going to beat it and let you talk in peace."

"Don't worry about it, Mike, we're good," I said, and got up to follow Jack to his room. Mike shrugged, flopped down, and closed his eyes. Once we'd shut the door behind us, I took my time choosing my pajamas and Jack walked around to the front of the bed, crossing his arms.

"Listen, before you scream at me…"

"Jack," I said, "you should ask yourself if that's really how you want to start this. If you truly think it's a good idea to start this conversation with the suggestion that I'm the one being irrational when I just had to find out on a goddamn TV program that *she* got to go see you and *I* didn't. Think about how that made me feel. Do you not trust me? Because otherwise, I really don't get it."

I could feel myself flushing from head to toe. He didn't want me to get defensive? Well fine, I'd go on the offense. Jack tried to tell me I was jumping to conclusions, but I spoke over him, raising my voice: "What was the phrase you used: *No more secrets, I promise*? What happened to that? And another thing: how would you feel if the tables were turned? You nearly lost your damned mind when Curtis came over here, and I've only ever seen him outside of class a handful of times! How in the hell do you think I feel knowing *she* was there?"

"It's not the same," he said. And before I could start yelling again, he added, "Vivian knows what it means to go through this. You don't!"

My heart was pounding, and I was almost scared. I hadn't expected things to get so heated so quickly. Frustrated, Jack ran his hand through his hair. I had two options: I could get even angrier and start a screaming match, which was tempting, or I could be an adult and try to restore peace, which was boring.

"Maybe that's true," I said, drawing a breath, "but does that mean I didn't have the right to be there and support you?"

"It's not that easy."

"What do you mean, it's not that easy? It's not that easy to put me on a list, come out and see me, and let me lend you a hand? What the hell do you think it feels like, knowing everyone got to go see you there but me?"

"Jen, dammit, listen to me! Rehab isn't some cakewalk! It gets ugly in there! *I* got ugly in there! I said some nasty things to people, things I still regret, and I didn't want to do that to you. You can't imagine the person I became. And I didn't want…"

"Jack, listen to me." I walked over to him, cradled his face in my hands, and looked at the little green flecks in his chestnut-brown eyes, which were sadder than I'd ever seen them. "Let's get one thing straight. I need you to believe—I need you to stop everything right now and believe—that I'm not going to turn around and run off every time you do something wrong. OK? Because I won't. Never. I'm with you. I'm here. And I'm not going to leave. What can I do to get you to understand that?"

He mumbled, "It's not you, Jen. It's just…"

"Whatever." It was time to put the issue to bed. "It's fine. You didn't tell me. It is what it is. I hid things from you before, I wish you hadn't hidden this from me, but I'll deal with it, it hurts, but we'll get past it. She's your friend, so I'll try to… I don't know…get along with her or whatever. If it will make things easier, I mean."

I tried to smile reassuringly, but I couldn't manage it when I saw his expression, which had changed from nervous to…cautious? *Oh no.*

"What?" I asked him. I could sense I wasn't going to like what I was about to hear. Instinctively, my hands dropped to my sides and I turned away.

"There's something you need to know."

"What?" I asked.

"Remember when I told you I…that I didn't do anything with anybody for the year we were apart?"

I turned back at him and glared. I didn't like where this was going. Not one bit. "Oh, so that was a lie? Is that what you need to tell me?"

"I mean, I… OK, I kissed some people, you know. And with some people it went a little farther than that. Don't think I was out there just hooking up with just whoever, though."

"What about Vivian? Does she count as *just whoever*?"

"It's not that simple," he said.

"Oh, it's not? Because it sure sounds like it is. You either slept with her or you didn't. Tell me what's complicated about that? You do realize you lied to me, right, Jack? You asked me to be sincere, and I have been one hundred percent honest with you since then, and now it turns out you lied to me about sleeping with someone?!"

"I didn't know how you'd react!"

"How the hell do you want me to react?!" I screamed. "You want me to clap for you? Tell you, *hey, great job*, Jack? Ask for details?"

Furious, I turned around to walk out, but he grabbed my arm and stopped me. "Jen," he begged. "I'm sorry. I was wrong."

"Did you think I couldn't take it? I mean, we weren't together at the time. You didn't owe me anything. But now you supposedly *are* with me, and you still can't be honest with me?"

"*Supposedly?* What the hell is that supposed to mean?"

I couldn't believe that was what had gotten to him out of all the things I'd just said. "Drop it, all right?" I told him.

"No, I'm not dropping it. Vivian is my friend. And it was my birthday. She'd been having a tough time, I had, too…and it just happened. It was right after that when I had my relapse. There's the story. We've never done anything again since. No kissing, no nothing. I swear."

"Jack, please. Don't lie to me again. I can't take it. I've seen her. She's charming, she's hot, she's a literal fucking movie star. How can you expect me to believe you're not into her?"

"I do like her, we hang out, but as friends! I'm not attracted to her! I don't even see her in that way."

"Great, why'd you sleep with her the first time then?"

That caught him by surprise. His mouth fell open, and unable to find an answer, he decided to strike back at me: "Well what about your charming, hot friend that you just happen to share half your classes with? How many times have I had to hear the name *Curtis* this year? You don't see me losing my shit over it!"

"Please tell me you're kidding! First of all, Curtis and I don't even hang out anymore, he's seeing somebody and he hardly even answers my texts. And second, you *did* lose your shit, like an absolute child, the first time he came over, and you haven't stopped whining about it since. Third, I'm pretty sure he's more into guys. He's never even hinted at the possibility of us doing anything."

"Of course not. He's probably putting on an act to try and get in your pants later."

If that wasn't the most ridiculous thing Jack had ever said, it was pretty far up there, and Curtis cracked up laughing when I told him about it. It was funny, but that didn't mean I wasn't pissed off. We were out on the lawn in front of the fine arts building, and he actually shook as he lay back on the grass.

"The *act* I put on," he repeated. "Please tell me he didn't actually say that."

"Of course he did! I couldn't make that up."

"What, is he living in the nineteen-seventies? Is he one of those idiots who's like *bi people don't exist*? You know what, I don't care. What happened afterward? Did you have make-up sex?"

"No. We just argued some more and then slept with our backs turned to each other," I said.

"That's how all the greatest love stories end."

"I'm glad you think my life is so funny," I told him.

"Seriously, though," he added, "I get being angry, but you guys *were* apart when he got with Vivian. He couldn't change his past by the time you came back, and the real message here is that he wanted to be with you again and was scared he'd lose you. And that's nice, in a way. I wonder if there's not other things going on, too. Like maybe if you weren't so worried about your grades, you'd be more chill about it."

That was a possibility. The mere mention of school made me check my watch. Grades were getting posted online that day, and I was so nervous, I'd asked him if we could be together to give each other moral support.

"OK," I admitted, "maybe you have a point. Maybe my nerves have been a little frayed. But you can't act like him lying to me about sleeping with her isn't a big deal."

"I don't know," Curtis said. "I just don't see it that way. Maybe it's because I'm a guy. Anyway, you'll probably come home and find out he's bought you flowers."

"Screw flowers. I want a cake."

His phone dinged. It was time. I sat there in a panic as he opened the page on his phone. If his grades are bad, I won't even look at mine, I thought. That was silly, but it gave me something to hang on to while I was waiting in agony.

"All right," he began, "here goes: pass, pass, fail, pass, fail. Not bad, right?"

"Curtis! You're so smart! How did you fail two classes? They'll put you on academic probation."

"Whatever, I saw it coming. I'll be fine. I don't know what the hell I want to do with my life, anyway, I was already thinking I might go back home for a few months and try to get my head together."

"You're unbelievable," I said, taking out my phone and navigating to the page. Heart pounding, I added, "I guess this is it. Let's see. A, great. B, OK, sure. A, amazing… Oh my God, Curtis, I passed everything! I just got one C! I can't believe it!"

I jumped up so high that I sent my phone flying, but I didn't care—I could get a new one if I had to. Curtis was excited, too. We fell on the ground and hugged and rolled back and forth, while the other students stared at us, perplexed. I didn't care. I'd set a goal for myself, and I'd accomplished it. I was still overjoyed when I got home that afternoon, so much that I could hardly remember being angry the night before.

Mike and Sue were sitting in the living room when I arrived. I skipped in, and she observed, "I guess you're not fighting after all."

"Excuse me?" I asked.

Mike explained: "We were arguing about what the hell had happened between you guys that would make my brother go into the kitchen to try and cook dinner. We figured he had to be making up for something he'd done wrong."

I turned and saw Jack wearing a pair of red oven mitts and pulling a casserole dish out of the oven. He hadn't heard us—he had on his noise-canceling headphones. I grabbed his phone off the counter and saw he was listening to a cooking tutorial on YouTube. It was so sweet. I walked in there without thinking and tapped him on the shoulder, hoping to see what he was cooking.

"AAAH!" he screamed, twitching and dropping the dish, sending whatever it contained—it was some unidentifiable black-and-red mush, and in all honesty, it looked atrocious—flying across the kitchen.

We both stood there staring briefly at the disaster. "Oops," I said.

Jack took off the oven mitts with a defeated gesture. "There goes my first and last attempt at cooking lasagna."

So that charred, runny mass was supposed to be lasagna? I had the feeling I had saved our household from certain death. I to conceal my disgust as I told him, "I'm sorry, Jack. It looked…great."

"You don't have to lie," he said, removing his headphones.

"Did you decide to cook to tell me you're sorry, or are we celebrating because the school year's officially over?"

"I was more thinking the second, but if you'll accept this as an apology, I'm cool with that, too."

"It's just two words," I told him.

"Fine," he said. "I'm sorry. I shouldn't have hidden something like that, and especially not for so long. But I meant what I said. There are no feelings there whatsoever. She's my friend, that's all. And she doesn't have feelings for me, either. I know she was mean to you. It's because she's got this…idea about you, because of the things I told her a year ago. I've been trying to get her to understand that it was complicated, and that isn't who you are or were, but she's struggling with it."

"Look, Jack, there's something I need to admit to myself, too: I did it. I did leave. I made up that story about Monty because I thought I knew better than you what you were supposed to do with your life. I can't keep pretending otherwise. So let's make a deal: you focus on your things, and I'll see if I can soften Vivian up. And if not, it doesn't matter. But I don't want you to have to worry about it anymore. You've already got too much on your mind."

"Does that mean you forgive me?"

"How about we do this: I'll clean up your lasagna disaster, you make me your famous chili, and we'll agree to forgive each other."

"NO!" Mike and Sue shrieked in unison.

"Don't listen to them, they're just a couple of haters," I said.

"Deal!" Jack shouted. He got to work, and I turned to Mike and Sue, who were groaning with disgust. I stuck my tongue out at them.

17

SHRILL SERGEANT

My theory is that nobody actually likes September. Kids have to go back to school, summer's over, the leaves start falling off the trees, it's back to the grind…and Jack and I had to come back from vacation.

It wasn't all bad: I had a killer tan, and I'd enjoyed myself in Greece. We'd been there nearly two months, but for me, the trip had been too short. Jack being Jack, he said we could just stay there. Even on the plane, he kept telling me that as soon we got to the airport, we could go to the counter, buy a return ticket, go back, and never return home.

But we had things to do. My semester was starting, he needed to promote his film… Marvelous as just giving it all up sounded, we couldn't ignore our responsibilities.

Jack had made me a promise when we were in Greece, and when we got back, I planned on making him stick to it. I wanted him to teach me to drive. I didn't like being so dependent. It was time to learn how to take care of myself.

He was surprised, but not enthusiastic, and whatever goodwill he might have felt about the whole thing vanished when Mike told us he wanted to tag along. And so one day, there we were, Jack in the driver's seat and me to his right, with Will in the back seat trying to relax while Mike stuck his head between us and announced: "That's right, ladies and gentlemen, you are now present for the first-ever driving class of the young and alluring Jennifer Brown! Will she make it? Will young Jackie still have a car when it's all over? Soon, all shall be revealed!"

Jack pulled the emergency brake and said, "Stop joking around!"

"He's just mad because in his heart he knows I'm a natural, I'll be driving better than him in no time," I informed Mike.

"Sure," Jack said snidely. "Just remember, when you need a shoulder to cry on the fifth time you fail your driving test, I'm here for you."

I rolled my eyes and got out. Jack sighed and did the same. Once we'd changed places, I rubbed my hands together enthusiastically. "So this is what it feels like to be you," I said.

"I'm already regretting this," he replied.

"Ross!" Mike exclaimed. "Don't be such a loser. She's going to do great."

Will, who had come along, added, "And worst-case scenario, if she wrecks, you can finally buy a car that actually looks cool."

Will and Mike buckled up. I think secretly they hoped a disaster would happen. I'd invited Naya along for moral support, but I think she and Will were more worried about their baby than my desire for independence, and prudently, she decided to stay home. I was excited, though. Humming to myself, I started touching all the buttons, flipping the levers, putting on the windshield wipers, hitting the turn signal when I tried to turn them off, honking the horn.

The guys mentioned that they'd taken bets back at home on how I would do. Everyone had agreed I'd screw it up—the only question was how bad—so when Jack said he'd taken my side and was sure I'd be great, I knew it was a lie.

"Shut up, y'all!" I said. "Now where's the, uh, start button?"

Jack buried his head in his hands and moaned, "My poor car...there's no way it will survive."

"Have faith," I encouraged him.

"Jen," he replied, "I'm begging you. Please, please don't ruin my car. It's the thing I love mo—it's the thing I love second-most in the world."

"After his bed," Mike said. Will pulled him back into the back seat and Jack got serious.

"Let's start with the pedals."

"Cool, where are those?"

A look of horror crossed his face, and I rushed to add, "Jack, I'm kidding!"

"Get out," he said. "I've changed my mind. I'm driving us home."

"No!" I responded, grabbing his arm. "It really was a joke. Give me another chance. I'll be careful, I promise."

Jack thought it over, then relaxed and told me about the clutch, the accelerator, and the brake. He must have been the last guy in the world to own a stick shift, but I thought that was for the best. If I could drive his car, then I could drive anything. As if I'd never been in an automobile before, he pointed out the gears, the hand brake, how the steering wheel worked—all things I knew, but I decided to be polite and listen along. There was only one thing I wanted: to hit the gas and take off. But I restrained myself. When the explanations were done, Jack looked down into his lap as though preparing himself for a certain death.

"It's time," he said, turning the key for me. The motor roared, and I said, "Let's go!"

Mike checked his seatbelt and asked, "What do you think Naya and Sue will do if we die?"

"Throw a party," Will answered. "Just think, it'll mean twice as much room for the baby."

"And one less parasite on the sofa," Jack added. "Now Jen, let's get this thing going before I change my mind. And take it easy, please."

I put it in first and stalled out. On my second try, Jack rested his hand on top of mine to reassure me. I knew he was nervous, but he made sure I knew he believed in me: "Easy now. You're already in first. Let's start over…"

I did as he said, and slowly, the car crawled forward. I tried to contain my excitement as I squeezed the wheel. Ten miles an hour! I was doing it! I smiled and looked over at Jack. "Am I doing OK?"

"You're doing great, babe. Now we're going to try to reach that post over there. Keep your speed up, turn a little, and…hey, what are you giggling about?"

"I don't think I've ever seen you this nervous," I said. "It's cute."

As he reproached me—*Jen, please*—I tried to listen close. Jack thought I was being too hesitant and cut the wheel a bit. We passed the post, and he told me to speed up and pull into a lot ahead of us. We went on turning circles, parking, restarting for what must have been an hour. When it was done, I felt better, and I think Jack did, too.

Will was the first to congratulate me, giving me an affectionate squeeze on the shoulder. "You look surprised," I said, mocking him. Mike pretended to pat himself down to check if anything was broken, and thanked God we were all still alive.

Jack shook his head, relieved, and announced, "Now it's time for the big test: You want to drive us home?"

I was nervous, but I nodded. We weren't far away. I wouldn't have to take any busy roads. I proceeded slowly, nearly stopping at the speed bumps, and when everyone joked that I was being too cautious, I cut loose and sped up to twenty-five miles an hour. I finally felt relaxed. But then I heard a scream:

"JENNA, WATCH OUT! CAT!"

I stomped on the brakes so hard the car shook and everybody lurched forward. Jack's arm shot across my chest, and I felt the seatbelt knock the wind out of me. I was gripping the steering wheel so tight, there was no blood left in my knuckles. Of course, there wasn't a damn cat in sight.

I heard cackling from the back seat. Mike. Jack turned and screamed, "What in the hell is wrong with you?!"

"I thought it would be funny," he replied. "Anyway, drivers need to be ready for stuff like that. Alertness, that's the most important thing when you're behind the wheel."

"You're literally the stupidest person I've ever met," Jack reproached him.

"Shut up, man," Mike said. "I think I broke my nose." Apparently, he had struck it against my headrest. It served him right.

"I don't really want to do this anymore," I told Jack, and he responded, "That's probably for the best," switching places with me and speeding off as Mike complained that he was bleeding on his T-shirt.

Jack added: "One more thing, Jen: don't even think of apologizing to my brother. He deserves it. I hope it's a permanent injury."

This wasn't the first episode of that kind. Mike had been acting weird ever since we'd been back. His arguments with Jack were getting more personal, and his jokes and pranks were more annoying than ever. And every time someone pointed out the obvious, that he was acting like a child, he'd pout and stew for hours.

He wasn't the only one who had changed, though. Naya's pregnancy was making her crazy. And that, in turn, was making Will crazy, because he had to spend all his time with her. Lana had fallen head-over-heels for some guy. Curtis had dropped out and gone home, where he was supposedly working in a coffee shop. And Sue…well, Sue was like a mushroom, you couldn't expect her to change very much.

Mike stumbled into the apartment holding his nose, and Sue looked up gleefully, saying, "Please tell me someone finally punched you out."

"It was an accident!" I clarified.

She sighed and looked back down into her book, unimpressed.

As Will joined Naya in the kitchen, where she was cooking up some monstrosity, Jack announced, "I'm proud to say that Jen was driving like a dream until my moron brother scared her."

"Yeah, he's actually letting me take the car out tonight on my own," I told Sue, waiting to see how Jack would respond to the provocation.

Sue and Mike chuckled as he said reluctantly, "Yeah, sure, if that's what you want."

I smiled and threw my hands around his neck, kissing him on the cheek. But he turned so that our lips met, and what was meant to be an innocent peck turned into something a little racier.

"Good lord," Sue groaned. "Like we didn't have enough cheesiness around here with Will and Naya. Now we've got to put up with the two of you."

"Seriously, guys," Mike said.

Jack let me go a moment, grabbed a pillow, and tossed it at his brother. "Don't be jealous, buddy. I'm sure you'll meet a lovely girl someday. Not."

Mike went to throw it back, but Sue caught it, smoothed it out, and set it down on her lap. On his way to join Will for a smoke, Jack caressed my face gently. I wasn't sure where all this was coming from, but I wasn't going to complain.

Naya emerged from the kitchen a few minutes later with a tray of what she called chocolate cookies. They were charcoal-black and shriveled, and the dough must have been too liquidy, because they'd run together into two giant perforated blobs. They barely looked edible, but with Naya acting like a madwoman lately, we knew it was better to feign enthusiasm.

"It's my first try," Naya said. "I'm working on some recipes for when the baby's born. I want it to really love me."

"Sugar *is* the way to a kid's heart," Sue said. In the meantime, Mike had managed to peel away one of the cookies and was eyeing it up cautiously, trying and failing to find a spot that wasn't burned to a crisp.

"Mike, just eat it!" Naya said.

"I'd better not," he responded, setting it carefully back on the tray. Right away, he knew he'd made a mistake.

Tears instantly formed in Naya's eyes. "I know! They're horrible!"

"No!" Mike corrected himself, biting off a teeny corner, which he chewed up and swallowed reluctantly. "They're not that bad." He ran to the kitchen for a butter knife and started scraping off the charred part. "See? They're still OK inside."

"I'm a horrible cook," Naya said. "If Will had made them, they'd have turned out perfect. I'm going to be a horrible mom, too." She sat beside me, leaned back, and began to whimper, her bottom lip quivering.

"You're going to be a great mother!" I told her.

"It's not true. I'm not built to take care of another person!"

From the kitchen, where he was still scraping a cookie down to nothing, Mike called, "I think you're taking this a little too far over one failed cooking experiment. I can barely turn an oven on, and you don't see me whining about it."

"It's not about the food!!!" Naya shouted.

"The burnt cookies are a metaphor for her future as a mother," Sue noted with raised eyebrows.

Naya stormed off to her room, and I followed after her. Over the summer, Will had bought a bunch of stuff for the kid, and most of it was still in boxes. There were toys, a crib, and a high chair. He was clearly excited about the big day. I couldn't help but smile, even if Naya was crying on the bed rubbing her belly.

"Naya, honey, what's up?" I asked. "Do you need to talk?"

Looking down at her stomach, she replied, "I just don't think I can do this."

"Why?"

"It's not like everyone says, Jen. I'm not excited, I'm not happy, I don't feel some maternal instinct welling up inside me… I thought it would be like a Lifetime movie, but the excitement just isn't there. Every time I see one of those happy mothers hugging her kid at the park or something, I can't stop telling myself, that just isn't me."

"Being a mom isn't something you feel, Naya. It's something you learn, something you grow into."

"You think?" I saw something like grief in her eyes.

"I don't think, I know. Do you really believe all the mothers out there were just born with the knowledge of how all this works? Give yourself a chance, Naya. You're making a lot of progress, and uh…you're getting better! You didn't burn the cookies as bad as you burned the pizza you made that one time."

"I just wish there was a webpage with some halfway decent advice."

"Naya, there are a million webpages with more information about parenting than you could ever possibly need."

I pulled out my phone and opened my browser. *Google, save me now*, I thought. I didn't know what I'd do if I had to deal with Naya's whining for the next three months. Of course, everything I found was stupid. Eventually, I settled on a list of questionable-looking *Mommy Hacks*. It was better than nothing. Or so I hoped.

"Here's some stuff," I said. "One, aromatherapy."

"Pass."

"Yoga?"

"Pass. My feet are so swollen, I can hardly stand. How am I supposed to do yoga?"

"OK, here's one," I said. "Scream therapy. Promises to relieve all the tension in your body. They say it's best to do it into a pillow to keep your neighbors from worrying."

This seemed to interest her. "I'll skip the pillow, though," she told me.

We stood, and she began to limber up as if for a workout. It was ludicrous, but I was in it to win it. The disciplinarian in me was coming out. Naya was no longer my friend, she was a grunt than needed to be whipped into shape.

"Ready?" I asked.

"Ready!"

"Set?"

"Set!"

"I can't hear you, soldier. LOUDER!"

"READY!" Naya shouted.

"READY FOR WHAT?"

"I'M READY TO BE A MOTHER!"

"I CAN'T HEAR YOU!" I repeated.

"I'M READY TO BE A MOTHER!"

"WHAT KIND OF MOTHER?"

"THE BEST MOTHER IN THE WORLD!"

"AND WHAT KIND OF BABY ARE YOU GOING TO HAVE?" I asked.

"A HAPPY BABY!"

"HOW HAPPY?"

"THE HAPPIEST BABY IN THE WORLD!"

"SAY IT LOUDER!" I encouraged her.

"THE HAPPIEST BABY IN THE WORLD!"

We went on like this until Jack opened the door, asking, "What the hell is going…?"

"AAAAAAAAAAAAH!" Naya shrieked, so loud that Jack panicked and ran straight into the bookshelf, knocking several volumes to the floor. Naya shook her arms, letting out the adrenaline, and said with a smile, "Jenna, this really works!"

"See? All you had to do was blow off a little steam!"

"You're the best!"

Jack was cowering like a frightened animal when Sue walked in, looking livid. "Who the hell's getting murdered in here?"

"Seriously," Mike said from behind her. "Our neighbors came downstairs to complain."

"Naya was just letting out some bad energy," I explained.

"You guys should try it!" she added enthusiastically.

Sue started to say, "This is bullsh—" but before she could finish, we heard Mike bellowing like a dying buffalo. I nearly jumped out of my skin. Jack stuck his fingers in his ears.

"You dumbass, you scared the shit out of me," he said.

Mike, enthusiastic, shouted, "It really does work! Jen, you try!"

Jack, trying to make peace, announced that if one more person tried to…

I sucked in a breath and screamed as loud as I could. My throat ached when I was done. Naya and Mike applauded. Jack and Sue shook their heads. That was when Will came around the corner, panting.

"Naya, are you all right?" he said. "I was on the roof smoking and I heard the screams. Did your water break or something?"

"They're just relieving tension," Mike said. Will couldn't believe his ears.

"It works," Naya told her boyfriend. "I feel a hundred percent better. I'm ready to take on the world! I'm not going to let that dumb stove beat me! I'm going to go make another batch of cookies!"

As she skipped away, everyone else in the room turned and scowled at me.

That night, as I was trying to fall asleep, I wondered if helping Naya had been such a good idea. I could hear her grunting and groaning, telling Will all the nasty things she wanted him to do to her. It had been better when they were fighting and everyone could finally get a good night's sleep.

"Those two are killing me," I said.

Jack's face was half-buried in his pillow. He turned and said, "Please remind me why we didn't stay in Greece?"

"Because we have responsibilities?"

"That's the worst reason I've ever heard."

I smiled and reached up, pretending to slap him, but he caught my hand. "Remember that night you got all drunk...?"

"We said we weren't going to talk about that!"

"And you threw a can of beer at a cop car!"

"Jack, we had a deal!"

"No, Jen, our deal was I wouldn't tell anyone else about it. We never agreed that I couldn't bring it up."

"Cheater."

He thought it was hilarious. It still embarrassed me every time I thought of it. I'd remember that night till the end of my life. But it wasn't my fault! If a place has an open bar, they should be required by law to tell you how much alcohol is in the cocktails! The details were blurry, but the things I remembered included: dancing on the bar top, shouting at a policeman, throwing the famous can at his car's windshield and shouting that my rights weren't being respected. If it hadn't been for Jack and his million-dollar smile, I'd probably be locked up in a Greek prison for the next decade. I wasn't proud of any of it, but Jack loved lording it over me.

"Don't laugh," I told him. "Remember how you forgot your suntan lotion when we went to the beach, and you played it all cool like *oh, I don't need it*, and then you returned to the hotel that night looking like a boiled lobster? Or that night you fell asleep holding onto the bottle of insect repellent like it was your teddy bear?"

"What did you want me to do? There were mosquitoes everywhere! I can't help it if they weren't biting you."

I laughed, but stopped when I heard Will and Naya slamming against the wall.

"Do they have to make so much noise?" Jack asked.

"I try to let her off the hook because she's pregnant," I said. "When I get pregnant, I hope people will cut me some slack, too."

Wait—had I really just said that? Had he noticed?

I looked over and saw him grinning with narrowed eyes. "What are you getting at, Mushu?"

"Sorry! That just slipped out! Come on now! Obviously, I don't want kids now!" I corrected myself. "Someday it would be nice, though… right?"

"It could be now for all I care."

"Uh…" I responded. "I don't know that we're in the best place in our lives right now to take care of a baby…"

"It's never too early to dream," Jack joked. But it didn't exactly seem like a joke. I could tell as his face lit up and he added, "Imagine how handsome our kid would be. A mix of the two of us. Definite model material."

"How humble of you."

"We couldn't do it here, though," he said, looking around. "It's too crammed in. One thing is Will and Naya, it's not like I can kick them out anyway, but could you imagine if there were *two* kids in this apartment? Kids need space to run around. They're like little animals. When I was small, my parents always had me out in the yard, because I was basically a one-man wrecking crew inside… No, this place won't do. But I'll do another film, make some real money, and we can buy a mansion. Problem solved. Or you could use those paints I got you to do one of those abstract pieces, like a line across a canvas, and sell it to some idiot for a hundred million dollars."

"Jack, why are we talking about this now? Relax a little."

He blinked with surprise, then looked at me close. I wanted to know what he was thinking, but before I could ask, he continued: "Sorry, I've just never been in a position to actually think about something like that before. Having a home, a family."

Was he blushing? I thought so, and that wasn't something Jack did often, which meant his words must have been sincere. Was it painful for him to admit that? Because I didn't want him stressed, or worried, or tense. We had all the time in the world, but for some reason, the topic of children had made him frantic. He almost seemed resistant as I wrapped my arms around him.

"How come?" I asked.

"I don't know. I always thought I'd end up living alone. The same way you can just tell Will and Naya are one of those unbearable couples who end up with five kids, two dogs, a cat, a hamster, and a beach house for the summer, I just knew the best I could hope for was to be the cool uncle who travels and brings back presents from exotic countries. And cool Uncle Jack, you know, part of what makes him cool is his bachelor lifestyle."

"You know things aren't just black-and-white like that, right? There are many shades of cool and not cool. And everybody's life is its own adventure. Like, imagine if you were cool *dad* Jack and you took your kids traveling with you and they brought back gifts for Uncle Will and Aunt Naya and their cousins? That could happen."

I almost got a smile out of him, and I thought I could see him trying to ask himself if that was really possible.

"But you'll have time to think of all that later," I said, resting my face near his neck. "The important thing right now is for you to do what *you* want."

He grinned malevolently and said, "I'll get to work on that." I screeched as he lowered his head into my chest, reached under my shirt, and started reaching upward, tickling me. Just as he touched my breasts, I heard the door open.

"Guys, the neighbor came down, and...oh. Sorry."

Mike was standing there on the threshold, gawking.

"Has no one ever taught you to knock on the damn door?" Jack asked. "What do you want now?"

Mike seemed to need a second to remember why he was there. "The neighbor's at the door. The nasty one. He's bitching about the noise again. I didn't know what to tell him. I usually sic Sue on him, but she's out."

I couldn't help but laugh as Jack cursed and got out of bed, walking past Mike, who—thank God—didn't make his usual dumb, pervy comment about how he could step in while Jack was busy. Instead, he just walked off to the living room, looking lonely.

18

FAMILIES AND SHOTS

I was in the bedroom painting, or really just playing with my brushes. I dipped them in different colors, laid down a few strokes, cleaned them off, switched them out, and never managed to even make an outline for a proper picture. I felt I could sit on the edge of the bed staring at the canvas all day and never find any inspiration.

"You're really going?" I asked. It sounded pathetic.

"Yup," Jack said unenthusiastically, taking clothing from his dresser and stuffing it in a travel bag.

"Till when?"

"Till Friday, I think. Can you live without me for three days, Michelle?"

I growled at him. "I get that film festivals are important, but isn't it a little ridiculous, telling you one day before you're supposed to be there that you're invited?"

"It is what it is. If it makes you feel better, I'm not pleased with it, either."

I stared at the brushes sitting there in front of me. I knew why I hadn't been able to get anything done: I was used to having him there all the time, and I was missing him already. But he had things to do, and I knew that the film promotion was important. And three days wasn't that long, even if it was hard to deal with, him leaving so abruptly.

You could hide his passport, I told myself.

"I'll keep you up to date on the goings-on around here," I said, standing up and carefully folding the clothes he'd tossed to the floor before layering them in his suitcase.

"I'll do that!" Jack said. "I'm still trying to decide what I'm taking."

"Be honest with me," I said. "We both know you're making a mess because you know I won't be able to stand it, and I'll be incapable of stopping myself from cleaning it up."

He batted his eyes at me innocently, and I put down the socks I was in the process of rolling. "I changed my mind. You do it yourself."

"I think I love you a little less," he called after me as I walked into the hallway on the way to the living room.

"Liar," I answered him over my shoulder.

"OK," he said, "I am lying. But if you see a photo of me and you don't like my outfit, you can blame yourself."

Naya was on the couch reading one of her baby books. Mike was watching TV. Will was pacing in the kitchen, and Sue was in the shower. I dared to sit in her chair, since it was close to Mike's, and he'd been acting so glum lately. He didn't even look at me. He just went on flipping through the channels.

"Nothing good on today?" I asked.

"Nope."

But he stopped hitting the button when he found a show about people who tried to fix their terrible tattoos. He turned up the volume loud.

"I've always wondered who would get a tattoo like that," I remarked when they showed a guy with bacon and eggs tattooed on his forearm. "Maybe he lost a bet? I'm sorry, I wouldn't go through with it. Would you get a dumb tattoo just because you lost a bet?"

"Maybe."

I was trying, but Mike preferred to treat me like I didn't exist. It was painful just sharing a room with him, and I was grateful when my cell phone rang. I looked at the screen: Spencer. Should I pick up or not? The last time he'd called without warning, it had been to tell me my grandmother had died. I couldn't stand the thought that horrible news was waiting for me on the other line. If that was true, though, what was the use in ducking it? I picked up.

"Hey, Jenny," he said, sounding weirdly cheerful. "How's it going?"

"Same old, same old. What about you?"

"I'm great!"

I breathed a sigh of relief.

"Is everything cool?" I asked. "You're not much of a phone guy. Do you need something?"

"Actually, sis, I've got good news. I'm going to a convention. I've been invited to give a speech on new methods for training young athletes. Believe it or not, I'm actually kind of a big deal these days. But the main thing is, the convention's at your school. I'm coming in tomorrow. And I was thinking, how cool would it be if you and I painted the town red?"

I was surprised enough that everyone in the room could tell. Naya glanced over, trying to figure out what I was thinking. Excited, I asked Spencer, "When are you coming?"

"Don't strangle me, but I'm actually flying in today. I've been meaning to call you all week, but I just kept forgetting. It's a short trip: I'll be around tonight and tomorrow, and then I have to get back to work. If you're busy, don't worry about it, I realize it's insanely short notice."

"To hell with that! I'm dying to see you! I'll try to make it the best two days you've ever had!"

Spencer seemed as emotional about it as I was, and I couldn't hide my smile when I hung up. Sue had walked out of the shower by then and was standing in the living room in her pajamas, hair still damp, looking at me with the same curiosity as Naya. "Who was that?" she asked.

"My older brother! He's coming for two days!"

Sue's nose wrinkled. "Your brother must be special. I could never get that excited about mine."

"You have a brother?" I asked.

"I have seven siblings," she answered. "And every one of them is unbearable. Tell me about your brother, though. Is he hot?"

I didn't see that question coming. It might have been the first time Sue ever suggested she could be a normal person, with normal urges and needs. Apparently, I wasn't the only one who thought that: Will started laughing in the kitchen, too.

"I don't know!" I replied. "He's my brother!"

"So what?" Sue asked.

"Yeah, he's hot," Naya butted in tranquilly.

"Leave him alone, Sue," I warned her. "He broke up with his girlfriend recently, and I think he's still getting over it."

A moment later, Jack walked out, asking, "What are you guys talking about?"

I've never been fond of goodbyes. Especially not at the airport. But still, I stayed by Jack's side all the way through security. He had a big crowd around him: Joey, the main actors, two makeup artists, two security guards, and three or four others I didn't know.

The festival was in Italy. It was a long flight, and they'd land in the morning and get to work right away.

"Write me and let me know once you're settled in," I told Jack.

"No," he joked, and I responded, "Don't make me kill you."

He was ten minutes away from his gate, and I felt the pressure to make it perfect, because I knew he had to go soon and I didn't want to waste a single second. Jack tossed his bottle of water in the trash can and I looked over at Vivian, who was standing with another actor a foot away. Her expression was mistrustful, and I wanted to snap at her, but I'd told myself I'd try to work on that relationship. Maybe we would never be best friends, but we could try to be cordial, or at least I could.

"You nervous?" I asked her and her friend, thinking addressing both of them would make it less awkward.

Vivian said nothing, but the guy responded, "Yeah. We're used to it, though, at this point. We've been at this for months."

"Maybe you can give Jack some pointers, then," I told him.

"Ross will be in perfectly good hands," Vivian said. "Don't you worry about it."

She was being mean, and she wasn't even making an effort to hide it, but I refused to argue with her, especially just then.

"I'm sure he will," I replied cattily.

We scowled at each other for a few seconds while the poor actor asked himself what was going on. I felt a finger under my chin turning my head—Jack was beside me, asking me if everything was all right before looking menacingly at Vivian.

She huffed, uttered something incomprehensible, and walked off. Her companion soon followed.

I hugged Jack around the waist and felt his shoulders slump. "She wasn't bothering you, was she?" he asked.

"No, not in the least. And the guy with her seems like a sweetheart."

"He's all right. He's a professional. That's more than you can say for a lot of people."

Joey interrupted us: "Sorry, lovebirds, but we can't miss this flight…"

"Just wait a second," Jack said, then whispered to me, "I don't know if I can go three whole days without you."

"Take baby steps," I told him. "Just focus on how you're going to get through the next few hours in an airplane with all these people."

He kissed me, and I sank into him as he held me, one hand on the nape of my neck and the other on the small of my back. I wasn't ashamed to show how much I cared about him. I wasn't worried about who saw. I opened my mouth, let his tongue slide in, forgot everything, just felt... When he stopped, it was as if he was already disappearing from my grasp. I tried not to let him go, but he said with a smile, "Jen, I'd stay here doing this all day, but Joey standing there staring at us is kind of ruining the moment."

"Stay anyway."

"Don't tempt me."

"I'm kidding," I told him. "I know your fans need you. Now give them what they're asking for and go enjoy doing whatever it is famous people do."

"Jack Ross!" Joey yelled just as we started to kiss again.

"It's not my fault, Joey," Jack called back, "she's using her witchcraft to try and keep me off the plane." Then he turned back to me. "Are you going to think about me when I'm gone?"

"No," I kidded him.

"You're lucky I know for a fact that you adore me."

After one last kiss, he walked over to his manager, who guided him through security. Over his shoulder he called out, "Behave while I'm gone, Mushu."

I responded, "Try not to miss me too much."

And then he vanished in the midst of the crowd. I stayed there a minute longer, unsure what to do, then decided to walk over to arrivals, since my brother would arrive an hour later. There was a café close by where I could wait for him. Since I knew I'd have time on my hands, I'd brought my laptop to study. It was past time to put my nose to the grindstone. I didn't want to find myself in the same boat as Curtis.

Some students from our major had a group chat, and I was checking that out when Spencer texted me to tell me he'd arrived. I put away my computer and went to wait for him amid the mass of people leaned against the railing. When I saw him, I shouted and waved my hands, but he couldn't see me, so I walked around to the side. We hugged, I had to jump off the ground to wrap my arms around his neck, and he laughed as I started kicking my legs like an excited little girl.

"Did you really miss me that bad?" he asked.

As he set me down, I replied, "So what if I did? Is that a problem?"

Rubbing the top of my head, he said, "You look good, sis. Better than when I saw you in February. Happier, that's for sure."

"I guess the time away from you has done me some good."

He pretended to wipe away a tear as we walked to the exit. He was too tough to tell me he'd missed me, too, but I could tell.

Despite my driving lessons, I still didn't have a license, so we took the train home. Along the way, we brought each other up to date on the family, our lives, our friends, and other goings-on. He was happy to hear I'd started running again, but disappointed when I told him I was only doing three miles a day. That made me feel bad, so I took the stairs up to the apartment when we got home.

"Nice place," he said as I opened the door, fingering a piece of wallpaper that had started to peel away. I told him it was hard to keep the place spotless with so many people coming in and out all the time.

"Ready for your big debut?" I asked him.

"I was born ready."

I edged past him into the living room, where everybody was sitting there just as they had before I left.

"Spencer," I said, "you've met most of these people, but I'll just go through the motions anyway. This is Naya and Will. They were at Grandma's funeral. This is Mike, Jack's brother. Jack, like I told you, is away traveling. And this is Sue, our other roommate."

Everyone turned and inspected him, pretty tactlessly if you ask me.

"Guys, this is my brother Spencer," I added. "I told him he could spend the night here."

"Of course!" Naya said, smiling. "Take a seat! We're dying for you to tell us all the embarrassing stories from Jenna's childhood!"

I'd have preferred we skip that, but I was glad there was *someone* welcoming there, not just Mike channel surfing like a zombie and Sue absorbed in her magazine. I guess whatever intrigue she'd felt the day before about my brother's looks had evaporated.

Spencer grinned, flopped down beside Will, and said, "I'm afraid I'd need way more than one afternoon for that."

"Jenna said you're here for a convention?" Will asked.

"Yeah, I have a speech in like two hours," Spencer responded. "It's not that big a deal, but they invited me and they're paying my airfare, so what the hell? Besides, it was a good opportunity to visit my little sister. I should probably go ahead and add that I'm supposed to be spying for Mom and Dad."

"What are you going to tell them?" I asked him.

"Honestly, we don't talk much, and as far as I can tell, you're not pregnant, so there's still no Shannon-level disasters on the horizon. I'll just tell them everything's great. They won't believe me, but whatever." As he said this, he noticed Naya's belly and rushed to correct himself: "Not that there's anything wrong with being pregnant! I'm just saying..."

Naya laughed mischievously. Since she hadn't said a word up to now, Spencer addressed Sue directly: "So, are you a student, too?"

Sue sighed, already bored. "Yeah."

"I assume you're majoring in communications?" That was a good one, and all of us chuckled.

Sue looked up and responded, "Psychology. I'm interested in what makes people think."

"Sounds complicated," Spencer said.

"It's not. Most people are simpler than the average lab rat." She stood and tossed her magazine aside on her way to the kitchen. "You want a beer?"

"Sure," Spencer said.

Hold on—was there some kind of attraction here? When Sue was merely cranky, that was a cause for celebration in our home. At her worst, she'd give Satan a run for his money. But here she was playing hostess, and if I wasn't mistaken, I had actually seen her smirk. And there was no doubt that my brother was checking her out. Even as he opened his beer and took a sip of it, he didn't take his eyes off her. *Ewww...* Will and Naya could tell where my mind was and were both grinning as Sue and Spencer struck back up their conversation. After a few seconds, Mike barged outside to smoke. I guess he was jealous, but surely he knew by now Sue would never give him the time of day.

I had thought I'd need to stay close to Spencer's side so he wouldn't feel out of place. But I now realized the only person out of place was me. So I announced that I needed a breath of fresh air and headed up to the roof.

I hadn't been up there in ages, and I'd never been nuts about climbing the fire escape. Even when Jack helped me up there, I tended to get scared. But I told myself it was time to be a modern, independent woman, then I cursed Mike, then I stuck one leg through the open window. I climbed up clumsily, one step at a time, shaking the ladder slightly to make sure it wouldn't collapse on me. When I got to the top, I noticed it was freezing.

I found Mike standing close to the ledge, one hand in his pocket and one holding his cigarette. He blew out a mouthful of smoke, looking utterly self-absorbed. I thought about startling him—getting him back for when he'd terrified me in the car the other day—but I didn't want to send him flying off into the abyss, so I just said, "Hi."

He must not have wanted company, because he froze when he heard me.

"Hey," he said tentatively. It sounded almost like a question.

"You mind if I hang out up here?"

He shrugged, confused. I think he was asking himself what I wanted. He looked away and took another drag of his cigarette. When he was calm—which rarely happened—he looked a lot like Jack. Shorter, with longer hair, but otherwise nearly identical. He could feel my eyes on him, and I think it was starting to bother him, because he said, "Unless you're studying me for one of your paintings, could you stop looking at me like that?"

"Sorry, I, uh… I didn't realize I was staring."

"Did you need something?"

"Actually, I wanted to ask you something," I said. "Mike, are you OK?"

"Why wouldn't I be?"

"I don't know, but you've been acting strange for a while now. And when you just took off just now, I thought maybe the thing with Sue and my brother had pissed you off."

"What thing with Sue and your brother?" he asked.

"I mean, if I had to lay money on it, I'd say they're probably going to hook up. And you and Sue, you're like superhero and sidekick, so I thought you were upset. I've kind of always assumed you had feelings for her."

"Sue's just a friend," Mike said, flicking his ashes off the edge of the roof. "Whoever she wants to sleep with, that's her choice."

"Fine, understood. So let's just pretend you're not upset right now. That still doesn't explain the past couple of days. Ever since your brother and I got back from Greece, you're so quiet. You've been treating Jack and me like we barely exist."

Mike looked away. "I don't know what you mean." He dropped his cigarette butt, crushed it out under his shoe, and tried to walk away. When I stopped him, he exclaimed, "Jen, what do you want?"

"I want to know what's wrong. I want to know why you refuse to actually talk to anyone. And most of all, I want to know if we did something to hurt you. Because if so, I promise you, we didn't mean to, and I'd do anything I could to make it better!"

For a brief moment, he looked as if he would open up, but that impression quickly vanished as he jerked his arm away and started pacing.

"Is it because we left you here?" I called out, desperate to find some explanation. "Did you want us to ask you to come along?"

"What the hell am I going to do in Greece?" he shouted. "It's not you and it's not Jack, OK? It's my band. We broke up. It's over."

I was speechless. Mike's head was hanging low, his shoulders were slumped. I reached out to hug him, but then I let my arms drop—I wasn't sure it was appropriate. "I'm so sorry, Mike. What happened?"

"The bass player got picked up by another band, and he took the rest of the guys with him. Now they're supposedly in a *supergroup*. I guess I wasn't *super* enough for them, so now I'm on my own."

"Maybe you could sing for someone else?" I offered. "Naya told me you were taking vocal lessons, she said you were getting better. Or this could be the moment to go solo! All you need nowadays is a computer and some mixing equipment, you don't even need any backup musicians anymore!"

"I don't know, Jenna… I don't feel like doing anything, to tell the truth. I've been at this for ages, it's never gone anywhere, I should probably just give it up."

To hell with it, I thought: if I was him, I'd sure want a hug, so what was holding me back? I squeezed him tight and felt him patting me on the back, almost as if he were consoling me. "I'm sorry, Mike," I murmured. "If you want, you and I can be a band. I used to play the triangle. I'm really good at it!"

I could feel the laughter shaking his torso—timid, not like the boisterous laughter I was used to from him, but perhaps that meant it was more sincere. "The triangle?" he asked sarcastically.

"Yeah. And I could sing harmony, too!"

He held me a long while in silence, and when he let me go, he didn't look angry anymore. "I've got an idea," I told him. "How about we go downstairs and watch your favorite show about tattoo disasters? I'm freezing up here."

Mike nodded and we took the ladder back down.

"I'm alive. Can I hang up now?"

It was two in the morning, and I had managed to stay awake until Jack arrived at his hotel. I was grouchy, but I couldn't blame anyone, him calling had been my idea. That first night alone, especially, I needed to at least hear his voice for a second. I knew if I didn't, I'd never fall asleep in that big empty bed without him. I'd actually tried to tell Spencer he could use it, thinking that crashing on the couch with the TV on would feel less lonely, but just as everyone had predicted, he had wound up in Sue's room. And even if things seemed better with Mike, I wasn't going to push the envelope by sleeping in the same room with him. I didn't trust him not to try something, and Jack would kill him if he found out.

Holding the phone in one hand, I grabbed the blanket and sheets with the other and pulled them under my chin. Then I hugged his pillow, which smelled of his shampoo. I put the phone on speaker so I could lie back and hold it up. I looked at my wallpaper: a photo of Jack winking and sticking out his tongue.

"Jen," he said, calm, tender, but exasperated, "you should get some sleep. You sound exhausted."

"So?"

"There's no need for you to stay up. I can call you in the afternoon."

"I like talking at bedtime. That's when the secrets come out."

"Bedtime for you, maybe. Over here, the sun's been up for hours. But anyway, how are things? You haven't destroyed the apartment yet, have you?"

"No, but I thought the building was going to collapse from all the bumping and grinding. First it was Will and Naya, which I'm almost used to at this point, but I'm sad to inform you that when they were done, my brother and Sue started going at it."

"Your brother and Sue? I swear, I leave for one day and it's like the world tilts off its axis."

"Tell me about Italy," I asked him. "Now that everyone's done boning, I can hear Mike snoring on the couch. He sounds like a sawmill. So I doubt I'll fall asleep anytime soon."

He chuckled and yawned. "There's not much to tell. The airplane landed, I guess you figured that out. I slept most of the flight. Our ride to the hotel was an adventure, because the driver was talking a mile a minute and no one could understand a word he said. I only got here ten minutes ago."

"You're all at the same hotel?" I asked.

"Yeah. But Vivian's at the other end of the hall! Don't worry, I promise there's no way we'll...hey, are you laughing at me?"

"I am," I said. "I'm not used to you being nervous. It's cute."

"Jen, have some respect for my reputation as an insensitive man."

"Jack, I trust you."

"I know, but I want you to *really* trust me."

"OK," I said, "we'll make a deal. Go do your work, don't do anything stupid, prove to me Vivian's just your friend, and I'll agree that I overreacted. Then we can put the whole thing behind us."

"How will you know if I'm lying?"

"Let's get one thing straight," I told him. "There's no girl who can compare to me, so I'm really not worried about it."

"Is this a new you, or have you just been keeping this sassy side of yourself hidden from me all this time?" he asked.

"I'm the same woman," I said. "I'm just trying to be less timid."

"Oh, we should get in some practice, then," he murmured slyly. "I've got an idea. You could tell me what you have on. Or better yet, what you don't have on. That way, we can see if you're telling the truth or just boasting."

Putting on my sexiest voice, I purred, "Well, let's see here… I have on a T-shirt from a very erotic amusement park…some cotton pants… I've got my hair pulled back with a scrunchie…"

"And underneath that?"

"There is nothing underneath that."

"Are you lying?" he asked.

"No. Do you want a photo?"

I could almost feel the steam coming out of his ears. "Hell yes, I want a photo. Two photos. A photo album, if you've got time for it."

"I wonder what you can do to convince me."

"Jen, this is torture. You know how I get."

I started laughing. I was telling the truth, though. I usually slept in panties and a T-shirt, but I hadn't done the wash today, so I had raided Jack's closet for something to wear to bed.

"OK, we'll let it go, then. Maybe we can resume tomorrow. I'm not exactly in a sexting mood right now anyway. I'd love to keep talking, but I need some sleep, and you've got to get to work, right?"

"For sure."

I smiled and said, "Don't overdo it, Jack. You're gonna knock their socks off, but that takes energy, and I don't want you getting sick or stressed out. I need you back in the condition I left you in." I kissed the screen as I heard him laugh.

"Love you, Jen."

"Love you, too, Jack."

We both hung up at the same time. I looked at the ceiling a moment, then down at myself, and tugged at my pants until they revealed the curve of my hip and one side of my buttocks. I took a photo, then erased it. Then another. Then ten more.

When I finally found the right angle, I sent him the picture and grinned.

See? I wasn't lying ☺

A few seconds later, I got my response.

Thank you. You've made my dreams tonight much more interesting.

19

THE RESCUE SQUAD

I slept better than I thought I would, and after waking up earlier than usual, I threw on my headphones and running clothes and walked down the hall on my tiptoes. Mike was still asleep on the couch. I closed the door softly, thinking he'd remain that way for a while, but when I got home an hour later, all the guys in the house were up and about. Will greeted me as I stole a piece of toast from my brother's plate, licking it so he wouldn't take it back from me.

"What the hell kind of host does that?" Spencer asked.

"The hungry kind," I replied.

Mike laughed, so I decided that made us allies and took the stool beside him. Spencer yawned and pushed his mug toward Will for more coffee. I had rarely ever seen him groggy, and I must admit, I found it funny.

"Long night?" I asked.

"Conventions, am I right?" Mike joked.

"Jen's still a child about these things," Spencer announced.

"Yeah, and you're a grandfather," I teased. "I remember I used to have a brother who could make it through a one-night stand without moaning and groaning about how he needs more coffee the next day."

"Wait and see, sister," he responded. "When you're my age, I'll be the one laughing at you. Anyway, I'm just getting the lead out before my morning run. Which will be your second morning run. I hope you don't mind."

"Spencer!" I shouted pointlessly. He was already on his way to Sue's room to change. Will and Mike grinned as I headed for the door. On his best day, Spencer would have smoked me—he had eight inches of height on me and probably seventy pounds of muscle. Thank goodness his, er, *extracurricular activities* had worn him out. He took off like lightning, but soon enough, he had to slow down, and I managed to match his pace without coughing up a lung.

It was getting close to midday when we stopped in a park. I tried to buy an ice cream at a nearby shop, but Spencer forced me to get an energy drink instead. I drank it despondently as we sat on a bench. At least it was orange-flavored, I thought.

"You can have your ice cream when I leave," he said dismissively.

"Need I remind you of how many times I've watched you eat an entire box of chocolate cereal?"

"Jen, we barely ever see each other nowadays. Just let me play the responsible older brother for a few hours."

I smiled and took another sip. We were sweating and our cheeks were flushed, even though it was starting to get cool out and most of the pass-ersby were in long sleeves.

"What time do you have to go?" I asked him.

"The gate opens at eight, so I've got time. By the way, my presentation went great, thanks for asking."

"What did you expect me to do, crack Sue's door while you two were getting it on to ask?"

"Yeah…maybe it's best you didn't. Anyway, for your information, I nailed it. Oh, and I wanted to ask you something: I heard you got back into painting?"

"Yeah," I said. "Jack gave me a set of oils and charcoals for my birthday, and I've really been enjoying myself. You remember how much I loved it when I was in high school?"

"I've got to tell you, sis, your face literally lights up when you talk about him," Spencer observed.

"Shut up!"

"Hey! Respect your older brother! Anyway, I mean that in a good way. He's a nice guy. I like him. It's a relief seeing you with someone who's not a total douche."

I looked away, and Spencer wrapped an arm around me. "Sorry," he added. "That was over the line. I shouldn't have brought him up."

No matter how much time passed, I didn't think I'd ever feel comfortable talking about Monty. I could still remember too well what it all felt like, and I wondered if it would always be that way. My greatest wish was simply to forget he existed.

At least he hadn't tried to get in touch with me again. Maybe now that he had Nelle to boss around all the time, he'd forgotten me. I sure hoped so.

Spencer asked, "Are you up for another mile or two?"

"No, I'm good. Remember, recovery's important, too. Hey, since you mentioned him, have you seen Monty?"

They lived down the street from each other. It wasn't exactly a stab in the dark. "I've caught sight of him," Spencer said. "But only once or twice. He knows better than to try to talk to me. If he came within a foot of me, I'd beat him to a pulp."

"What's up with Nelle? Are they still going out?"

Since the funeral, I'd started to feel bad about how I'd treated her. Her timidity, her defensiveness—I had been the same way when I was going out with Monty.

Spencer scratched his chin, unsure how to respond. "She's around. I wouldn't say she's doing great, let's put it that way. I'm not one for gossip, but I don't think that's exactly a secret. She's thin as a reed, she never leaves the house, she got fired from her job…her parents came and asked our parents for help, because they went through the same thing with you."

"I think you mean they refused to go through it with me. Dad I can give a little credit to, he did tell me to go to the police before he caved to the pressure from everyone else in town. But the way Mom acted was just despicable. I know I shouldn't complain, I'm sorry, I just felt burned by the whole situation. If you and Shannon hadn't had my back, I don't know what I'd have done."

"I know, Jenny. And I do get why you're angry. I'm not sure what Mom and Dad told them. I prefer to stay out of it. It's a sad situation, but it's not my business."

I nodded and said, "You know what? I changed my mind. I could do another mile or two."

That afternoon, back in the apartment, while Spencer was in Sue's room gathering his things, I realized how much I'd miss him, and I wished he could stay a little longer. It felt like he'd only just arrived.

I walked him to the front door of the building and asked, "Are you sure you don't want me to go to the airport with you?"

"Nah. I'm a grown-up, Jenny, I can manage one train ride on my own. There's no point in you wasting the fare."

"Sure," I said. He reached up and mussed my hair. "Are you ever going to stop doing that?" I complained.

"Yeah. When you grow up."

"I'm turning twenty-one in February! When are you going to admit I'm grown?"

"Maybe when you're forty, we can talk."

I stuck out my tongue, and he chuckled, then waved, slung his backpack over his shoulder, and walked off toward the train station. I stood watching until he turned the corner and disappeared.

It had been cold outside, and I'd gone down in only a T-shirt. When I returned to the apartment, I walked to the bedroom and put on one of Jack's hoodies. Mike and Sue were in the living room. Naya and Will were out for a romantic dinner.

"Aw, you look so sad," Sue said. "You want some milk and cookies?"

"I'm not hungry," I responded.

"I'll take some milk and cookies," Mike said.

"I didn't offer them to you, parasite."

Mike smiled, looking almost as carefree as he had before Jack and I went on vacation. I sat down next to him and sank back on the couch. I guess they must have seen the worry on my face, because they started pelting me with questions about whether I missed my brother or missed Jack or was worried about school or was on my period, and finally, just to get them to shut up, I cried, "It's not that! It's not any of the stuff you're saying! It's a friend. I'm worried about a friend. Or not a friend. I don't know what you'd call her. Remember how we got high together that time and I told you both I'd had an anxiety attack because a friend hooked up with my boyfriend? Well, it's her."

They nodded, understanding now, and Sue said, "Got it."

"They're together now," I continued, "and according to Spencer, things aren't going well. I got that impression too when I saw her at the funeral. And I've tried to call and check on her, but she won't pick up."

"You can call her from my phone, maybe she'll pick up if she doesn't recognize the number," Mike said.

"What if she hangs up on me when I start talking?" I asked, almost preparing myself to be disappointed.

Sue responded wisely, "At least you'll know you tried."

Hands shaking more than I'd like to admit, I grabbed Mike's phone and dialed her number, which I still knew by heart. Then I turned on the speaker, and my two roommates leaned in to hear better.

Every ring was like an eternity. Nelle had never been the type to pick up right away. In fact, she'd never been much of a phone person at all, and I wouldn't have been surprised if she'd missed the call. But on the third ring, I heard scratching noises on the other line and saw on the screen that someone had picked up. Then I heard her voice: "Hello?"

She sounded normal. Tired, maybe, but normal. "Hey, Nelle," I said. "Don't hang up. Please."

She waited a few seconds in silence, as though trying to restrain herself. "Why are you calling? Do you have a new number, or...?"

"I'm calling from a friend's phone."

"I don't want to talk to you," she told me after a short pause.

"Wait!" I heard her phone moving and just knew she was about to hang up. "I just want to ask how you're doing. That's all. Tell me that, and you can hang up if you want afterward."

"I'm good. Are you happy now?"

"Tell me the truth."

"I did."

"Nelle, I talked to Spencer. I know everything. I know you lost your job, I know you're not eating..."

"I didn't *lose* my job, I quit, OK?"

I closed my eyes and took a deep breath. "Nelle, listen... I know what you're going through right now. I was in the same situation. I know it's..."

"Jenna, you don't know a damn thing about my situation! You left! You don't even know me anymore!"

"How am I supposed to? You don't call me, and you don't pick up when I call."

"I can't pick up, all right?"

I heard her take a deep breath. She was quiet for so long, I looked at

Sue and Mike, who were staring at the phone attentively. I thought Nelle would hang up, but then I heard her again. "It's not that easy."

She was speaking in a soft tone, so different from the excitable, energetic voice I was used to. She sounded as if she were very carefully measuring her words, as if there were things she knew she couldn't say.

"Trust me, Nelle. It's not as hard as it seems."

"Who are you to tell me that?" she asked.

"I was in the same situation as you."

"No, you weren't, Jen. You don't understand. You lived far away, you had a group of friends helping you, you had people who cared about you. I'm here, locking in all day with him. No matter where I go, I can't make it far before he finds me."

"He left me alone," I said.

"Because you're hours away."

"Do like Jenna, then," Sue interrupted us. "Go to school. You can come here. Registration is still open."

"Who the...?" Nelle asked.

"Or don't go to school. Just come here," Mike said. "What have you got to lose?"

Nelle was babbling: who were these people, how dare I let them listen in on our conversation, this was private, and so on. I told her they were my friends, and even if they were nosy, they were right. She should come. She'd be safe, and she could build a new life here. When she protested that it wasn't that easy, I reminded her that her parents had money running out their ears, and they loved her and were scared of what Monty could do to her. They'd do whatever it took to get her away from him, I had no doubt about that.

"We'll come pick you up!" Mike burst in. "We can take my brother's car. If Jen asks him for it, he'll definitely say yes."

Sue didn't look convinced. "How many hours' drive are we talking?"

"Five, more or less," I told her.

"I'm sorry to interrupt you guys," Nelle called out, "but I never said I was coming. And you're rushing me."

"If you're letting a guy push you around and abuse you, then you should be rushed," Sue objected.

"Monty's going to be furious," Nelle said.

"Let him be," Mike told her. "You won't be around to see it."

After a couple of seconds' silence, Nelle conceded, "OK, I'm in."

Convincing Jack to lend us the car was easier than I'd imagined. All I had to do was say the word *emergency* and he agreed. His only condition was that Mike not drive, which meant for the first time we'd be seeing Sue behind the wheel.

It wasn't what you'd call an easygoing trip. Sue kept stopping for coffee—she wasn't tired, I think she was just bored. Mike sat in the back, unable to shut up, literally just singing or making noises when he ran out of things to say. And I couldn't stop chewing my nails.

It was weird, arriving back in my old neighborhood with those two. Sue had never been there, and Mike couldn't remember it, so I pointed out the sights. They were surprised at all my stories. I don't think they imagined so much could happen in such a small town.

"Where's your friend live?" Sue asked when she stopped at a stop sign.

"Two streets farther down. It's close to my parents' place."

"Are we going to visit them?" Mike asked, sticking his head in between us.

After a moment's hesitation, I said, "I don't really know that we should."

One thing I liked about the two of them was they weren't pushy: they knew your limits, and even if they liked a good bit of gossip, they never felt the urge to pry.

Sue parked Jack's car across the street from Nelle's house. We were all nervous as we got out, but I felt better when I noticed there were no vehicles around. Not Monty's car or motorcycle, not even Nelle's parents' car. She was definitely alone.

It felt strange climbing the porch steps with Mike and Sue on either side of me. I did it as quickly as I could and rang the doorbell. Nelle opened almost immediately. She looked frantic, dragging her rolling bag with a backpack slung over her shoulders. She'd obviously been waiting.

Whatever hostility she'd felt toward me was gone. In her eyes, all I saw was fear and hope.

"Hey," I said. "This is Mike and Sue, you met them over the phone." The two of them waved at her.

"Is that the car?" she asked.

"Yeah," I replied. "Did you tell your parents?"

"They know everything," Nelle said, shutting the door. "Can we go now? Please?"

I nodded and bent down to pick up her bag. Nelle was pale as a sheet. I wondered why, but then I saw the same thing she had seen: Monty was standing there on the sidewalk.

He was just as I remembered him, except even more muscular. I'd heard he'd been kicked off the basketball team and was now working at a gym. He was dressed in his work clothes—a tight, stretchy shirt and gym pants—and had on a pair of headphones, which he removed when he saw us. I guessed his shift had just ended.

"What the…?" he started, looking at Mike and Sue. Then he saw me, dropped his bag next to him, and said, "Oh, OK, I get it."

That was enough to terrify Nelle, and I started asking myself what we should do. Nothing occurred to me at first, but I knew one thing: even if Monty did scare me, I wasn't like her. I wasn't going to panic. I would never let him have that power over me again. My hands weren't sweating, and my brain was working fine. My fear was just something rational, I told myself, but that didn't mean I had to let it control me. I looked straight at him and saw the fear burning in his eyes. Before he could speak, I said, "You can't be here. I've got a restraining order against you."

At first, Monty didn't respond. Then he laughed sarcastically and, calm as could be, wrapped the cable of his earbuds around his phone, slipping it into his pocket.

"What kind of shit have you been telling her, Jenny?" he asked, making my name sound like an insult. "Did you tell her to leave me? Is that it?"

"I told her the truth," I said. "That's all."

Monty tipped his head to one side. "You know what I think? I think you can't stand for people to be happy without you. And it gets under your skin that things are so great with Nelle and me. Because that means the problem wasn't me, it was you."

I could have laughed as he went on, "What brought you back here? Aren't things good with your new boyfriend? It's ironic that you were so desperate for me to leave you alone, and now here you are again…"

"Oh, please, Monty. I had to change my number to get you to leave me alone. You even used my grandmother's death as an excuse to get back in touch with me. You literally still go hang out at my parents' house!"

"What am I supposed to do?" he asked. "We live in the same town. I have reasons to go over there. Plus, I may as well remind you, you moved halfway across the country and refuse to talk to them. What's weird is that you don't understand how that might bother them."

Before I could open my mouth again, Mike grabbed my wrist and said, "We're going. This conversation is pointless, and you don't owe him an explanation." I had never seen Mike so serious before.

Sue agreed. "He's right. Let's get out of here."

Nelle grabbed her backpack, which she'd dropped in a moment of panic. Mike picked up her rolling bag, and the four of us walked down the stairs. I was surprised that Monty didn't move at first. He just stared, and when Nelle made it to the sidewalk, he asked, "Are you for real? You're not even going to bother to say goodbye?"

He was staring daggers into her, but I told her, "Just ignore him."

Nelle moved quickly. She was clearly desperate to reach the car. But Monty stopped her, grabbing her arm and saying slowly and coldly, "I'm talking to you. The least you can do is look me in the face."

Nelle turned. Her lips were pale, and her hand was squeezing the strap of her backpack so tight her knuckles had turned white. I charged forward before Sue and Mike could stop me and grabbed his wrist, pulling it away. Surprised, he asked, "What the hell are you doing?"

"Let her go," I warned him.

"Stay out of this," he said.

"Don't order me around. I'll do what I want," I responded.

I was surprised at the firmness in my voice and my posture. Nelle stepped back while Monty scowled at me. This was the first time since I'd known him that I'd seen hesitation in his eyes.

"Let her go," I repeated, softly but sternly.

I remembered how Jack had confronted his father. He hadn't been violent. He had made it clear that he didn't need to put on a show to get his way. And that inspired me to do the same with Monty.

"She's my girlfriend, Jennifer," he told me. "She's none of your concern."

"She's my best friend, and she is my concern. Especially when I see the guy who nearly ruined my life trying to do the same to hers. It's over, Monty. Let her go."

To everyone's disbelief, he did. Nelle stepped back, and Sue caught her so she wouldn't fall. Monty turned to me and came so close I had to look up to see his eyes. But I didn't let him intimidate me. I didn't move, didn't flinch, didn't blink. I just stared back and waited.

"You think you're brave, huh?" he asked, one eyebrow arched. "Well, let me tell you something, Jenny. You're the same insecure chick you were back in high school. The only thing that's changed is you've found a couple of morons to defend you. I'll tell you what's really sad, though. I can tell you're still in love with me. Not with Jack-off Ross. With me. That's the only real reason you're here. It's pathetic."

I laughed in his face, as loud as I could. "You think I'm in love with you? Monty, please. I may be insecure, but I could never fall in love with some oaf stuck in a small town who pretends to be a basketball star when he couldn't even hold onto his spot on a feeder team. You're a loser, and you've always been a loser, and that's why you've always tried to hurt other people, to make yourself feel better. I love Jack. I never loved you. And I doubt anyone else ever will, either."

That felt good. Letting it all out was like drawing in a breath after scaling a mountain. A huge weight had been lifted off of me. But if I'd taken inspiration from Jack's confrontation with his father, I'd forgotten one important thing: Monty and Mr. Ross were two different people. Where Mr. Ross had frozen, Monty leaped at me, ready to grab me by the neck, and I barely had time to get away.

Nelle and Sue froze, but Mike, who had been in his fair share of scrapes, jumped in and shoved Monty backward, shouting, "Don't you dare touch her!"

None of us had expected that, least of all Monty, who grimaced, confused, and asked him, "Or what? Because I sure as hell know your little ass isn't going to do something about it."

That was personal, and Mike didn't hesitate to throw a punch at Monty's face. But he was slow, and Monty blocked him easily and answered back with a harder, faster blow. We could hear the crunching of bone, and Mike bent over and held his nose. Irrationally, I grabbed Mike to protect him, even though I knew there wasn't much I could do. I didn't have anything like Monty's strength, and I wasn't sure if I was prepared for what might happen if I hit him.

As it turned out, though, I didn't need to, because Sue jumped in to take my place, dealing him a swift kick between the legs that buckled him over and knocked him to the ground. He rolled back and forth groaning, coughing, and trying desperately to catch his breath.

"Come on!" Sue screamed.

We ran around Monty to the other side of the street, me holding onto Nelle's arm, Sue trying desperately to take out her keys. Mike hurried along, holding his nose and laughing despite the blood. "Sue, that was amazing!" he said. "That dumb bastard will probably never have kids!"

"It's a bad time for your jokes," Sue called back to him.

Out of the corner of my eye, I saw something moving. Monty, I thought, terrified. But then I saw it was my mother and froze. She was wielding a broom, coming up behind Monty, who had stood and was staggering toward us. My eyes were like saucers as she raised her weapon and struck him in the back of the head.

"Leave them alone," she shrieked, raising the broom and bringing it down over and over. "You piece of trash! You dog! You nasty, nasty person! I called the cops! They're already on their way. You'll learn your lesson this time!"

With these words, she broke the broomstick over his back. Monty tried to grab the half Mom was still holding, and when he couldn't, he covered his face and took off running, stopping only briefly to pick up his gym bag.

All of us had stopped and were gawking at Mom, who was breathing hard but looked proud of herself. Proud and worried, obviously.

"Are you all OK? Did he hurt you?" she asked.

I was too stunned to speak. I simply pointed at Mike, whose nose was gushing. Mom moaned and hurried over to take a look. I heard more footsteps, slow and heavy. It was Dad. He looked exhausted and rested his hands on his knees, only speaking after nearly a minute had passed and he'd caught his breath. "OK, it's OK, you're safe," he said.

We walked to my parents' house, where Mike stuffed his nostrils with tissue until he finally quit bleeding. We asked Sue how she'd managed to floor Monty, and she just laughed and said she'd taken karate lessons as a kid. Mom hadn't actually called the cops, but her threat had worked. Monty didn't come back, and he didn't dare to call, either. My parents said we shouldn't travel that night. It was dark, and we'd been through a traumatic experience. Sue, who looked exhausted, didn't argue with them.

For the first time in a while, I felt at ease in my own home. Dad and Mom made beds for Mike and Sue in Spencer and Shannon's old rooms, and Nelle slept in my bed with me. We stayed up talking till around two. After brushing my teeth, I peeked in to check on my roommates. Sue was lying flat on her back like a vampire in a coffin. Mike was splayed out with one leg hanging off the bed.

Dad came out to meet me in the hallway. "Sorry I didn't make it in time to save the day," he joked in a whisper. "I don't run as well as I used to. Don't tell anyone, though."

I didn't laugh or smile. He had a lot of explaining to do, and I wasn't going to let him off that easy.

"Jenny, I know we haven't treated you the way we should have," he continued.

"You've got that right."

"You deserve to be angry."

"Right again."

"I'm trying to say I'm sorry, OK? And I want you to know you're welcome here again."

"That's great, Dad," I told him, "but it's a little late for words. You went for months without talking to me, you kicked me and my friends out of my grandmother's funeral, and you turned your back on me for getting a restraining order against Monty when you're the one who convinced me to go to the cops. I appreciate you guys being there for us tonight, but that doesn't change what's happened. We're leaving tomorrow."

I didn't wait for an answer, I just pushed past him and walked into my room. Nelle was already in the bed in her pajamas, lying on top of the covers and looking at the ceiling. When I shut the door, she admitted in a soft tone, "I heard your conversation. I'm really sorry."

"Don't be. It had to be talked about."

I pulled up the sheets and got into bed beside her, turning off the lights and thinking in silence.

"Some night, huh?" Nelle murmured.

"I'll tell you one thing: if someone had said a week ago I'd be lying in my bed in my parents' house with you, I'd have told them they were out of their mind."

She laughed and swatted at me. "I'm not good enough for you?"

"I'm sorry to break this to you, Nelle, but you're not really my type."

Grabbing a pillow and hugging it to her chest, Nelle said, "Thanks for coming."

"Don't mention it."

"I'm serious. Thanks for pushing me. After the way I treated you when your grandmother died…"

"Seriously," I told her, "I'd rather not talk about it."

I had managed to put the bad things out of my head, and there was no point in her stirring them up.

"Sure," she agreed. "Good night, then."

"Good night," I said, turning my back to her and starting to drift off.

Nelle spoke again: "Thanks for helping me even though we're not friends anymore."

Opening my eyes, I replied, "You'd have done it for me." That wasn't true. We both knew it wasn't true. But she didn't argue.

"I can see your treehouse from here. Remember how I spilled a soda on the rug and then you never let me back in there again?"

"You deserved it."

"We were happy then," she said. "And I ruined it. I'm sorry."

That memory had made me grin. But the apology…something about it didn't sit right with me. I had wanted it before. Now I wasn't so sure.

"It wasn't your fault, Nelle," I told her. "It wasn't our fault. Neither of us can blame ourselves."

After that, we finally fell asleep.

I don't know who was more surprised the next day, the twins or Spencer, who had been planning to drop in to see our parents and instead found all of us having breakfast at the kitchen table.

I was ready to go back home, so I made sure the conversations were kept short, and by nine, we were all in the car. Or everyone except for me was. I had the trunk open and was stuffing Nelle's things inside. My parents came out to say goodbye, looking doubtful.

"Be careful on the road," Mom said. "And stop and eat something."

"Sure."

"Call when you get in," Dad added.

"All right," I said.

When I closed the trunk, they surrounded me. "Honey, we're sorry," Mom said. I wanted to respond, but I didn't know how I felt. It wasn't anger—at least, I didn't want it to be—but something inside me was resistant to just pretending the last two years hadn't happened. To avoid any discussion of it, I hugged them both and got inside, and they wished everyone a pleasant trip.

I fell asleep several times on the ride home. Mike and Sue sang songs on the radio together. At first, Nelle refused to join them—she always had been a little self-conscious—but at some point I woke and heard her screaming so loud, I thought she'd burst a lung. I tried sticking my fingers in my ears, but it was pointless.

Jack called while we were on the road. I got Sue to turn down the volume and responded. "Please tell me you're back home," I said.

"Indeed. You know what's not, though? You. Not to mention my car. I thought you'd be back by now. You're in trouble. Though if you've managed to find a way to get rid of Mike and Sue forever, I might let you off the hook."

"Sorry, Jack. We're almost there."

"Don't say you're sorry. This relationship's full of surprises, that's what makes it fun. You want to tell me what the emergency was?"

I looked over at the rest of the group. Everyone was staring away, but I could tell they were all eavesdropping, the gossips. I remembered Monty raging around like a monster, and I almost lied to Jack to keep him from worrying, but I remembered our agreement: no more lying.

"Don't get mad," I said. "It's not as big a deal as it sounds like, it's just…" Slowly, tentatively, I told him everything that had happened, leaning my head against the window. Jack didn't reply or interrupt me, and that only made me more nervous. I needed to know if he was upset, and what kind of mood he was going to be in when we made it back. When I was done, everyone else in the car was as eager to know his reaction as I was.

"Are you angry?" I asked.

"I don't know," he confessed. "If I'd been aware of what you were doing, I probably wouldn't have let you use the car. That was dangerous, it could have gone bad."

"It didn't."

"But it could have."

"But it didn't!" Sue shouted. "Stop being so dramatic."

Jack sighed.

"Give Sue some credit," I told him. "She's the one who put Monty on his ass."

"OK, I guess I'm starting to like her a little better." We got off the phone soon afterward, and my excitement built up right until the moment when we were pulling into the parking lot. We had dropped Nelle off on the way—her parents had paid for a hotel room for her until she could find a place to stay, and she said she preferred to be alone when she heard how many people were living in our apartment. I didn't blame her—she probably needed the solitude after all she'd been through.

"So that was the famous friend your ex cheated on you with," Sue said in the elevator.

"I can understand why," Mike said. "She *is* hot. Don't be offended, you've got a way better personality, but…"

"Shut up, idiot," Sue snapped and nudged him with an elbow.

"I'd just as soon we not talk about it," I interjected.

I was nervous when I walked into the apartment, but the sight of Naya and Will there on the sofa looking happy calmed me down. Jack was sitting across from him. Will asked if we'd brought back presents. Sue asked him if Jack's car still being intact counted. Jack looked exhausted. I figured he must have taken a nap at least, but maybe it hadn't helped. His suitcase was still under the bar by the kitchen.

I wasn't sure what he was feeling just then, but when he walked past me to the bedroom with a bare nod—no hug, no kiss—I realized he was probably in a bad mood.

"Jack," I said as he disappeared down the hallway, and he called back, "Not now."

Everyone's eyes turned to me. After a moment's hesitation, I grabbed his suitcase and dragged it back to the bedroom. When I shut the door behind us, I found him lying on the bed with a pillow on top of his head.

"Not now," he repeated.

"Just let me explain…"

"There's nothing to explain, Jen. We agreed we would talk about things, and I trusted you, and you used that to do something you knew I wouldn't approve of."

"There wasn't time!"

"There was. There's always time to call. But as I said, I don't want to talk about it. I'm exhausted." I knew that was the end of it. He turned his back to me and to the entire world. And since I wouldn't get anywhere with him in that moment, I left him alone.

20

CHRISTMAS WITH THE FAM

As the weeks passed, I had to get used to Jack's absences. He'd leave for a few days, come back with souvenirs, usually food, from wherever he'd been, and soon he'd be gone again. He seemed happy. He liked having something to do, and he liked meeting his fans and his favorite actors, directors, and producers. The energy of the film world was a rush for him. That was something he couldn't hide.

And he was getting better and better known. Not just in town, but in other cities, other countries, other continents. He was made for the camera, and the little jokes he cracked in interviews made the whole world fall in love with him. Sue dedicated herself to getting views for all the videos he posted online; apparently, she'd taken a class in SEO, and she was determined to make his stuff go viral. As for the rest of us, we were stuck in the twentieth century, waiting for him to show up on television.

It wasn't the best time for me, though. I was feeling lonely at school without Curtis. Hanging out with my classmates was dull without him, and as I struggled to get through the material, I started to realize how much he had helped me. To tell the truth, I was getting mopey. It was Will who pulled me out of it. He encouraged me to start my own study group, and even if it wasn't the best thing I'd ever done, it did help, and my grades certainly improved.

After one of our weekly meetings in the library, I saw a flash on my way down the stairs. I looked around but didn't see anyone taking pictures, and I forgot the whole thing until the following week, when a major magazine published an article about Jack with my photo in it, describing me as his girlfriend. I had thought I was angry until Jack called from Argentina, so furious that it took Will, Naya, and me to try to calm him down.

"Stop telling me to chill out!" Jack screamed over speakerphone. "Who the hell do these people think they are? They can't just invade my privacy like this! Some psycho on the internet is going to look at that picture and figure out which school Jen goes to, and then there will be all kind of stalkers following her around."

"Jack," I tried to reassure him, "it'll be fine. The article's been out for a while already, and I haven't noticed anything weird. I don't even think the photo's that clear."

"If a single person bothers you," Jack said, "that's it for any contact with the press. I'll move to Tahiti and they'll never hear another word out of me."

I didn't like that he was angry, but I was glad we could have a normal conversation about something. He had been weird ever since I'd gone to get Nelle. Not confrontational, just unable to relax around me. I had wanted to sit down and talk to him about it, but between one thing and another, it was hard for us to get a moment alone, and I think in a way we were both avoiding it, too.

Naya was now eight months along, and attending classes had started to be too much for her. Will finally managed to convince her to finish off her semester at home, and fortunately, her professors were understanding.

There was just one little problem. Or not so little. Having a pregnant, bored, nervous, stir-crazy Naya in the house was a challenge none of us were ready for.

Sometimes she would cook all day. Other times she'd lie on the sofa immobile. She might get a wild hair and go on a cleaning frenzy while chewing out Sue and Mike for being messy. Every day, there was at least one crisis. We all started entering the house with our guard up in case a shoe or a plate might fly past when we walked in the door.

Will had gotten an internship at a financial company. The hours were long, and he came home exhausted every night. And that left me staying up with Naya, watching movies and series and just talking. Because of her hormones or her nerves, she spent most of the day in bed, then when night came, she was full of energy and wanted company.

One night, while she was playing with her heartbeat monitor, I asked her, "As much as you play with that thing, I've got to say it's weird that you don't want to know if it's a boy or a girl."

I dipped a tortilla chip in some queso—that was one of the things Naya had cravings for, and I wasn't so rude that I'd let her eat alone!

Naya passed me the headphones so I could hear the heartbeat, too, as she said, "Honestly, I just want it to be healthy. That's all I keep thinking about."

"Have you guys talked about names?" I asked.

"Yeah, lots. Will hates them all, though."

"Tell me some."

"I really like Gabriella, Michelle, and Kim."

I took off the headphones and objected, "Not Michelle…"

"It's not because of you, it's because of the Beatles song. I can sing it to her when she's little. It sticks in your head, don't you know it? *Michelle, ma belle, these are words…*"

"Please, Naya. I love you, but your singing voice is like nails on a chalkboard."

"And Gabriella is the girl from *High School Musical*. And Kim is—"

"Naya, don't say it—"

"For Kim Kardashian!"

"I swear, I'm trying not to judge you, but try a little harder, please." I told her. "What's Will want?"

"He likes Jane. I don't know why. He just does. I mean, we could go with Michelle Gabriella Kim Jane. That way nobody gets the shaft."

Nobody but the kid, I thought.

"What if it's a boy?" I asked.

"It's a girl," she replied solemnly.

"How do you know?"

"A mother knows these things!"

It struck me that one of the reasons God invented obstetricians was because mothers *didn't* know these things, but she seemed so certain that I didn't want to contradict her.

Mike and Sue almost never left the apartment anymore. Sue had finished her degree but hadn't bothered looking for a job, and with no band and no ambition, Mike just hung around keeping her company. They spent all day watching movies and TV and eating. Jack called them bums every chance he got, but it didn't seem to have any effect. Sue had money from something or other, so she could afford to loaf around. Mike didn't, but he had a gift for squeezing anything he wanted out of his mother.

Mary had come over a few times. Her visits were always unnerving. Mike ignored her, Jack was curt with her, and only Agnes's occasional presence made those moments tolerable.

I think Jack was disappointed in her. Time kept passing, and the divorce she'd promised never happened. Jack's father had moved into an apartment on his own, but after the separation, things screeched to a halt, and I think Jack feared they'd backslide, so he wouldn't let himself get his hopes up.

Nelle had gotten a place of her own. Or rather, she'd found a place and her parents were paying for it. She wasn't interested in going to school—she said it wasn't for her—but she did take all kinds of stupid online classes that allowed her to add lines to her résumé. She had a LinkedIn page, but no one was getting in touch with her because she had no relevant experience in anything. She didn't care, though. She was enjoying her free time.

Things had changed between us. We weren't close the way we had been when we were girls, but we still met up to talk sometimes. Our discussions were short and trivial, but they were something, and I appreciated them. No matter what, she had been an important part of my life.

I was telling Jack about her one day when he said, out of nowhere, "I get where she's coming from. School sucks. I've honestly been wondering why you don't quit."

He was lying on the bed looking at his phone, but this was something he did sometimes, acting distracted when he really wanted to talk about something serious. I was sitting on the ground at the time, mixing paints and looking at a blank canvas.

"Excuse me?" I said. "What are you talking about?"

"I don't know. You've been complaining about school constantly lately. You don't need a degree for anything. Maybe you should drop out."

Passing a streak of green paint over the canvas, I said, "Look, I may not be in the most enthusiastic phase right now. But that doesn't mean I want to quit."

"You said Nelle was taking online classes. You could do that. Or something else, if you wanted. I just feel like you're wasting all your time doing two things that aren't going anywhere."

Two things: he meant my painting and school. Jack didn't understand dedicating yourself to something that didn't bring an immediate payoff. He was like Mike in that way: they both thought you had to be having fun all the time. For me, though, it was different, and as many times as we'd had this discussion, he never would understand. I liked painting, and I didn't want to give it up. And the same went for school. If I started something, I needed to finish it. Jack didn't understand how backward my family was, he didn't know how hard I'd had to fight to get them to even consider college. That had been an accomplishment on its own, and I wasn't going to give up now.

Instead of responding, I gave Jack a menacing look that told him we weren't going through this again. He grunted to show his disagreement, but he didn't insist. Instead, he asked, "What are you working on there?"

"Something ugly. It's an abstract painting of you not listening to me when I tell you how I want to live my life."

I meant it as a joke, but there was a grain of truth to it. I held up the canvas as Jack was rolling his eyes, and when he was done being sarcastic, he stared at it a moment. "It's not bad," he said. "My mom says a true artist doesn't imitate reality, they create their own, or some mystic shit like that."

I thought those words over and fell into a brief trance thinking about what they meant, and when I heard the alarm on my phone, it nearly made me jump out of my skin. Only as I was about to turn it off did I remember. "Shit! It's six! Jack, why didn't you say anything? I need to shower! Dinner's at eight!"

I didn't wait for his response before taking off down the hall. I managed to slide into the bathroom just before Sue, promising her I'd be in and out in no time. With a brush and a nail file, I tried frantically to scrape out the paint from under my nails. When I was done, I hurried back to the bedroom, where Jack had cleaned up my art supplies. That wasn't like him. He must have realized what a rush we were in. He'd opened the sliding glass door to air out the room a bit. I was so busy digging through the dresser, I didn't notice the cold creeping in until I was throwing on my bra, panties, and leggings.

Jack tried to calm me down: "You know, it's fine if we show up late, they're not going to shut the door in our face."

"It's Christmas, Jack! We can't be late on Christmas!"

"Technically, Christmas is tomorrow. Today is Christmas Eve."

I didn't answer, because I was too busy trying to pull up my wool dress while Jack calmly slipped on his cracking sneakers and looked in the mirror to make sure his hair was sufficiently messy. Men! That was all he had to bother with. I pulled up my boots, grabbed my purse, ran back to the bathroom to throw on some makeup. Once again, I had to cut Sue off to do it.

"JENNIFER!" she shouted.

"I promise, it'll just be a second this time."

She nearly ran me over when I came out, begging Jack to put my toiletry bag in his backpack, because our suitcase was full. On my way out the door, I felt my heart skip a beat and shouted, "The charger! I almost forgot my charger!"

Jack waited patiently as I discovered another four or five things I'd almost left behind. When I was finally ready, it looked like we were going to be late.

Naya, sitting on the couch wrapped in blankets, shouted at us to have a good time. "Drink extra for me!" she added, and Will, sitting next to her, said, "Yeah, actually, don't do that."

The two of them would be having Christmas Eve dinner in the living room, with candlelight. Naya thought it was romantic. Will was so worn out, he was just happy not to have to leave the apartment.

Mike was going with us. He'd gone down to the garage early to smoke a cigarette before we left. Jack ordered him to put it out before he got in. We were going to the lake house. Agnes and Mary would be there. I assumed—I hoped—Mr. Ross wouldn't.

Jack had told me I could invite my family. I thought better of it. Things were already tense enough in my life without bringing more problems onboard. I didn't really know where Jack was at with his mother by this point, and with them there, anything could happen.

I had already been home once more, for my mother's birthday, and it hadn't been especially comfortable. Of all the people I talked to, the one who seemed most sane was my nephew Owen. He dressed me down for promising to come over the summer and changing my mind; he asked how Spot the stuffed horse was doing; and he told me that was the last toy I could ever steal from him. My conversations with my siblings and parents weren't half as entertaining.

In the car, Mike asked if we could put on some music to pass the time, and if he could pick it. Jack didn't answer, and when Mike reached for the dial, Jack swatted him away, putting on a boring classic rock station. Whenever a song he knew came on, Mike sang along at full volume.

In the time since we were last at the lake house, several lots had been sold nearby. Houses were going up, and Jack complained that it was turning into a subdivision. Soon all the peace and quiet would be gone.

"All good things must come to an end," Mike said solemnly.

"Unlike you," Jack said. "I assume you'll be with us till the end of time."

Mike ignored him, finally getting his way and changing the station.

When we arrived, Jack parked and unloaded our luggage. Mike dragged his suitcase carelessly through the snow, tracking mud onto the immaculate porch steps. Mary must have known who was ringing, because Mike was the only one who would have stood there pressing the button over and over.

"I heard you the first time," she told her older son with a smile. They hugged just as Jack came up behind them.

"Hey, Mom," Jack said, walking right past her.

"Jennifer!" his mother said when she saw me, and gave me a tight hug. "How are you? How are your grades? Jackie says you've been complaining about school."

"I'm making it," I said, which was true, though she'd probably hoped for a bit more enthusiasm. I noticed Mary was swaying a little, and she had a full glass of wine in her hand. Was she drunk? We'd only just arrived! I didn't say anything, though, as I shut the door and walked through the vestibule and into the kitchen, where Agnes had taken a gigantic turkey from the oven and started spooning sauce over its golden skin. It looked delicious, and Mike was hovering around her, ready to steal a bite.

Agnes was usually warm, but today she was on a mission, and she waved at me vaguely before getting out the knife to carve it. I heard Jack murmur next to me, "I'm going to take our things upstairs."

I followed a few feet behind him, wondering if he was planning on giving me the silent treatment the whole time we were there. I wasn't sure how much longer I could take that from him, and to tell the truth, I didn't think I deserved it. We were staying in his childhood bedroom again. When he tossed our luggage on the bed, I took out my contact lenses and put on my glasses. Jack left while I was doing it. I found him in the room at the end of the hall where I had seen his father once playing piano.

Should I have left him alone? Maybe he needed some space. But my worries got the better of me. "You OK?" I asked as I walked in.

His back was turned to me. I took a seat beside him and looked at him out of the corner of my eye.

After a moment, he asked, "Do you think it was a bad idea to leave the apartment in Will and Naya's hands?"

I was sure that wasn't what was bothering him, but I played along. "I don't think Will's going to let her wreck it, if that's what you're worried about."

Jack smiled. "Great, I feel better already."

"Just think how nice it's going to be there when Naya gives birth and we have a crying baby keeping us up at all hours. That's what you've always dreamed of, isn't it?"

He grimaced. "You know, you're not the world's best at putting someone in a better mood."

"I never said I was!"

Jack hid his face in his hands. "I can't believe it's actually going to happen. I don't know if Naya's ready to be an adult."

"Well, she's there. Once they get married, that's the last box to check off."

"Will won't ever get married," he said. "He doesn't believe in marriage. Naya doesn't, either."

I'd heard them say that, but I never bought it. If I knew Naya, she'd do it for the photos alone.

Jack continued, "Anyway, who the hell gets married when they're in their early twenties?"

"Some people do. My mom was nineteen when she got married, and her sister was twenty-three. Of course, they were both pregnant."

"So the women in your family don't just have tons of kids, they also get married when they're fresh out of high school."

"Well," I said with a shrug. "Shannon bucked the trend. She got pregnant early but just has one kid so far, and she never got married. Since I haven't done either, I'm the odd one out."

"For now," Jack said, getting down on one knee. I was so shocked, I almost flew through the roof.

"JACK! That's not funny!"

"It is, though. I wish you could have seen your face!"

He cackled for a long while, then an uncomfortable silence returned. Jack cleared his throat and sat a little farther away from me. I toyed with a thread hanging off my dress.

"You do know you can tell me about whatever's worrying you, right?" I said.

Jack looked me in the eye. I thought he would speak for a second, but then he pursed his lips and lied. "I told you, I'm fine." Once again, a door was shutting in my face.

Downstairs, we found Agnes plating everyone's dishes. She'd put on her reading glasses because, according to her, she hadn't made quite enough vegetables and no one could get an extra ounce. An eternity passed while she made sure everything was perfect, but no one complained, and nobody touched anything until she had joined us and given us her blessing to dig in.

I couldn't call it a comfortable meal. Mike, Agnes, and I were the only ones who spoke. Mary swilled wine the whole time, and Jack just stuffed his face. I don't think Mike noticed anything was wrong, but Agnes certainly did. By the time dessert was over, Mary could barely stand, and she didn't even notice when she spilled wine all over the tablecloth as she announced, "Time to open the presents!"

"Don't we usually wait till midnight?" Mike asked.

"Who cares? Santa's not watching!"

Jack said nothing as he watched her stumble off. He didn't even rise from his chair until I touched his forearm. Only when we were handing out the presents did things get a little less awkward.

Mike hadn't bought anyone anything, but he sang everyone a song to make up for it. It was…better than some of his other music? I couldn't say much more. Agnes baked everyone cookies, and we ate them while we opened everything else. Mary gave Jack and Mike concert tickets. Mike hugged her, Jack just nodded. For me, she'd gotten a smartwatch to wear when I was running. I gave her some earrings with peace signs, which overjoyed her. I'd bought Mike a jean vest, which he seemed to like, and for Agnes, I got a video game.

I didn't get to hand Jack his present before he gave me mine. He was grinning a little too much for my liking as he handed it to me.

"Should I be worried?" I asked.

"It's going to be the best present you've ever gotten," he promised.

I wasn't convinced when I opened it, and even less when I saw it was a T-shirt with an arrow pointing toward left that said, *I don't deserve him*.

"You love it, don't you?" Jack said. "Just be sure I'm always standing in the right place when you wear it."

"You know what?" I responded. "I'm actually glad you got me this, because now I won't feel guilty about your present."

I handed him a package, and he opened it, intrigued. His eyebrows rose as he looked at the T-shirt I'd gotten him. "Are you serious?" he asked. He held it up. It read, *Call me if you need a babysitter*.

The whole time, Mary went on drinking. She'd almost killed a whole bottle of wine on her own since we got there. She was slurring her words, swaying from side to side, leaning on me, laughing obnoxiously. Jack's face didn't give away how he was feeling, but I could tell by the tension in his shoulders that he was angry.

At one point, I got up to pee, and Mary said, "Hey now, don't run away." She grabbed me around the shoulders, accidentally knocking me to the sofa. She thought it was funny, but that was as much as Jack could take.

"Can you stop being an idiot?" he hissed.

Mary tried to rock herself back up. "I'm just trying to have fun."

"No," Jack said, "you're drunk, and it's making everybody here feel weird. Maybe you could lay off the sauce for five minutes?"

Mary kept smiling, but it was clear her son's words had affected her as she stood and walked to a chair a bit farther away. In a soft tone, she told Jack, "Sometimes, you can be just like your father."

Jack didn't react at first. Mike and Agnes watched him, afraid of what he might do. He blinked, then seemed to finally absorb her words, and stood. "How dare you compare me to him!"

"How dare you treat me the way he does!" his mother responded.

"You're drunk, Mom, I'm just trying to get you to sober up!"

"No, you're trying to humiliate me!"

"Mom, you're acting pathetic. But why should I be surprised? You were pathetic when Dad was beating us and you tried to pretend we were a perfect little family, you were pathetic when you sat there with me in the restaurant swearing to me that you'd leave Dad, and you're pathetic now, acting like this is just a fun old Christmas with no family drama whatsoever!"

Mary absorbed the blows better than I'd have thought she would, setting down her glass and standing to look Jack in the eye. With six feet of distance between them, they looked like two duelers ready to face off.

"You think you're the only one in this family who's suffered," Mary said softly. "Well, I'm sorry to inform you otherwise. Your brother suffered, I did, your grandmother..."

"It's not the same!" Jack screamed. "He never did the things to you that he did to me!"

"Jack, physical violence isn't the only kind of abuse."

I didn't approve of her being drunk, using alcohol as a crutch to finally speak her mind, but she was right about that. It didn't appease Jack, though. "What are you trying to say? That he hurt you as bad as he did me? Nice try, but I don't think so, Mom."

"All I'm saying, Jack, is your pain doesn't cancel out ours."

That wasn't an accusation, it was a confession, something she'd clearly been keeping locked away a very long time.

Jack looked confused. Angry. Unsure where to turn. He wanted to bring an end to the argument, but he didn't know how, and I was sure he didn't want to say something he'd later regret.

"How fucking convenient this is," Jack said, so furious his voice was trembling. "For years, you stood by and didn't say a word. I had to swallow your depression, I had to swallow Mike's addiction, I had to swallow Dad always being on my ass, I had to swallow Grandma never lifting a finger to help us. And I never opened my mouth once to complain. Never. And now I do something—now I stand up for myself—and all you can talk about is how I'm trying to *cancel out* your pain? What about my pain? Did you ever think about my pain?"

Mary looked down. "I did, Jack. And I'm sorry you had to go through that. I really am, from the bottom of my heart. But…"

"No buts!" Jack screamed. "Do you not get it? I always was there for you, for Mike, for everyone. But who was there for me? Who? You've never in your life worried about anyone else, and you don't have the right to go throwing this shit in my face now!"

"I've tried, Jack! How many times do I have to ask your forgiveness for not being there when you needed me? I'm trying, now! You think he didn't treat me badly? You think my marriage was a bed of roses? I didn't have anything left to give, Jack. I tried to protect you. But what did you want me to do, run away? You remember how your father used to lose control! If I'd taken you away, he would have found me, he could have pulled strings, he could have gotten custody of you. Look at you now, you have your own lives, you're grown-up, I'm the one who's alone. I'm literally stepping out into unknown territory with this divorce. I don't know what's going to happen to my home, my work, my galleries. He's threatening to take it all away! But I'm trying to turn the page. I thought I was doing the right thing by separating from him. But you still won't forgive me. What do you want me to do, Jack?"

Mary's eyes were desperate, and Jack wouldn't respond. He wouldn't even look at her, and neither would Agnes or Mike. She was struggling to control her emotions as she added, "You have to believe me. It isn't as easy as it looks."

I met eyes with her, but I didn't want to get involved. I had already pissed Jack off when I'd taken his car to get Nelle. I wasn't about to add insult to injury. And yet, what his mother was feeling was real, and I knew what she was talking about. Against my will, I found myself addressing her: "It isn't easy, Mary. I know. It isn't easy to leave a relationship like that. Especially when it's all you've got."

Jack shook his head. "Are you seriously taking her side?"

"No, Jack," I answered. "I'm not taking anybody's side. There are no sides, don't you get that? This is exactly what your father wanted, for you all to fight with each other. He exploited your vulnerabilities when he was here, and now he's gone, and he's still doing it. He's the bad guy in this story, not any of you."

I was fidgeting. I couldn't help myself. I didn't like the situation, and I didn't like being on the spot. And most of all, I didn't like seeing Jack in this state.

He looked from me to his mother. That hard, angry facade started to crumble. He clenched his teeth to keep us from knowing what he was thinking. It didn't matter, though. He was an open book to me. Looking at the ground, he murmured, "All I wanted was for you to protect me, Mom."

I had looked down, too, to keep myself from crying, and I didn't see Mary's expression as she said, "I'm sorry, Jack. You needed a mother, and I wasn't that for you."

"I wanted someone to let me know I wasn't alone," he said.

"Jack," Mary responded, "I know you don't believe me, but I'll do anything to be sure you never feel that way again. Not you, not Mike, not anyone in our family. I swear. Just give me a chance. Just one chance."

Jack lifted his head, and Mary started to take a step toward him, but then stopped. When she'd gathered her courage and finally wrapped her arms around him, Jack didn't pull away. He even rested his face against her shoulder.

Agnes sighed. "If I'd known the night was going to turn out this way, I'd have drunk a bottle of wine myself."

Mike laughed nervously. Mary grimaced at the two of them, and Jack walked out onto the back porch. The cold didn't seem to bother him as he continued toward the dock, where he walked back and forth, alone. I started to follow him, but Mary stopped me. "Leave him alone a while," she advised me. "He needs to decompress. I do, too. I'm going to head upstairs. Between the argument and the alcohol, my head's spinning…"

"I'll join you up there," Agnes said, taking off the Santa Claus hat she'd been wearing. "I'm too old for these kinds of family feuds."

On her way out, Mary whispered something to Mike, who nodded. When they were gone, and Mike was staring out the window at his brother, I told him, "You know, if you need to talk to him alone, I'll leave you here."

"Don't feel like you have to run and hide, Jenna."

"It's fine," I told him. "I should try to get some rest anyway."

As I left the room, I heard the patio door open. I don't know what Mike and Jack talked about. When my curiosity got the best of me and I looked out the window, all I could see was Jack kneeling down and clutching his head in both hands and Mike there next to him on the snowy ground, concentrating. I took off my glasses, put on my pajamas, and got into Jack's bed. Everything that happened swirled in my mind briefly, but in an instant, I was asleep.

It was still dark when I opened my eyes and felt Jack getting into bed. His hands were frozen as he hugged me, but I didn't complain. I felt the tension drain out of him as he held me close and rested his cheek on mine.

For the first time in a while, it felt honest for us to touch each other, and I savored it a moment before turning toward him. I could see the tears on his cheeks glistening in the moonlight.

"I'm sorry," he said.

"I'm sorry, too," I said.

"I don't like the way we've been lately, and I don't like us spending so much time apart. I'll drop the traveling and—"

"Stop, Jack," I interrupted him. "What's been going on with us these months has nothing to do with you going away."

"It hasn't helped."

"But it's your job. And even if you weren't working, I'd still be in school. I don't want any of this to change, and you shouldn't, either. This is our life. We have to learn to deal with it."

He thought this over, and, unsure what else to say, I ran my finger along the top of his knuckles and held his hand. "I saw you talked to Mike."

"He's the one who talked, really," Jack said. "I just listened. You know how hard it is for him to shut up."

I laughed softly. Jack pulled me into him again. It wasn't a time for words, but even without them, I slept more calmly than I had in months.

21

JAY AND ELLIE

This is going to sound bad.

Terrible, actually.

But the better and better Jack and Mike got along, the more I started to resent their relationship.

Or not their relationship exactly. More like the effect it had on everyone else. Jack loved to joke around and laugh, and all of Mike's jokes were based on getting on other people's nerves. That made a terrible combination. Whenever they were together, Sue was screaming at them to get out, Naya was shrieking about how she needed peace and quiet for her baby, Will was defending Naya, and I was locked up in the bedroom with my headphones on trying to ignore it all.

I was worried about Naya. She was ready to pop, and I couldn't help but fear Jack or Mike would do something stupid and her water would break right there on the couch.

That worried me especially during the baby shower. Will had been against having one—he said it was one of those dumb things people on TV did, and they didn't need their friends to buy them presents—but Naya insisted, and he was too good a guy to put his foot down. Her timing was terrible, with my midterms around the corner, but I couldn't just opt out, so I found myself there blowing up balloons with Mike and Sue while Will cooked—wisely warning Naya against helping—and Jack put up posters and a strand of letters that read *Congratulations!*

The mood was festive, and I was in a good mood, despite everything, until Jack turned to me and asked in a soft voice, "So, what did you get her?"

Shit! I had forgotten to buy a present! Before I could send out an SOS, Naya walked over to me with a beaming expression, almost waddling because her belly was so big. "Jenna, can you go check on Will in the kitchen?" she asked. "He won't let me set foot in there."

"Why could that be?" Sue remarked sarcastically.

Mike laughed, and all the air in the balloon he'd been blowing up flew back into his mouth, causing him to cough. Naya rolled her eyes and said, "Thanks, you're the best!" before I had the chance to wriggle out of it. I grunted, and noticed Jack was looking down at me with a knowing expression.

"Let me guess: you didn't get her anything."

"Shhhh! Don't let her hear you."

"Jennifer Michelle, you are a real piece of work."

"I'm busy, Jack! And I never know what to get people on occasions like this." I tried to justify myself. "It's a baby, what are you supposed to buy a baby?"

"Did your sister not have a baby shower when she was pregnant with Owen?" he asked.

"You're kidding, right? She didn't want anyone to know she was pregnant till the last minute. She basically vanished until she was almost ready to give birth."

Jack reached out for more decorations. I handed them to him, and he started taping them up. "You can relax," he said. "Once more, I've covered you. I got her a present from both of us."

Mission accomplished, I thought.

"You are a literal dream come true," I told him.

"I know. You can pay me back later."

I pinched him, he yelped, and then he went on with his work.

"You're not going to tell me what it is?" I asked.

"It's a surprise."

"Jack, the surprise is for the person getting the gift, not the one who's supposed to be giving it."

"I don't care, I don't want to ruin it, Jen, and I hope this won't offend you, but you've got a big mouth. And Naya's persistent. If she decides she wants to get a secret out of you, you'll crumble in a matter of seconds."

I wanted to defend myself but he was probably right, so I nodded, left him to his work, and went to the kitchen to help Will.

Lana soon showed up with her new boyfriend. I don't think anyone but Naya bothered to learn his name. Chris arrived with a big basket of Swiss chocolates, which Naya tore into like a badger, almost clawing Mike when he tried to get a piece. A few other people from college came, along with friends of Naya and Will from high school, and finally Curtis, who positioned himself strategically across the room from Chris. It was a small group, but it wasn't a big apartment, so it felt crowded, especially when the music started playing. Will and I kept going back to the kitchen to refill the trays of food, Sue reprimanded people for making a mess, Naya flitted from person to person, and Jack, who had business to attend to, spent most of his time on the phone.

It wasn't boring. I'll give them that. And the food was amazing. Will had made chocolate truffles—I had no idea he had it in him—and I could only stop stuffing them in my mouth when Naya stole them off my plate.

At one point, Naya grabbed Will's hands and sat him down next to her. I couldn't tell what they were discussing, but a few seconds later, she brought her hands up to her mouth, cupping them like a trumpet, and announced, "Present time!"

Will tried to protest, but she told him, "I don't care! I want my presents!"

Everyone sat wherever they could, and we passed Naya the gifts one by one. She tore off the paper, which was her favorite part, then passed the boxes to Will to examine each item and thank whoever had given it to them. They got pacifiers, a huge pile of clothes, stuffed animals, rattles and other toys, a bassinet, a cradle, a carrier backpack, and enough soaps, shampoos, and lotion to keep the kid clean and moisturized until retirement age.

The whole time, Naya kept looking over at Jack and me. She was obviously anxious to know what we'd gotten her, and she was making the others curious, too. Eventually, she unwrapped the last gift in the pile and Will said ominously, "There's only two people left."

I glanced over at Jack as he reached into his jacket and removed a red envelope with a gold ribbon. Naya snatched it out of his hand. "What is this?" she asked suspiciously, taking out several sheets of paper. I wondered the same myself. Will and Naya scanned the tiny writing. "What is this?" she repeated.

Will leaned in closer, then looked up to find Jack grinning. "Wait a minute…"

"That's right," Jack said.

Nervous, frustrated, Naya said, "Can someone please explain to me what's going on?"

Jack took pity on her, stood, and pointed to a line on the first page. "It's the deed to this apartment."

What the…

Naya still didn't get it, and Will had to explain to her, "Babe, he's giving us the apartment."

You could have heard a pin drop as Naya absorbed the news. Everyone was staring at her. I don't think anyone could believe it. Jack laughed at me and winked.

At last, Naya asked, "Are you seriously giving us your home?" Her voice was an octave higher than usual.

"It's your home now," Jack said. "I hope you like it."

Will handed the papers back to Jack. "We can't accept it. It's too much."

"Will," Jack said. "You can take it, and you should. It's three bedrooms, the location is great, and it's one fewer thing for you to worry about once the baby comes. I know you guys have been looking around and haven't been crazy about anything you've found. Well, now you don't have to worry about it. Enjoy."

In the ensuing rounds of congratulations and hugs, Jack peered at me slyly. "I was curious to see what look you'd have on your face," he said.

"Jack, seriously! You gave them your home! I can't believe it. You better watch out, though. Naya hates anyone else taking the spotlight, and she could already be plotting her revenge. Do you think they'll give Sue and Mike the boot?"

I saw the two of them hugging Naya and Will. I guess they'd need to ingratiate themselves to their new landlords.

"I think I can convince them not to," Jack said. "We need to talk about you and me, though. We're going to need to move out to make room for the baby."

"Have you found another apartment?"

"I actually had something bigger in mind. I want to buy a house with a big yard. But that's a choice for both of us, and what you think matters, too."

Unbelievably, he was serious. I wanted to tell him he was moving too fast, that we should stop and think, but he vanished into the crowd. The party went on for another hour or two, and then, as the food and drinks were finished off, the apartment emptied out and we started cleaning up. I was exhausted by the time I finally lay down with Jack in the bedroom. I pulled the covers up to my nose and rested on my back, my head sinking into the pillow. Jack turned off the lights and asked me what I was thinking.

"I was wondering when your next trip was. I've gotten kind of used to having this big old bed all to myself."

He grunted and reached over to pinch me, and I tried to shimmy away.

"Good, Michelle," he responded. "I'll keep that in mind the next time I get the call for an overseas meeting."

"What are you going to do? Not come back?"

"It depends on how many sexy photos you send me."

"I believe you mean tasteful adult photos," I said.

"Call them what you want. If I don't get an emergency supply to help me make it through the next dry spell, I might have to resort to drastic measures…"

Our door opened, and Mike stuck his head in. "Hey guys."

"What do you want?" Jack asked.

"I was just saying hi."

"Mike, it's midnight. You weren't just saying hi," Jack said.

"Sure. Well, the thing is, Chrissy is snoring really loud, and I—"

"No," Jack cut him off.

"You don't even know what I was going to say!" Mike protested.

"I do. You want to know if you can sleep in here. And the answer is no," Jack said sternly.

"Why don't you go sleep with Sue?" I recommended. We both knew that wasn't going to happen, though, and I wasn't surprised when Mike tried to convince me to go in and wake her. It was true Chris was snoring loudly. With the door open, we could hear him in our bedroom. After a moment's discussion, Jack told him he could sleep on the floor, and Mike lay down, bundling up under a tiny blanket that barely covered his feet.

As we could have guessed, it only took him a moment to start complaining. I looked at the ceiling and tried to tell myself this wasn't happening.

After hearing Mike turn around and curse for the third or fourth time, Jack said, "For God's sake, just come up here," and Mike jumped between us. They immediately started bickering again, and I almost shouted, "Can we just try and get some sleep?"

But obviously, Mike couldn't let the night end without another one of his stupid jokes. "What's it like, finally being in bed with the handsome brother?" he asked.

"It's terrible," I responded. Mike kept trying to talk until Jack issued a few death threats. Then, despite his complaints that he wasn't tired, he started snoring. By now, I suspected I'd be awake till morning. Jack sighed and covered his ears.

"What did I do to deserve this?" he asked.

I shushed him and he grumbled, "What? Are you afraid I'll wake the six-foot baby resting beside us? This idiot has ruined my night."

"We'll have lots of nights together, Jack."

"Not enough, if you ask me." That got a smile out of him, and we each turned on our side and tried in vain to get some rest.

"Uuuuuggghhh!!!"

I looked up from my cell phone at Naya. She was lying on the sofa with outstretched arms. Mike ignored her, focusing on changing the channel. Seeing that no one would come to her aid, Naya tried again: "Uuuuuuggggghhh!"

"What is it?" I asked her.

"Finally, somebody's taking pity on me," she said.

"For what?" Mike butted in.

"I need help getting up! I've got to go pee!"

Mike grimaced. "How many times a day to you have to pee? I swear, it's every five minutes."

"I'm peeing for two, have a little respect," she said.

I knew Mike wouldn't lift a finger, so I stood, gave her my hands, and waited for her to drag herself up and stomp to the bathroom. When the door closed behind her, I sat back down. "Mike," I said, "why don't you ever leave a show on for more than five seconds?"

"There's nothing good on."

"We could watch a movie. I could text Jack and ask him for a recommendation."

Mike sighed and said, "He's in Holland, leave him alone." Mike was acting crabby again, the same way he'd been when Jack and I had gotten back from Greece. Everything anyone said seemed to get on his nerves. I'd had it, and I decided today was the day to grab the bull by the horns. I snatched the remote from his hand and turned off the TV.

"I've had enough of this, Mike. I need you to tell me what in the hell's going on with you! Why does every little thing I do or say piss you off? Did I do something to you?"

"No…"

I sensed some doubt in his voice and scooted over closer to him. "Is it the band thing again?"

"No."

"Then what?"

"It's complicated," Mike said.

I was frustrated, but I took for granted that once again, my efforts at talking had failed. And despite my irritation, I decided to be understanding. "OK, man. Well, if and when you want to be honest with me, I'm here. But for now, try not to treat everyone else like dirt. We're all going through things."

He frowned. "I don't mean to treat you badly. I like you a lot."

"I like you, too, Mike. We've been through a lot together." I reached over and grabbed his hand. "And whatever you need, you know you can count on me."

I smiled at him. But instead of smiling back, he lurched forward and kissed me on the lips. It caught me so off guard that my brain needed a few seconds to register what had happened. First I froze, then I jumped back as if I'd just stuck my finger in a light socket. Mike jerked away too as I shouted, "What the hell are you doing?"

I tried to figure out what to say, but I didn't have much time, because Naya shouted, and we looked over to find her with her hand over her mouth and the hem of her skirt soaking wet. Mike asked, "Did you just piss yourself?"

Naya shook her head and said, "Sorry for the drama, guys…but I think my water just broke."

None of us knew what to do. We were probably the three least responsible people in the house. I shouted Will's name and took off running for his bedroom. He jumped out of bed and shouted that he was asleep. "Come quick!" I told him. "Naya's water broke!"

That got him moving in record time. Before I knew it, he had on a shirt, pants, and shoes, and had slung over his shoulder the two bags he kept packed for emergencies. He got on one side of Naya, and Mike got on the other. Will grabbed the keys, and the two of them walked her to the door.

"Are you OK to drive?" I asked. Will looked frantic, but Sue was gone, and I doubted he wanted Mike or me behind the wheel of his car.

Just then, the door opened, and we all turned to Jack, who rolled in his suitcase and announced, "Guess who decided to come home early?"

I can't imagine what he thought when he saw the state we were in, but he soon understood the situation. He dropped his suitcase by the door and grabbed his keys.

"Get your car and wait for us downstairs!" Will shouted.

Jack didn't need to be told twice. He rushed away while I hit the elevator button about a hundred times in a row. Naya was already hyperventilating, saying, "Oh God… Oh God… I can't believe a baby's going to come out of me… What if it can't get out?"

"Everything's fine, Naya," I said, smoothing down her hair.

"It's not! There's no way it'll fit! It's going to get stuck!"

"It won't," Mike said, patting her on the arm. "You'll see, it'll be totally smooth."

"Shut up, Mike!" Naya shouted. "Don't think I didn't see what you did!"

Will looked at us, confused, before we all crowded into the elevator. Naya screamed as I hit the button for the first floor. With his usual impeccable sense of timing, Mike started defending himself, saying, "It's not what it looked like, OK, Naya? I can explain."

Will warned him, "Mike, I don't know what you did, but this isn't your moment. Shut up and give me a hand."

I had been staring at the ground the whole time, but when I felt the cool air rush in, I started rubbing Naya's back. Jack was already downstairs waiting for us, and he helped Naya into the car. Will, Mike, and I piled into the back seat, and Jack took off like a race car driver. For once I was fine with it, and I told him, "I never thought I'd be thankful for your reckless driving, but good job."

"Shit, shit, shit shit!" Naya screamed from the front seat.

"Don't curse in front of the kid!" Will said.

"The kid can't hear me! And I feel like I'm getting ripped in half!" Naya shouted. "It hurts! I'm dying."

Will rubbed her shoulders and said, "Mike, get your phone out and time the contractions."

Mike objected, "I don't know what a contraction is."

"Jesus, you idiot," I said, getting my own phone out and tracking them as best I could. It only took us ten minutes to get to the hospital, but there were two in that time, which I was pretty sure meant this was serious. Jack screeched to a halt at the intake area, and Will and Mike struggled to get

Naya out. I rode with Jack into the parking deck, and when we'd parked, we took off running. The women in reception sensed who we were with and pointed down a hallway, and soon we found everyone in one of the patient rooms.

Naya had already changed into a hospital gown and was lying on a stretcher. Her chest was rising and falling quickly, and her face and neck were bright red. Mike was holding one of her hands, and she was twisting his fingers mercilessly. Every few seconds, she would shout, and Mike's eyes would open wide with fright. Will, in a panic, was pacing back and forth.

"Jenna, come here!" Naya called to me. "I need you!"

Will hurried over too, but she turned away from him, saying, "Not you. You're the one who did this to me! No, I'm sorry, babe, I didn't mean that, it's just…"

She couldn't talk more because tears filled her eyes, and she looked at him lovingly for a moment before pain overtook her face.

"I'm dying!" she said. "And that stupid doctor said he can't do anything till my contractions start coming every two minutes. This is horrible! I've changed my mind! I don't want to be a mother! Can't they just take it out now?!"

"Babe," Will told her calmly, "I know it hurts, but you're doing great, everything's going fine. You're not dilated enough yet, and we have to wait."

Jack asked, "Does it really hurt that bad?" Naya responded by unleashing a string of curses that reminded me of the girl in *The Exorcist*, and, worried that she'd kill him if he said something else stupid, I dragged him out of the room, saying, "Let's grab something to drink."

Jack didn't put up much resistance. As I slid a dollar into the drink machine, he complained, "In my defense, Jen, this isn't the welcome I had hoped for."

"What were you hoping for?"

"You in your birthday suit, maybe."

I tried to elbow him, but he ducked me and grabbed the bottle of water that shot out of the machine.

"You could try to be a little more romantic," I told him.

"I can be romantic in a couple of days. Right now, I'm dealing with primal urges."

Him talking about sex reminded me of what had happened just before we left the apartment. I wasn't sure whether or not to tell him. His reaction would be like a bomb going off. Maybe it was better to wait? As I wavered, Will walked over, grabbed the bottle of water from Jack, and said, "Get two or three more of those."

We did as he said and went back to Naya's room, where we waited until the nurses kicked us out. After that, all of us but Will lingered out in the hall—as the father, he must have had special permission to be inside. Chris showed up half an hour later with his parents, and last of all came Sue and Lana, who looked furious to be running into each other. *Some welcoming committee*, I thought.

Waiting for a baby to be born was a new experience for me. With my sister, they induced labor, and in an hour, Owen was out. For that matter, this was the first time any of my friends had been pregnant. I was nervous, and it felt like the ordeal would never end. Jack and I passed the time coming up with names.

"I think Kim is awful on its own," I told him. "And the thought that she likes it because of Kim Kardashian just makes me want to pull my hair out."

"She could call her Kylie, after Kylie Jenner," Jack said.

"Shut up," I told him.

"Maybe it'll be a boy anyway," he said. "If so, I like Jeremy."

"Why?"

"I don't know. It's not too long and not too short. It's not common, but it's also not weird. It's just right in the middle."

"So you're saying you want mediocre kids," I ribbed him.

"Easy there, Michelle. We're talking about *a* kid, not kids."

We talked over a few others: Elizabeth, which I thought was elegant and Jack thought was boring; John, which was pointless, because it was the most common name in English; Jay and Ellie, which were the two we agreed on, leading Jack to say, "We should get to work, then. Little Jay and Ellie aren't going to make themselves!"

The conversation started getting dull, and we examined Naya's and Will's families, who were acting like they'd be struck by lightning if they so much as looked at each other. Chris noticed the awkwardness and tried to start a conversation, but it didn't go anywhere. Jack whispered in my ear that both sets of parents were divorced. I guess that was part of the problem.

I had almost fallen asleep when Will finally opened the door. He was smiling, and I breathed a sigh of relief.

"We did it!" he said. "They're resting, but everything was smooth. The baby's healthy, and Naya's doing great, too."

"What is it?" Naya's mother shouted.

"A little girl," Will shouted. "I hope all of you are ready to meet Jane."

22

NEW ROOMMATE

Jack huffed and puffed and beat the pillow with his fist.

"For the love of God, don't they make muzzles for babies?" he asked.

I tried not to laugh. I was as tired as he was, but my attitude was a little more realistic. Naya had brought Jane home a month ago now, and ever since, our nights had been filled with the baby's wailing. She cried like clockwork starting at eleven each night, and not what you'd call softly. She made sure everyone knew something was wrong, and nothing anyone did ever calmed her down.

I heard Will's footsteps in the living room. He was walking her back and forth and rocking her, which irritated Mike, and when they started arguing, that only made the whole thing worse.

"She cries all night and sleeps all day," I murmured. "She doesn't have a regular biological clock yet. It'll get better with time."

"I think she's doing it on purpose," Jack said. "I think she's an evil baby and she's been sent here to drive us all insane. Probably all babies are that way, like mogwais, cute at first, but then you turn your back and they become gremlins."

How sweet.

"What about little Jay and Ellie?" I asked.

"I've changed my mind. We're doing great now. Why mess with success? Let's leave the kids to other people."

I laughed until I heard Jane squealing again. "Dammit," Jack said and jumped out of bed.

"Jack, it's not the baby's fault," I said as he reached the door.

"I know. I'll take it out on her parents."

I had no choice but to follow him out. Will was sitting down in the bedroom cradling Jane in one arm while she wailed. Sue was pacing back and forth. On the sofa, Mike had his eyes closed and was trying to pretend none of this was happening.

"What's up with her?" Jack asked.

"Do you not think I'd have tried to fix it if I knew?" Will replied slowly.

"She hates us," Mike groaned. "That's what it is."

I asked where Naya was, and Will responded almost bitterly that she was sleeping. Unsurprisingly, a neighbor soon knocked on the door. Ten times this month, someone had come to complain. I understood their frustration, but I don't know what they expected us to do. Soundproof the whole apartment?

Ordinarily, I opened the door to talk to them. I always tried to be calm, explain the situation, and apologize, and it usually worked, though the angry guy upstairs was a pretty tough customer. The main thing was to keep Sue away from the door, because letting her get past you, you ran the risk of a charge for accessory to murder.

I got in front of Jack before he could go unload his rage on someone. Of course, it was the guy from upstairs. He had a nasty expression on his face, and I feared I wouldn't get rid of him as easily as usual.

"Good evening," I said.

"You want to tell me what in the hell's going on with that kid?"

"We're trying to calm her down," I said, as always.

"Well, it's not working, so try something else!"

Before I could respond, Jack's hand came from behind me and rested on the doorframe just over my head, making a loud slapping sound that got my attention as well as the neighbor's. As the neighbor narrowed his eyes, Jack hissed, "Back to piss and moan some more?"

The neighbor was standing uncomfortably close, with his finger extended and a scowl on his face. "That kid won't stop crying," he said.

"Well, thanks for telling us, we had no idea," Jack replied.

"It's annoying."

"You're annoying."

"If it's not parties, it's an argument. If it's not an argument, it's somebody having sex. If it's not that, it's this damn baby. You're making it impossible to live here."

"Then move," Jack told him. "Or buy a pair of earplugs."

"You can't stand here and tell me you think this is normal," the neighbor objected.

"How about this," Jack said. "I've got a solution that will work for all of us. At the end of the hall, there's a window with access to the fire escape. You can climb up on the roof, throw yourself off, and make everyone's day. No more crying baby for you, no more bitching neighbor for us."

He slammed the door in the man's face.

"Jack!" I reprimanded him. "I don't know if you should have said that. That guy looks like he could be violent."

"I'll get violent with him if he comes back here one more time. I'm tired of his bullshit. It's hard enough dealing with people's attitudes *inside* this apartment without having someone I don't even know coming to me to complain."

Poor Will. When we walked back, I noticed the deep bags under his eyes. He looked like he could fall asleep on his feet. In despair, he looked over at Mike and asked, "Dude, can you hold her a minute?"

Mike was scared of the baby, but he didn't have any other option, so he took her, hands shaking, and held her against his chest. Miraculously, silence ensued. She had stopped crying. Everyone was shocked, Will most of all.

"Mike, you're amazing!" Sue said.

Jack waved me back to the bedroom. "Come on, fast, let's go to sleep."

Mike whispered, on the verge of panic, "Don't leave me here! I don't know what to do!"

"He'll help you," Sue said maliciously, pointing to Will, who was on the couch and had already fallen asleep. "Have fun babysitting!"

I saw the look of horror on his face as Jack shut the door carefully, lay down on his stomach, and closed his eyes, leaving me nowhere to squeeze in.

"Jack, make some space for me," I said.

"No. Just sleep on top of me."

"You asked for it," I mumbled and flopped down on his back. He grunted from discomfort but was too lazy to move. After a moment, I added, "There's no way you can actually sleep like this."

"I can, though. I'm doing it."

"Liar. You're talking to me."

"I'm sleeptalking."

"Yeah, you're an idiot, too," I said.

"I never told you otherwise."

I started bouncing up and down, shaking him. The thing with the neighbor had gotten my blood pumping, and I wasn't tired anymore. "Get up," I told him. "I want to talk. I don't think I can fall asleep yet."

"Listen, Jen," he said wearily, "I got on my knees at Christmas time, I asked you to marry me and you laughed at me, and that means the *for better and for worse* clause in our vows isn't active yet. So seriously, much as I love you, you're killing me. Just let me sleep."

"Fine. Give me some space then."

"Whatever." Jack rolled onto his side, and I climbed between the sheets. He looked so cute there with his eyes closed, his lips fluttering when he breathed out. I covered him with a blanket and tried to go to sleep myself.

Naya had turned into a zombie. She wandered around the apartment in a pink robe, her hair poking out in all directions, her eyes surrounded by worrisome black circles. She usually had the baby in one hand and a bottle or toy in the other.

There were days when I offered to take care of Jane so she could go out for a little bit, but I couldn't always deal with her. School was taking up tons of time, in class, in my workshops, and when I had to study. And when I needed to relax, I preferred to do it by calling Spencer or Shannon or drawing, not by changing a baby's diapers.

Still, there were days when I felt so bad for Naya. Like one afternoon when I'd gotten home early and taken a long hot shower, and I came out to find her passed out on the couch with Will—asleep, they looked like the perfect couple—while Jane stared back and forth between Sue, Mike, and the TV.

"There she is," Sue said when I emerged. "Superaunt. I'll bet you'll be popping out a baby of your own pretty soon."

"Not funny, Sue," I replied.

"I'm not kidding," she said.

That was one of those moments when ordinarily, Mike would have cracked a joke, but all that was over ever since he'd kissed me. I hadn't told Jack about it. I was pretty sure I should, but it was long ago enough now that I didn't know how to bring it up. And at a certain point, I think I just decided it was dead and buried.

I had expected Mike to apologize, but unsurprisingly, he never did. Instead, there was just distance. No more pervy comments, no uncomfortably long hugs. In fact, he barely looked at me. It was better in a way, but I also didn't like the weirdness that had settled in between us.

Will jolted awake, looked around until he saw his two girls, then smiled and relaxed, rubbing his eyes. "Hey, Jenna."

"How's the world's best father doing?" I asked. He smiled, I think. Or maybe it was a frown.

"Do you guys know if Naya fed her?" he inquired.

A half-full bottle was dangling from Naya's sleeping hand. I grabbed it and set it on the coffee table. "I'd say yes."

"Cool," Will said. "Well, if you all will excuse me…"

"Time for another nap?" Mike asked.

"Yeah. The other forty were just for practice," Sue interjected.

I took a look at my phone. Jack was supposed to come home for dinner—he'd gone to help his mother with something—but it was eight, and I was starting to wonder. He'd seen her more often since our Christmas dinner disaster, and it seemed their relationship was improving. He acted like visiting her was an obligation, but I had the feeling he enjoyed it. I'd hoped he'd write me to tell me how things were going, but when I didn't see any messages from him, I read a couple of class emails instead.

I zoned out until I heard arguing. I looked back up to find Naya awake and scowling at Mike. "Are you guys OK?" I asked. He was looking down, with a guilty expression.

"We're fine," she said, "it's just that Mr. Why-Don't-I-Kiss-My-Brother's-Girlfriend thinks he's qualified to give me advice about *my* relationship."

"Naya…" I began.

"Don't get into it, Jenna. He's an idiot, and he needs to learn to keep his trap shut."

"I'm sure he didn't mean what he said," Will objected.

Mike started rubbing his temples. "Naya, please, don't bring that up again. I know it was a mistake, but it's in the past, and it would be better if it stayed that way."

A part of me agreed, but I also remembered what Jack and I had discussed. No more lies, no more secrets. It was a question of respect. At the same time, I had to think about my own sanity and the sanity of everyone in the apartment. Was this really the time for Jack to have another one of his breakdowns, when all of us were already so on edge?

As I asked myself this, I crossed eyes with Mike, who threw up his arms and shouted, "What do you think, Jenna? Do you want my brother to know? Because, fuck it, if you do, I'll tell him."

"Mike, for God's sake, don't curse in front of the girl," Will said.

Sue, who had remained silent up till then, observed, "I really doubt that's a good idea. Mike clearly regrets what he did. I think that's enough. All of us make mistakes."

"A mistake is doing it once," Naya responded. "This is the third strike for Mike. There's seven of us in this apartment now, that's way too many, especially if one of us is going to criticize other people's relationships and constantly try to undermine Ross, who's done so much for us. If he confesses to Ross and they make up, fine, but otherwise, he can go. I'm not going to sit here and cover up for him anymore, and I'm not going to keep listening to his bullshit."

Sue and Naya scowled at each other, then looked at Mike and me.

"I *can* tell him," Mike said. "I'm not scared, if that's what you guys think."

I didn't know how to respond, so I told him, "Do whatever you want. I don't care."

A few minutes later—following a stressful silence—Jack opened the front door, walked in whistling, and stopped as he noticed how awkward the situation was. "Is something up?" he asked.

"Come here, honey," Naya said to her daughter, picking her up and walking to the bedroom. "The adults have something they need to talk about."

Jack looked confused. "We do?"

Will was as nervous as I was. Mike was even worse. He was opening and closing his fists, and a thin film of sweat had appeared on his brow. Sue's lips were pursed as she observed the scene.

"OK, seriously," Jack announced. "I'm going to need you guys to tell me what the hell's going on now."

"Something happened," Mike admitted. "And it's past time I told the truth. I kissed Jenna."

I wished he hadn't just come out with it like that. He could have prepped Jack, made an excuse, something. I felt like a soldier on a battlefield waiting for a grenade to land and explode. For a few seconds, Jack stood there staring, and I even began to wonder if maybe he didn't care. But then a shadow fell over his face. "Tell me you're kidding."

"I'm not," Mike said. "It was the night Naya gave birth. I tried to kiss her, she pulled away from me. That's it. End of story."

Did he hope just blurting it out would make it seem like less of a big deal—one of those things that just happens, like bad weather or a burst pipe? I don't know, but it didn't work. The tension grew in Jack's body as he turned from his brother to me. There were too many emotions in his face for me to grasp what he was really feeling. "You didn't tell me," he said quietly.

"I'm sorry," I responded.

"You said we'd tell each other everything. And as for you, Mike… You're a miserable piece of shit."

Will stood, his hands slightly raised, as if he were trying to calm a wild animal, and warned Jack not to say anything he'd regret.

"Oh, don't you worry," Jack said. "I won't regret any of this."

"What do you want, Ross?" Mike asked. "I admitted it. I was sincere. That's a lot for me."

Jack smiled bitterly, enraged, and said, "Oh, should I go get you a prize now? A cake, maybe? You think since you admitted it, that makes it OK? I'm not supposed to be pissed off now? You've never been able to change, Mike, and you never will. You're a bum, a loser. You don't even deserve to be talked to."

"This was different!" Mike argued.

"Every time you fuck up, it's *different*. And then you come to me and call me brother and tell me it's important to make peace, but you never actually try to improve. And whenever I treat you like an adult in the hope you'll be responsible for your actions, you go off crying about how no one loves you. Has it ever occurred to you that maybe no one should?"

That was cold, even for Jack. Mike grimaced and looked away. But Jack wasn't done. He turned to me, unable to speak, and that silence hurt worse than any words. Then he stepped to Will. "Did you know?"

Will nodded. "I'm sorry, man."

"You're sorry?" Jack roared. "Screw you, too, Will. Seriously. All of you leave me alone. Every one of you is pathetic."

He stomped out of the apartment without another word, and none of us knew what to say.

The next morning, Jack still hadn't shown his face, and I had to get up early for an exam. I hoped I hadn't bombed, given how little sleep I'd managed to get. I couldn't stop thinking about whether my relationship was over—all Jack had asked for from me was honesty, and I didn't know why that was so hard to give him. And so when Naya met me in the hallway and said, "I think my daughter hates me," I was happy to be able to focus on someone else's drama.

In her daughter's defense, if someone tried to put a diaper on me as ineptly as Naya was doing with Jane, I'd probably hate them, too.

"Don't be ridiculous," I said, "she's just uncomfortable."

"It's not the diaper, Jenna, it's everything. I'm not good at being a mom, and Jane knows it. She hates me, I'm absolutely certain of it. Can babies feel hatred? Have you ever read anything about that?"

"Come here," I said, scooped Jane up, and took her gently back to the changing table.

Naya apologized for being a pain. "I know I complain too much."

"It's not that," I responded, "it's just that you let any little thing get you down. Like this. It's not instinct, it's something you learn, but it's hard to get any better when you fall apart any time something doesn't go perfectly. Now watch."

I put Jane's favorite rubber duck beside her, then gripped the baby's ankles softly. She blinked her pretty little eyes. Naya looked as concentrated as a student taking notes. I unstuck the tabs, opened the diaper, and, noticing Jane had a slight rash, rubbed her down with a little ointment. When she was changed and clean again, I picked her up and handed her back to Naya. "See? Good as new."

"You're magic," Naya said.

"I had a lot of practice with my nephew."

"Can you come watch me the next time I change her? I really do want to get it right."

"Of course," I told her. "I'm an expert."

Naya held Jane to her shoulder and rocked her as she put away her things. The baby grabbed a lock of her blond hair and started sucking it. She only ever did that with Naya, and I couldn't help laughing at it, because Naya had always been obsessed with her hair. But having kids can make the vainest person less self-centered, and Naya had given up trying to stop her.

"How was your test?" she asked as we walked toward the living room.

"Horrible."

"How was class?"

"Horrible, too."

"Man," Naya said, "it's a barrel of laughs around this apartment lately."

Maybe I should have sugarcoated things, but in that moment, I couldn't. I was drowning, and I was unable to focus because I could barely sleep between the baby and my issues with Jack. After the test that day, I'd walked out of class and overheard everyone saying how easy it had been. I had barely waded through it, and I didn't want to even consider how ridiculous half of what I'd written was.

I needed to move forward, not backward, though, so I spread out my notes for my other classes on the coffee table and started studying. Will was there with his laptop—he'd been glued to it since his internship started—and Sue was in her easy chair chitchatting with Mike. Naya started complaining that her boobs hurt. I tried to ignore her.

I could have gone to the bedroom, but of course I didn't feel like it. Everything there reminded me of Jack, and the thought of Jack reminded me that I had a very unpleasant conversation in store for me. With the TV on, I could hardly concentrate, and I thought Mike and Sue should have the decency to turn it down. But they were locked in one of their usual spats. They started throwing pillows at one another, and one of them missed and scattered my notes. Jane grabbed one of my sheets of paper, crumpled it, and stuffed it into her mouth. As I was picking my stuff back up, I growled, and everybody realized I was at my limit. They fell silent, and I inhaled and exhaled three times, trying to regain control of myself. I was stomping around, gathering my papers and trying to get them in order, when Jack walked in, still wearing the same clothes he'd had on the night before. Worst of all, Vivian was with him.

I hadn't seen her since our less-than-pleasant encounter at the airport. She smiled, but I knew how sincere her smiles were. Since I'd told myself I'd try to play nice, I managed to muster an expression that wasn't quite disgust. Jack looked irritated as he glanced back at her. "OK, I'm home," he said, "you can leave now. I told you I didn't want you to come up."

"Well, I'm here now, and you can't kick me out," she said.

Jack turned to me. "What's your problem?" he asked. "You didn't call me, you didn't send me a single text. I could have died and you wouldn't even know."

It was true. I'd thought he needed his space, and plus I had studying to do.

"He didn't die," Vivian said. "He was with me. Luckily."

She reached into her purse, pulled something out, and tossed it on the coffee table. It was a bag of cocaine. Jack went pale. Jane started crying from the noise, and Naya tried to calm her down. All I could do was stare.

"I was having a party," Vivian informed us, "and he showed up, and I caught him buying that."

"I didn't take any of it!" Jack rushed to say.

"But you bought it! And once again, it's because you're upset over Jenna! I told you if you got back with her, you'd fall into the same trap, Ross. I know you, and I don't like to be right, but..."

The unmistakable sound of paper tearing made everyone stop and turn. My notes, my precious notes—in a rage, I was tearing them to shreds. My fists were shaking as I began screaming, "I. CAN'T. TAKE. IT. ANYMORE. I'm sick of this shit!"

"Not in front of the baby!" Will chastised me.

"To hell with the baby! You think the baby knows what a swear word is? You think a creature that can't do anything but eat, sleep, and piss in a diaper is really worried about hearing a bad word? You think a *word* matters to that baby more than the fact that every single person in this house is fucking insane? That's right, I said everyone! I can't take it with your petty dramas any longer!"

I'd never lost it like that, but it did something for me—I felt like a new person! My heart was pounding as all the exasperation of months flowed out of me.

"You don't have to be like that," Naya said.

"Oh, I don't!" I turned toward her. "Who are you to tell me that? You haven't stopped bitching for one second since Sue and I found you crying in the bathroom! If it's not the baby, it's Will, if it's not Will, it's us, if it's not us, it's how you've chipped a nail, if it's not your nails, it's your goddamn cooking! Nothing is ever good enough for you! You whine about literally everything! Do you not notice that everyone else here gets by just fine without needing to be reassured every two seconds? Maybe you should try comforting someone else for a change instead of constantly crying for everybody to come comfort you!"

Hearing a throaty giggle, I turned to Sue, who pretended that she had been coughing. Too late. Now she had a target on her head.

"Something funny, Sue?" I hissed. "Because if I'm being honest with you, I'm over you never taking seriously any of the seventy million problems we have in this apartment. You sit there in your chair like a queen and act like you're so much better than us, like none of the things that bother us matter, and that gives you the right to laugh everything off. Well, I'm sorry to bring you back down to earth, but you're no better than anyone else here. Being nasty doesn't make you smarter than the rest of us, it's just that you're too weird to have friends of your own, so you don't know what it means to worry about other people or care about them or get upset for them. I don't know if it's because you're scared of getting hurt or what kind of complex you've got that you can't just open up, but you can get one thing through your head right now: you're just as crazy as everyone else in here."

Mike had frozen, as though praying that if he played dead, he might be immune to the onslaught. But it didn't work. He was my next victim, and I was far from finished.

"And you...kissing me! Seriously! Because if there is one thing you have got to know: Never, Mike, never in a million years would I ever dream of hooking up with you! And even if I would, are you really that much of a creep? Do you not have one ounce of respect for your brother? What the fuck is wrong with you? Are you such a loser that the only way you can feel good is to bring everyone down to your level? Has it ever once crossed your mind to try, I don't know, being a better person? What about telling your brother you're sorry for constantly mooching, constantly putting him down in subtle ways, constantly treating whatever's his like it's yours? You piss and moan all the time about how nobody loves you. Maybe you could try to make yourself worthy of being loved!"

I was hyperventilating by now. But I wasn't done. I picked up the bag of cocaine and threw it back at Vivian. Surprised, she caught it in midair.

"As for you, don't even get me started," I said. "Jack's best friend—didn't you call yourself that? You're supposed to be his best friend, and there you are rubbing your hands together with malicious joy at the thought that he might relapse. Because that would give you the chance to talk more garbage about me and tell Jack once again how I left him in the lurch and how I'm such a bad influence. Let me tell you something: I might have screwed up, but I've always treated Jack like an adult, while you're running around in the background mommying him, picking up his phone and not telling him I've called, secretly trying to keep him away from his friends like he'll relapse if he has to come in contact with reality. And then, when he's at his lowest, you what? Go to bed with him! I may not know you, but I can see where you're coming from, and that's been true from the first time I met you. I tried to keep a good attitude about you for Jack's sake, but that's over. You may think I'm some dumb small-town girl, but I've seen right through you from the beginning. And it's past time you stopped judging others and took a look at yourself."

I was almost done. I only had one left. I took a deep breath before turning to Jack. He had entered in a huff. Now he was cowed, waiting for his turn. I think I even saw him shrink back when I looked at him, just before he sat down and defended himself: "Don't start in on me! I didn't do anything wrong!"

"Oh, you don't think disappearing the entire night is doing anything wrong? Or running away any time things get uncomfortable? Or expecting me to always go chasing you down? Has it ever occurred to you that facing your problems might help actually solve them, so you won't have to drag them around forever? When it comes to other people, you're perfectly happy throwing their mistakes in their face, but I guess since you had a hard childhood, you're not responsible for anything you do. Look, I admit it: I left, I had secrets. Fine, well you had secrets, too. So I didn't tell you Mike kissed me. I'm sorry, but I tried! And then when the truth came out, you ran away before I could apologize, and who did you run to but Vivian, to a party where you knew you might relapse. Is that what you wanted? To fall down a black hole and have everyone worried and asking once again, *Oh, no, what are we going to do about poor Jack?* Well, sorry, but it's time to grow up and cut that shit out. So the next time you're upset, just come out and say it. Because I can't deal with this circus every time one of us makes a mistake. It was cute at first, but I'm over it."

By that point, I could barely breathe. No one dared to talk to me but Sue, who said, "You're a little—"

I cut her off. "I'm a little over it. You're right. I wanted one thing tonight: to look over my notes in peace so I wouldn't bomb another fucking test. So even if everyone here seems to think I'm wasting my time, or that school is something I just do for fun and my grades don't matter, please, let me get on with it."

I picked up the scraps of paper. The ones I'd torn, the ones Mike had stepped on, the ones Jane had put in her mouth. When I had them in a pile, I stomped off down the hall, turning back once to say, "All of you need to get your heads examined."

I was grateful that no one stopped me, and even after I shut the door, there was a long silence. When they did start talking again, I shut them out. I had work to do. I opened up my laptop and transcribed everything. At least that way, I wouldn't have to worry about a baby drooling over all my hard work.

Hours must have passed by the time Jack knocked on the door and walked in. He was cautious. Whatever mission he thought he was on when he first arrived at the apartment, he had better ideas now.

"Hey," he said.

He closed the door behind him and looked around. I think he was trying to find something he could joke about to break the ice, but when that didn't work, he smiled innocently and began, "About what you said…"

"Do you really want to get into that again?" I asked.

"Not really, but… I just wanted to say…you're not all wrong. But also, I don't think your degree is a waste of time. I'm sure no one else does, either. It's admirable that you've stuck it out, we all respect what you're doing. And the same goes for painting. I realize I was a dick about that. I didn't mean to be, I just say stupid shit sometimes."

He was bouncing back and forth from his heels to his tiptoes, intimidated, which wasn't the way I was used to seeing him. He crossed his arms. "I know you're waiting for me to say something, but I don't know what."

"You do, though," I said. "Of course you do."

He looked up at the ceiling. It was clearly painful for him to say those magic words. But when he realized he had no choice, he sighed with resignation. "I'm sorry."

A smirk crossed my face, and I looked back down at my notes.

"Aren't you going to say something?" he asked.

"I'm busy."

He grumbled and started to walk out. Before he made it, I called out, "Jack?"

He looked back, curious.

"Were you really going to relapse?" I asked.

He hesitated. "For a minute, maybe. But then I stopped. I realized right away that I had a lot more to lose than I did to gain... Now keep hitting the books. I'll let you know when dinner's ready."

23

BEGINNINGS, ENDINGS

I didn't know what it was like to watch a person grow up. With Owen, because he didn't live with us, I didn't follow the process slowly. Certainly not enough to understand how the people around them could affect a young person's life.

Jane had been with us for a few months now, and she no longer cried the way she used to. She was more manageable, and it was easier to figure out what she liked. My white blouse with the big buttons, which she always tugged at every time I wore it. The music Jack put on, which always made her bounce her head back and forth and gurgle in a way we thought meant *more, more,* until she finally got too tired and Will had to put her to bed. Sue said she didn't care for her much, and I had the feeling it was mutual: she frowned when she had to hold the baby, and Jane would scream and wriggle every time Naya tried to hand her off to her. Mike was Jane's favorite: if he was around she'd stop crying, would eat the foods she normally spit up on her shirt, and would fall asleep no matter how agitated she had been. Whenever Will and Naya couldn't take her wailing anymore, they'd turn to Mike. He was resistant at first, but soon he was every bit as crazy about Jane as she was about him.

The nightmare began not long after her first birthday, when she started walking on her own. She'd turn up out of nowhere, grab whatever was at hand, hide things in her parents' bedroom or give them to Mike... She was funny, too, though. She loved multicolored clothes, she loved having her hair put up in pigtails, she liked these ugly, fluorescent bracelets, and she liked her mother putting makeup on her. They had the same green eyes, and Naya was proud that her daughter took after her.

When Jane started talking, she didn't seem to know who *mama* and *papa* were and would use those names with whoever was holding her. Fortunately, Naya and Will didn't care. She also said *yes, no, bye-bye*, and *poo-poo*. This last one was Jack's fault, and it was her go-to word when she didn't like something. When she was mad, she would scream it over and over as she crawled off and hid under one of the beds.

She and I eventually got along. When she first arrived in the world, I was so busy studying that I barely had time for her. I had to start my last year of school; Jack was traveling all the time. Will was working, Sue was looking for work, things were hard all around. But if I ever had a bit of free time, I'd take her to the bedroom to paint, and that opened up a new world for her. She'd see me and start shouting *Pay! Pay!* That was her way of saying *paint*. She loved nothing more than covering her palms with the stuff and stamping them on paper. Before too long, she learned how to hold a brush.

We were at that one day when Jack came to the door to announce it was time to eat.

"Shh!" I joked. "Can't you see the artist is at work?"

Jack smiled, walked in, and scooped her up. She shrieked when she had to put the brush down but started laughing when Jack tossed her up and down in the air. As he placed her on his shoulders, she waved at me and said, "Bye-bye!"

I put everything away, fixed my hair, changed into a different T-shirt, and went to the living room. Since we had a baby in the house, we didn't eat as much junk food anymore. Well—most of us didn't. Jack and Mike were far from grown-up in that regard and showed no interest in the cutlets and salad Naya had made that night.

"What do you guys want to watch?" Will asked. "A movie, a series…?"

"How about a reality show?" I asked.

"How about I kill myself?" Jack responded.

I stuck out my tongue at him. I hoped Naya would take my side, but she was too busy trying to get Jane to eat. Mike said, "Series," Jack said, "Movie," and we all looked over at Sue for the tiebreaker.

When she pushed her food around her plate instead of saying anything, Will said, "Everything all right there, Sue?"

She looked up, crestfallen, and announced, "I found a job."

Everyone congratulated her, and Mike asked, "Why do you say that like it's a bad thing?"

"Because it's in another town," she responded. "If I say yes, I'll have to move."

Her expression stressed, Naya inquired, "What are you going to do then?"

"I've got to take it," Sue responded. "I can't just sit around here forever. We all knew this would happen someday, right? That we'd eventually have to move on?"

She was trying to feign indifference, but I could tell that she was upset. Her voice was soft, and she kept staring at the floor, as if she didn't want to look us in the eye. "It's not starting for a while," she added, "so there's no need to be dramatic. There'll be time for goodbyes and all that."

Mike couldn't believe what he was hearing. It hit me weirdly, too. It felt somehow like I was being abandoned. I tried to remind myself that this wasn't a movie and we couldn't just go on pretending our lives had never changed. I took for granted that we'd be friends forever, but we were growing up. There was no getting around it. My graduation was around the corner, Naya and Will were parents now, Jack was a big director with meetings every other week. We couldn't hold onto the past. All Sue had done was remind us of that.

Jack was thinking the same thing I was thinking, but I didn't find out until that night when we were in bed. We had been talking about this and that for a while when he asked out of the blue, "Do you want to keep living here?"

"Wow," I told him, "that was abrupt."

"Sorry. It's just that what Sue said got me thinking. I told you we'd move a long time ago, but then it kind of fell by the wayside. I'm ready, though, I think. I want a place with some land."

I turned onto my elbow and raised my head onto my hand. Jack looked nervous, as though he didn't know how I'd react.

"Why do I get the impression that you're not telling me everything?" I asked.

"I just… I had an idea, but I don't know what you'll think of it. The lake house. You told me before you liked it. And it's Mom's now, she got it in the divorce. And she and I were talking the other day, and she said two houses were too much for her. It's a lot of upkeep, and she's not working as much as she used to, and she said it's just not worth it for her. If I don't take it, she's just going to put it on the market."

"Is she just going to give it to you?" I asked, admiring the boyish grin on his face.

"Not outright. There will have to be some kind of financial arrangement. I don't really know the ins and outs of it. It's part of my inheritance, but it's Mike's, too, so I'll need to buy him out of it eventually. But that's for lawyers to deal with. Whatever it is, I can manage it. I'll probably need to make another film, though."

"I like your confidence," I said. "I'm assuming you'll just snap your fingers and a project will fall out of the sky?"

I already knew the answer. His manager had been on his case, studios had been chasing after him, and if he wanted the opportunity, it was there for the taking. His first film was still getting streamed like crazy. He was a success. There was no other way to put it.

Pathetically, I hadn't even seen his movie yet. I must have been the only one. But I wanted to see it with him, I thought that would make it more special, and every time I brought it up, he changed the subject. I began to worry he was embarrassed of it, so after a while, I quit trying.

"Do you have a subject in mind?" I asked.

"I was thinking horror."

"Great. I'll be the first person in the world with a boyfriend who's made *two* movies I can't watch."

"You don't want to star in it?" he joked.

Speaking of stars, he and Vivian were still friends, despite everything. I still didn't like her, but we were at least cordial after my explosion. We were never going to be super besties, but at least we didn't scowl at each other every time she came around now. That in itself was progress.

"I'll leave acting to the pros," I said. "But please, remember to invite me to the premiere this time."

Jack must have had the lake house on his mind for a while, because the very next day, he set up a meeting with his mother and a lawyer. I tagged along, and when nearly everything was done, Mary walked around with me while Jack signed the papers. She showed me her old studio and said, "I was thinking this could be yours."

She was calm, but something in her voice, a certain sorrow in her smile, told me she would miss the place. The divorce had been hard on her, and it had done serious damage to her career. She couldn't bring herself to paint or take photos anymore. Nothing seemed to move her.

"Maybe you and I could paint together here," I reassured her.

"I think I may have lost the taste for it."

"Then you can be my manager! Who knows the art world better than you?"

Mary smiled and shook her head. We stepped into the garage, which I think she wanted to show me because it had all the boys' old things: toys, bicycles, surfboards… Everything was covered in dust, and I sneezed as soon as I stepped in there.

It was beautiful around the lake house: quiet, serene, surrounded by nature and the sounds of birds. But it was far from our friends, and I wasn't sure I was ready for that. Jack must have sensed that on the drive home, because he asked me, "Are you having second thoughts?"

"No… I mean, sort of. I'm excited for us to live together out here, but…"

"You're not ready to say goodbye to everyone?"

I nodded. After a second's thought, Jack proposed, "Why don't we do this: we'll wait till you graduate and then we'll see how we feel. The commute would be a huge headache anyway."

That I thought I could accept. I looked forward to enjoying my final months of living together with my friends, just taking it easy. But of course, that was the farthest thing from reality. I had an internship, final projects, exams, and when I had a free second, I usually wanted to paint or talk to someone from my family on the phone. And that left little time for hanging out.

Jack was up to his ears in work. He and Vivian were writing a script together and would spend hours in the bedroom with the door shut, coming up with ideas and characters. I sometimes painted in there while they were doing so, and once or twice I threw out an idea of my own.

Jane was out of her screaming phase, so we were finally able to sleep at night, and with so much to do, we'd pass out as soon as we lay in bed. Then, every morning, the alarm would go off at six, and the whole cycle would start over again. Jack and I barely even had time for each other outside of the holidays and family events.

My birthday was so close to Jane's that we decided to celebrate them both on the same weekend, inviting everybody out to the lake house. There was only one rule: nobody was allowed to do any work. I had a great time. We all did, I think. I was twenty-three now, and Jane was two. The poor thing ate so much cake that her stomach hurt for a week.

I remember how funny it was when Mike got the idea to build a bonfire, and for some incomprehensible reason decided to ask Naya to help him out. They went for wood, which they piled up sloppily on the lawn before spending ten minutes trying to light one corner of a log. Jack and I went out to check on them. The smoke had blackened their faces, and Naya had burned her thumb. We shook our heads as Will came to the rescue.

"You know, guys, the usual approach is to start with some twigs or newspaper…"

Mike and Naya exchanged confused glances, and Naya said, "I guess that makes sense."

Mike said, "Not to me. Wood's wood, what's it matter how big it is?" Will pushed him aside and arranged the kindling in a pyramid. I took Jane's hand, and she helped me arrange a circle of stones around it, then we went and gathered some pine needles and tore newspaper into strips.

Naya and Mike had done next to nothing, but that didn't stop them from spending the whole night bragging about what an amazing fire they'd built.

With so many things pulling me in different directions, graduation day came upon me before I even realized it. I had wanted to skip it, but Jack never would have let me. And so I found myself up in the front row, in my stupid robe with my stupid pasteboard on my head, with a pink dress underneath that I'd spent a small fortune on and that no one could appreciate. As I felt my sweat soaking into it, I told myself a T-shirt and shorts would have been smarter.

I looked back at the audience and found my parents out there. They'd driven up with my brothers and my sister. Our relationship still wasn't the greatest, but I was happy they'd come. Agnes and Mary were sitting next to them and talking away, and Mike had his arm around Owen, who was much bigger than I remembered him.

He didn't even ask about Spot anymore. That made me sad. I still set him on top of my pillow every time I made the bed. Poor Spot, he deserved to be remembered, but children are fickle. Owen was probably into Minecraft now.

Naya, Will, Lana, Sue, Curtis, and Chris were all out there waiting to scream my name. But we were called out in alphabetical order, so they'd have to wait a bit. Jack caught me looking at him and gave me a thumbs-up. He knew I was nervous. I smiled to reassure him.

All the students were on edge. It was silly, because we all knew we'd made it, we'd seen our grades weeks ago, but it still felt like something could go wrong. My heart pounded harder and harder the closer they got to my name. All I had to do was cross the stage, take the diploma, shake the dean's hand, and stand with the rest of the group. Surely, I could manage that without stumbling or doing something stupid.

Or could I?

The person next to me got up. She seemed to walk over in slow motion. Then the dean looked down and read the next name. *Jennifer Michelle Brown.*

Of course, he had to read out my middle name. I was sure Jack thought that was hilarious. I did the same as the others, heard the clapping as I climbed the steps, the dean smiled and congratulated me, and I accepted my diploma. My palm was sweating as I turned to face the camera. My smile must have been less than convincing, because I've never felt so stressed in my life.

When I saw the flash, I walked toward the other graduates on the stage and waved at my friends and family. They were all standing up and applauding, and Jane, resting on Will's shoulders, was shaking her little hands in the air.

There was a party in one of the quadrangles with waiters carrying passed hors d'oeuvres, mothers and fathers crying, graduates breathing one last sigh of relief. Some people were continuing on to grad school, but for me, the ordeal was done. And I was proud: the first person in my family to graduate from college.

Everyone congratulated me one by one, even the twins, which was an unprecedented event. I was tired, though, and soon I wanted to go home. I held out till midnight for other people's sake, and when I couldn't take it anymore, I said I needed some sleep. Happily, everyone else was done by then, too.

As soon as I set foot in the apartment, my body released that balled-up tension. Jane was already sleeping, and Will and Naya took her to bed. Sue and Mike chatted in the living room. Strangely, I wasn't ready for bed yet. I asked Jack if he wanted to have a beer with me. He said, "You've made me an offer I can't refuse."

We sat together on the folding chairs on the balcony, me in my pink dress and heels, him in a button-down shirt and pleated pants—which I think was a first. I don't know which of us looked goofier.

"I want you to know," he remarked to me as we were two beers in, "I don't put on dress clothes for just anybody."

"Poor baby, how you've suffered. I'm sure you'll get me back when you have your next premiere and I have to go in some designer dress."

We had gone back and forth about it, and I'd decided to go, though I dreaded the idea of watching a horror movie in Dolby surround. I'd had nightmares about that damned nun for years. But Jack had insisted, and of course I couldn't leave him on his own.

"You'll have to get used to it. That's what rich people do," Jack said.

"Great. Just what I've always dreamed of. Are you going to get a corny sports car, too?"

"I don't know," he replied. "I like my car."

"What about a second house? Or a yacht. Or a hot-air balloon."

"I was thinking more like a honeymoon…"

Oh no. Was this happening? I looked at him. His usual silly smile drained away, and he looked serious. He cleared his throat. He was nervous. This better not be a joke. Could it be…?

"That's been on my mind lately, you know," he began. "I don't want to rush it. But it just keeps making more and more sense to me, and I don't see the point of waiting." He took my hand. "I talked to your sister to get her advice, and she freaked out of course, she was so excited. Your parents like the idea, too, your mom even made some recommendations on how I could propose. As for my grandmother and mom, you can only imagine. They've been calling me almost every day asking me when I'm finally going to pop the question…"

I tried to say something, but I was frozen. I couldn't believe this was real. I wanted to pinch myself to make sure. Jack went on: "Jen, I know you and I are young and we haven't been together that long. And I know it hasn't always been good. We've had arguments and disagreements, and we'll probably have more. But that's part of the deal, right? And no matter what, we want to be together, and together is how we're going to get through those things. I could never imagine saying that to anyone else. You're the only person in the world I can see myself living my whole life with. And so…"

He reached into his pocket, and my heart started pounding like a drum. My cheeks were burning, my palms were sweating, I could hardly draw a breath. He took out a little velvet box and squeezed my hand.

"The first time we were together, it didn't last long. Three months, but even then, I couldn't imagine myself without you. A lot has happened since, but there's one thing that's stayed the same. And that's my certainty that a life without you just isn't a life I want to have. And I may be rushing things, and it may be cheesy… I mean, I know it's cheesy, it's the cheesiest thing I've ever done, and it sounds even worse now than when I was practicing it in the mirror, but I don't care. I want to be with you. And I know we don't need a piece of paper that says we love each other, but maybe it's nice anyway. So I'm putting myself in your hands. Jen…will you marry me?"

My heart ordered me: *You idiot, if you don't say yes now, you and me are done.* But I wasn't sure what words to choose. The box in Jack's hand was open—I could see the streetlight glimmering off the yellow gold of the ring. My mouth was hanging open, my body was paralyzed.

"Now would be a good time to answer," Jack reminded me. "I'd recommend *yes*, but hey, it's your call."

At last, I cleared my throat and started nodding frantically. Jack looked at me incredulously.

"Yes," I whispered.

"Was that a yes?"

"Yes!"

"For real?"

"Jack, yes! Yes! Now put that damn ring on my finger before I freak out!"

He did it, and I looked down at the glimmering stone and then back at him. I wasn't sure who was more surprised, or if it was surprise, relief, or terror that we felt. This was a huge step, a step I hadn't been sure I was ever going to take. But once it was done, I knew I'd made the right choice. I sighed with relief as Jack asked, "I guess this means we need to organize a wedding?"

I smiled, flashed the ring at him, and said, "I guess it means you'll have to start calling me Jennifer Michelle Ross."

We opened two more beers. And two more after that. And several more. I lost count as the sun started coming up, but I didn't care.

Not every night is made for worrying.

24

ROO-ROO

Jack was lying on the carpet with Jane in the living room, and she was staring at him. He'd fall silent, she'd smack the toy in front of her with her fist, he'd pretend to be scared, and she'd crack up laughing. This from the guy who said he didn't get along with kids.

Sue kept shooting them nasty looks because she was trying to read a book, but she didn't complain, and for her, that was saying something. Will could tell she was agitated and thought it was funny, but he didn't bother saying anything.

"How about this one?" Naya asked. "It's perfect!"

I looked at her laptop screen, unconvinced. She had found a page about theme weddings, and one of the examples was Disney, and she was elated as she carried on about how she could be Cinderella, I could be the Beauty from *Beauty and the Beast*, Sue could be Grumpy, and so on.

"I guess that makes Jack the Beast," Will said.

Jack shrugged as if it didn't really bother him.

"That's sweet, though! You'd be a great Beast," Naya reassured him, but I interrupted her to tell her I didn't think a Disney wedding was a memory I would cherish for the rest of my life.

Jack agreed, and I said it was probably a bad idea to look for wedding ideas on the internet. "Why can't we just do a normal wedding like every-one else?"

"Because a normal wedding is boring!" Naya objected.

"Naya, imagine me telling my mother she has to come to my wedding dressed as Mrs. Potts or whatever. She'd probably kill me."

"Jenna's right," Will said. "What's the point of stressing over trying to be original? They should just do what everyone does: rehearsal dinner, wedding, reception, honeymoon."

"You're not taking this seriously!" Naya growled. "Weddings are sup-posed to be special. It's the most wonderful day in a person's life!"

"Whatever," Jack said. "I'm leaving all that stuff up to Jen."

"Thanks a lot," I responded. "You know it's your wedding, too. You could try to help out."

"But I just don't care, Jen!" Jack objected. "I care about marrying you, but the when and how are irrelevant."

"Irrelevant!" Naya shouted, as though she were about to burst into tears. "Isn't that sweet. I'm sure you'll make an incredible husband."

Will turned down the volume on the TV and asked, "Why are y'all even talking about this? There are people who organize weddings for a living, you should just hire one of them."

"That would cost a fortune," I said.

"Babe, your husband-to-be is loaded," Sue reminded me.

"It's not just about the ceremony," Naya continued. "You need to think about the setting, the guest list, the food…and now that Jack is who he is, you can't just do some reception at his mother's house with a cake from the supermarket. People will come with expectations, and you can't disappoint them…"

"Can we please chill?" Will asked. "It's not your wedding, Naya, and we know Jack couldn't care less. So it's really about Jen and what she wants."

I did have something in mind. I'd tried to pretend it wasn't a big deal, but I'd been thinking about it much more than I'd have cared to admit. And since I was terrified at what nonsense Naya might propose next, I came out with it: "What I've really always wanted to do is get married on a beach." Since nobody responded, I went on, "I mean, it's just an idea. If Jack doesn't like it, then…"

"Why on a beach?" Sue asked.

"I don't know. I hate the idea of everyone having to put on a tux or evening gown and there being a section for the bride's family and another for the groom's, and a priest being all solemn and whatever. I wish everyone could just relax, wear whatever they want, kick their shoes off and walk in the sand if that's what they feel like."

Naya was horrified, but Jack agreed. "I love it. No more need for debate. We're having a hippie wedding on the beach."

By now, I'd had enough of the subject—it was something private, between Jack and me, and not a proposal the whole apartment got to vote on—so I asked, "What are we doing for dinner?"

"Well, Jane's sleeping at her grandmother's tonight, so that means we don't have to eat healthy for once," Will said with relief.

"Burgers!" Naya announced.

Jack responded, "I don't know, maybe my lovely bride wants one of her nasty barbecue pizzas."

"No way," I said. "I got a slice yesterday and I thought I would puke just from the smell. It's weird, but that's been happening to me a lot lately. Believe it or not, I could go for a salad."

Sue was shocked that I'd turned down barbecue pizza. Will and Jack were relieved and were debating between tacos or Chinese. Naya, though, was staring at me with a panicked look on her face. Out of the blue, she stood and said, "Jenna, come with me. Feminine emergency."

I followed her to the bathroom. She forced me down onto the toilet seat and looked me dead in the eyes.

"Jenna, when was the last time you had your period?"

That caught me off guard. "I think it was on May fifth?"

"You do know it's June seventeenth, right?"

That silenced me a moment. I think my brain simply refused to admit what she was implying. She rested her hands on my shoulders and asked, "Are you absolutely sure?"

I nodded. And I was regular as clockwork.

"Do you guys use protection?"

"Uh…"

I remembered the night of my graduation almost a month ago. We had laughed, gotten drunk, stayed up late, and wound up in bed. I didn't remember many details of that night, but I was pretty sure there hadn't been a condom in the wastebasket in the morning.

Reading the panic on my face, Naya cursed before rushing to reassure me: "OK, OK, no need to panic yet. We still don't know anything for certain. Do you have a pregnancy test?"

"Why would I have a pregnancy test?"

"For emergencies!"

We'd been in there long enough that I was worried people were getting suspicious. And in this case, *people* meant Jack. Like magic, he knocked at the door. "Is everything all right in there?"

"No!" Naya responded, before I hissed at her and made her correct herself. "I mean, yeah. Great. Everything's great."

Jack clearly didn't buy her performance. He burst in, worried, stared at us from head to toe, and asked me what was going on. He knew me too well to think that I was fine, and I could feel the blood draining from my face and my fingers shaking.

"Are you sick or something?" he said.

"Not exactly," Naya answered for me. Her presence was unhelpful, to say the least.

Unsure how to proceed, I began, "Jack, you remember my graduation night...?"

"Not much," he responded, grinning.

"Yeah, exactly. I don't remember it too well either. And now it turns out that I'm late."

It took him a few seconds longer than it took me to grasp the significance of that. When he did, he started stuttering: "B-b-but... I wore a condom, I'm sure I did."

"Are you?" Naya questioned him.

Looking at me almost apologetically, Jack said, "I really thought I did."

"Well, it's time for a test. I'm going to go see if I still have one," Naya announced, like a parent chastising her children. She soon returned, holding the test out sternly. I quivered as I peed on the little strip, shook the stick off, and started waiting. Five minutes it took. Five minutes that felt like five eternities. I had forced Naya and Jack to go out in the hall while I was taking it. Now they were both back, standing in front of me with arms crossed. Jack ran his hand through his hair, I rubbed my arms to try to get warm, Naya held the test and looked at it closely, waiting for a little telltale stripe to appear.

Hoping to distract me, she asked what we had going on over the next few days. We were planning on doing some shopping: we needed furniture for the lake house, materials for the reno, and we were thinking about taking Mike away for a trip to the lake house, because he was having another one of his lonely phases. "Keep talking," Naya told me, which I did, just babbling to not think about the emergency at hand. Poor Jack, I must have been driving him insane.

When the five minutes were up, Naya interrupted me and said, "OK, showtime."

Everything moved in slow motion as she brought the test out and scrutinized it closely. She seemed to be taking forever, and in a huff, I said, "Dammit, Naya, are you going to tell us the results or what?"

"Eh… I think it didn't work."

"Excuse me?" Jack murmured.

"There's no lines on it at all. I just remembered that these things expire, and I bought this one just after Jane was born, so…"

"NAYA!" I screamed, and she apologized profusely.

It was getting late and there was nothing open nearby, so we decided to wait for morning, even though I knew there was no way I could sleep. I kept telling myself I couldn't be pregnant. I didn't *feel* pregnant, and I always took it for granted that I'd know as soon as I was. I was nervous all night. I couldn't enjoy my dinner, and all through the meal, I could feel the pressure of Jack's eyes on me. We conversed and pretended to laugh, but I don't think our act convinced anyone.

When we got in bed, I told him, "Don't stress about it. We'll find out tomorrow and we'll decide what to do then."

"Sure," he said distractedly.

Hoping it would cheer him up, I added, "How about we go back to talking about the wedding? We still haven't picked a day, but I was thinking sometime next June would be nice."

"June's too hot."

"May?"

"It rains too much in May."

"How about April?" I asked.

"Yeah, April, I like that. Mid-month, though, when it starts to get warmer. The sixteenth, maybe. Does that sound good?"

He smiled like an angel as I agreed, "Yeah, April sixteenth sounds good."

"Well, that's one thing we can clear off our plate," I told him.

"Great," he said. "Good night."

Weirdly, he was calm, and he managed to fall asleep without much trouble. I wasn't so lucky. I felt hysterical thinking about the pregnancy, but I tried to talk myself into happiness: I thought how beautiful Jane and Owen were and reminded myself I really wanted children… I was older than Naya and Shannon had been when they gave birth. What did I have to worry about? And yet…

By one in the morning I couldn't take it anymore, so I threw on some clothes and stole Jack's car to drive to the nearest Walmart, a half hour away. A while later, I was back in the bedroom, tugging Jack's shoulder softly. At last he woke. "Wh-what the…?"

"Come, Jack. It's urgent."

He struggled out of bed for a few seconds before following me out like a mummy, only opening his eyes once we were out in the hall. "Why are you dressed?" he asked.

"I went to get a test. Now lower your voice or you'll wake Mike."

I walked him into the bathroom. Shut the door. Sat on the lid of the toilet. Pointed to the test, which was on the edge of the sink. As Jack's eyes widened, I told him, "There's a minute left."

"A minute," he said. "OK. I can survive a minute. Everything's fine. No matter what, everything's fine."

Ordinarily, I would have smiled at him. This time, I just couldn't.

"What will you do if it's a no?" I asked.

"Jen, I'm more than happy to keep trying as many times as you need."

"And if it's a yes?"

"I guess we'll go buy a crib and I'll go on eBay to see if anyone's selling *Kill Bill* baby sheets."

I shook my head. "I'm being serious, Jack."

"Trust me, I'm being serious, too. If it's just you and me, I love that. But if there's a little Jay or a little Ellie in that belly of yours, then you'll be making a dream come true for me. Now is that minute up yet?"

"Forty seconds, Jack."

"What if we had three kids?" he asked.

I chuckled nervously. "I'm not even sure if I want *one*."

"Come on, now! One's nothing. Five is too many, obviously. But two is too few. Look at me and my brother. I'm sure the fact that there were just two of us left lasting psychological damage. So we're talking about three or four. Unless you want six. Seven, obviously, is out. Seven's an unlucky number…"

"Three, Jack. Three's my limit."

"Fine. What should we name the third? Rufus? We could call him Roo-Roo. It would be cool."

"You've had a lot of stupid ideas," I said, "but that is possibly the worst one ever."

"Tyler, then."

"Tyler could work. Now shut up. This thing is ready, but I don't know if I'm ready to look at it."

Jack could tell how worried I was as I looked at the time on my phone. He brought a hand to his chest. "I'll tell you one thing, Jen. I've never prayed in my life, but I'm praying now."

"What for?"

"For a positive, obviously."

"I wish I was as confident as you about this whole thing," I said.

I felt his eyes on me as I looked down.

"So…?"

"Well," I said. "One line is negative. Two is positive. The problem is, I can see like five lines now. I don't have my contacts in."

"Jesus, Jen, you're killing me! Give me that thing!"

He grabbed the test and stared at it, not saying anything for a few seconds. Only when I bugged him did he look me straight in the eyes and say, "Looks like we're going to have to make a trip to the baby store, Michelle."

25

NEW STAGES

"No way."

"But…"

"Did you not hear me?" I asked. "N. O. That spells *no*."

"You're so boring."

I looked closely at the sheets he was showing me—the famous *Kill Bill* sheets he'd brought up before—with their illustrations of swords and blood and people in black-and-yellow suits. I shook my head and kept pacing through the bedding aisle.

"I'm not sleeping with those," I told him.

"Not even if this comes with it?" He waved a hand from his chest to his abdominals.

"Not even," I said, reminding him that we'd made an agreement: every choice we made there that day we had to both agree on. Mike, shuffling behind us and eating an ice cream, butted in: "Can I add something?"

"No," Jack responded.

We stopped in the aisle and looked back at him. I hadn't been wild about the idea of having him act as our personal decor consultant, but that was Mike—you just couldn't get rid of him. Snubbed, he skipped off ahead of us, amused at his brother's annoyance. I took Jack's arm, trying to be grateful that I'd even gotten him out the door. Shopping had never been his thing, and he was even more wary now that he was starting to get recognized in public. Already, two people had noticed him, and one had snapped a photo.

He grumbled again, and I reminded him that he was the one who had insisted on getting new furniture.

"I was young and innocent!" he protested. "I had no idea what the consequences would be."

"Well, you've got to deal with them now. And that means going to the baby section."

I was surprised that remark got a smile out of him. But then, I'd been surprised at how happy he had been ever since we found out I was pregnant. I mean, I was, too, but I was terrified as well. I wasn't sure I was responsible enough to bring another life into this world, and didn't know how I'd handle such a big change. It was exciting, but when I really thought about it, I could feel the ground sink beneath my feet. So I tried to take it one step at a time. And that meant shopping. Not that we needed much: Will and Naya had given us Jane's old things. The hip carrier, the Montessori mirror, the nasal aspirator...half this stuff I had never even heard of, but apparently you had to have it all now—that's what I'd learned from all the Facebook and Instagram accounts about modern parenting Naya had shown me.

"Jack, what the hell are you doing with all those frames?" I asked, emerging from my trance.

"Baby photos...that's a thing, right? Don't tell me we're not going to take a bunch of photos of our kid?"

I smiled, but then I saw that one of them had a stock photo of two grandparents cradling a child, and that reminded me of an issue I hadn't intended to bring up yet. But Jack could read me like a book, so there was no point in hiding it. "Listen, I wanted to ask you something," I said. "I know we haven't talked about it yet, but..."

"No," he said softly. "I'm not telling him anything."

I knew who *him* was. Jack's father, of course. We hadn't talked about him in forever. Why would we? He was a mean old man, and he'd never done much for either of us. But things had changed. We were getting married and having a kid. Were we really going to shut him out forever? I knew I couldn't force Jack to reconcile with his father, and I didn't even want to. But I needed him to know that the option was open.

"Whatever you want to do, I support you one hundred percent," I said gently. "I don't care if you tell him about the kid, I don't care if he doesn't come to the wedding, it's your call. I just want you to know that if you ever do decide to tell him, I'm OK with it."

Jack thought it over for a minute, looking at the same stock picture that had made me wonder about all this, and shook his head. "Our child deserves to grow up in a loving family, not around someone like Dad."

"Perfect," I said. "I won't bring it up again. He's your father. That means everything that has to do with him is your decision."

He tried to play it cool, but I could tell he was relieved. I didn't feel the need to add anything as I grabbed his arm and dragged him down another aisle. When we finally finished, we had two loaded shopping carts and very little desire to deal with the stuff inside them. We discovered Mike waiting for us by the door with a bag of gummies in his hand, which he didn't offer to Jack and which he hid behind his back when Jack tried to snatch one.

I had a way with *Uncle Mike*, though, as I'd taken to calling him. When I reminded him I was eating for two now, he let me have as many as I asked for. Thankfully, the brothers got along, more or less, as we drove to the lake house. We'd been taking things out there bit by bit for the last two weeks, and by now, all that was missing was our clothing, which we'd left for last.

I should mention that Mike was now a part of this *we*. I noticed one day he'd slipped a bag of his things in with ours when we were packing, and I'd mentioned it to Jack. There was a big fight about it, then the two of them stopped talking to each other for a while. Mike said he didn't understand what the big deal was: technically, the house was half his, and all he was asking for was to stay in the guesthouse for a few months, just until he found a job. But in all the years I'd known Mike, he'd never once had any steady work, and Jack and I both feared *a few months* meant forever.

Not that I minded so much. The guesthouse was far enough away that I assumed we'd have our privacy—more than we'd had in the apartment, at any rate. Jack refused to bend, though, until one day when he said out of the blue, "OK, Mike. You win. But there's a catch: you're not sticking around for free. There's not going to be any more scrounging. You're an adult, and it's time you lived like one. The property needs a gardener. If you want the job, you're hired. I'll include room and board at the guesthouse as part of your wages."

"Gardening sucks, though! Can't I be your chef instead?" Mike asked.

"Mike," Jack responded, "you couldn't boil an egg if your life depended on it. You can be the gardener and live in the guesthouse, or you can find something else. That's the deal. Take it or leave it."

There was no danger of Mike finding anything else, so now we were stuck with him.

As we dropped everything off, I looked in a corner where a stack of canvases stood wrapped in brown paper. Those were my dreams: my paintings, the ones I was hoping to make my name with. Mary had told me they were good, and she was planning a show for me at her gallery. She saw something in me, she said, but I'd need to work my fingers to the bone; I was too raw. She gave me assignments to improve my technique: portraits, still lifes, landscapes. She was an expert, so there was no point in arguing, and I did everything she said—anyway, I loved it, and I was excited to see if these finished pieces would go anywhere. Even though I'd gone through countless tubes of paint, I still held onto the box Jack had given me. It was there on the table now. Just before we left, as Jack and Mike were dropping the last of our shopping bags in the corner, I looked at it again, winking at Jack and asking, "Are you guys ready?"

We had spent our last night at the apartment, and we were having a special dinner to say goodbye. I was looking forward to it, because of the celebration and because I was starving, too. But I wasn't too excited about Naya's cooking. She had insisted on taking care of everything, which was sweet of her, but even after years of motherhood, she still couldn't cook to save her life. When we got back, everyone was sitting on the sofas and chairs. Naya had already set out our meal. It was at least recognizable as spaghetti—the kind of mushy, sludgy spaghetti they serve at a high school cafeteria. Everyone dumped parmesan cheese on the pasta until it looked like a little hill of snow, and that helped us swallow it down without too many complaints.

At one point, Jane jumped up with a smile and ran over to hop in Mike's lap. After all that time, they still had a special connection.

"Christ, I hope she develops better taste in men one day," Sue joked.

Naya asked how the preparations were going at the new house, and when she could come see it. I said she was welcome any time, but she should really give us time to furnish it. That sounded so *adult*, but I guess we were adults now. I mentioned that, and everyone argued with me: Naya said she was a *young adult*, a *post-adolescent*, still a kid, basically. When Mike joked she'd soon be one of those middle-aged women who lies about her age, Naya asked, "I just want to make sure, you guys are taking him with you, right?"

"As long as he behaves," I said. "He's staying in the guesthouse. That's conditional on him staying out of our hair."

"I'm not a dog," Mike butted in, "I can speak for myself. Anyway, I have an important role at the lake house, I'm the gardener, in case you haven't heard. So Dad will have to shut up about how I've never made anything of myself."

"You must be proud," Sue said, "taking your brother's money to live on his property."

"Our property," Mike fired back. "And I've been meaning to tell you, I've got a queen bed. It's too big for just me. Maybe you want to come live with me, Sue."

"I'd rather sleep on the floor of a gas station bathroom," she replied. "Anyway, this is my last night here, too. I've got to start my own job."

I never thought there was much love lost between them, but every time Sue reminded us that she was leaving, Naya got all sentimental. Jane could tell, and threw her arms around her—it said something that a little child was better able to handle life's ups and downs than Naya, but so it goes. "You guys all up and decided to leave me on my own!" she wailed.

Will reminded her, "Excuse me, I'm here, and your daughter's not going anywhere, either."

"Whatever," Naya complained. "It's different. We'll never have our old life back, and it makes me sad."

"It's not so far," I told her. "Sue's an hour away by car, and the same for us. You can come visit whenever you want." Jack had zoned out watching TV, but when I nudged him in the ribs, he nodded, probably unaware of what we were talking about, and said, "Yeah, for sure."

That got a smile out of Naya, and her good mood lasted until we went back into the bedroom to get the last of our things. Then she started whimpering again and asked, "Can't you guys just stay one more night? Please?"

Will touched her shoulder. "Babe, this has to happen, OK? Life goes on. Jenna's going to have a baby, they've got a new home…it really is time."

Naya nodded and watched us packing up. It was heartbreaking, seeing how sad she was, but what was I supposed to do? On an impulse, I said,

"Let's do a selfie!" That was music to Naya's ears, even if everyone else in the apartment found it horrifying, especially Sue, whom I grabbed and pulled into the crowd as she protested, "I don't do photos!"

"It's just one! For old time's sake! Naya's right, we're going to look back on these years one day and we'll wish we could have them back," I told her. "And it'll be good to have a photo to take a little trip back in time."

I guess that was convincing, because she stopped struggling and we all piled in on the couch, except for Jane. She'd fallen asleep and looked like a little angel, so we left her there. Once we were in our places, with Sue in the middle, a couple on either side of her, and Mike behind us grinning like an idiot, Naya shouted, "SMILE!" We heard the click of the camera a second later.

As Naya stared at the photo and said, "Amazing," Jack reminded me we had to leave. We hugged and said a long series of goodbyes. I had to grin as Naya needled Jack about his cool attitude until he finally admitted that he'd miss everyone.

"I knew you were a softy deep down," she shouted, squeezing him tight. "You can go now. I just needed to hear you tell us you loved us."

"I didn't say I *loved* you guys, I said I'd miss you," Jack countered.

"Same difference," she said, sticking her tongue out at him.

Tired of the back-and-forth, Mike declared himself tired and we walked out into the hallway. I felt a knot in my throat. I guess Naya wasn't the only cornball in our group. This really was it—the end of something. And I was ready for what was going to come next, but that didn't mean there wasn't a part of me that longed to stay behind with my second family. For better or for worse, we had all chosen each other, and looking back, I don't think I could have found better people to spend my college years with.

Grinning, I said, "You guys behave, all right?"

A tear rolled down Naya's cheek, Will smiled, and Sue stood there with her arms crossed.

"You, too," Will said.

Jack grabbed my hand. Sue finally managed to show a human emotion, asking, "We are going to hang out again, right? You guys said so. I'm taking that as a promise."

Impulsively, I threw myself at her and squeezed her until she screamed for me to let her go. "Group hug!" Naya called out, and everyone wrapped around us. We swayed together a few minutes longer, then Mike, Jack, and I walked down to the car.

As I watched the highway roll past us in the nighttime, everything was silent except for Mike snoring in the back seat. I looked over at Jack, who seemed pensive. His hand was on the gearshift. I reached over and grabbed it.

"I'm remembering something my therapist told me about stages in life," I told him. "How every time a door closes behind you, a new one opens."

He smiled. "Does it lead to a better place or a worse one?"

I laughed. "What we've experienced together has been incredible, Jack. But something tells me the future is going to be even better."

"I think so, too."

I pulled his hand into my lap and felt his thumb tracing out the edge of my engagement ring. When he reached the diamond in the center, he looked over at me and asked, "Are you ready for the next stage, Jen?"

I didn't have to think twice. I just smiled and nodded.

"I sure am."

Epilogue

APRIL SIXTEENTH

I took a deep breath and stared into the mirror.

"You look great," Shannon told me. "Stop being such a worrywart."

"It's fine," my mother chided her. "If she feels nervous, that's natural. But honey, you *are* gorgeous. I can't tell you how proud it makes me that one of my children is finally getting married."

She wiped away a tear, and to distract her from the tension, I said, "Yeah. I wouldn't keep my fingers crossed for the rest of them."

"I still have hope for Shannon," she admitted. "The other three…well, we'll just have to see."

Shannon said we should go outside, and I reminded her Dad was supposed to come up first. She nodded and said they'd give me a little time to myself. Then she squeezed my arm and said, "Good luck out there."

As the seconds passed slowly, I reexamined myself. My makeup was nothing fancy—I hadn't wanted it to be. My hair was tied back in a bun with a few loose strands framing my face. That was a last-minute change, against my stylist's wishes, but it was a humid day and my curls wouldn't play nice. I ran my fingers down the edge of the dress. I had thought it was perfect when I bought it, and even though I was anxious now, I had to admit, it looked amazing. Simple but elegant, strapless, form-fitting, with a flounced skirt… Even Dad liked it, and he groused about everything.

I was going out barefoot. Everyone was. I wished I could have seen the look on Mom's face when Shannon told her that was the dress code. I grinned at the thought and smoothed out a slight wrinkle as I heard a knock on the door. It was Naya, who peeked in and said, "Can I? We've got a slight emergency."

"What is it?"

"I think he needs his mommy."

Naya pushed her way in, holding Jay in her arms. He was screaming like a banshee and pulling Naya's hair as she tried and failed to keep his little arms at bay.

"I'm sorry," she said, "I just suck with kids. I tried with Jane, but I could never calm her down the way Will could, not to mention Mike."

"It's fine," I said, smiling and taking hold of my son, who instantly relaxed. "What's up, Jay?" I asked. "Why are you driving Auntie Naya crazy? Let me guess, mean old Sue did something to make you angry?"

Sue walked in behind Naya and murmured, "You wish. The one who should be complaining is me. I've never had to wear such a ridiculous dress in my life."

Sue, Naya, and Shannon were my maids of honor, and they had on matching light-blue gowns with their hair hanging over their shoulders. Naya loved it—she looked good, and she knew it—but Sue had hardly stopped carping since I first mentioned the idea.

"Let me remind you, Sue, it is my wedding," I chided her.

"And that's supposed to be my fault?"

"Besides," I added, "you actually look good."

"Mike's told her so five times," Naya informed me.

Sue rolled her eyes. "I need a guy my age."

"Mike is your age," Naya responded.

"I mean mentally. Mike has the brain of a five-year-old on his best day."

As I laid Jay down on a blanket, I asked what everyone was doing, and Naya told me they were all gathered on the beach. Spencer had walked off by himself, she said, and was reading and rereading the text of the ceremony. I still remembered the day he told me he'd gotten ordained as a priest online. I'd heard of people doing that but never thought it was real, but Spencer had done it, and now he was excited to officiate our marriage. The idea gave me nightmares at first, but it was exactly the kind of crazy thing that Jack loved, and he convinced me it would be fun. Spencer and I had grown close over the past few years, and it meant a lot to me that he wanted to be a part of my wedding. My brother Spencer—the guy who used to get mad at me and throw food in my hair—would now be standing in front of me as Jack and I read our vows.

I didn't want to ask myself what could go wrong, because I wouldn't know where to start.

"You've got five more minutes," Naya reminded me. "Ross is already standing there waiting. I can't believe I'm about to watch Ross walk up to the altar. That was something I never thought I'd see in my life."

"Have you talked to him?" I asked.

Sue laughed. "I caught him raiding the appetizer table. His mom saw him and told him not to stain his tux, and he lost his shit and yelled at her to leave him in peace."

Once Jay was asleep, I wrapped him up tight and handed him off to Naya, telling her my mother would take care of him. Sue and Naya walked out, and I shut the door behind them, gathering my courage as I waited for my father to arrive. I tried to remind myself that everything was taken care of—Jack had spared no expense, and the hotel that was handling the catering and everything else was top-notch. All I needed to do was make it down the aisle without tripping.

With nothing else to do, I kept wrapping the strands of hair on the side of my face around my fingers and letting them go, watching them bounce slightly like little springs. Finally, I heard a knock and my father's voice saying, "Jenny, are you ready?"

I opened up with jittery hands and said, "No, but I guess I never will be."

"Does that mean we should go downstairs?"

"Yeah."

Dad patted me on the cheek and said, "It's going to be great, honey. We should get a move on, though. I don't want your husband-to-be to have a heart attack."

"Have you talked to him?"

"Yeah. He seems nervous. In the two or three minutes we chatted, he must have adjusted his tie fourteen times."

"Jack can barely even tie a tie," I informed Dad.

"I know. I had to help him with it. Again."

I giggled as we walked downstairs, exited through the back patio, and walked onto the beach. There was a little trail of rose petals leading to the altar. Normally, I would have thought that was cheesy, but my mind was racing and I hardly noticed them. "I don't think I've ever been this nervous in my whole life," I said.

"Listen," Dad replied. "We've still got time to catch a cab and hightail it out of here."

I giggled, holding a bouquet of flowers tight to my chest. I didn't even remember where I'd gotten it from. My whole body was trembling.

"I don't know what's up with me. The hard part's over, right? Jack and I live together, we've got a kid. All I've got to do is go up there, say *I do*, and get on with my life. But I'm still freaking out. I feel like I need to throw up."

"You'd better do it now, then," Dad told me. "Because you definitely don't want the photographer memorializing that."

"I'm good," I replied. "Let's go ahead and get it over with."

He offered me his arm, and I took it, standing next to him. I drew in two deep breaths, and we started walking. As we topped the slight hill, I saw the chairs with their light blue upholstery arranged in two groups. There were flowers, a wooden arch, balloons, wreaths…and the guests— not too many, because we'd wanted an intimate wedding. Just Shannon; Owen; Sonny and Steve; Mary and Agnes; Sue, Mike, and Will; Jane and Naya; Lana and some guy I assumed was her latest hookup; Chris; Curtis; Vivian; some actors from Jack's films; Joey; Nelle; a couple more family members; some other faces I didn't bother looking at as I saw Spencer standing in front of the archway smiling from ear to ear.

Then there was Jack. The sight of him actually relieved me—he was more uptight than I was, if that was possible. He couldn't even bring himself to glance at me. I was in a trance as the music played and we proceeded up to the altar. I thought Jack would crumble to pieces as my father clapped him on the shoulder before taking his seat.

Spencer started talking, and my eyes got lost in Jack's tailored black suit, which was so sexy I almost forgot we were in public and I couldn't throw myself at him—not yet, anyway. We met eyes, and I realized he must have been thinking exactly the same thing. He grinned and mumbled, "I'd hoped you'd wear something see-through, but I guess I'll settle for this."

I didn't respond. All I could do was stand there stiffly and wait for the kiss that I knew was coming. Jack took my hand and recited something, but I didn't even absorb the words, and finally, Spencer growled at me: "Jenny!"

"What?"

"Try and pay attention," he muttered under his breath.

A few people in the audience giggled, and I felt the blood rush into my cheeks. Jack was trying to be serious, but he couldn't help smirking as he squeezed my hand and tipped his head slightly toward Spencer, who repeated, "Do you, Jenny, take Jack to be your lawfully wedded husband?"

When I didn't respond right away, Jack grunted, "You're scaring me," and I responded in a whisper, "Don't be scared," before nearly shouting, "I do."

Jack smiled as he slipped a golden ring on my finger, and I thanked him as I did the same to him, feeling immensely grateful for that moment, even if my hands were shaking so much I could hardly stand it.

At last, Spencer declared, "By the power vested in me by the internet two months ago, I now pronounce you man and wife. You may get it on!"

"Spencer!" Mom shouted from the audience.

"Sorry," he corrected himself. "Jack, you may kiss the bride."

Jack cradled my face in his hands; I felt the heat of his flesh and the cold metal of his ring, and it made my heart speed up. I closed my eyes. It was a short, soft, tender kiss, and a few seconds later, he pulled away.

I thought he'd say something—he always did—but before he could speak, Spencer threw his arms around us both. Sonny and Steve came up and did the same, and soon half the guests had joined them.

Dinner was served on the hotel's back patio. I had finally relaxed, even if I was a little concerned at the fact that my brothers were allowed access to an open bar—that felt like a recipe for disaster. Thankfully, they behaved, and the most embarrassing thing that happened was the toast Mike proposed, which consisted mostly of him cracking stupid jokes at our expense. Naya said a few words, too—as many as she could manage between sobs—and it was nice, despite everything. Everybody knew everybody, we didn't feel a need to make excuses, and the mood in general was generous and friendly.

The minutes passed, then the hours, and food and alcohol were swallowed in large quantities. People danced, drank, ate, laughed, and danced some more... I couldn't have hoped for anything better.

I was waiting at the bar myself when the photographer came over. She was a small girl with dark hair and expressive blue eyes. Her camera was almost as big as her head. She congratulated me and added, "I hope this isn't a bad time, but I was thinking of trying to snap a few pictures just as the sun goes down. It's really nice, with that last bit of light off of the sea."

It was a good idea, especially because there were hardly any photos of Jack and me alone—every time we tried to take one, some guest or other crashed into the scene. I told her yes and grabbed my new husband, pulling him down the path. As we walked, I asked the photographer about her job. I was surprised to find out this was her first wedding—she normally did real estate photos, baptisms, things like that. I remarked that my sister had found her, thanks to a profile of a band on a music website.

"Oh, that," she said. "Yeah, that's my boyfriend's group."

"That hot guitarist with the tattoos is your boyfriend?" I asked. Shannon had shown me the website when we were shopping around for photographers and he was an impressive specimen, to say the least.

"Excuse me," Jack said, clearing his throat. "Perhaps this is a good time for me to remind you that you're married, and you can't just go gawking at hot guitarists on the internet anymore."

"It's my sister's fault," I protested as the photographer, whose name was Brooke, told us where to stand. We posed for about twenty minutes, but soon the sun was so low that we had to call it quits. Brooke showed us the shots on her digital camera, and they were incredible. She really had an eye.

I was about to compliment her when I heard what sounded like a lion's roar: my twin brothers, who were running over with mischief in their eyes. They lifted me off the ground before I could react and took off toward the water. I screamed for Jack's help, but he was in the same situation as me: Naya, Sue, Will, and Mike had picked him up, too.

Before I knew it, my beautiful wedding dress was soaking wet and I was floating in the ocean. Furious, I shook my head and shouted, "Sonny, Steve! Get back here, you bastards! I swear to God, I'm going to drown both of you!"

Mike, who couldn't let a second pass without making a smartass remark, said, "You'll never get them to come back if you talk to them that way."

I crossed my arms, fuming, as he grinned at me, his tuxedo shirt clinging to his chest. I guess his brother had been harder to handle than I was, so instead of throwing him in, he'd just plunged in with him.

Jack swam over, pulling off his jacket and tossing it to the shore. "Hello, my dearly beloved," he said. I ignored all the people standing on the beach, some laughing at us, others stripping down to get in the water themselves. Jack grabbed my waist, pulled me into him, and gave me the kiss I wished I'd gotten at the altar—long, deep, intimate.

"I've got to tell you, Michelle," he said, "when you told me you wanted a wedding by the water, I wasn't so sure, but now I'm one-hundred-percent on board."

"Two things," I replied. "One, don't call me Michelle or I'll file for an immediate divorce. Number two, what changed your mind?"

"Take a look at yourself."

I glanced down and saw my entire body was visible through my dress. I screeched, and Jack said, "Don't worry, I'll cover you. But just a pointer, in case we ever renew our vows: I don't think you're supposed to wear pink panties under a white dress."

"I did it for you," I told him.

"Good, because I've been thinking about what comes next all day. And don't tell me you haven't, too."

I laughed, but he stopped me, kissing me again.

"I don't know," I said. "The whole sleeping together on your wedding night, that's so cliché, right? I was thinking I'd throw on some jeans and go hang out at the bar for a few more hours."

"Michelle!" he uttered in shock. "How dare you say you prefer anything on this earth to being in the buff with your new husband! And trust me, I paid for the champagne, it's not *that* good."

"Are you telling me you are that good?"

"I'm the best thing you've ever had," he said complacently. I had to let him have that, it was true.

We kissed again, and I warned him, "I'm not kidding about the Michelle thing, though. I may love you, we may have a child together, but I will walk right out that door if you keep it up. Every time I hear it, it's like nails on a chalkboard."

"I like it, though!"

"I don't care, Jack. A deal's a deal. You can take it or leave it. And it goes without saying, you'd better not dare call me Mushu."

He thought it over for what felt like an eternity. Then I saw a playful gleam in his eyes. "Fine," he said at last. "From now on, I'll call you one thing and one thing only: Mrs. Ross."

Read how Jenna and Jack Ross
first fell in love in
BEFORE DECEMBER.

1

AN OPEN RELATIONSHIP

"An…open relationship?"

"Yeah. Exactly."

My boyfriend was beaming. I wasn't. Not in the least.

"What's that?"

"Jenna, I think the name kind of gives it away."

He had to be joking.

Or should I say: he'd *better* be joking.

He had just dropped me off in front of my dorm! Literally! I hadn't even had time to get my suitcase out of the car, and already he was thinking about changing everything about our relationship.

"Monty, do we have to talk about this right now?" I grumbled. "How did you not get around to it before?"

"Uh…I just didn't."

"Are you serious? We've spent the past two days together."

"I know, but…I just didn't know how to bring it up. It never felt like the right moment."

"Oh, but I guess now is just perfect?" I asked.

"Jenna, don't be like that. I've got to go, and I had to tell you before leaving. It's not something you'd want to talk about on the phone, right?"

"No, it isn't."

I sighed and decided to relax a little bit. I was nervous about college, out of my comfort zone, and it wasn't right to take that out on Monty. Especially when he was about to leave. Being angry at each other the last time we were together... I didn't like that idea.

But what was I supposed to tell him? I looked at him awhile, dwelling on that innocent smile of his—too innocent for the person he really was.

Then I realized I hadn't really thought about what would happen to us when I stayed here and he went back home. He was finished with school. Or at least that's what he told himself for now. Our town had a NBA development league team, and he was going to focus on that. He only liked one thing, really. Playing basketball. All day long.

Me, though... I'd been so busy getting ready for college, wondering what life in the dorms would be like, that I hadn't even considered that we wouldn't see each other for a long time. Too much time, I guess. He had to train and I was taking a full load, so daily contact was going to be a hard ask. Plus, it's not like I had money to go see him all the time, and I doubted he'd want to come out here to see me. I could already hear the excuses: *Babe, I just had practice and I'm beat...*

At least we'd see each other for Christmas. But December was so many months away.

I tried to focus again on the conversation when I realized he was waiting for an answer.

"I don't know what to tell you," I admitted. "I'm not even sure I understand what it means to...have an open relationship. I just don't know what one is."

"It's simple. Look, you and me, we're a couple, right?"

"I think so," I joked.

"Perfect. So we love each other, we appreciate each other, we respect each other, but...we've both got our needs."

"Our needs?"

"Yeah."

"What needs, Monty? Like eating?"

"No, Jenna."

"Drinking?"

"Not exactly…"

"Sleeping?"

"Jenna, I'm talking about sex."

"Huh?" I blushed and looked around, wondering if there was someone nearby who could hear us. "S-s-sex? Are you…?"

"Could you stop looking around like we're plotting a murder? We're just talking about sex."

"I don't like talking about sex," I said.

"I know." He rolled his eyes. "Still, though. Sexual needs are real needs, right? I mean, I don't know about you—you're kind of asexual—but me…"

"Do you even know what it means to be asexual?"

He ignored me. "I do have my needs."

"Wait." My voice went three decibels higher. "Are you telling me you want to sleep with someone else?"

"What? I'm not…"

"I hope this is a joke," I said.

He held my face in his hands and told me, "All I'm proposing is that if at some point…you know, like if we feel the need, we can just do it."

I pushed him away. "And might I know why you'd ever feel the need to sleep with someone who wasn't me?"

"I don't. Not now," he said, looking almost offended.

"Oh, you don't. Then should we go back over what you meant when you described an open relationship to me just now?"

He knew what I was getting at, and he tried to cover it up by touching me again, but I dodged him. I could tell he was upset. I lowered my head.

"I'm sorry," I murmured. "But I'm really nervous and…"

"I know." He relaxed and took a breath. "I know it sounds weird," he went on, "but open relationships are a thing now. And scientists have shown that couples in open relationships stay together longer."

"I'm sorry, who are these scientists?"

"And I'm not even saying I *do* want to do it, but…how long are we going to go without seeing each other? Three months?"

"Almost four," I said. "But you're ducking the issue…"

"I don't think it's good for the body to go that long without doing it, Jenna."

I scowled. "I went seventeen years without doing it with anyone and I was perfectly fine."

"Yeah, but when you're a virgin, it's different. You don't know what you're missing, so you don't suffer when you don't have it." He grabbed my hand and pulled me softly toward him. "Come on, babe. You know I love you, right?"

"Yeah, Monty, but…"

"And you know that won't change. No matter what happens. Or who happens." He laughed at his own joke. "You get me. That's why I'm with you, why I love you, because you've always understood me perfectly. And you know I have my needs, Jenna. So…what's the problem if I give a little love to someone else when you're not around?"

"That's a very fancy way to avoid the word 'cheating,' Monty."

"It's not cheating if both people consent to it."

"Right. So you're asking for my consent for you to sleep with whoever you want."

"Hey, it's not just me. If you meet a guy, you can sleep with him, too."

Honestly, I didn't find that very consoling. "Did it ever occur to you that I might not want to sleep with anyone else?" I asked.

"Great! Then don't. But at least you've got the right to change your mind, you know?"

"So you mean that if I walk into the dorm right now and meet a guy and I like him and I want to sleep with him, you don't care? You know you don't believe that."

"That's not what I'm saying, Jenna."

"What are you saying then, Monty?"

"We don't even have to sleep with anyone. It's just, with us having a long-distance relationship, we could have the right to…you know…be in situations, and if a person's there and we're super-attracted to them, then fine, we can do what we want with them. Without resentment, without reproaches, without jealousy."

He was still holding my hand, and I wanted to pull it away. I didn't like what I was hearing at all. "I don't know, Monty. It sounds a little weird."

"Come on…" He smiled and gave me a kiss on the lips. "It'll be fun. Plus, we can have rules."

"Rules?"

"Of course. To make you more comfortable. Like, every time one of us does something with another person, they have to tell. That would be best, I think."

"I don't want to know what you do with other girls," I told him.

"OK, fine. We won't enter into details. We'll just let each other know it's happened."

"Monty…"

"Now it's your turn to set a rule."

"I never even said I wanted to do this," I argued.

"Well, let's imagine you agree. In that case, what rule would you pick?"

I turned it over in my head a moment while he looked at me expectantly. "Well…no friends. I don't want you hooking up with any of my friends. And I won't hook up with yours."

"Sounds good."

"Are you actually telling me you don't mind if I sleep with other people?" I asked.

"Jenna, if it's just sex, then I don't care." He cupped my cheeks again. That was a thing he did when he was trying to convince me of something. "That's what an open relationship is. You might sleep with someone else, but you know you love the person you're actually with. And that's how strong our relationship is. Cool, right?"

I wasn't sure *cool* was the word I'd use to define the situation, but he wasn't going to give me any peace till I said yes, so finally I shrugged and responded, "If that's what you want…"

He smiled and grabbed the back of my neck to kiss me. I let him, even though I wasn't feeling it. Then he took my suitcase out of the trunk and left it on the ground next to me.

"Great, well we'll…"

"I'll take it from here," I told him. "You should go. Otherwise you'll be home late."

Surprised, he asked, "Do you really want to go inside alone?"

"Yeah, I really do."

"Jenna, I don't mind lending a hand."

"I've got it." I gave him a peck on the cheek and he smiled, and I told him to call me when he got in.

"And you text me and let me know how things are," he said.

To tell the truth, I'd expected a more emotional goodbye. But instead I got a pat on the cheek and he hopped in his car and took off. I saw him wave as he hit the gas.

For a moment, I regretted telling him to go. But it was better that way. I needed to absorb the fact that from now on, I'd probably be spending a lot of time by myself. I had to get used to it, and the sooner, the better.

I turned toward the building and started dragging my suitcase, stomach tight from my frazzled nerves. I felt like a soldier headed out to fight her first battle.

My dorm was close to the Humanities, where I'd be studying. Looking at the worn redbrick façade, I thought it probably hadn't changed much in decades. There was a huge poster hanging on one of the walls that said something about women's rights. That made me smile as I took the stairs inside, huffing and puffing because my bag was so heavy.

Inside it was packed. The place itself looked old-fashioned, but there were so many people there, I forgot about that right away. I had to glance around a moment to find the reception area. There was a blond guy in huge glasses behind the counter, not much older than me, and he seemed stressed as he shouted something to a young man who was leaning against the wall. I wondered why he was there. It was a girls' dorm. Maybe he was someone's brother or cousin?

Anyway, it wasn't my problem. I stood there behind him, waiting for him to finish.

"Ross, I can't let you go up there," the guy behind the counter said. He sounded tired, as if he'd already repeated this several times. "On day one, only family members can go up. And no guys. You know that."

"'You know that,'" the other one repeated mockingly and grinned.

The blond guy turned red in the face. "Could you take me seriously for once in your life?"

"Could you give me a break for once in your life?"

"Ross, this is a girls' dorm—"

"Thanks, I didn't notice—"

"And you're not a girl."

"Neither are you, and you're working here."

The guy behind the counter got angry and groused, "Look, I'm here because this is my job and I'm trying to do it to the best of my ability!"

"Perfect. Then you can be the one to go tell Naya she has to take her own suitcase upstairs."

The guy behind the counter froze. "No. You tell her."

"Me? I don't think so, buddy. That offer's expired. I tried to be a gentleman, but you won't let me." He shook his head. "I guess it's going to have to be all your fault, Chrissy. Too bad. I liked you. But no worries, I'll come to your funeral to tell you goodbye, OK?"

The blond guy—what kind of name was Chrissy?—looked at him as he decided what to do. "Let Will do it," he said. "He's her boyfriend. That counts as family for my purposes."

"Do you think I'd be here if Will could come?"

"No," Chrissy said. "I guess not."

"Bingo," the other one replied.

"Why couldn't he come?"

"Our dear friend Will is busy and thinks I'm his errand boy."

The receptionist asked if whatever this Will was doing was more important than his girlfriend.

"What do I care?" Ross replied. "I literally just got up twenty minutes ago. I slept two hours. Maybe less. I'm dying to go back to bed. And this suitcase is like a ton of bricks. And I'm hungry, Chrissy. All I want to do right now is go home and eat my cold leftover pizza from last night and sleep away the next decade."

Ross paused and then leaned over the counter. "So will you let me take Naya's suitcase upstairs so I can get on with my life, or are you going to keep telling me no?"

Chrissy was flushed. He seemed to be having some kind of short circuit. Was it really such a big deal to let a guy go up to one of the rooms? With all those people in there, who'd even notice?

"Fine," Chrissy murmured, defeated. "But get a move on! If someone sees you…!"

"I'm a discreet man. You know that," Ross said, smiling from ear to ear.

The blond guy seemed to finally realize I existed, and his face turned serious once again. He nodded his head toward me and said, "Look, Ross, as you can see, people need my help, so…"

Without even looking at me, Ross picked up the suitcase and started making fun of him again. "Yes, I can see you're a very busy man."

"How can I help you?" Chrissy asked me as his acquaintance wandered off toward the stairs. I tried to look friendly and said, "Sorry, I didn't want to interrupt…"

"I wish you had," Chrissy replied. "He's unbearable. Anyway, what's up? You're staying here?"

"Yeah. My name's Jenna. Jennifer Michelle Brown." I showed him my license, which he stared at for a moment.

"Jennifer Michelle. Strange combination." He tried to find me on his list.

"My parents are very imaginative," I murmured.

ABOUT THE AUTHOR

Joana Marcús, born in Mallorca in 2000, divides her time between her studies, her books, and her pets. Since she was little, she's loved writing. Her first compositions were short stories, and it wasn't until she was thirteen that she found the courage to publish her first complete story on Wattpad, where she is still writing today.

Instagram: @joanamarcusx